Darkness & Light

BOOKS BY JOHN HARVEY

In a True Light
Flesh & Blood
Ash & Bone
Darkness & Light

The Resnick Novels
Lonely Hearts
Rough Treatment
Off Minor
Cutting Edge
Wasted Years
Cold Light
Living Proof
Easy Meat
Still Water
Last Rites
Now's the Time:
The Complete Resnick Short Stories

Poetry
Ghosts of a Chance
Bluer Than This

As Editor
Blue Lightning
Men From Boys

Darkness & Light

JOHN HARVEY

AN OTTO PENZLER BOOK

HARCOURT, INC.

Orlando   Austin   New York

San Diego   Toronto   London

Requests for permission to make copies of any part of the work
should be submitted online at www.harcourt.com/contact or mailed
to the following address: Permissions Department, Harcourt, Inc.,
6277 Sea Harbor Drive, Orlando, Florida 32887-6777.

www.HarcourtBooks.com

First published in Great Britain by Random House UK Ltd.

Selection from D. H. Lawrence's *Sons and Lovers*
courtesy of Random House, Inc.

Excerpt from "Dante's Tomb" from *Collected Poems: 1937–1971*
by John Berryman. Copyright © 1989 by Kate Donahue Berryman.
Reprinted by permission of Farrar, Straus and Giroux, LLC.

Library of Congress Cataloging-in-Publication Data
Harvey, John, 1938–
Darkness & light/John Harvey.—1st U.S. ed.
p. cm.
"An Otto Penzler book."
1. Ex-police officers—Fiction. 2. Nottingham (England)—Fiction. I. Title.
PR6058.A6989D37 2006
823'.914—dc22 2005037771
ISBN-13: 978-0-15-101133-9 (alk. paper) ISBN-10: 0-15-101133-8 (alk. paper)

Text set in ITC Caslon 224
Designed by Kaelin Chappell Broaddus

Printed in the United States of America
First U.S. edition
A C E G I K J H F D B

For my editor, Susan Sandon, without whom...

She said to me, half-strangled, "Do that again.
And then do the other thing."

—John Berryman,
"Dante's Tomb"

The thought of being the mother of men was warming to
her heart. She looked at the child. It had blue eyes, and a
lot of fair hair, and was bonny. Her love came up hot,
in spite of everything. She had it in bed with her.

—D. H. Lawrence,
Sons and Lovers

Darkness
&
Light

Chapter 1

1965

BEHIND HIS SPECTACLES, THE BOY'S EYES WERE LIKE bevelled glass.

Alice Silverman turned in her chair and adjusted the window blind so that the late summer light fell muted into the room. All the surfaces—the pale wood table, the backs and arms of both chairs, the long low cabinet of shallow drawers—hummed with a shimmer of honeyed dust. Each drawer in the cabinet was marked clearly with the name of the child to whom it belonged; some, those of the youngest, had an animal brightly painted beside the handle, a dolphin, a diplodocus, a brown bear with outsize feet and a big red bow at its neck.

Close to Alice's slim wrist rested the unlined pad on which, occasionally, she noted down words or phrases in a neat hand, or otherwise doodled, crosshatching dark corners that might be clouds or trees. Between herself and the boy there were sheets

of unmarked paper, some coloured, some plain, and near them
a wooden box filled with pencils, chalks, and crayons.

"There's plenty of paper here," Alice said. "You could draw
something. Make me a picture."

Barely a flicker of response in those eyes.

"It's difficult, isn't it?" Alice said. "Part of you wants to, but
part of you doesn't."

Still nothing.

She had asked him before, not asked him, chivvied him, told
him. Needing a response. Something she could push against.
Not wanting him to be too comfortable. None of those namby-
pamby social-worker questions—What had he done in the holidays? What was his favourite group, the Beatles or the Stones?

Alice looked at him and the boy shuffled awkwardly on his
chair until he was sitting almost sideways, head down, face
angled away.

The Stones, she thought, it had to be. For her, at least. The
words to "Mother's Little Helper" running through her head.
The thrust of Jagger's skinny hips, the cruel lewdness of his lips.

A shiver ran through her and she sensed the boy stiffen as if
somehow he had noticed.

THE REFERRAL HAD COME FROM THE BOY'S TEACHER INI-
tially, not based on any one particular thing, more an accumu-
lation of incidents that had alerted her to some underlying
malaise that went beyond the norm. Sudden mood swings, out-
bursts of temper, tears; several occasions on which he'd soiled
himself in the playground, or once, in class, an incident, quite
possibly misinterpreted, between himself and the school secre-
tary when they had been alone in her office, something vaguely
sexual.

Alice had read the reports, hummed and hawed, finally found
a place in her schedule. Almost five years now since she had
finished her training, three since taking up her post with this

authority. The younger children, seven, eight, nine, she felt less anxious with, more in control. Boys like this, though, edging eleven, slightly built but with something threatening about them nevertheless, something confrontational beating just beneath the skin...

Sensing the allotted time drawing to a close, Alice allowed herself to glance down at her watch; capped and uncapped her pen, then told herself not to fidget. A cup of tea and a biscuit: two more sessions and then she was through. Another day. Tonight there was a Buñuel at the Film Society. *Viridiana*. Maybe she'd go along, take her mind off work, relax.

"All right then," Alice said, as brightly as she could. "I'll see you again next week."

Chapter 2

WHEN ELDER HAD FIRST TAKEN RETIREMENT AND MOVED down to Cornwall—could that really be close to four years ago?—one of the things he'd promised himself was that he'd learn the names of all the trees and flowers that grew close to wherever he set down roots. But high in the peninsula between Zennor and St. Ives, on a narrow strip of land between moor and sea, there were no trees—or precious few—and the flowers that pushed through, hardily, each spring, remained for the most part anonymous. Red campion he knew, and foxglove; bluebell, of course, and primrose, but little else. The pocket guide he'd picked up secondhand was tucked, half-forgotten, among the books that were crammed, higgledy-piggledy, along his shelves.

This morning the sky was pale over the sea and smudged with gray inland, darkening over the old tin mine at Sperris Croft; the only sign of sun a faint reddening blur around the hills to the southeast. On the radio the night before, the forecast had been for a dip in temperature by as much as ten degrees, and, over the higher ground, rare for April, a light fall of snow.

Elder made coffee and toast and hunkered down in the one comfortable chair with a book: *The Fox in the Attic* by Richard Hughes. The farm labourer's cottage he rented had lain empty for the better part of a year before he had moved in, its owners' plans to gentrify it for the holiday trade stalled amid family recriminations and a shortage of cash. The stone walls, thick enough to withstand the wind, were still, in places, unplastered, and where plaster had been slapped haphazardly into place it remained unpainted, taking on a pinkish hue that reminded Elder of faded marble. An oil-fired stove, on which he cooked, was the main source of heat, adequate to the needs of someone living alone, as long as he was prepared to wear several layers of clothing through the winter and required no more than a single shallow bath a day.

For the first eighteen months, the radio had been his only link with the outside world, but then, under some pressure from his ex-wife, Joanne, and the few friends who insisted they wanted to stay in touch, he had a telephone installed. A land line, there being no signal for anything else. It scarcely ever rang.

After the better part of an hour, Elder set aside his book, stretched, and stepped outside. Colder, yes, but not by that much: Perhaps the forecast had been wrong. Fifteen minutes later, boots laced, waterproofs fastened, woollen hat pulled down over his ears, he set out on a path that would take him through Nancledra to the opposite coast and within sight of St. Michael's Mount. Now into his fifties, Elder had chosen a lifestyle that kept him fit at least.

Returning that afternoon, fortified by a pastry from the baker's in Marazion and the two apples, Coxes, he had taken with him, he saw, from the top of the lane, a swathe of white moving fast across the sea, a band of palpable hail and snow.

Secure indoors, he shucked off his coat, eased off his boots, and set the kettle on the stove to boil. Before the tea had brewed, pieces of hail the size of quarters were rattling against roof and windows, sufficient to drown out the first tones of the telephone from the corner of the room.

Elder covered one ear with his hand as he spoke.

Joanne's voice in reply was faint at first, but clear enough to make his stomach lurch. His first fear always, that something had happened to their daughter, Katherine. Something else.

"What's wrong?" Elder asked.

Joanne's laugh was quick and not altogether true. "Does something have to be wrong, Frank?"

Probably, Elder thought. "You're all right, then?" he said.

"I'm fine."

"And Katherine?"

"Katherine's fine. She's got exams coming up soon."

"She'll do okay?"

"She's working hard."

Katherine was taking her A/S levels at college and hoping to go on to university that autumn, either Loughborough or Sheffield Hallam, to study for a degree in sports management. Well, why not? In Cornwall, Elder was certain, it was possible to get degrees in surfing and wave technology. And athletics, running, had for a long time been an important part of his daughter's life.

"How's Martyn?" Elder asked.

There was no reply.

The owner of a small chain of hair stylists and beauty salons, Martyn Miles was both Joanne's employer and her erstwhile lover, the man with whom, unbeknown then to Elder, she had enjoyed a lengthy affair. When Joanne and Elder separated, she and Martyn Miles had set up house together, since which time he had moved out again, once if not twice. Elder was reminded of the painted wooden figures who had lived in a model Swiss chalet on his parents' sideboard, popping in and out with each change in the weather.

"You remember Jennie?" Joanne said. "Jennie Preston?"

"Not really, no."

"Petite. Blond. She's in sales. Beauty products. Hair care, you know? We met her for a drink in the Lace Market. A couple of times."

"No, I'm sorry."

"She's got a sister called Claire. Older. Bit of a sad case, according to Jennie."

Get to the point, Elder thought.

"It seems she's gone missing. Claire."

"Missing?"

"Almost a week now. No note, no message, no phone call: nothing. It's not like her at all. Poor Jennie's going crazy."

"She's reported it to the police?"

"They didn't seem very interested."

"She did report it, though?"

"Yes. And all they said, basically, was she's a grown woman, no sign of foul play, there's not a great deal we can do."

"That's probably true."

"Frank, it's driving her crazy."

"You said."

A slight pause. "She wonders if you'd help."

"I don't think so."

"Why not?"

"She lives up there? The sister? Claire?"

"Yes."

"Then I'm three hundred miles away."

"You don't have to be."

"Don't I?"

"When was the last time you were here?"

"Round Christmas."

"So come up for a few days. See Katherine. You could meet Jennie; talk to her, at least."

"What good would that do?"

"I don't know. Set her mind at rest, if nothing else. Maybe

there are things she can do herself, things she hasn't thought of. Just having someone else to talk to, someone who takes her seriously, that would help."

Elder could feel the helplessness of it, rising like cold water over his feet and around his ankles.

"Come on, Frank. It's not as though you're actually busy down there, after all."

That's the point, Elder thought, a lot of it at least.

"Let me think about it," he said. "I'll get back to you."

"You promise?"

Your promises—what did his mother used to say?—they're like pie crusts. His mother had said a lot of things. "I promise," Elder said, and set down the phone.

HE DID RING, TWO DAYS LATER, ON MONDAY. IN THE MEAN-time, he'd contacted the Nottinghamshire force and, after exchanging a few barbed pleasantries with officers he used to know, got himself put through to the sergeant in charge of Missing Persons.

Claire Meecham had been reported missing by her sister on Tuesday the twelfth of April. A statement had been taken but no follow-up set in motion. After all, it was little more than a week. And how many thousands disappeared each year? Just walked away, without so much as a by-your-leave. Hadn't Elder done so himself, in a way? And the proportion of cases in which some crime was involved was, he knew, small.

But Katherine—his relationship with his daughter had not always been the best these past few years, and this business with Jennie's friend, it was a good excuse to see her again. He would drive up the next day.

AT THE LITTLE CHEF ON THE A46, MIDWAY BETWEEN EVE-sham and Stratford-upon-Avon, he stopped for a pot of coffee and an Early Starter, a breakfast special that seemed to be always available, no matter how late in the day. After that it was a short distance to the Fosse Way, the old Roman road that would take him, straight as a die, to the outskirts of Leicester; a short stretch of motorway beyond that and he would see the signs for Nottingham South, then follow the single carriageway in past the power station, the old training college, the Clifton estate.

He'd heard this radio programme about a writer—Graham Greene, was it?—his centenary. How he'd lived in Nottingham early on and not thought much of it, a bit of a dump, drab and dark by his account, but something about it nonetheless, something that meant once you'd lived there, it never quite let you go.

Elder eased left off the overpass and followed the broad curve of road round and down into the city centre; five minutes, ten at most, and he would be at Joanne's home in The Park, a private estate of large, mostly Victorian houses in the lee of the Castle walls. Not that there was anything Victorian about the narrow, architect-designed space that presented little more than a flat, gray wall and two small windows to the passing world.

Joanne answered the door with a promptness that suggested she'd been half-waiting for his arrival—his or someone else's—and gave him a quick smile as she stepped back for him to enter, the wood floor of the hall so pale and unblemished, he felt almost obliged to kick off his shoes.

Elder followed her through into a living area made spacious by dint of a raised ceiling and an almost sheer glass wall that gave out onto the stone patio and garden beyond.

"How was your journey?"

"Oh, you know."

"What was it? Six hours?"

"Nearer seven."

"You must be exhausted."

"I'm okay."

She was wearing a silver dress that scarcely seemed to touch her body save, perhaps, at her hips. Her hair—darker now?—had been spun into a soft coil at the back of her head, a few stray hairs reaching down to rest against her neck.

"Let me get you something. Tea? Coffee? A glass of wine?"

There was a glass of white wine on the low centre table, half-empty or half-full? A little short of three in the afternoon.

"No, it's okay. I'm fine."

"You're sure?"

"Sure."

"Well, sit down at least."

For Christ's sake, he just stopped himself from saying, I've been sitting down half the bloody day—uncertain what it was about her, about this house, that was weevilling so rapidly under his skin.

He perched at one end of a long settee that in his memory had been white, but was now a delicate shade of mauve, toning in with the faint grayish blue of the walls.

Joanne disappeared into the kitchen and returned with her glass close to full; sitting opposite him in a cushioned S-shaped chair, she lit a cigarette and released a slow wraith of smoke into the air.

"I spoke to Jennie. She'll meet you this evening."

Elder nodded. "Okay."

"Frank, she's really grateful to you for doing this."

"I haven't done anything."

"You will, though. I know you will."

Elder let it pass. "How about Katherine?" he said. "Does she know I'm here?"

"Of course. She said she'd ring, try and sort something out."

"Good of her."

"Come on, Frank. She's busy, studying. You should be pleased."

"I am. I'd like to see her, that's all."

"I'm sure you will."

"This flat she's in, how's that working out?"

"Fine as far as I know."

"Why anyone in their right mind would choose a run-down place in the arse end of Lenton..."

"Instead of living here?"

"Yes."

"Frank, she's nineteen years old. She's got a life of her own."

"I know, I know."

"You can't mollycoddle her forever."

"There's been a lot of that."

"You know what I mean."

"I know."

Elder leaned back and for a moment closed his eyes. If he was never himself free of the time Katherine had been snatched off the street by a confessed murderer, imprisoned, and abused, then how much worse must it be for her? How hard for either of them to forget that much of the blame was attached to Elder himself?

"Perhaps," he said, "I'll have that cup of coffee after all."

As Joanne walked past the window, the sun came out as suddenly as if someone had just switched on a light, and Elder could see the outline of her breasts and thighs beneath the swivel of her dress.

Following her through to the kitchen, he leaned against the jamb of the door and watched as she spooned coffee into the bottom of the cafetière.

"When I asked you about Martyn on the phone, you didn't answer."

"That's because there was nothing to say."

"You're not seeing him?"

"Seeing him?"

"I mean, he's not living here any more?"

Joanne pushed down the plunger in the cafetière too soon.

"Why is it, Frank, every conversation with you, I feel as if I'm being interrogated?"

"I'm interested, that's all."

"Oh, yes?"

"Yes. Of course."

"Martyn moved out last June, you know that. Or you did."

"I thought he'd moved back in."

"Not really. We did try—what did you say?—seeing each other for a while after that. It never really worked." She poured coffee, barely dark, into wide china cups. "All those young girls hanging round him, not much older than Katherine. I couldn't compete."

"That's nonsense."

"Is it?"

Sliding his coffee along the work surface toward him, she lit another cigarette.

"You're not sleeping with him, then?"

"Sleeping?"

"You know what I mean."

"Not afraid of the word, are you, Frank?"

"All right, fucking then. You're not fucking him anymore, is that better?"

For a moment, she held his gaze. "Only when he wants to, Frank. And, like I say, that's not often these days."

Pushing past him, she went back into the other room.

Chapter 3

ELDER BOOKED INTO THE PREMIER TRAVEL INN, ACROSS from the BBC building at the head of London Road. The room was anonymous and clean, with a firm bed and a small TV and a view down over the canal as it made its measured turn toward the law courts and the railway station. A solitary fisherman sat on a folding stool by the canal's edge, one rod near his right hand, another resting on a trivet some few metres off. A pair of moorhens ducked their scarlet-tipped beaks beneath the grayish water by the opposite bank.

Still angry with himself for behaving like an adolescent with Joanne, Elder stripped off his clothes and stood in the shower longer than was necessary, as if washing some sense into himself were even a possibility.

Away in Cornwall, he scarcely thought of her for weeks on end and thought little positive when he did; there was no real sense of missing her, of wanting things to be as they once had been. And when he did see her, more often than not it was like

meeting a friend with whom you've fallen out of touch, whatever there'd been between you so far in the past as to be mostly
forgotten.

Strangers.

Elder laughed.

Jealousy then, is that what it was?

Jealous of Martyn Miles after all this time?

Fuck!

He slammed his open hand against the tiled wall and turned
the shower high. A burst of cold then out. The small reassuring
roughness of clean, well-laundered towels; his body in the mirror taut as he stretched, no sign of flab, not yet. He'd wanted her,
that was the thing, wanted her as she moved past the screen of
glass and then again, when she stood in the kitchen, close. *Only
when he wants to, Frank.* Her skin when she'd stared up at him,
so pale it was almost as if the light showed through, faint purple
shadows below the eyes. *Only when he wants to.*

Elder let the towel fall and stood naked in the centre of the
room, head down, eyes closed, slowly unclenching his fingers
until they were no longer fists.

IN THE TIME SINCE HE'D MOVED AWAY, BARS HAD SPRUNG
up like brightly coloured sores across the centre of the city.
What was it? Four hundred licensed premises within a radius of
little more than a mile? A half million pounds changing hands
on Friday and Saturday nights? Come two o'clock, the pedestrianized streets would be awash with puke and piss, young men
in short-sleeved shirts eager for the chance to lash out with a
word, a threat, a boot, at worst a knife; and girls, no matter the
weather, dressed (if that was the word) in the skimpiest of
clothes, their backsides, as the singer put it, out to the world.

Even midweek, early in the evening, finding somewhere for a
quiet drink without the ubiquitous soundtrack pumping, bass
heavy, through the sound system, was difficult if not impossible.

Jennie Preston had done her best. A corner bar just off the main street in Hockley, caught between the bland brickwork of an NCP car park and the philanthropic splendour of Victorian textile factories since turned into exclusive apartments or lecture rooms for the new city college. There were deep leather armchairs in twos and threes around the walls, tables scattered here and there across a well-scored wooden floor, and stools along the bar itself. Not many people yet: a small cluster of men drinking bottles of imported lager; two women straight from work, heads close together over a bottle of chardonnay; a solitary man, newspaper folded open, doing the crossword at the bar, and pausing every now and then to ponder a clue and check his watch. The music was mostly instrumental—organ, was it? Saxophone? Dinner jazz, Elder thought it might be called.

He knew it was her the moment she walked in.

Petite, Joanne had been right; without her heels, Elder doubted if Jennie Preston would have topped five feet. She was wearing a rust red suit, the skirt just above the knee; her blond bobbed hair, streaked here and there a darker colour and falling in a line that followed the curve of her chin, was expertly cut. Living with a hairstylist for nigh on twenty years, almost despite himself, Elder had learned a little about these things.

"Frank." She walked toward him, hand outstretched, and he rose to meet her. "Frank Elder, yes?"

"Yes."

"It was good of you to come."

He gave one of those half nods, half shrugs to suggest it was fine, he hadn't overly put himself out.

"What are you drinking?" Jennie asked.

"I wasn't yet. I thought I'd wait."

"Wine then. Red okay?"

"Yes, let me…"

But she was already on her way to the bar, heels clipping the floor. Only one of the men in suits failed to turn and look.

A few minutes later she was back with two large glasses, which she set carefully down before fetching an ashtray from another table.

"You don't mind?" she asked before lighting up.

Elder shook his head.

"How about merlot? You don't mind merlot?"

"Not as far as I know."

"I saw this film a while back, and this guy in it, a real wine buff, you know the kind, he and his friend are just about to meet these two women for dinner and he says, if one of them orders merlot I'm going to get right up and leave." She smiled. "But you don't feel that way?"

"No."

"Then cheers."

She touched her glass to his and drank. Even in that subdued lighting her makeup showed clear and bright.

For fifteen minutes or so they chatted about her job and how she had first met Joanne, some years back now, repping shampoo and conditioner into the salon Joanne managed; Jennie a foot soldier back then, not East of England sales manager as she was now, with several hundred accounts to look after—and cold calling, for her, thank God, a thing of the past.

She asked Elder about Cornwall. Didn't it get lonely? The winters, they must be the worst. And Katherine, she'd only met her a couple of times, but she was lovely, a lovely girl—and after what had happened—to have put that behind her as well as she had and get her life back on track—he must be really proud.

Elder supposed that, when he could avoid the guilt, that's what he was.

"My sister," Jennie said. "My sister, Claire."

"There's still no sign?"

Jennie shook her head.

"And it's how long now?"

"The Sunday before last. Nine days."

"There's been no phone call, no letter, nothing?"

"Nothing."

"And you've no idea where she might have gone?"

"None."

Jennie reached for her bag and lit another cigarette. There were more customers in the bar now, the lighting had been dimmed further, the volume of the music eased up. Little more than silhouettes, people drifted past outside in twos and threes.

"I called round on the Sunday afternoon," Jennie said, "the bungalow in Sherwood where she lives. She moved into it after Brian—her husband—after he died. Five years ago, cancer. The kids had gone, grown up, and I suppose she thought, you know, a new start. New lease on life."

For a moment Jennie's voice cracked and she looked, hastily, away.

"You went to see her," Elder prompted.

"Yes. It's been a habit to go round every couple of weeks. Sundays. Just, you know, a cup of tea and a chat. Try and take her out of herself a bit."

"She needed that?"

"Oh, yes, I think so." Jennie drank the last of the wine from her glass and dragged on her cigarette. "I got there a bit later than usual. Four, four-thirty, I suppose it was. Somewhere around there. It wasn't dark yet, but getting that way. There were no lights showing inside, none at all, and I remember thinking that was strange. Then I thought she might be lying down, taking a nap; she gets these headaches sometimes, migraine I suppose, and the only thing she can do is lie down in the dark until it goes away. So I knocked a few times, and rang, and then when nothing happened, I let myself in. Claire had wanted me to have a key.

"I called, called out her name, and then when there was no reply, went into the bedroom. I was certain that's where she'd be, under the covers, you know, fast off." Jennie paused. "There was just this bear, this old bear, propped up against the pillows. We'd had it since we were kids, hers first and then mine; somehow she'd got it back. Ratty old thing it is now, only one eye. And she wasn't anywhere. Claire. Not anywhere."

"She'd known you were coming round?"

"Not really, I mean, not for certain. But she'd have assumed it, yes. Like I say, it was what we did. Besides, she was never out, not that time of day. She'd be watching a film on TV. Ironing a few bits and pieces. Reading."

"She wouldn't have popped out to see a friend?"

"She doesn't have friends. Not that way. Oh, a few people she knows to say hello to, neighbours, but no one close. Not the kind you can just call round to, on spec. Besides, she wouldn't do that; she's not the sort."

"And there was nothing to indicate where she'd gone?"

"Nothing. Believe me. I checked her clothes, the wardrobe, her things in the bathroom—in case she had gone away for the weekend and not got back, though God knows where. But it was all there, everything was there, in place, the way she always kept it, neat and tidy. Everything except bloody Claire."

Fiercely, she stubbed out her cigarette in the ashtray. Elder carried the glasses back to the bar and returned with fresh ones, more merlot. It tasted all right to him, but what did he know?

"What you've got to understand, about Claire..." Jennie weighed in again as soon as he sat back down, "she isn't like me. She doesn't stick her face out, get on with things. She's never..." Jennie leaned back and pushed her hair away from her face. "When we were growing up, our mum, she walked out. Packed her bags and left. I don't know, I suppose it had been going on for years, her and my dad, falling out, this and that. They say kids notice these things, but no, we didn't. Not me, anyway. Even thinking back, I didn't notice a thing. But one day—whatever the reason, whatever brought it to a head I don't know, Dad never said—she just upped and left. Kiss on the cheek, pat on the head. Gone. I was five. I didn't understand, didn't have a bloody clue. She'll be back, I thought, she'll be back. Tonight, to-morrow, the day after. She never was. Not once."

Jennie leaned back and drew smoke down into her lungs.

"I can understand that. Now. Not leaving like she did, not that. But once you have, once you've gone, the only way you could hope to make it work, live with yourself, must be to make a clean break. Forget. They say mothers never can, but I don't know…"

Someone passing close to the back of Jennie's chair brushed against her and apologized.

"My dad took it bad. Never made a fuss or anything, but you could tell; later especially, you could tell. Claire, she was a good deal older than me, fourteen. She looked after me when Mum left. Had to, more or less. After Dad died, especially. She left school as soon as she could and got a job. She could have gone to university, she was bright enough, but no. It wasn't even a job she liked. Just paid a few bills, that's all it was, marking time. Soon as Brian married her, she packed it in. Stayed home, looked after the kids. Two. Two kids, Jane and James." Jennie shook her head. "That was her life, the children, the house."

She sipped some wine then cradled the glass in both hands.

"One day—university, whatever—they're gone. And then Brian got sick, lost weight, three months and he looked like a stick. Six more months the doctors gave him but he hung on close to three years. I sometimes think it was our mum leaving made him cling on how he did. As if he wasn't going to go and leave us, no matter what. And, of course, she nursed him, Claire, all the while. Did everything."

For a moment, Jennie closed her eyes.

"When he died, the first few months, she was brilliant. Me, I thought she'd fall apart, but no, all the funeral arrangements, she handled those, boxed up Brian's clothes for charity, put the house on the market, found herself a job. Just back in an office, nothing special, but a job all the same. When she sold the house, she gave a chunk of money to each of the kids and bought the bungalow with the rest. And then she stopped: as if she'd run out of steam. That was five years back. Now it's work that bores her silly five days a week, the weekly shop at Sainsbury's and that's all. Jane comes back to see her once in a while—not as often now as she used to—and once in a while Claire goes down to see her. At least she did when Jane was still in London. She's in Bristol now, getting an MBA."

"And the son? You said there was a son?"

"James."

"Where's he?"

"Australia. Went out for six months, some kind of transfer from the firm he was working for, and stayed."

"She wouldn't have gone out to see him? That's not a possibility?"

Jennie shook her head. "Without telling anyone? Without telling me or Jane? No."

"But you've checked all the same?"

Jennie smiled a little with her eyes. "I've checked. The last contact they had was a phone call a couple of weeks before Claire disappeared. James is always on to her to get a computer so they can keep in touch by e-mail, but Claire says no, she wants to hear the sound of his voice."

"They're close, then?"

"As close as you can be a few thousand miles away."

"It puts a lot of pressure on you."

"I try." Tears threatened the perfection of her face.

Elder hesitated, drank some more wine. "I don't suppose you thought to bring a photograph?" he said.

But of course she had. Two, in fact. Head-and-shoulder shots, the kind you take yourself in cubicles at post offices and railway stations. A serious-looking woman with a roundish face and dark, rather lank hair. Late fifties, Elder would have said. That at least.

"It occurred to me not so long back," Jennie said, "I didn't have any recent pictures of her, not since Brian passed on, so I asked her if she'd get some taken. Told her I'd pay. I thought she'd go to a proper photographer, in town. What she gave me were these."

Elder nodded and slipped them back into the envelope.

"What I'd like you to do," he said, "is make a list of anyone you can think of with whom she might have been in touch— the children, of course, and anybody else. I know, I know, you say she didn't have many friends, but think about it again and if you do come up with anyone, note it down. Where she worked, the details there, I'll need those, too."

"You will help then?"

"I'll do what I can."

"Thank you."

"Just don't get your hopes up, that's all."

Immediately, he saw the fear flood her eyes.

"I mean, about what I can do. As far as your sister's concerned, my guess is she's fine."

"Then where is she? Why doesn't she get in touch?"

"I don't know. But she'll have her reasons, I'm sure."

Eighteen years earlier, Elder had been involved in an investigation into the disappearance of a teenage girl from a caravan site on the North Yorkshire coast; when she was found, years later, she was living in a small town in New Zealand, facing out across the Tasman Sea. She had had her reasons, too.

Outside on the street, Jennie looked small beside him, but having made a trip to the Ladies had recovered, her face back in place. No longer as if she might break.

"This list you want, will tomorrow afternoon be okay? I can fax it to your hotel."

"That's fine."

"Okay." She took a step away. "I'm just in the NCP. Can I give you a lift?"

"Thanks, no. I'll walk."

Jennie held out her hand again. "What you're doing, I'm really grateful."

Elder edged a smile. "The bungalow, you think it would be all right if I went out and took a look?"

The hesitation was momentary, no more; Jennie slipped the key off the ring and into his hand. She'd already given him her card with her various numbers, address, and e-mail.

"We'll be in touch," she said. "Yes?"

"Yes."

He watched her pass through the car park entrance, then set off along Stoney Street in the direction of his hotel.

INCONGRUOUSLY, THERE WERE MORE FISHERMEN NOW, hooded and wrapped against the cold, small green lights alongside them puncturing the night. Car headlights flickering in the waters of the canal. Elder had tried sleeping: been unable to sleep. He'd opened his book, but failed to concentrate, no matter how much the story was pulling him in. *After what had happened—to have put that behind her as well as she had and get her life back on track. After what had happened.* The killer he'd been chasing had abducted his sixteen-year-old daughter, Katherine, and taunted him with what he'd done, what he might do. By the time Elder had finally caught up with him, Katherine had been subjected to savagery and pain she would never forget, her life hanging from a thread. *You nearly killed her, Frank.* His wife Joanne's words. *You. Not him. Because you had to get involved, you couldn't let things be.* Beneath her anger there was truth, a kind of truth that skewered them all together even as it rendered them apart.

Now the man who had damaged her most was in a secure unit in Broadmoor, and Katherine, after a period when she'd seemingly run wild and courted risk, as if, perhaps, nothing more terrible could possibly happen to her, had gradually reined herself back in, resumed her studies, begun to sort out her life.

You must be proud.

Just to think of it for one second made him catch his breath.

He tried another chapter of *The Fox in the Attic* before turning out the light.

At four-thirty he woke, rimed in sweat. Something, an image, pulling at his brain. It took him several moments to realize it was from the book, not the last section he'd read, but something earlier: unforgettable. Two men walking out of the sea marsh side by side, save for the misted rain the only things moving amid the unremitting gray; two men with shotguns, the taller carrying, slung across his shoulder, the body of a dead child. A girl. Elder could see it. Clearly. Her thin legs bouncing lightly against his chest.

Chapter 4

ELDER STOOD ALONE IN THE CENTRE OF THE ROOM. Someone, presumably Jennie, had pulled the beige curtains partway across the picture window, and had placed the free newspapers and meagre post on the small table just inside the front door. Patterned, machine-made lace hung down close to the glass, keeping out prying eyes. Antimacassars were draped neatly across the back of the two-seat settee and its matching chair. A cushioned footstool stood neatly in between, and, near that, a coffee table finished in beech veneer. A dresser that had come, Elder thought, from the larger house where Claire Meecham had lived previously, stood against the rear wall, its shelves busy with picture plates and china dogs and framed photographs, the two largest displaying her children in mortarboards and gowns, degree certificates held proudly across their chests. Smaller, centrally placed, was a picture of Claire and Brian, bundled up against the cold on some English sea front—

Scarborough, Filey, Skegness—clearly half-frozen but, just as
clearly, smiling. Happier times. As much as ten years before?
He picked up the photo and held it toward the light. Claire
would have been in her forties then, roughly the age Jennie was
now, but looking older. Rounder of face, her hair turning naturally gray. A comfortable fifty or more. Comfortable.

Elder stepped back.

The air in the room smelt stale.

The kitchen was neat and narrow, tea and coffee clearly la-
belled in squared-off plastic jars; Horlicks, Ovaltine, a blue-
and-white-striped J-cloth draped across the plastic bowl in the
sink. Pinned to the wall by the rear door, a Woodland Trust calendar showed the days up to the weekend on which Claire had
disappeared marked off with single diagonal lines. "Bank" was
written inside one square in letters almost too small to read,
"Doctor" in another. "Library" several times.

At the far end of the garden, a small flurry of sparrows and
blue tits was squabbling around a pair of half-empty bird feed-
ers. So far as was known, Claire had gone to work on the Friday
as normal, returning home at the usual time; on Saturday she
had apparently caught the bus to Arnold for her weekly shop
at Sainsbury's: Jennie had said there were milk and chicken
breasts newly in the fridge, fresh bread in the bin. There was no
car: not anymore. Brian had always done the driving; somehow
Claire had never learned.

A fluffy pink bath mat hung over the edge of the bath; a
green and red acrylic toilet seat cover. The bedroom was larger
than Elder had expected, its walls a dusky pink. The one-eyed
bear that Jennie had mentioned was no longer on the bed, but
propped up on a chair between dressing table and wardrobe.
There was a small clock radio on a cabinet beside the bed, a
box of coloured tissues, and a book club edition of Daphne
du Maurier's *Rebecca*. Elder had read it, had read several of

du Maurier's books, in fact, after visiting the author's house in Cornwall. He had preferred the one about pirates and ship-wreck. What was it? *Jamaica Inn?*

The wardrobe doors sprang open easily. Dresses in olive green and shades of gray and brown; a suit in sombre black. Skirts and blouses, evenly matched. Pairs of shoes lined up along the floor. On the surface of the dressing table were mois-turizing creams and oil of evening primrose, a few items of makeup, more tissues, a brush and comb.

The two top drawers, as he'd expected, held mostly under-wear, tights, several nightgowns, a small selection of thermal vests; below, neatly folded, were sweaters and cotton tops and cardigans. Elder slid the last of the drawers back into place then opened it again. The edge of something white was just showing between two shades of green.

Not white but lightly embossed cream; one of those semi-stiff card folders they give you with enlargements of your favourite photographs. This one showed a woman whom Elder, at first glance, failed to recognize as Claire: fully made-up, glass of wine in hand, her hair stylishly rolled, wearing a blue off-the-shoulder dress that emphasized the cleavage of her breasts.

In the photograph with Brian she'd looked happy, yes, con-tent, but this was something different. Exultation. Delight.

Elder sat at the dressing table and switched on the light. His first thought was that the picture had been taken some years earlier, when she was younger; but no, behind the lipstick, the foundation, and the blusher, this was recent, he was sure. Claire, if not today, then not so many weeks or months earlier.

There were two narrow drawers beneath the mirror and he slid open first one and then the other. In the first were bits and pieces of inexpensive jewellery—bracelets, earrings, a plain sil-ver necklace with a cross—in the second, resting inside a piece of folded cloth, was a vibrator, ridged along the sides and with a smooth and bulbous head.

Well, Elder thought, somewhat surprised, why not?

TRUE TO HER WORD, JENNIE FAXED THE INFORMATION Elder had asked for to his hotel. An address and phone number for Claire's daughter, Jane, in Bristol; phone number and e-mail address for her son, James, in Melbourne, Australia. The organization where Claire had been employed was called Midas Holdings and had offices on Castle Gate. Jennie thought her boss there was called Tranter, but other than that, she hadn't been able to come up with a single name from among the people with whom Claire worked.

Elder dialled the number Jennie had given him for herself and got through to her voice mail; the reception on her cell was patchy, just time enough to ask her to meet him that evening at the hotel before the signal went completely.

The walk up through the city to the Central Police Station was uneventful, Elder close to losing count of *Big Issue* sellers who, despite failing in their pitch, cheerily exhorted him to have a good day.

Neil Grimes, the DS from Missing Persons, had promised him five minutes and kept him waiting in reception for three times that long before coming, heavy footed, downstairs, a burly reddish-faced man in some danger of outgrowing both the sweater and jacket he was wearing.

"Let's talk outside," Grimes said. "I could murder someone for a fag."

They walked round the corner to Shakespeare Street, diagonally across from a bar Elder remembered as Russell's, though it seemed now to be called something else.

"You were on the force," Grimes said, after his first long drag. "Up here. Major Crime. A few years back now."

"Been checking me out?"

"I doubt I'd be stood here talking to you else."

Elder nodded. "Claire Meecham. She was reported missing…"

"A week yesterday, aye. Off on a cruise, most like. Sommat of the sort. Back any day, you'll see, complete with tan and duty-free."

"Her sister's positive she'd never have gone off like that, without a word."

A wry smile cut across Grimes's face. "Handled many mispers, did you? When you were in the job?"

"A few."

"'Cause if you did you'd know folk can wake up one morning, pack a bag, and walk out the door wi'out bothering to slip the lock or feed the chuffin' cat."

"Folk fall in harm's way, too."

"You think that's what's happened here?"

"I don't know."

"Aye, right." Grimes took one more pull on his cigarette and nipped the end between finger and thumb; he'd save the rest for later.

"The sister," Elder said, "she thinks you might not be giving it all the priority you could."

Grimes laughed. "And you are?"

Elder shrugged. "I said I'd poke around. A favour, that's all. Didn't want you to think I was going behind your back."

"No skin off my nose," Grimes said, beginning to walk back toward the station entrance. "Anything does crop up, you'll give us a shout?"

"Of course."

"No quarrel then, have we?"

The two men shook hands, and Elder, realizing he hadn't had lunch and hearing his stomach grumble, went off in search of food.

HE'D ALWAYS LIKED THE FRENCH CAFÉ ON KING STREET
and was pleased to find it still in business. He asked for a ham
and cheese baguette and ate it while he browsed through that
day's *Post;* his copy of *The Fox in the Attic* was too big to fit his
jacket pocket. A mistake.

Still hungry, he had a crêpe with sugar and lemon before his
coffee. Time for a stroll down past the Theatre Royal toward the
Arboretum before heading back to the hotel to meet Jennie.

Later that evening he would phone both of Claire's children,
hoping to catch James before he set off for work, and then, the
next day, check out Midas Holdings. Maybe go back out to the
bungalow and speak to some of the neighbours. He'd been in
the city a good twenty-four hours and so far had made no attempt
to get in touch with Katherine. And yet he could do all this: ex-
pend time and energy on someone he only knew from an empty
bungalow and a couple of photographs. Because it was easier,
easier than dealing with someone you knew almost too well.

He knew that Katherine was living in a student house in
Lenton, though he had never been there. The cell number he
had for her was no longer current. The distances between them
growing greater all the time.

ELDER BOUGHT A BOTTLE OF JAMESON AND TOOK IT
into the hotel and up to his room. Switched on the TV then
turned it off again. Four walls. Back down in Cornwall, early
evening, he would pull on his coat and walk out across the
fields, the shapes of animals bulked close in the gathering dark,
the last light stretching in a pale ring across the rim of sea.

When Jennie arrived, later than she'd intended, she was
angry with the traffic, frustrated by the incompetence of other
drivers, the idiot she'd just been listening to on the car radio, a
thin film of sweat on her upper lip.

"Best not ask what kind of a day you've had," Elder said, edging a smile.

"Best not."

They sat in the far corner of the lower-level bar and at that hour had the place almost to themselves. Driving or not, Jennie was in sore need of a gin and tonic, and Elder had a small scotch to keep her company. Once she'd settled and lit a ciga-rette, he slipped the photograph from between the pages of his book.

"My God!" Jennie exclaimed, knocked back. "Where on earth did you get this?"

"One of the drawers in her bedroom. Tucked away."

For a moment he thought she was going to question his right, but she bit her tongue.

"You've not seen it before, then?" Elder said.

"Never."

"Any idea where it was taken?"

Jennie looked at the picture again. "None, I'm afraid."

"Nor the occasion?"

She shook her head.

"It is recent, though?"

"It's difficult to say. For sure, I mean. But, yes, I think so. The last couple of years at any rate." Jennie took the photograph in both hands. "It's amazing. Claire in that getup. Don't get me wrong, I think she looks fantastic. It's just I've never...I've never seen her like this, that's all."

"So dressed up or so happy?"

"Either. Both. Anyone would think she'd won the lottery. At least. And that dress—she used to make me feel like a real slap-per if I showed half the cleavage she's flashing there."

"You're sure you don't know where it is? Where it was taken?"

Jennie shook her head. "It's a reception of some kind, isn't it? A wedding, maybe? I just don't know."

"Could it have something to do with the place she worked? A retirement party, perhaps? Christmas?"

"It's possible, but..." Jennie reached for her glass. "If you did know, do you think it would help? I mean, do you think it's got anything to do with whatever's happened? Where she's gone?"

"It might. It obviously meant something to her, enough to hang on to. Although why keep it hidden? From what you say, her daughter aside, you were about the only person to go and see her. Regularly, at any rate. Would she feel the need to hide it from you?"

"Not really, no." Jennie smiled. "Not once I'd got over the shock."

"What about Jane?"

"I don't really know. She'd be surprised, certainly. But any more than that...If it was James, it might be a different matter."

"His mother, you mean. Looking sexy and having fun."

"It's not what boys want, is it? Where their mothers are concerned."

"Probably not."

Jennie gave the photograph one more look before setting it down.

"There was something else," Elder said.

"Go on."

"It probably wouldn't be worth mentioning, but for the impression you'd given."

"About Claire?"

"Yes."

"Is this something else you found ferreting through my sister's drawers?"

Elder nodded. "A vibrator."

"What?"

"A vibrator."

"My God! I didn't know she had it in her." And then Jennie blushed full red, realizing what she'd just said.

"I didn't mean..."

"I know."

"I always thought that as far as Claire was concerned, sex was, well, it wasn't something she considered very important. So I'm surprised. And I suppose, in a way... well, yes, I suppose I'm pleased." Jennie brushed the ends of hair from her face. "I'd ask you, though, the same question as before. How does finding those things help find her?"

"And I still don't know. Except that it suggests she wasn't quite the person you took her for. Not altogether."

"You mean she was leading another life?"

"It doesn't have to be as dramatic as that. But the more we can find out about her, the more chance we have of discovering where she is."

Ten minutes later they stood at the top of the stairs outside the hotel; the traffic, into and out of the city, had started to calm down.

"You've got far to go?"

"Not far."

Elder realized he had no idea where she lived, whether or not she lived alone. The only rings she wore were on her right hand.

"I might be a bit difficult to get hold of for the next couple of days," Jennie said. "Sales conference. Best leave a message on my cell if you need to get hold of me."

Back in his room, Elder poured himself a shot of Jameson before reaching for the phone.

Chapter 5

JANE MEECHAM'S VOICE WAS SHARP AT FIRST AND shrill, not at all pleased that her aunt had given her number to a total stranger; but then once Elder had explained the situation and the nature of his involvement, she mellowed. Not much, but a little. Her concern over her mother's whereabouts and whatever might have happened to her seemed real enough.

Did she have any idea where her mother might have gone? She did not. She'd thought about it and thought about it, racked her brains, but no, nothing.

Except...

Except what?

She had a vague memory of her mother mentioning one of the neighbours trying to talk her into going off on holiday, the pair of them. Some Saga tour or other. Ages ago now. A year, maybe more. No, sorry, she couldn't remember the neighbour's name. By now, she could even have moved away. But if not, surely she shouldn't be that hard to find?

When was the last time, Elder asked, she'd seen her mother?

A good couple of months now. January. Since starting this course, just about every minute was spoken for. London, it had been. She'd been back there for the day, shopping. The sales. Her mother had come down to meet her on the train.

How had she seemed?

How did she ever seem? The same.

Elder paused, registering the taint of frustration in the daughter's voice.

"Tell me the truth," Jane said then. "Do you think she's all right? I mean, do you think something's...happened to her?"

"I don't know," Elder said. "I honestly don't know."

"As soon as you do..."

"I'll let you know."

"Thank you."

Less than ten minutes later, she rang back.

"Look, Mr. Elder..."

"Frank."

"Frank, I've been worrying, ever since you called—I mean, do you think I should be there? Now? Helping? I don't know how, but doing something..."

"I don't think so. To be honest, it's difficult to think what you might do."

"You're sure?"

"I'm sure."

"Only I didn't want you to think I don't care."

"I don't think that."

"And you will call if anything..."

"I'll call."

Elder dialled the number for her brother, James, in Australia, but he was out or, at least, not answering: Elder left a message asking him to call back. The television offered a choice of buying a studio flat in Greenwich for a cool quarter of a million, or a broken-down villa in Tuscany in need of renovation and repair for considerably less. When the phone rang again and he picked it up, expecting it would be James, or Jane again, it was Katherine.

THE NEXT MORNING STARTED BRIGHT AND CLEAR: THE sky a pale but definite blue. There was still a decided nip in the air. Elder found the place Katherine had mentioned without difficulty: a narrow delicatessen and café with a few stools across the front and more down along both sides. She was already there when he arrived, sitting in the window corner, reading through some printed notes, yellow highlighter in hand.

"Hi, Dad."

"Hi."

She put her face up to be kissed, her cheek smooth against his lips.

Her hair was cut short, neat against the nape of her neck, spiked up a little at the front; her face a little fuller than the last time they had met.

"Sorry if this is early," she said.

"No, it's okay."

"I've got a class at ten. Then I'm busy the rest of the day."

"You want another?" he asked, pointing at her almost empty cup.

"No, thanks, I'm fine."

"Okay. Do I wait here or...?"

"You order down at the back."

"Right."

"And Dad..."

"Yes?"

"I wouldn't mind a piece of cheesecake, actually."

There were several people in front of him, mostly waiting for sandwiches and coffee to go. Elder looked back at Katherine as she ran her highlighter across a piece of text: faded red basketball sneakers, blue jeans, sleeveless black sweater over a pale top, denim jacket bunched on the stool behind. Something about the way she sat there, concentrating, one hand occasionally pushing up through her hair, made his breath catch low in his throat.

You must be proud.

He fumbled in his wallet for a five-pound note.

"So," he said, as he slid onto his stool, "how's it all going?"

"Oh, you know."

"Interesting?"

"This? Sport psychology. It's okay. Common sense, really; most of it, anyway. It'll help when I'm at uni." She smiled. "That's the idea, anyway."

"How's that going? University. You've got a place?"

Katherine shook her head. "Nothing definite yet."

"But you should know when?"

"Oh, soon."

"And this is where? Loughborough?"

"Loughborough or Sheffield."

His coffee arrived, along with Katherine's cheesecake.

"I asked Mum how come you were here, but she went all mysterious."

"It's no secret." He told her, briefly, what he was doing.

"More white knight stuff, then?"

"Sorry?"

"Those books you used to read me when I was little. Princesses asleep in the tower, waiting for Sir Whatever to ride up out of the west."

Elder drank some coffee; enjoyed watching her wolf down her slice of cheesecake, four, five bites and it was gone.

"Whatever happens," he said, "I should be around for a few more days. Perhaps we can get together when you've got more time? Go out for a meal, maybe?"

"Yes, sure." She was already stuffing things inside her bag.

He wanted to ask if she was still seeing her therapist, but somehow didn't dare.

"Thanks for the cheesecake."

"Any time."

A kiss that landed just below his ear and she was out of the door and gone. Elder felt strangely numb. Without the need, he stirred his coffee carefully before drinking any more: it was good and it was strong. Enough to give his heart a jolt, or was that something else?

MIDAS HOLDINGS ANNOUNCED ITSELF WITH A DISCREET gold panel attached to the outside wall. Elder spoke his name and business and was buzzed on through. Several interior walls on the second floor had been taken out to make the main space open plan, but Simon Tranter had an office of his own, with a view down onto a garden at the rear. Dark shrubs and a neat patch of lawn.

Tranter was young, younger than Elder had expected, but then most people these days usually were.

He offered coffee and Elder declined.

Tranter sat back down behind his desk. "You wanted to talk about Claire Meecham."

"Yes."

"I'm not sure how much I can tell you."

"Anything might help."

"Well, she's industrious, thorough, far too experienced for what she was doing here—she should have been an office manager somewhere at least. But this was what she wanted. Or so it seemed."

"So when she failed to turn up for work..."

"I was surprised, naturally. I phoned her home, but there was no reply. Thought, you know, she'd been taken ill. When she didn't turn up again on Tuesday, I sent somebody round. It was so unusual, you see. But the place was locked up, nobody in."

"And this was all without warning?"

"Absolutely."

When the phone on Tranter's desk started to ring, he pressed a button and it went away.

"Does she have any particular friends here?" Elder asked. "Someone she might have talked to more than anyone else?"

Tranter was already shaking his head. "It's not as if she was standoffish, not exactly; she was always polite, friendly enough on the surface, but, well, she's quite a bit older than most of the other staff, for one thing, and then, you know, she always seemed to be one of those people who preferred to keep to themselves. Which was fine. She came in promptly, did her job. Sandwiches at lunchtime, I believe; sometimes she'd eat them at her desk. Off home at the end of the day. That was Claire."

"You sound as if you're not expecting her back."

"We'll keep her position open for another week or so, but after that we'll have to advertise." Tranter glanced, none too subtly, at the executive clock on his desk. The seconds ticking digitally away behind a perspex screen.

"Just one other thing," Elder said. "At Christmas, does the firm have any sort of—I don't know—party, get-together?"

"New Year, yes. Kick-start things after the holiday. Buffet dinner, free bar up to a point. DJ. People appreciate it."

"And Claire, she would have gone along?"

Tranter laughed. "You don't really know a lot about Claire, do you? Kicking and screaming, you wouldn't have got her to anything like that. Not in a million years."

Elder thanked him for his time.

QUITE A FEW OF CLAIRE MEECHAM'S NEIGHBOURS WERE either out or simply not answering the door. "No Free Newspapers," read the signs. "No Circulars." "No Unsolicited Mail." Those who did respond looked out warily, ready to say no to whatever he was trying to sell: God or cheaper gas or a trial subscription to the local health club and gym. Several, seeing Elder there, recognized him for what he once had been, and their faces fell, anticipating the worst: an accident, an arrest, a death.

Gladys Knowles, though, was chirpy, more than ready to talk, bored with her own company and daytime TV. There was a flourish of pink in her permed gray hair, a bright, birdlike look in her eye, and a pair of unlaced sneakers on her feet.

"You've not come about the drains?"

"Afraid not," Elder said.

"I didn't think so. Too much to expect. I've only rung the bloody council half a dozen times since Tuesday last and that's not enough to get 'em out of bed."

Elder smiled.

"It's not funny, you know. You should smell it out back, or better not. Like one of them saunas mixed with Skegness at low tide. I've a good mind to bottle it and take it down there, shake it under their noses. Let 'em know what it's like."

"Claire Meecham," Elder said, taking advantage of a pause for breath. "I was wondering if you knew her at all?"

"From across, at forty-three? Nothing wrong, is there?"

"Not necessarily, no."

"Only I was thinking, just yesterday, I've not seen her for— ooh, a good few days now, it must be. Not that we were in each other's pockets, understand, but I'd see her putting her bins out, you know how it is, tripping off to work of a morning. Down to get the bus, regular as anything. Set your watch by her."

"Her sister hasn't heard from her in a while, that's the thing."

"And she's worried sick, I dare say."

"She's concerned."

"These days you'd need to be."

"You've no idea," Elder said, "if she might have gone off on holiday? Maybe with someone from round here?"

"Holiday?"

"Her daughter said she thought one of the neighbours had suggested they might go away together."

"That'll be Mrs. Parker, then. This side, at thirty-eight. Set back off the road. Parker by name and nature, too." Gladys tapped the side of her nose. "Always coming round, trying to get you to sign some petition or other, refugees or a new pedestrian crossing. Collecting for Oxfam. This—what is it?—tsunami. Wanted me to join her book group, that was the last thing."

"And you didn't fancy that?"

Gladys pursed her lips. "Too clever by half."

A GREENPEACE LOGO WAS DISPLAYED BESIDE THE FRONT door of number thirty-eight, immediately above another heralding membership in the neighbourhood watch. "Welcome" was picked out in four languages on the mat, but no one was home.

Elder went back to his car, propped his book up against the wheel, and proceeded to read. He was almost at the end of his third chapter when a spindly figure came bicycling down the street, sedate rather than speedy, a woman wearing a striped woollen hat, scarf, and gloves, a dark green anorak, and a long skirt over boots. Not taking any chances with the weather. A straw shopping bag wobbled from the handlebars as bike and rider slowed to a halt.

Elder slipped his bookmark into place.

"Mrs. Parker?"

Her face swivelled sharply in his direction. "Ms."

"I beg your pardon. Ms."

"What can I do for you?"

"I was wondering if we could talk about Claire Meecham?"

She looked at him carefully. "Just let me take this around to the back and then you'd best come in."

WHAT LOOKED TO ELDER LIKE A SOUTH AMERICAN BLANket was draped across a deep settee; a black-and-white cat sat curled on an easy chair, interested enough in Elder's arrival to peer out from beneath one paw, but no more. Framed on the wall was a photograph of a younger Ms. Parker at the head of a demonstration, shouting at the heart of a police cordon and holding a CND banner defiantly aloft.

"Anti-Polaris demo," she said. "Holy Loch. Useless, of course. Polaris was decommissioned and in its place we got something worse. But you do what you can. Either that or go under." She looked at him keenly. "I presume you don't agree?"

"It depends."

"You are the police, though?"

"Not exactly."

"Name and not rank, then."

"Elder. Frank Elder."

"Marjorie Parker."

"Ms.," Elder said, smiling.

"I'm sorry about that. Insisting, I mean. It's just these stupid assumptions. After a certain age, if you're not Mrs. then you might as well be dead."

"You're clearly not that."

She brightened. "I expect you'd like some tea?"

"Thanks, that would be nice."

"Chamomile, peppermint, or Assam?"

Elder opted for Assam.

When it arrived, accompanied by a plate of biscuits, he summarized Claire's sister's concerns.

Marjorie Parker set down her cup. "I knew she wasn't there, of course. No lights at night, that sort of thing. I mean, you notice. In fact, I telephoned the police myself. Because of the place standing empty as much as anything else. Had to wait two days before someone came back to me. We have the matter in hand, that's what he said, the young officer who called. Wouldn't tell me any more. In hand. As if poor Claire were one of those old cars you see abandoned with 'police aware' pasted to the windscreen. Six months like that before someone finally comes and tows it off for scrap."

Nodding, Elder drank a mouthful of tea.

"You said 'poor Claire.'"

"Yes, I did, didn't I? I thought of her that way, I'm not sure why. Wrong of me, really. She had no problems with her health, at least none that I knew of. She seemed perfectly competent, held down a good job."

"Yet still 'poor Claire.'"

Marjorie Parker gave it a little more thought. "I got this impression, I suppose, of someone who'd given up on life too soon."

"And you thought she should resist that?"

"Don't you?"

Elder wasn't sure. "People make their own choices. It's not always possible to understand why."

"What you mean is, don't interfere. Leave well enough alone."

"That's not for me to say."

"You'd think it, though. And say it, too. Behind my back if not to my face. People do. Interfering old busybody. And worse." She sighed. "When you've lived your life thinking it's a duty to help, to be concerned, it's hard just to sit on your hands and do nothing. Appreciated or not."

"And you tried to help Claire?"

"I always tried to find time to talk to her, yes. Suggested one or two little things she might find interesting. Exhibitions at the Castle, or out at Lakeside, that sort of thing."

"And how did she respond?"

"Oh, politely enough. She came along with me on one occasion and seemed to find it interesting. She even talked about taking a course, I remember, though I'm not sure if she ever did." She paused for another mouthful of tea. "I tried to convince her to come away on holiday once. Ten days in Egypt. Fascinating it would have been." She smiled. "You'd have thought I'd asked her to come to the moon."

"So she never went out at all?"

"Hardly ever. That's to my knowledge, of course." Another smile. "I'm not my sister's keeper, however it might appear. I do go away myself, usually to see friends. And Claire used to visit her daughter, of course. But no, in the ordinary way of things, I don't think she ventured out more than was necessary."

"And you're not aware of people coming to visit her?"

"Aside from her sister, you mean?"

"Yes."

"Not really. Her daughter used to pop up from time to time, but I haven't seen her in quite a while now. As I say, it was more often Claire who went to see her."

"You wouldn't happen to remember when she did that last?"

"I think I do, as a matter of fact. Yes, it was—let me see—four or five weeks ago. Maybe a little more. I met her at the bus stop, that's how I know. She had a small suitcase with her, so naturally I asked if she was going away. Just to London, she said. Jane's coming up from Bristol for the weekend."

"And this was when?"

"February, I'm sure. I could probably find the exact date if you think it's important."

"It might be, yes."

A small Letts diary provided the answer. "Here we are. The last but one weekend in February, that's when it would have been. I remember telling her I was going to London myself the weekend after. A CND conference at Westminster Hall."

Elder rose to his feet. "You've been generous with your time."

Marjorie Parker escorted him to the door. "I had a good friend once," she said. "Went out for a walk and took a fall. Banged her head. Nothing too serious. Someone passing took her to Accident and Emergency. When the triage nurse asked her name, she realized she didn't know. Three weeks it took her before she could remember a thing."

"And when she did, she was okay?"

"Right as rain."

"Let's hope it's something like that in Claire's case," Elder said. "At worst."

"I hope so." She held out her hand.

"One of your other neighbours," Elder said, "she mentioned a book group."

"Oh, yes."

"Claire didn't belong?"

"No. I asked her, of course. But the response was just the same. She wasn't much of a reader, that's what she said. Why do you ask?"

"No special reason."

"She'll turn up, I'm sure."

"Yes, I expect you're right."

Elder walked back across to the bungalow and let himself in. He stood for several moments in the semidarkness of the curtained room, breathing in the same stale, unlived-in smell. In the kitchen he ran the tap, then drank water from a glass. When he turned back the calendar, sure enough the weekend of February the nineteenth and twentieth was marked with a cross. Elder looked again. In each month the word "library" was written clearly several times. Not much of a reader, that's what Ms. Parker had said.

Chapter 6

1965

SHE HAD BOUGHT FLOWERS TODAY, FREESIAS, AND LEFT them in the outside office; bought them on a whim and carried them inside a cone of patterned paper as she walked to the clinic. The smell of them was still faint on her hand.

The boy was talking very little, if at all; still avoiding her eyes. There had been an incident at school. One of the other boys, older, had called him a name and in response he had attacked him, tried to hit him with a chair. By the time a teacher had arrived to break things up, the older boy, stronger, had been on top, punching him, pinning him down. Alice had the letter in the briefcase that was now down by her side, the report.

There was a piece of gauze on the boy's right cheek, close to the ear, sticking plaster holding it in place.

"Tell me what happened," Alice said.

Not as much as a glance, a shrug.

"Your eye, you've taken quite a bang."

Nothing. Still nothing. As long as he was staying in the room, some part of him wanted her to know, wanted her to under-stand. But what? He was making her feel cut off, numb.

"Something happened at school," she said. "You got into a fight."

The boy closed his eyes.

Let it rest, Alice told herself; let it go. Move on.

"Not at school," he said. So quiet, she could only just make out the words.

"You're sure?"

"Course I am." Quicker, louder, almost angry.

"Where then?"

"Home. At home."

"You bumped into something."

"Don't be stupid."

"What then?"

"He hit me."

A nerve ticked at the corner of Alice's left eye.

"Who hit you?"

"He did, of course."

"Who's he?"

"My dad, who d'you think?"

Alice smoothed her hands along the table's edge.

"He hit me. Round the face with the back of his hand. And then he held me down and punched me hard."

"That isn't true."

"Course it's fuckin' true. He fuckin' punched me. My dad. Here. See? Fuckin' here!"

The boy yanked the plaster from his face and the gauze stuck there for a moment before floating down. The smell of urine totally overpowered the last lingering scent of freesias from Alice's hand. His father, she knew, had been killed in a road ac-cident when the boy was three.

Chapter 7

ELDER WAS BANKING ON THE FACT THAT CLAIRE Meecham had used her local library, rather than make the journey into the city centre and the main library on Angel Row. The woman at the information desk was a well-rounded forty, with glasses and straw-coloured hair that was mostly piled up around her head and held in place with pins. She was trying, ever so politely, to disengage from an elderly man who could have stepped out of a Lowry painting, flat cap on his head and a long raincoat hanging loose around his shins. Steam trains, especially the old London and Northeastern Railway, were evidently his thing.

When finally she'd shuffled him off in the direction of the reference section, she gave Elder an apologetic smile.

"Stand here all day and talk to me if he could. I've switched off, of course, long since, dreaming of summer beaches and piña coladas while he's mithering on about the 7:47 from Grantham to Hartlepool. Or wherever. What can I do you for?"

Elder explained, keeping it as low-key as he could.

"And you think she might have come in here? One of our regulars, like? The name rings a sort of bell, but I can't be sure."

He showed her the photographs Jennie had given him, and her face brightened.

"Oh, yes. Mitchum, isn't it? No, Meecham. That's it. Meecham, Claire. It's usually me on duty when she phones."

"Phones?"

"To reserve one of the computers. It's either that or take potluck, you see. There's two we keep for drop-ins, the rest you can book in advance." She nodded toward the computer room to the right of where they were standing. "You can see how busy it is now."

"And Claire booked ahead?"

"Most often, I'd say so, yes."

"Evenings?"

"Yes. She might have come in earlier, of course, I'd not necessarily have known. But as far as I know it was evenings. Not so far off closing."

"So she wouldn't stay long?"

"Not really, no." The librarian shook her head and a few hairs loosened themselves out of place. "Not like some of them. Sit there all day if you'd let them. Two hours, that's the maximum now. It used to be three, but Health and Safety reckoned as how that was too much without a break. Repetitive strain injury, I suppose. Aside from going boss-eyed."

She laughed and Elder smiled along.

"You wouldn't know what Claire Meecham particularly used the computer for?"

"Oh, no. Everyone gets their own PIN, you see, when they first sign on. All they have to do then is sit right down and log on for themselves. Sometimes, if it's kids in there for their homework and you think they might be up to something, surfing for something saucy, you might take a wander past, lean over their shoulder, and give them a fright, but no, unless people are having difficulties and ask for help, you just let them get on."

"And that was Claire, in and out, getting on."

"No more than ten minutes sometimes. If that."

"She could have been just checking e-mails, then?"

"It's possible, yes. More than likely, now I think about it." Taking off her glasses, she polished them against the front of her jumper.

"These drop-in computers you mentioned," Elder said. "I don't suppose there'd be one free now?"

The librarian smiled her best smile. "As a matter of fact, there is."

AS ELDER UNDERSTOOD IT, THE MOST LIKELY E-MAIL AC-count for Claire to have was one of the big five or six: AOL, Hotmail, BTinternet, Virgin or NTLworld. If that was the case and if she had used her own name, or a version of it, he was in with some chance of tracking down the account. After that, and only then, things might begin to open up. They would also—no small thanks to the Freedom of Information Act—become more difficult.

A little more than an hour in, the librarian sneaked him a cup of instant coffee and a jammy dodger. His back was starting to ache and he was beginning to realize repetitive strain injuries were more than a cheap way of getting time off to go and watch the cricket.

After a brief stroll around the stacks and a swift perusal of the DVDs, he settled down again and another hour later he struck gold.

claire.meecham3@hotmail.com

Elder's elation as he logged on was punctured almost immediately when the server asked him to type in his—her—password.

Eight letters. Eight numbers. Some combination of the two. Most people, he knew, despite warning, used something instantly memorable and close to home, just as they did when choosing a PIN for their credit card or ATM. Own birthday, maiden name.

The only person who could provide that information easily, he thought, was Jennie, and she was off at her sales conference, waxing enthusiastically about conditioner and dermatologically tested shampoo.

Short of any other ideas, he decided to give the librarian one more try. "There's no way, in the circumstances, you could help me with Claire Meecham's password?"

He might as well have been asking the name of the driver who took the last express from London via Nottingham to Crewe.

"I haven't got a clue, my love," she said, "and even if I did…"

ELDER THANKED HER AND WENT BACK OUT ON TO THE street. The temperature had dropped by some three or four degrees and it was starting to rain. An April shower.

There was a phone box midway along the small parade of shops, and he fumbled in his pockets for coins. Not too surprisingly, Jennie wasn't answering her cell and when he tried Jane he got her answerphone. Leaving the number of his hotel was not the most useful, he realized; out here in the real world he would have to get himself a cell phone.

He drove into the centre of the city and parked at the parking garage on Fletcher Gate, just finding a space on the tenth floor. There was a Carphone Warehouse close by Waterstone's.

The last and only other time he'd tried to buy a cell phone, he'd had the same problem: convincing the eager young assistant that all he wanted was the cheapest piece of equipment possible, no extras, no frills. He would have to drop it back at the hotel later and leave it on charge. Which meant locating another pay phone to call Maureen.

Maureen Prior.

Elder's sergeant when he had first joined the Nottinghamshire Police eight years before, Prior was now a detective inspector in the Force Crime Directorate—as the Major Crime Unit was now known—and looking to go higher, boards and the like already taken, just waiting for her spot.

After an on-again, off-again flirtation with Starbucks and Pret A Manger, Prior had reverted to what she liked best: a little café where coffee was still just coffee, and a bacon roll was still a bacon roll.

Elder was placing his order when she hurried in, oval face breaking into a smile; for a moment, he thought she was going to give him an impulsive hug, but she settled for a handshake instead.

"Good to see you again, Frank. I was wondering when you'd get in touch."

"You knew I was here then?"

"Neil Grimes said something to Willie Bell; Willie told me. It's a small city, Frank." Her expression midway between a grin and a grimace.

She'd had her hair cut shorter, Elder thought; still the same clothes, though, anonymous and dark, the kind that go unnoticed in a crowd. A good copper, Maureen, one of the best.

"Busy?" he asked.

She made a face. "No more than usual. Senseless stuff for the most part. Shootings. Drug related. Rival gangs. Kids with too much time on their hands and something to prove, or so they think. Buy a gun, steal a car. Life's cheap, Frank. For some. Friday last, for instance, these two youths bumped into each other coming out of the cinema, eleven at night. One of them's got his girlfriend with him, wants to act big. Walks across to his car, takes a .22 from where it's hidden in the boot, goes over and shoots the other guy in the neck. Seventeen years old."

Elder shook his head.

"Or this," Prior said. "Close to one in the morning a call

comes in, someone's driving a BMW up and down both sides of Mansfield Road, on and off the pavement, bouncing off parked cars. A patrol car goes out to investigate, and sure enough the Beamer takes off. Ten minutes later he's lost control at the head of Sherwood Rise, swung broadside into a group of people on their way home from a party. Two in hospital with broken limbs, serious loss of blood; one fifteen-year-old girl pronounced dead on arrival at City Hospital. And the driver—the driver, Frank, half out of his head on alcopops and vodka, he was younger still. Thirteen."

"I don't envy you," Elder said.

"You know what it's like, Frank. You try not to let it get to you. Do what you can."

"Yes," Elder said, remembering. He'd managed not to let it all get to him for the longest time, but then, somehow, he'd lost the knack.

"You're up here playing hunt the thimble," Prior said.

"Something like that."

"Any joy?"

"Not much."

"You've seen Joanne?"

"When I arrived."

"And Katherine?"

"She managed to fit me in between classes."

Laughing, Prior shook her head.

"What?" Elder said.

"You sound so grudging."

"Do I? I don't mean to."

"As if you expect the poor girl to drop everything and come running, just because you've deigned to come out of hiding."

"Is that what I'm doing? Hiding?"

"You tell me."

Elder fidgeted on his chair.

"So I should just leave her alone?"

"All I mean, Frank—Katherine, you shouldn't expect too much. You're the one went off, after all, left her to get on with her life—maybe that's fair enough. And now she's doing the same. Without you."

Elder shook his head. "Easy enough said, Maureen."

"Let her make the running, at least. You've got to do that. If she doesn't want to get too close, that's what you have to accept. You're here now, but for how long? Once this business is sorted, you'll be gone."

"I suppose so. Though if it hadn't been for her, I doubt I'd ever have agreed to come in the first place."

"And she knows that?"

"I don't know."

"Of course she doesn't. Not unless you've told her. She thinks you're just here because of some investigation. Seeing her, it's incidental. The icing on the cake."

"It's not like that."

"Then tell her."

"I can't."

"Why ever not?"

Elder shook his head. "It'd be putting too much pressure on her, that's why. And like you said, she wants to live her own life, she's made that clear enough."

"She's still your daughter, Frank."

"She's almost twenty years old."

"And damaged."

"What?" Elder looked as if he'd been slapped.

"She's damaged, Frank. Those things that happened, all that she went through. That's not going to go away."

Elder hung his head.

"She needs you, Frank. You can see that. She needs to know you care."

"Christ, Maureen..."

"What?"

"Back off, will you. Give us a break."

"I'm sorry." Her face relaxed into a smile. "Getting judgmental in my old age."

"You mean you weren't always?"

She made a face.

Elder's coffee was barely lukewarm.

"How long will you be around?" Prior asked.

"It really does depend. Now I've started on this thing, I'd like to see it through."

"And she's been missing, this woman, how long?"

"Ten, eleven days."

"Frank..."

"What now?"

"That long, likely something's happened to her or she doesn't want to be found."

Elder exhaled slowly and leaned back in his chair. Around them, the café was filling up. Even here, music was playing; music from another era but music all the same.

Prior was on her feet. "Frank, I've got to be getting back."

"Sure."

He walked with her to the door.

"You'll keep in touch?"

"Of course."

He hesitated while she walked off, low heels clacking against the tiled floor. Another moment and she was out of sight. Despite the fact that they had worked closely together in the past, she had never pushed him about personal stuff in that way, and he couldn't help but wonder why she was doing it now.

When he got back to his hotel, there were two messages, one from Jennie, one from James Meecham in Australia.

Chapter 8

BY THE TIME ELDER HAD TRACKED DOWN JENNIE IT WAS
evening, and wherever she was there seemed to be some kind
of a party going on: loud voices, music, and laughter. He guessed
the conference bar.

"I have to try and figure out your sister's password," Elder
said, his voice already raised.

"Her what?"

"Password."

"What for?"

"Her e-mail account."

"Her what?"

"E-mail account. It seems she..."

"Look," Jennie interrupted him as the noise swirled round
her. "This is hopeless. I'll ring you back in five minutes. Okay?"

Without waiting for a reply, she broke the connection.

When she called him back it was from the quiet of her hotel
room. "If I heard you right, Claire has an e-mail account?"

"Apparently, yes."

"She doesn't even have a computer."

"It looks as if she used one in the library."

"What on earth for?"

"That's what I need to find out."

"And to do that you need her password."

"Exactly."

"I haven't got a clue."

"Most people use birthdays. Dates they know they'll remember. Her own, her children's, her dead husband's."

"I know some of them; the rest I can probably dredge up given the time to make a few calls. Why don't I get back to you in the morning?"

"Okay, good. Names, too. I assume she changed her name when she got married?"

"From Cowdrey to Meecham, yes."

"Any middle name?"

"Alexandra."

One letter too many. "If there's anything else you can think of that might be useful, let me know when you call."

"Will do."

Elder gave her the number of his cell just in case.

BY TEN THE NEXT MORNING, ARMED WITH MOST OF THE information he wanted, Elder was logged on to one of the library's computers and starting to work through the most likely combinations, searching for Claire's password.

It took time, but less than he had thought.

cowdreyc

As simple as that: she'd gone back to who she was before.

Elder thanked his stars that, like most people, she'd eschewed being clever for something obvious: no wonder Internet and bank fraud were as prevalent as they were.

Two clicks and the most recent contents of her inbox were there on the screen. Claire, it seemed, had been a subscriber to

no fewer than three Internet dating agencies. Personal intro-
ductions for compatible partners, country-loving singles, and
unattached professionals.

I was intrigued by the description you gave of yourself, said
Norman from Northampton, *and would very much like to meet
you.*

Please send a recent photo, pleaded Roy from Leicester,
nude if possible.

I am a recent widower, wrote Gary from Kettering, *semi-
retired, energetic, warm and sensitive. Hoping to meet a lady
to share experiences and happiness with. Please do reply.*

There were seventeen unopened messages dating back to
the day on which Claire had disappeared. Scrolling down, he
paused over a pointed but fairly innocuous promise of a lost
weekend in a Cotswold hideaway, complete with brass bed and
open fires. What Elder was looking for, aside from a clue as to
where she might be now, was something that would explain her
mid-February trip to London.

Then there it was.

*Delighted that you've decided to accept my invitation. Will
meet you at St. Pancras as planned. Stephen.*

There was no sign of Claire's response. She seemed to have
been scrupulous, in fact, about deleting whatever mail she'd
sent herself: that folder was empty. Neither were there any in-
coming messages that went back beyond the turn of the year.
No matter: if necessary, and with a court order, any IT expert
worth his salt could trace—what was it called?—her audit
trail—without difficulty, he was sure.

This was as far as he could go for now. Composing the message in his head, he clicked on Stephen's e-mail address.

stsinger7@aol.com

JENNIE WAS INCREDULOUS. "SHE'S WHAT? SHE'S BEEN
what? No, no, no, don't tell me. I heard what you said."

"It seems as if she went down to London mid-February. Spent

the weekend with a man named Stephen. Stephen Singer. Ring any bells?"

"None at all."

"I've arranged to meet him. Tomorrow afternoon."

"I'm coming with you."

"There's no need."

"I'm coming."

"Okay."

"Let me have the address and I'll meet you there."

"MUM'S BEEN DOING WHAT? DATING? ON THE INTERNET?" James's voice had taken on a decided Australian burr. "Well, good for her."

Not exactly the classic Freudian response Elder had expected.

"It doesn't bother you then?"

"Nah, why should it? Little surprised, I suppose. Everyone over there's so uptight, sitting round behind twitching curtains, criticizing. Thank God it's not like that over here. It's why I like it." He laughed. "That and the surf. Being twenty minutes from the beach. Great for kids. You got kids?"

"One. Grown-up now."

"I was going to say, if you had kids, bring 'em out. Holiday of a lifetime." He laughed again. "Course they might never go back."

"Your aunt and I..."

"You mean Jennie?"

"Yes. We're going to talk to someone your mother had met through the Net."

"You think he might know where she is?"

"Not necessarily. Not directly. But what he does know might help."

"And they were what? Having an affair? Mum and this bloke?"

"It seems as if they spent the weekend together, beyond that we don't know."

"My bet, that's where she is now, off in some love nest some-where. That's the case, I'm pleased for her. Couldn't be happier. After all that time nursing my dad, it's what she deserves. She's still a youngish woman, right? Fifty-five nowadays, it's not old. Not old till you're past sixty, these days. If that."

Elder liked to think he was right: right about all of it.

"You find out anything, anything at all," James said, "you'll let me know, right?"

"Right."

It had been like talking to someone no more than a couple of streets away, yet at the same time, a long, long way off. Another life.

AS IT HAPPENED, JENNIE CALLED HIM AND SAID SHE'D meet him between eight and eight-thirty; they could have some breakfast and then drive down to London together in her car.

No argument.

She arrived early, wearing a black quilted vest over a white shirt with loose sleeves, dark cord jeans tucked into brown mid-calf boots. Smart but casual. The weekend. Elder thought that kind of vest had some special name, without remembering what it was.

He chose scrambled eggs and bacon from the buffet, toast that had stood for too long, coffee, and juice. Jennie asked for an omelette, freshly cooked; filled a bowl with yoghurt and fruit, with a sprinkling of nuts.

"Conferences," she said as they sat. "Drink too much, smoke too much, too much of the wrong kind of food. That and blokes hitting on you when they've drunk enough to get the guts to do to."

"That happens?"

Jennie's eyebrow arched. "Only all the time. Guys there are in a minority, anyway, so they're always going to think they're in with a chance. And if you've got any kind of clout in the company, like me, that's enough to give them fantasies of bending you over some executive desk."

She spooned up a portion of yoghurt and prunes.

"What do you do?" Elder asked. "Situations like that."

"Oh, kid them along, try and pass it off as a joke. If that doesn't work, tell them to go home to their wives and kids."

"And then? If that still doesn't work?"

Jennie licked something from her lips. "It doesn't usually get much further than that." Her omelette arrived and she nodded thanks. "One time when it did, this fellow was being a real pest, I got Derek to come and meet me. That's my boyfriend, partner, whatever it is you're supposed to say these days. Derek. He lifts weights, right? Least he used to. Atlanta Olympics. And he's still big. As in B-I-G, you know?" Jennie laughed. "I didn't have any problems after that. Not with that jerk at least."

They were on the road by nine fifteen, Jennie's car a sporty little Mazda that she drove this side of reckless, passing almost everything in the outside lane.

"You always go this fast?" Elder asked, concern in his voice.

Jennie grinned. "You want fast?"

Elder tightened his seatbelt and did his best not to look concerned.

Closer to London, speed cameras and the volume of traffic slowed them down, and Jennie switched on the CD player. "Listen. You know this?"

"'Fraid not."

"Boz Scaggs. Some name, yeah? The voice, though. Blue-eyed soul, I think that's what it's called."

Easing up the volume, she sang along.

Chapter 9

STEPHEN SINGER LIVED IN A TINY MAISONETTE IN HAMP-
stead, South End Green, to be more exact; the ground floor and
basement of one of a row of older terraced houses, no more
than a stone's throw from the southwestern edge of the Heath.
Each room was small with low ceilings and mostly book-lined
walls. He doubted if Jennie's Derek would have been able to get
through the front door, even on his knees.

Stephen himself proved to be a sprightly sixty with graying
hair and the neat suggestion of a beard, and not tall, five six or
five seven at best. He was sporting a Fair Isle cardigan over a
faded purple shirt, green canvas jeans, and, despite the temperature outside, open sandals on his feet.

There was music playing from one of the other rooms.
Mozart? If it was classical, Elder usually assumed that's what
it was.

"Coffee? You'd like coffee? Or I could manage tea?"

Coffee was fine.

They sat angled toward one another, knees almost touching.

"When I first bought this place," Stephen said, "long, long before I retired, I thought of it more or less as a pied-à-terre. Oxford, that's where I was teaching, where I spent most of my time. Then, when I took early retirement, and gladly I might say, I came here to live. Almost ten years ago now."

He looked around as if he could scarcely believe it had been that long.

"My sister..." Jennie said, jerking things to the matter at hand.

"Of course, of course. Claire. From what you said in your e-mail, Mr. Elder, I can see you must both be sorely worried. Very sorely indeed."

"You haven't seen her?" Jennie said. "Since whenever it was?"

"Since February. No."

"Nor heard from her?"

"No."

"You're sure? No phone calls, letters, e-mails?"

"Nothing." He gave a slow shake of the head. "I only wish I could say there were."

"The weekend that you spent together," Elder said. "Was that the first?"

"Yes. I mean, no. Not exactly. We'd met twice before, just for the day. Once at the end of January, and the other occasion was in November. November last."

"And this was where?"

"In London. We met in central London and spent a few hours together before Claire caught her train home. It was only on the last occasion that she came here, to the flat. I'd invited her, you see, to stay." Breaking off, he glanced at Jennie a shade anxiously. "Stay for the weekend. We'd got on so well, at least that's what I'd thought. My presumption, at least. At first she said no, she didn't think it was right; didn't think she was ready, that's what she said. And then she changed her mind."

"Do you know why?"

He gave a birdlike shake of the head. "Not really, no."

"You must have asked."

"Of course. 'I'm here now,' she said, 'isn't that enough?' It was."

"Did you sleep with her?" Jennie asked, an edge to her voice.

"I'm sorry. I don't think…"

"Did you sleep with her, for Christ's sake?"

"Yes. Yes, I did. We did. If you're concerned, it was something she was entirely comfortable with. There was never any suggestion of…"

"All right."

"I just didn't want you to think…"

"All right. I said all right." Jennie swung her head away.

"The weekend generally," Elder said. "Would you say it went well?"

"Yes. Yes, I think so. We went to Tate Britain on the Saturday. 'Turner, Whistler, Monet.' It was crowded, of course, but a marvellous exhibition. Quite breathtaking. Claire was very appreciative. Later in the afternoon, we had a stroll on the Heath. I made dinner here. On Sunday morning there was a concert at Wigmore Hall. She caught the train home midafternoon."

"Happily?"

"Yes. I think we'd both had a splendid time. I had, I know. And Claire, Claire sent me a lovely card. Just a little thank you, you know…"

"You've still got it?" Jennie said quickly.

"Yes, of course."

"Let me see."

Stephen got up and went into the other room, returning moments later with a postcard Claire had presumably bought at the exhibition. On one side there was a reproduction of Whistler's *Nocturne in Blue and Gold;* on the other she had written in a neat, rounded hand: "Dear Stephen, So many thanks for a delightful weekend. Affectionately, Claire." A solitary kiss.

"You said you haven't seen her since?"

"That's right."

"There's been no contact at all?"

"On Claire's part, none."

"And on yours?"

"I wrote several times."

"Wrote?"

"Yes."

"Not e-mailed?"

"No. It's so impersonal. And besides, she'd given me her address. She hadn't wanted to, I realized that at the time, and perhaps it was wrong of me to insist. But I did want to see her again, and it seemed the best way."

"Clearly not," Jennie said. "Persuading women to do things against their will, it rarely is."

Stephen started to say something, but fell silent.

The Mozart, if that's what it had been, had come to an end. There was the sound of a dog barking outside, faint and then loud. Cars passing. Someone whistling as they walked by.

"Did Claire say anything," Elder asked, "anything at all about any other relationships?"

Stephen shook his head.

"Nothing about any other men she might have been seeing, been involved with?"

"I didn't ask."

"Even so..."

"I did ask her, just in the way of conversation, if she'd made use of the Internet before, to meet people, and she admitted that she had."

"Admitted," Elder said. "That's an interesting word."

Stephen looked at him. "Because it implies guilt, you mean?"

"I suppose so, yes."

Stephen considered it a moment longer. "I think for people of my age, there is that connotation. Something secretive, furtive. I dare say for some that's a great part of the attraction."

"And for Claire?"

"I don't think I'd go that far. Although I did get the impression that she liked to keep that aspect of her life quite compartmentalized from the rest."

NOT SO MANY MINUTES LATER, THEY HAD LEFT STEPHEN Singer on his doorstep and were walking up toward Hampstead High Street in search of lunch.

"So," Elder said, "what did you think?"

"Of Stephen?"

"Yes."

"I'm not sure. A bit self-controlled for my liking. Bit too clever, too. Oxford, was it? But I suppose he seemed decent enough."

"Trustworthy, then?"

Jennie glanced sideways. "Yes, I think so." She shook her head. "I really don't know."

They walked on up the hill. "Did you believe him? When he said he hadn't seen Claire again."

Jennie stopped in her tracks. "Didn't you?"

"I don't know. My first inclination is to say yes, I do."

"But?"

"But one thing I've learned, first inclinations, first impressions, they're not to be trusted. Not always, anyway."

"So you think he might be lying? He might have seen Claire more recently, that's what you mean? You think he might know what's happened to her, where she is now?"

"Whoa, whoa. Not so fast. That's one hell of a leap."

They stood aside to let a pair of joggers go past.

"But it's possible?" Jennie said.

"It's possible."

When Elder recommenced walking, Jennie fell into step beside him. The implication was clear in her mind, but best unspoken: in one way or another, Stephen Singer could have done her harm.

"There was something about where he lives, didn't you think?" Jennie said, as they turned on to the High Street. "That place of his."

"How do you mean?"

"I don't know. There was this atmosphere. Sort of strange. Unreal. The size of it, for one thing. It made me feel like Alice, *Alice in Wonderland,* remember? When she goes into the White Rabbit's house to look for his gloves? And it all gets smaller and smaller around her until she's trapped and can't get out. It felt like that."

"When we get back," Elder said, "I'll have a word with a friend. See if we can't find out a few things about Stephen on the quiet. Just in case."

"She was taking a risk, wasn't she?" Jennie said, a few moments later. "My sister. Meeting people like that. Mind you, once you've passed a certain age, if you do want to meet someone, a man, what else can you do? She's not exactly going to go clubbing, is she? Out on the town on a Friday night. And whatever I've learned about Claire recently, and that's been quite a bit, I still can't quite see her as the speed-dating type, can you?"

Though his experience of speed dating was precisely nil, Elder thought that was probably true. All else aside, Claire didn't seem the kind to rush into things without weighing up the pros and cons and being able to maintain some element of control.

"It's got to be something to do with all this stuff, though, don't you think?" Jennie said. They were outside a pub advertising Toulouse sausages and mash. "Meeting someone through the Net."

"It's all we've got to go on," Elder said. "For now."

It was two clear weeks since Claire had last been seen.

———

JENNIE DROPPED ELDER OFF AT HIS HOTEL, AND BEFORE she swung back out into traffic, rang Derek on her cell.

"Don't tell me," he said. "You're running late." A smile, not anger, in his voice.

"Think again. Five minutes tops."

"How come you're calling me then?"

"Thought you might want to start pouring the wine."

When she and Derek had become enough of an item that her friends had started asking her if she was thinking about getting married again, Jennie had been quick to disabuse them. Once, thank you very much, was quite enough. Besides which, she'd never really seen Derek as the marrying kind. He was there, most of the time, when she needed him, and that was enough. Enough for him, too, or so it seemed.

Two years this summer and they hadn't as much as moved in together, hadn't seriously considered it. Jennie had her house, Derek his flat: both had their space. Derek's was close enough to the city centre for him to be able to walk to work.

Along with his cousins, Derek ran the door at a number of the city's clubs and pubs. Bouncers, doormen, call them what you will. Most nights, Saturdays in particular, Derek would make the rounds, check that everything was cool, under control, sort out any little problems that had ensued. It's what he would be doing later on.

Most weeks, Tuesdays or Wednesdays, quiet nights, Derek would come round to her and they would order Chinese, watch a DVD in bed; other times, Jennie would go to his place and he would cook. Jennie kept a few things now in his wardrobe, had half of his bathroom cabinet to herself.

"So, Sherlock," Derek said, greeting her at the door with a generous glass of sauvignon blanc, "how was it?"

"Strange." Lifting her face toward him, she took the glass from his hand as he kissed her mouth. A moment later she kicked off her shoes.

"Strange how?"

"I don't know. Just—well, strange. Weird. Sitting there, all civilized, with this man who could know what has happened to my sister."

"You think he does?"

"I don't know. He says no, but..." Jennie took a big gulp of wine. "People lie, don't they? All the time."

She hoisted herself up on to one of the kitchen stools. Derek was in the middle of making some kind of pasta sauce—mushrooms, anchovies, onions, tomatoes—and was wearing a cook's apron over a white T-shirt and black linen trousers.

"The copper," Derek said, "ex-copper, what did he reckon?"

"Thought he was okay, I think. Believed him, or at least he said he did, about seeing Claire..."

"He did fess up to seeing her?"

"Yes. Three times." Jennie hesitated. "Slept with her, too."

Derek grinned. "Fast worker."

"It's not funny."

"I know."

"Said he wanted to see her again, but she said no."

"Couldn't have been up to much in the old bed, then."

Jennie shook her head.

"What?"

"Think that's the answer to everything, don't you?"

"No." He rested his hand on her shoulder and she shrugged it away.

"I'm not in the mood."

"Okay, okay. Relax. Stick something on the stereo while I see to this. Unless you want to make a dressing for the salad? Only not too much of that walnut oil this time, yeah? Just a touch."

Jennie set aside her glass and eased down from the stool. She thought she could probably do both, make the dressing and find a CD. That Jill Scott she'd given him for his last birthday...

Chapter 10

AWAKE EARLY AS USUAL, ELDER QUICKLY SHOWERED, shaved, and dressed; a pair of swans was drifting past as he walked outside and down the steps toward the water's side.

The last thing Jennie had said to him the previous evening, before driving home: "You don't think it's hopeless, do you? I mean, wherever she is, you do think she's all right?"

"Yes," he'd lied, "I'm sure she is."

What? Holed up in some country cottage, waking even now to the sound of birds and the promise of fresh coffee and warm bread, newly picked mushrooms, perhaps, and lightly poached eggs?

He walked briskly, lengthening his stride as he passed under the first bridge, taking himself past what had previously been a phalanx of slowly crumbling warehouses and had now become, for the most part, loft apartments or smart bars. An old British Waterways sign was still discernible in fading white, high to his right. When he and Joanne had first moved here, not so many years before, Katherine about to start secondary school and not yet on the cusp of her teens, everything had seemed to Elder full of promise. New jobs for Joanne and himself, in time a new house, new lives.

"Fuck!" he said to nothing and no one. "Fuck and fuck again!"

He kicked a stone out onto the canal and sent a bevy of ducks scattering noisily. Above, the sky had taken on that peculiarly leaden look that presaged snow. Mid-April, for God's sake. How could it snow?

Hands in pockets, he turned back toward the hotel.

Back in his room, he looked again at the printout he had made of Claire's inbox; there were ten addresses worth contacting, ten people to be asked about any possible contact with her, ten people to be visited and seen.

He thought again about Jennie's reaction to Stephen Singer, running over the morning in his mind and trying to see Singer as Jennie had seen him, feeling for the same off-key, slightly threatening atmosphere. Trapped? No, it hadn't been how he had felt. Maybe you had to be a woman, brought up on *Alice in Wonderland,* to understand? Or just a woman? Perhaps that was enough.

THE STUDENT HOUSE IN WHICH KATHERINE WAS LIVING had bins out front filled to overflowing, a blanket serving as a curtain draped across one of the upstairs windows, an oversize moose in the front window, coloured streamers dangling from its orange horns.

The young man who eventually came to the door was wearing scabby jeans, a blue woollen hat pulled over his ears, and nothing in between.

"Kate!" he called back up the stairs. "Someone for you."

He disappeared into the back of the house, leaving Elder on the doorstep. It was fully five minutes before Katherine emerged, a quilt round her shoulders, bare legs.

"It's not too cold out," Elder said. "I thought we'd go for a walk."

She looked at him as if he were truly mad.

BY THE TIME THEY ARRIVED AT THE PARK, THE FIRST FEW flakes of snow had started to drift aimlessly down, feathering in the wind. Katherine vainly protesting, Elder set off at a healthy clip down toward the lake, but by the time he had settled into a more sedate pace, she had hurried past and was urging him on.

From the far side of the water, the baroque towers of Wollaton Hall were only dimly visible through a haze of shifting white.

"Jesus!" Katherine said. "We're crazy. You know that, don't you?"

Elder grinned and for twenty or thirty yards he stayed close with her as she started to run. But Katherine had been a county athlete as a girl, and even out of training she had him comprehensively beaten.

When they reached the slope that would take them back to the stable block and its café, Elder was standing, hands on hips, bent double, desperate to catch his breath.

"That," Katherine said with a note of triumph, "will teach you to hoick me out of bed on a Sunday morning."

Elder grinned.

Along with large cups of hot chocolate, Katherine had a cheese and ham toastie, Elder a well-stuffed bacon roll. Leaning back against one of the long wooden seats and sheltered from the wind, they relaxed. There were a few families there with kids and dogs; an elderly couple in sensible walking gear; several singles thumbing through the Sunday papers.

They talked easily about Katherine's course, about some of the other students in the house, most of whom were already at university; skated over the subject of her mother and Martyn

Miles. Katherine told Elder when he asked that, yes, she was still in contact with her ex-boyfriend, Rob Summers, who was now studying for an MA in creative writing in North Wales, but just as friends. Nothing serious, okay?

Elder wondered if Summers was still supplementing his income by selling dope, but he forbore asking.

When, a little over an hour later, he dropped Katherine back at the house, she gave him a kiss on the cheek and a hug and promised to call him later in the week.

"Dinner, right?"

"Right."

Even now, watching her walk away was like watching a part of himself move out of reach.

He was almost back at the hotel, just pulling off the London Road roundabout, the snow now little more than an occasional flurry, when his cell began to ring. It was Jennie.

"Hang on a minute," Elder said, turning into the car park and coming to a stop in the first available space. "Okay, now I can talk."

Jennie's voice was high-pitched, the words tumbling out.

"It's Claire. Claire. She's here. I went round to the bungalow. I don't know why. Like I used to. You know, Sundays. I thought I'd just drive past, but there was a light on inside. I couldn't believe it. I let myself in and there she was. In the bedroom."

"Jennie, that's great news."

"No, you don't understand. She's dead."

Chapter 11

SOMEONE WAS GIVING THEIR LAWN THE FIRST CUT OF the season, the sound of the mower distant and low. The day had changed, soft light filtering through a faint straggle of cloud; the earlier snow, where it had settled, was long melted and gone. At intervals along the street, trees were coming slowly into blossom, pink and white. Jennie's car was parked at the curb, the door to the bungalow ajar.

The blinds in the bedroom had been partly opened, the faded pink of the walls muted and indistinct. Claire Meecham lay at the centre of the bed, eyes cloudy and open, covers pulled up toward her chin. Jennie was sitting, shadowed, at the side of the room, head down, fingers wound into a knot.

"Jennie…"

She raised her face for a moment, then blinked away.

"I'm going to put on the light."

Jennie shielded her eyes.

Elder stepped around the bed and lifted back the flowered quilt. At first glance, Claire was fully dressed save for her shoes:

cream-coloured blouse, black skirt. Her hair seemed to have been brushed neatly into place. Her left arm was angled across her body, the other close by her side. A silver chain was fastened at her neck, the ruby pendant resting against the faintest suggestion of bruising on her skin.

The ancient teddy bear, frayed and worn, was propped against the inside of the crooked arm, its single glass eye reflecting the light.

Elder lowered the cover carefully into place.

Dry and harsh, a sob broke from Jennie's throat.

"Come on," Elder said, "let's go into the other room."

Jennie shook her head. Makeup was smeared, wet, across her face.

"Come on," he said again. Reaching down, he raised her from the chair and led her into the living room, helping her down onto the small settee.

"You phoned the police?" he asked.

"No. No. I called you first. I didn't know . . . I didn't know what to do."

"That's okay."

Elder took his cell from his pocket, hoping Maureen Prior's home number would come to mind. Third time of trying, he got it right. She didn't seem too pleased at having her Sunday disturbed, but listened all the same. "Give me ten minutes," she said, and broke the connection.

Elder sat opposite Jennie while, fingers uncertain, she stripped the cellophane from a fresh packet of cigarettes.

"Tell me what happened," he said, "from when you arrived."

Her lighter flared.

"The police will ask you, take you back through it, more than once. It might help to go through it with me first."

Eyes narrowing, Jennie drew smoke into her lungs.

"There's not much more than I told you already. I'd gone out in the car to get petrol, cigarettes. Then, I don't know why, I came up here. It's not as if I was expecting Claire to be here or anything. I couldn't even get in; you've got the key. I just drove past, turned, and stopped outside. Sat there. And then I saw the light. Inside. I couldn't get out of the car quick enough. She's here, I thought, she's back. I raced up to the door, rang the bell, and knocked. Shouted through the letterbox. Claire, Claire, her name over and over again. And when I banged on the door again, harder, it came open. Just a little. It must have been on the latch. I went in and called again, tried here and the kitchen, and then I saw the bedroom door was shut, and so I thought that's where she must be, in there lying down, one of her migraines."

Jennie's fingers were tight on Elder's arm.

"When I saw her in the bed I thought I'd been right and I tip-toed round, not wanting to wake her, but just so happy that she was back. I looked down at her and thought, yes, she's peaceful, she's resting, when she wakes up she'll be better. And I bent down to kiss her, just on the forehead, and her skin, it was cold. I looked at her eyes and they were...they were..."

Jennie pitched forward and, her face against his shoulder, Elder held her fast.

Minutes later, when he heard the car arrive, he eased Jennie back against the settee and went to the door.

Maureen Prior was wearing a loose cotton jacket and blue jeans, not-so-new trainers on her feet, no makeup, hair pulled back off her face: Elder thought it might be the first time he'd seen her at a crime scene so casually dressed.

"You know how many weekends I've had off in the last month, Frank? How many since Christmas?"

"Not many, I guess."

"Too right."

Elder grinned sympathetically and got no response.

"This woman," Prior said, "she's the one you've been looking for?"

"Yes."

"Okay, let's take a look."

Elder turned and followed her into the bungalow. Within a short while, the whole panoply would be following in their wake.

Prior stood a while with Elder at her back, taking in the room. Technicians would record the scene before the pathologist set to work, but photographs and videotape, however accurate, were never the same, one remove always from the real thing.

Stepping forward, she snapped on gloves. "The skin here at the neck, Frank, it's scarcely bruised."

Pressure enough to have broken the hyoid bone? They would soon know. Elsewhere, where it was visible, the skin had taken on a marbled appearance, through which the veins close to the surface had become more conspicuous.

"She's been dead a while, Frank. From the state of the body, six or seven days."

Elder nodded.

"The person who found her," Prior said. "The sister—she's still here?"

"Yes."

"Holding up?"

"Just about."

JENNIE HAD BEEN TO THE BATHROOM AND REPAIRED HER face. Smoked another cigarette. She answered Maureen Prior's questions as straightforwardly as she could, glancing at Elder occasionally for reassurance.

"Is there anything you want to ask me?" Prior said when Jennie had finished.

Behind them, soft-footed, men and women in protective clothing moved patiently from room to room.

"Claire," Jennie said. "The body...what will happen?"

"She'll be taken to Queen's Medical Centre. There'll be a postmortem."

"She'll be cut open," Jennie said quietly.

"The pathologist will carry out an examination. Do what's necessary to establish the cause of death. Anything else that might help to clarify what happened."

"She'll be cut open," Jennie said again.

"Under Home Office guidelines..."

"Cut open and stitched back up." Louder now.

"Yes," Prior said.

Tears filling her eyes, Jennie fumbled for another cigarette.

"Is there anyone you want us to call?" Prior asked. "Someone you could sit with for a while? Family or..."

"That's my family, lying dead in there."

"I'm sorry. I know, it's just..."

"My family."

"What about Derek?" Elder said, remembering the name. "You want me to give him a ring?"

"No, not now. Not yet. I don't want to see him just yet."

"Hang on here a minute," Elder said.

Marjorie Parker was at home, watching the to and fro with interest. Of course, she'd be happy to provide Jennie with a cup of tea and a place to sit quietly, out of the way. Elder couldn't be sure how long it would be before someone from the local press came sniffing round, doubtless eyeing Monday's front-page headlines. Some officer in the know would already have made a call, earned himself a pint or two. Marjorie Parker, Elder felt, would give any reporter short shrift.

Back in the bungalow, Elder found Maureen Prior taking a last look at Claire Meecham's body before it was removed. The hair carefully combed and brushed; the body neatly dressed, laid out, at rest: everything similar if not the same.

"You know what this makes me think of?" Elder said.

It took her a moment to make the connection. "Ninety-seven?"

Elder nodded.

"Irene—what was her name?"

"Fowler. Irene Fowler."

"Long time ago, Frank."

"Even so," Elder said. "Even so."

EIGHT YEARS BEFORE, 1997, ELDER HAD BEEN NEW TO
the city; new to the Major Crime Unit, a detective inspector up
from the Smoke. The older officers, some of them, still called it
that. London—the Smoke.

Maureen Prior, recently promoted to detective sergeant, had
been given the job of showing him the ropes; somewhat grudgingly, Elder had felt. It would be a long time before he would win
her trust, even longer her respect.

The call had come through midmorning, Elder's third day on
the job. Irene Fowler, fifty-seven years old and the executive director of a small food distribution company, in the city for a DTI-
sponsored conference on expanding trade possibilities beyond
the EC, had been found dead, fully dressed, in her hotel bed.

One hundred and forty-seven separate witness statements
later, close to three thousand hours of police time, only two
suspects had emerged: both were arrested, questioned, and released. No one was ever charged with Irene Fowler's murder.

Elder's first murder investigation within Major Crime.

Its failure printed indelibly on his memory.

"If you're right, Frank," Prior said, "we need to talk."

TWENTY MINUTES LATER THEY WERE SITTING IN THE
front seat of Prior's five-year-old Honda, parked by the side of
Queen's Medical Centre, and drinking rancid coffee from the
cafeteria; Elder filling her in on what he knew of the background to Claire Meecham's murder.

Earlier, Jennie had convinced Elder she was all right to drive
herself home; she would come in to the police station the next
morning and answer more questions. For now what she needed
most was rest.

"They were close, then?" Prior said. "Jennie and her sister?"

"I think so, yes." A pause, and then: "I think she felt sorry for her."

"Sorry?"

"In a way, yes. That and some sense of obligation."

Prior nodded. "She'd got on in the world, I suppose—good job, smart clothes, snazzy little car—and there's her sister, living out in never-never land, no husband, no friends, old before her time."

"Something like that, yes."

"Except, from what you've said, that wasn't true." Prior gave the coffee one more sip, wound down the window, and poured the remainder out onto the ground. "Jennie might not have known it, but it wasn't true. Claire was out meeting people, making contact, going off for weekends, enjoying herself. Concerts, exhibitions, who knows what else? Having sex. And why not? Why shouldn't she? She wasn't the quiet little mouse her sister thought she was, waiting around to shrivel up. She had a life."

"And it killed her."

"We don't know that."

"We can assume..."

"Assume, Frank? Is that what we do?"

"You know what I mean."

"Right now, I don't think we're in a position to assume anything very much. There's a fifty-five-year-old woman in there, most likely dead from strangulation, but we don't even know that yet for a fact. Until this afternoon, none of us has the least idea what happened to her in the last what? Two weeks? We don't know who she's seen, where she's been, where and when she died. As the poet said, we know little more than bugger all."

"A secret life."

"Her prerogative, Frank. Her choice. Keeping herself to herself. It's what some people do."

Yes, Maureen, Elder thought. Isn't it just?

"Those e-mail addresses," Prior said.

"First thing tomorrow."

"Whatever we need to do to find out more—it may need a court order—I'll let the computer guys loose as soon as I can."

"People I've spoken to," Elder said, "I'll write it all up. You'll want to talk to them again."

"The man you went to see in London..."

"Singer."

"How did he strike you?"

Elder grinned. "You're asking me to assume?"

"I'm asking your opinion."

"I'm sorry, Maureen, but without a few more facts..."

She punched the fleshy part of his arm with her fist. "Come on, Frank. On a scale of one to five, guilty or not guilty?"

"Did he kill her?"

"Did he kill her?"

"Gut feeling, I'd say no. But could he have killed her, that's a different question. Time, opportunity, occasion, we could all of us kill anyone."

"Get out of the car, Frank, before I put your theory to the test."

Elder took his half-finished cup of coffee with him. "Your office still where it used to be?"

"Last time I looked."

He took a pace away. "Tomorrow, then."

"Tomorrow."

Elder's own car was on another level, the only space he'd been able to find.

"Oh, and Frank..." He turned his head at the sound of her voice. "You're not really walking away from this. You know that, don't you?"

On a scale of one to five, Elder thought, right or wrong?

Chapter 12

1997

"KATHERINE!"

No reply.

With a slow shake of her head, Joanne raised her voice and tried again. "Katherine!"

"What?"

"Have you got your eye on the time?"

No answer other than a dulled thump, Katherine throwing down a book or banging her heels on the bedroom floor. Joanne rolled her eyes and unleashed a sigh.

"I'll go," Elder said.

Katherine was sitting cross-legged on her bed, new school skirt stretched wide across her knees, white shirt unbuttoned at the neck, the tie that she'd been wearing when Elder had seen her last, tugged off and hurled across the room.

"Kate," Elder said quietly.

"What?" An angry flash of her eyes that he recognized all too well.

"What do you think you're doing?"

"What's it look like?"

Elder reached back and closed the bedroom door.

"Oh, God!" Katherine said.

"What?"

"Lecture number one. Katherine, you're not a baby any more. A little girl. You're a young person, a young adult. It's time you behaved like one."

"Exactly."

"Started taking responsibility for yourself."

"That's right."

"Well, that's what I'm doing, yeah?"

"Sitting on your bed and throwing a sulk instead of getting ready for school?"

"I'm not in a sulk. And I'm not going to school."

"That's ridiculous."

"Is it?"

"Of course it is."

"You've seen the place, it's horrible."

"It didn't seem too bad."

They had come up from London to meet the head teacher, the three of them, toward the end of the last school term. The other kids, those who didn't ignore them totally, staring at Katherine with what she'd obviously seen as hostility. The head teacher breathing platitudes, mission statements, and test scores; Katherine staring at her shoes, not looking him in the eye when he asked her a question, scarcely answering at all. Elder hadn't been able to get out of there fast enough.

"It's the same for me, you know," he said.

"What is?"

"Going into a new place, meeting new people, people you've got to work with—it's not easy, I know that."

"Then why do it? Why couldn't we have stayed in London?"

"You know why."

"Because *she* didn't want to."

"We agreed."

"That's rubbish."

"It's not. We sat down and talked about it, all three of us, and we agreed."

"I didn't agree to anything. And neither did you, not really. You only went along with it to please her."

"Your mother thought…"

"My mother got her own way, like always."

Like mother, like daughter then, Elder thought.

"Well, we're here now," he said, "and we'll have to make the best of it, won't we?"

Katherine's face was set in stone.

"Won't we?"

He leaned over and slid his arm round hers, kissed her on top of the head.

"Okay?"

"I suppose so."

"Good." Elder stepped back, crossed the room and picked up her tie. "Why don't you put this on and come back down? Still time for a bit of breakfast if you hurry. Don't want to be late, your first day."

"Dad?"

He was outside on the landing when she called.

"So's I'm not late, give me a lift, will you? Just this once."

When Katherine came into the small dining room, some few minutes later, her tie was back in place, worn at grudging half-mast, new school shoes on her feet.

"Is there any toast?"

"If you want toast," Joanne said, "you need to get up earlier. There's cereal in the kitchen, you know where it is."

"It's okay. I'm not hungry."

"Suit yourself."

"How about a banana?" Elder said. "Half? Have half with me."

Joanne clunked her spoon down against her empty bowl and left the room.

"What's got into her?" Katherine asked.

Elder kept his opinions to himself.

When he got back from taking Katherine to school, Joanne was upstairs, fixing her face. There was a light drizzle outside, the sky the same omnipresent slate gray it seemed to have been since they'd moved.

"I thought we weren't going to do that. I thought she was going to walk."

"It's just today. Besides, no sense in her getting there soaked."

She smiled at him in the mirror. "Be giving me a lift into town, then, will you?"

"If you like."

He sat on the bed, watching her apply one colour to another around her eyes. The same careful ritual ever since he'd first known her. "My line of work, people expect you to look your best." Joanne had been a hairstylist in a small Lincolnshire salon, models wanted, senior citizens half price Tuesdays.

"You must be getting bored," she said to his reflection.

"Not really. There's still quite a bit to do."

Elder had some leave coming and had opted to use it getting the place they were renting into shape: all right, it had only been a flat back in Chiswick, but a large one, stuffed to the gills, and here in this matchbox house it was hard to find a home for all they'd collected through fifteen years of marriage, especially the eleven years since Katherine had been born. Much of the last few days, Elder's time had been divided between carrying stuff to the nearest charity shop or ferrying it to the tip. Once things were settled, the salon Joanne was to manage open and running, they'd start looking for a house of their own, no rush, take their time, find somewhere nice.

"Want a cup of coffee before you go?" Elder said.

"Best not."

What passed for a rush hour tailing to an end, it was an easy enough drive into the city.

"Bit hard on her this morning, weren't you?" Elder said.

"She'll get away with murder if she can, you know that as well as me."

Hardly murder, Elder thought. Eleven, rising twelve, on the edge of her teens, if some of the kids he'd run into contact with in London had been anything to go by, they were lucky Katherine was as amenable as was generally the case.

"It's not easy for her, you know," Elder said, "moving round like this."

"It's not exactly easy for any of us."

"More difficult for her."

"Never mind, Frank," her hand resting on his knee, "at least she's always got your shoulder to cry on."

"And you haven't?"

"It's not your shoulder I'm interested in." Smiling, she let her hand slide up his leg.

"Careful, I'll have an accident."

Joanne laughed. "One kind or another."

Grinning, Elder glanced in his wing mirror and accelerated into the outside lane. With any luck, Joanne would be in the same frame of mind after Katherine had gone to bed.

He parked on Fletcher Gate and walked, holding Joanne's hand, down to the tiled passageway—an alleyway, he supposed—where the new branch of Cut & Dried was to be found. Joanne had worked for them in London, and Martyn Miles, the owner, had offered her the chance to manage the new salon they were opening in Nottingham.

"It's a fantastic opportunity, Frank," Joanne had said. "Starting from scratch. Everything from the colour of the walls to hiring on, it'll be down to me. And it won't be like London, Martyn

in and out all the time, his hands in everything: I'll have it all
to myself."

They'd made their first visit, the three of them, earlier in the
year; the premises empty and pasted over with signs saying
"Post No Bills." Weeks of accumulated mail inside the door.

"You know I want this, don't you?" Joanne had said, slipping
her hands into his pockets as she pulled him back against the
glass.

"I know."

"So?" Pulling him closer, her face had moved over his and, as
he closed his eyes, she had kissed him slowly on the mouth.

"God!" Katherine had exclaimed, and thumped her father on
the back.

Elder swung round, more amused than annoyed. "What?"

"Making a bloody exhibition of yourselves, that's what."

That was months ago and now they were here, Joanne reaching into her bag for the keys, the shop front shining and new,
and there was Martyn Miles stepping out of the door to greet
them, smooth suited, hair just so, a ready smile.

"Martyn, what are you doing here?" Joanne said.

"Thought I'd surprise you, see how things were getting on."
Kissing her lightly on the cheek, he offered Elder his hand.

"Good to see you, Frank. Settling in?"

"Just about."

"Nice city, you'll like it."

"Maybe."

"Mind you, you'll only see the seamy side, I guess. Your line of
work. Not like Joanne here. Eh, Jo? The smartest and the best."

Joanne smiled an awkward smile.

"How about a coffee, Frank?" Miles said. "Time before Jo and
I get down to business."

If he calls her Jo once more, Elder thought, I'll thump him.

"No, it's okay," he said. "Best be getting back."

"See you tonight then, Frank," Joanne said. "Around five. If I'm going to be any later, I'll ring."

No kiss.

Elder's footsteps hollow on the tiled floor.

Later that day, he called the Major Crime Unit and told the office manager he'd be coming in sooner than planned.

HIS DESK WAS SOMEHOW BACKED INTO A CORNER, AF-fording Elder a fractured view of a car park and little else. Little respect for rank, not that Elder was the only DI in Major Crimes, far from it, and he'd have to prove himself before pushing for a change of scenery. He'd met the superintendent when he came for an interview and briefly again this morning, a chance encounter on the stairs; the detective chief superintendent had shaken his hand and introduced him to the half-dozen other officers who'd been around—names Elder had largely forgotten already. There would be time.

"DS Prior will see you get settled in, show you around. Meantime, that's you over there."

A hand on the shoulder and he was gone.

The chair Elder sat in had a definite tilt to one side. The surface of the desk was scored with assorted scratches and scribblings, its front edge marked with small burn marks from cigarettes left smouldering—testimony to how long it had been in use. Days Elder welcomed the end of, when smoking in the office was the norm.

A bunch of files, mostly out of date, seemed to have been dumped at his station for no reason; most entries on the Rolodex were heavily scored through, replacement details hastily scribbled into corners; the screen of his PC was cracked and the hard drive had no power cord attached. The top drawer of the desk was jammed full of manilla envelopes and blank paper; below that, several local directories and a phone book dated

1994; among the folders in the bottom drawer he found a half-eaten pork pie, still in its wrapper, mould clinging to the pastry, the meat a virulent shade of green.

"I see you've already found your way to the canteen."

Elder dropped the pie onto the desk and swivelled in his chair.

"Maureen Prior," the detective sergeant said, holding out her hand.

She was medium height, medium-brown hair neither too short nor too long, light brown eyes; she was wearing black cord trousers and a black cotton sweater, her only adornment the leather-strapped watch on her wrist. Midthirties, Elder thought, give or take. The joke with which she'd introduced herself, if that's what it was, was the only one he would hear her make for the next several years.

"Why don't we get a cup of tea, anyway?" Prior said. "You can ask me whatever you need to know."

THE FIRST TWO DAYS PASSED QUICKLY ENOUGH, ELDER familiarizing himself with the system, the routine. The Major Crime Unit for the county was divided between two bases: Carlton, here toward the eastern edge of the city; and Mansfield, a tough former mining town some fourteen miles north. Murder, serious assault, arson, high-end robbery: cooperation, sometimes edgy, with the Drug Squad and Vice. At present, the unit was involved in a joint operation with the Leicestershire Force, looking into the unsolved murders of four women, all strangled, two in Leicestershire, one in Keyworth, one in Grantham. Close to overstretched.

Elder's second day, one of the other DIs invited him to join a bunch of them for a drink, early evening. As was often the case, early turned to late. By the time he got back home, Joanne was in bed and asleep, and when he woke her, half-accidentally, half-hopeful, she rolled away from him with, "Christ, Frank! You stink!" on her lips.

Day three, a little past eleven, that was when he got the call. "Sounds like it might be one for you," said the 999 operator, before putting it through. After listening, Elder thought she was probably right.

Maureen Prior was at her desk, using all but her little fingers on the keyboard of her computer.

"Royal Palm Hotel," Elder said, "you know where it is?"

Prior pressed SAVE, moved the cursor to EXIT and reached round for her bag.

Twenty minutes later they were in reception and being directed toward the manager. "This is unbelievable," he said. "Unbelievable in this hotel." His tie was a bilious shade of yellow, his accent middle eastern, his fingernails buffed like ivory. "Please, please, follow me."

The lift glided upward without seeming to move.

"The chambermaid," the manager explained, as they stepped out into the corridor, "Lottie, a good girl. She let herself into the room to clean, change bed linen, and so on. There was nothing, no 'Do Not Disturb' outside. The room should have been empty. At first she thought it was just the way the duvet had been left. Then she saw a face..."

He used his key to open the door and stepped aside, following the two officers into the room then closing the door again firmly at their backs.

"Someone sleeping, that's what she thought, a heavy night perhaps, and then..."

But neither Elder nor Prior was really listening. Their attention fixed elsewhere.

The woman's face was angled slightly to the left, a wedge of dark, almost black hair falling across her cheek, both eyes open, staring out. The collar of some kind of shirt or blouse was visible above the cover's edge, and behind that a faint but definite reddening, like chafing, of the skin. The skin itself was cold: no pulse beating at the temple, no life.

Not young, not old.

Elder looked across at Prior, nodded, and, between them, they lowered back the quilt.

It was the collar of a dress, soft gold with a faint pattern running through; short sleeves; a belt fastened at the waist and the skirt full length and slightly flared.

It was not a dress that had been slept in.

Not a wrinkle, not a fold out of place.

Not sleeping, then, but laid out.

The woman's arms were angled down, angled together, the left hand resting on the right; there was a gold ring with a small diamond setting on her right hand, and on the third finger of the left a slight indentation, a pale circle of skin where until recently she had worn a wedding band.

Elder moved away from the bed. "This is the woman the room was registered to?" he asked.

"I think so," the manager said. "I suppose."

"You don't know?"

He shook his head.

"You do know who the room was registered to?" Elder tried to keep the impatience out of his voice.

"Yes, of course."

"So?"

"Irene Fowler, that is what it says. Naturally, I looked."

"And you've no idea if this is her?"

"These last few days it was busy; the conference, we were full."

Elder walked across to the wardrobe and slid back the door; a third of the hangers were full, two more dresses, both full length, skirts and tops, a topcoat in beige, a dark blue pinstripe suit with wide lapels. What looked to be expensive underwear in the drawer; a cashmere sweater for the cold. Four pairs of shoes.

In the bathroom, a toothbrush and toothpaste rested inside a plastic cup. Hairbrush and comb. Lotions and creams. A towel, discarded, on the floor beneath the sink; another on the rim of the bath, neatly folded; the shower curtain pulled back.

"Here," Prior said.

When he went back into the room, she was holding up a black leather handbag, holding it with a ballpoint bearing the hotel's name.

"It had got pushed down between the cupboard and the bed."

She put down the bag and, before opening it, pulled on plastic gloves.

Personal organizer, lipstick, wipes, small comb, tissues, panty liners, ibuprofen, loose change; a wallet with sixty pounds in notes, store cards, credit cards, a driver's license bearing the name Fowler, Irene Patricia; date of birth, twenty-first of June, 1940; address, seventy-one Sheridan Avenue, Market Harborough.

"Interesting," Prior said. "Driving license, no car keys."

"Perhaps they're in her coat."

They were not in her coat: no keys of any kind.

"The maid," Elder said, "the woman who found her…"

"She would not have taken anything," the manager said.

"That's not what I meant. We need to speak with her, that's all."

"She is downstairs, in my office. She is very upset."

"We'll need to talk to the rest of the staff as well," Prior said. "Anyone who was on duty last night. This morning, too."

"They are not all here. They…"

"You'll give us a list. They'll be contacted, brought in."

"We'll also need a list of everyone who was staying at the hotel," Elder said, "those who were attending the conference, especially. Any outside speakers, guests."

"I can let you have the name of the conference organizer, of course. Also, there is a programme. I have copies downstairs."

"Good."

"Why don't you go down?" Prior said. "Maybe talk to the maid? I'll make a few calls, get things moving."

"Okay."

But before leaving he went back to the bed and looked down. Irene Fowler, fifty-seven years old, recently widowed or divorced; smart, well groomed, well educated at a guess, more than gainfully employed: Around the slight swelling on her neck there were purplish marks, no bigger than pinpricks, as if tiny blood vessels had burst beneath the skin.

The maid was Croatian, worried about her immigration status, confused. She had seen the woman once before, at least once. The day before, she was certain. Or maybe the day before that. She had come back to her room when it was being cleaned. Alone? Yes, alone. Some papers she'd forgotten. Papers, books, something. Polite. She had been very polite and nice.

Interesting, Elder thought: a businesswoman attending a conference, she would have a briefcase, at least; most likely a computer, a laptop; certainly a cell phone.

None of those things appeared to have been in her room.

By late afternoon, none of them had been found.

Earlier, a maroon Volvo Estate registered to Irene Fowler was discovered in the car park and opened without recourse to the keys. She had been a tidy driver: Aside from the car manual and an up-to-date road atlas, there was but little of the usual detritus—a blue-and-silver wrapping from a bar of Cadbury's milk chocolate; a chamois; parking tickets from Nottingham, Derby, and Leicester, all from within the last ten days.

When her ex-husband was finally tracked down and notified, he cursed and swore and broke down in tears.

There were children, too, grown-up now, but children just the same.

By the time Elder arrived home, Katherine was long in bed, and Joanne sat watching a screenful of doctors cracking open a man's chest; he didn't know if it was fiction or for real.

"Long day," Joanne said, reaching her cheek up to be kissed.

Elder mumbled something vague.

"There's pasta," Joanne said, "I could heat it up. Meatballs and tomato sauce."

"It doesn't matter."

"You've eaten already?"

"No, not really."

"Then you should." Switching off the set with the remote, she swung to her feet. "You can't go without food. Besides..." nudging him in the stomach, "don't want you fading away."

The light was still on in Katherine's room and she was reading her way through an abridged *Jane Eyre* for the second or third time.

"Shouldn't you be asleep by now?" Elder said.

"Dad!" The *a* dragged out so that it became two syllables, breaking in the middle.

"What?"

"You're always nagging, you know that?"

Elder ruffled his fingers through her hair. "How was school?"

"Fine."

"Really? I thought you were dreading it."

"It was okay."

"Not as bad as you feared then?"

She gave him the same exasperated look she'd first perfected at age five: a slow sideways turning of the face away, along with an upward rolling of the eyes.

"Five more minutes, okay?" Elder said. "Then it's lights-out for sure."

"Okay."

His supper was ready in a deep white bowl, new from Muji that day, Joanne never one to miss out on the chance to do a little shopping; Parmesan cheese, a small salad of tomatoes and spinach, a glass of red wine.

Once Elder had sat down, Joanne clinked her glass against his.

"What's this all in aid of?"

"Does it have to be in aid of something?"

"I don't know."

"Well, I did have a good day. We took on two new stylists and someone to do nails. A good girl, I think, to work reception. Martyn seemed pleased."

"That's good, then."

"You don't have to be so sarcastic."

"I didn't know I was."

"Like hell you didn't."

Elder sighed and smiled and shook his head. "I'm sorry."

"No probs."

Just occasionally, Joanne came out with something, some little phrase, that drove him up the wall.

When he'd finished eating, Joanne refilled the glasses and they carried them through into the other room. One of those singers she liked on the stereo.

"How was your day?" Joanne asked.

"Let's say not as good as yours."

In that light she looked beautiful and he knew he would have followed her almost anywhere had she asked: this place no better no worse than most.

When his hand rested high inside her thigh, she made no attempt to move it away.

FORENSIC EXAMINATION OF THE DEAD WOMAN'S BODY only told them so much. Death had been caused by strangulation, the hyoid bone broken, a loss of blood to the brain. Some kind of soft ligature had been used, most likely an article of clothing, one that left no readily discernible trace.

There was alcohol in her bloodstream, but not an incommensurate amount. There were signs of recent sexual activity, but nothing that suggested sexual assault. No trace of semen, inside or outside the body: assuming a condom had been used, it had been removed from the scene.

The most likely scenario, the investigating officers agreed, was that she had invited someone, a man, up to her room; they had sex together, consensually enough, but after that something had gone wildly wrong. If wildly was the word. The way in which the body had been left suggested composure, calm, a strange degree of detachment. Ritual, even. Care.

As Maureen Prior pointed out, there was no way of knowing for certain that whoever had made love to her and whoever had killed her were one and the same, though the circumstances suggested they most probably were.

For a while the former husband came under suspicion, as nearest and dearest often did, but delve as they might there was nothing there, nothing other than anger, sadness, and regret. One of the casual workers at the hotel had a record of minor sexual offenses—exposing himself, stealing underwear from launderettes, a single incident, unproven, of rubbing himself up against a woman on a crowded bus—and although both Elder and Maureen questioned him, separately and together, they could find nothing conclusive linking him to Irene Fowler's murder.

Links were sought, connecting the death to those from strangling that were already under investigation, but none were found. After three months, the file, still open, was shuffled to the bottom of the deck, the bottom of the drawer.

Case unsolved.

Chapter 13

ELDER FELT THE FIRST DROPS OF RAIN AS HE CROSSED Fletcher Gate to where Joanne had suggested they meet: a glass-fronted café-restaurant with a spiral staircase between the floors; Joanne seated on the upper level by the window, staring out.

"Frank, it's dreadful." News of Claire Meecham's murder had been the lead item on the local news, front page in the early editions of the *Post*. "Poor Jennie."

Nodding, Elder eased out a chair.

"I didn't know whether to phone her or not," Joanne said. "I don't know what's best."

"I saw her earlier," Elder said. "Just briefly. She didn't seem in too bad a state. You should ring her if you can."

He had been in to the Force Crime Directorate HQ to drop off the information for Maureen Prior as promised, and Jennie had arrived just as he was leaving.

"This is Derek," Jennie had said, introducing the man at her side.

Derek was tall and dark skinned, handsome and substantial in a pale linen suit. Elder's knuckles were still sore from shaking his hand.

He ordered a regular coffee and watched as Joanne sipped her latté. Outside, the rain was falling more steadily, making uneven trails across the glass. A tram climbed slowly past and stopped for passengers before turning down Victoria Street toward Old Market Square.

"It said in the paper she'd been strangled."

Elder nodded.

"Someone broke into the house and strangled her?"

Elder shook his head. "I don't think so."

"I don't understand."

"I think she was already dead."

"But how...?"

"Whoever killed her. I imagine he took her back to where she lived."

Joanne fidgeted with the rings on her hand. "Will they catch him, Frank? What do you think?"

"I don't know. I hope so."

"You'll stick around? Help?"

"I doubt it. They can manage well enough without me. Maureen's in charge of the investigation. Maureen Prior, you remember her."

"All the more reason, then."

"For what?"

"For you getting involved. You and Maureen, you were always a team."

"No. Maureen knows what she's about. Besides, I've packed it all in, remember? Done and dusted. Out to grass."

Joanne smiled with her eyes. "So you say."

"You don't believe me?"

"You got involved before."

"That was different. And pretty much a disaster. As you were at pains to point out."

"I'm sorry. There were some things I never should have said."

"But you were right. If I hadn't stuck my nose in, what Katherine went through would never have happened."

"You don't know that."

"Of course I do."

It hung among them, all three of them, his culpability, unwitting as it may have been, in the events that had led, almost, to Katherine's death.

Joanne looked at her watch. "I should be getting back."

"Okay. I'll stay and finish this."

"You'll see Katherine again before you go?"

"I'll try."

Joanne seemed to hesitate for a moment, then bent and kissed him quickly on the cheek. "Take care, Frank."

"Do my best."

He heard her heels on the stairs, then, moments later, watched as she crossed the wide street, hurrying a little against the rain. Five, ten yards along the opposite pavement before she was lost to sight. How much easier it would be, Elder thought, if she had become less instead of more beautiful with age.

KATHERINE HAD GIVEN HIM HER NEW CELL NUMBER, BUT when he tried it there was no reply; when he called round at the house there was no one in. Despite the rain, which continued to fall, he chose to walk back into the centre, across Castle Boulevard and along the canal. No matter how much he tried to shunt his mind toward other things, coincidences continued to bounce back and forth between the years: the way both women had been dressed then laid in their beds; the means of death itself, similar though not identical; the lack, as far as he knew, of any clear forensic evidence.

Near the edge of the marina, he stopped to watch four ducklings, the size of small fists, traversing the water in their mother's uneven wake.

What rankled most was that Irene Fowler's murderer had never been found, the case—his case—never closed. The same stupid, instinctive injured pride that had led him to become involved with such awful results before. Well, not this time. Inside an hour he would be packed up, checked out, heading west. He would call Katherine when he got back and explain; invite her down to Cornwall, the next break from her course.

As he turned from the canal side toward the hotel entrance, there was Maureen Prior walking toward him.

"Come to wave me off?" Elder said.

Prior shook her head. "I've come to take you to lunch."

"I don't think so."

"You're not hungry?"

"Something like that."

"Then you can watch me eat instead."

They drove out past the racecourse and parked by Colwick Lake, facing out across the flat expanse of water.

"Catching your own?" Elder said.

Prior reached round onto the back seat and lifted up a plain white plastic bag: inside were two chicken salad sandwiches, individually wrapped, and some Walkers crisps.

"That's it?"

"You weren't hungry, remember?"

"That was before."

She handed him his sandwich and started to eat. The sound of rain was light on the roof. There were two other cars parked farther along. A fisherman in a dark green waterproof and hood.

"Got the results of the postmortem earlier," Prior said. "Preliminary, at least. Nothing we mightn't have guessed. Quite severe bruising in the tissue beneath the skin. Fractured windpipe. Strangulation. The pattern of hemorrhaging matches the marks on the neck."

"Any other marks?"

"Some rawness around the wrists and ankles, not new. Faint bruising on the upper arms."

"She'd been tied up; pinned down."

Prior nodded.

"Rape?"

A shake of the head. "Probably not. Some evidence of sexual activity, vaginal, but no particular bruising or tearing."

A pair of ducks wheeled low across the water and skidded to a halt near the far bank.

"Anything else?" Elder asked.

"Not a great deal. No significant amount of alcohol in the bloodstream; a small trace of aspirin, but no other drugs."

"What about time of death?"

"Nearest they can estimate, ten to twelve days before the body was found."

Elder nodded. He got out of the car and in a few moments Prior followed suit. The rain seemed to be slackening off at last, though the sky was still sealed in gray.

"Claire Meecham went missing sometime on the weekend of April ninth, tenth," Elder said. "Now it seems as if she died just a few days later."

"We need to find out where she was."

"Who she was with."

They continued to walk around the edge of the lake. "Irene Fowler," Prior said. "You really think this is the same all over again?"

Elder smiled. "You told me before, don't assume."

"But if you did?"

He shrugged. "The similarities, they're there."

"Some are, agreed. But there are differences, too. Irene Fowler was murdered in a hotel, for one thing. That's where she was found. Claire Meecham was discovered at home, but that's not where she was killed. Someone had kept her body hidden for some little time and then gone to the not inconsiderable risk of taking her back and tucking her up in her very own bed. That's a lot different, Frank. A whole new ball game."

"Not necessarily."

"Of course it is."

Elder was shaking his head. "It could be an elaboration and nothing more. The basic things haven't changed. Two women of roughly the same age. The way the bodies were left. The way they were killed."

"I know. We can't ignore it, I know that." She glanced up at him. "We need your help, Frank. Going through all that stuff again."

Elder shook his head. "I don't think so. I fucked up last time, remember? If someone's going to trawl back through the Fowler case, it shouldn't be me."

He picked up a stone and sent it skimming across the lake.

"Yes, it should," Prior said. "You know it better than anyone else. And besides, you know how many investigations we've got ongoing right now? How many murders since the turn of the year? It's no secret, we're stretched to breaking. And now the chief constable's got the Home Office breathing down his neck, threatening to send in people from outside, another force."

"Better the devil you know—that what you're saying?"

"Something like that."

Elder picked up another stone and sent it sailing out after the first, remembering, in that instant, standing on the sand at Mablethorpe with Katherine when she was five or six, throwing pebbles at the turning tide; Joanne sitting behind a windbreak higher up the beach, with a thermos and a pile of magazines.

"Bernard Young," Elder said. "He's still the superintendent in charge?"

"I spoke to him this morning," Prior said. "He'll be glad to have you onboard. Civilian consultant, whatever the going rate. I should think they'll even help with somewhere to stay."

"How about the assistant chief constable? You can't just waltz it past him."

Prior glanced at her watch. "Bernard should be seeing him about now."

"Pretty confident, weren't you? That I'd come around."

"I've known you a long time, Frank."

It was true: And aside from the fact that she was good at what she did, he knew next to nothing about her at all.

What had she said about Claire Meecham? *Her choice. Keeping herself to herself. It's what some people do.* Though she didn't flaunt it, Maureen was an attractive woman, presumably with needs and desires of her own.

"Okay," Elder said, "I'll do what I can."

IN THE THREE YEARS THAT BERNARD YOUNG HAD BEEN detective superintendent in command of what had been the Major Crime Unit, he had seen its name changed, its staffing numbers and resources cut, the unit itself under threat of being closed down. "Two more years to retirement," he would tell anyone with an ear to listen. "Two more years and I'm off to this place I've got picked out in the Yorkshire Dales; reread every word of bloody Thackeray and breed tropical bloody fish."

That afternoon he was wearing a sad-looking serge suit, vest buttons undone, striped tie loose at the neck. The high colour in his cheeks suggested he'd been neglecting the pills prescribed to keep his blood pressure under control; either that or he'd taken a nip at the bottle of Lagavulin he was known to keep in his office desk.

The core of Maureen Prior's squad was gathered together: two detective sergeants, four DCs, and two civilians, one to manage computer access, the other to handle the flow of telephone enquiries and paperwork. Stretched thin was the term that came to mind.

"Some of you know Frank Elder here," Young said. "Most of you, I dare say. He was a DI in the unit and a damned good one—before he took a strop on and buggered off down to Cornwall, that is. But he's worked with us a time or two since, one way or another, and he's fit to do so again. Maureen'll fill you in on the details. What I'm saying is, give him all the support he needs. He's not an outsider, he's one of us. And you'll not need me to tell you how much we need a result here. Any of you with half an eye on the City ground'll know the way Forest have been playing they're set to flush 'emselves down the toilet, and if we don't keep our heads above water we'll likely do the same. So let's do the business on this, okay? Eye on the fuckin' ball."

Shuffling of bums on seats; murmurs of agreement all round.

"Now," Young said, rising to his feet. "I've got to put on a penguin suit and eat rubber chicken with the chief constable and the lord fucking mayor. If His Worship will excuse the expression. When what I'd rather do is be joining you lot down the pub."

With something of a flourish, he waved an arm toward Maureen Prior and wandered out of the room. Small conversations flared up and faded again as she got to her feet. Photographs of Claire Meecham and Irene Fowler were already pinned to the wall behind where she stood. Details and descriptions of how and where they'd died.

Clearly and concisely, Prior went through the connections between both cases. Two middle-aged women, strangled and their bodies treated in this perversely respectful way. Eight years between the two incidents. A long time. An interval that raised, some of them might think, distinct possibilities. If—and it was a big "if"—the same person was responsible, had they been in prison in the meantime? Out of the country? Or were there other reasons they still had to find? Other victims even?

Prior let this last question hang, disturbingly, tantalizingly, over their heads before moving on.

"So," she continued, "two murders, and the most recent, that of Claire Meecham, will be the major focus of the investigation. Frank here will be concentrating on Irene Fowler, trawling back through the files, reassessing evidence, reinterviewing key witnesses. That's what we've brought him in, primarily, to do. The rest of us will pitch in and help as and when he needs it, as and when we can."

Faces turned toward Elder, some appraising, others positive, smiling, a few thumbs-up into the bargain.

"Before we send him back in time, though, there's a few things Frank can tell us about Claire Meecham. He was looking into her disappearance, up to her body being discovered. Frank…"

She stepped aside, as Elder got to his feet. Quickly, he filled them in on what he'd learned about her background, her work history, perhaps most importantly, the life she'd kept hidden from her sister.

After answering a few questions, Elder sat back down.

"Right," Prior said, her final rallying cry. "We know a little, we have to learn a whole lot more. The last weeks of Claire Meecham's life in particular: where she was, who she was with. With luck and a well-placed kick up IT's arse, we should have a full computer history in the next two days: once we've got that, everyone she was in contact with in the past twelve months will have to be tracked down and interviewed. Up until then, we'll concentrate on those names that Frank's already pulled out of the file. Then there's family, friends, colleagues, neighbours, you know the routine. Check, prioritize, check again."

She didn't need to add that all relevant databases, including the sex offenders register, would need to be accessed and scrutinized.

"Claire Meecham and Irene Fowler," Prior said finally. "There may not be a link, but if there is we'll find it, I'm certain of it.

Just remember, nothing's written in stone. Stay open. Stay open and stay focused, okay?"

She stepped back.

"Any questions?"

THE NEXT MORNING ELDER MOVED OUT OF HIS HOTEL and into a serviced apartment in the Ice House, a converted seven-storey building close to the National Ice Centre. The apartment itself was sparsely but quite stylishly furnished, with a floor that was clean enough to eat off, should the situation demand, and a small balcony which afforded a view out across the city.

More by chance than design, he had stumbled over a small Italian restaurant close by, in the old fruit and vegetable market on the edge of Sneinton, a matter of minutes from his new base. Jennie assured him she would find it without difficulty.

When Elder arrived, a little earlier than arranged, more than half of the dozen or so tables were occupied. He took a seat in the far corner, between the wall and the smoked glass separating them from the street, and signalled to the waiter that he was waiting for someone else to join him.

He had managed to see Katherine the previous evening, a quick drink in the pub she described as her local, an old stripped-down boozer now mostly patronized by students, a few of the aging regulars relegated to the corners, where they sat facing inward, clutching their pints, doubtless complaining about the noise.

Katherine had seemed pleased enough to hear that he was sticking around a while longer, but preoccupied, her mind fixed somewhere else. When he taxed her about this, outside on the street, she told him she was worried about an essay she should have finished and handed in, one extension already and three days overdue. Elder had nodded understandingly, without quite believing it to be the truth. When was it, he wondered, the age at which children began lying defensively to their parents as a matter of course?

Now he glanced again at his watch and wondered about ordering a glass of wine. Jennie had said she might bring Derek with her, but when she walked in, some ten minutes later, she was alone.

"I'm sorry," she said, a little breathlessly. "Took me longer to find than I thought, and then I couldn't find anywhere to park the bloody car."

"It's fine," Elder said. "I've not been here long. Have a seat. Let's get something to drink."

The waiter was already heading their way.

Jennie was dressed more soberly today, smartly nonetheless, her makeup toned down. Attractive enough still to turn heads.

"So," Elder asked, "how've you been?"

"Okay, I suppose." Jennie lit a cigarette, slipped her lighter back into her bag, and released a slow plume of smoke. "I had to phone Claire's children—Jane was in a terrible state, wouldn't stop crying; James was not a great deal better, truth be told. And then, for him, there's all the business of coming over for the funeral, though until we know when it is..."

"I'm sorry," Elder said.

Jennie managed a quick smile. "I still don't think I've taken it all in. Not that Claire's dead, I know that. Just...you know... everything. Everything else."

The wine arrived and she emptied a third of her glass at a single swallow.

"It's like I never knew her, you know? Who she really was. And I don't know why she kept so much to herself. I don't know if she was embarrassed or ashamed or what."

"Perhaps she thought you wouldn't approve."

"Of her seeing men? Having a life?"

"It's possible."

Jennie shook her head in disbelief.

"After her husband died," Elder said. "Maybe she thought she had to behave in a certain way."

"The grieving widow."

"Something like that."

"That couldn't be further from the truth," Jennie said. "I was the one telling her to go out and enjoy herself. Begging her to. A good time, that's what she deserved. What she'd earned. After nursing Brian the way she did. I told her so. But no, that's all right for you, she used to say, that kind of thing, you're still young."

Jennie drank some more wine.

"If only she'd told me about it, meeting blokes through the Internet, all that. We could have talked about it together, had a laugh."

Only the need to decide what they were going to eat warded off more tears. After ordering, Jennie asked about the investigation, how it was going to proceed, and Elder told her what he could.

"This other murder," Jennie said, after listening, "the one from before, you think it's the same man?"

"It's possible. There are too many similarities to ignore. But that's all it is, a possibility."

"And that was what? Eight years ago, you said?"

"Yes."

Jennie leaned toward him. "Then why Claire? Why now?"

"That's what we've got to find out."

As the food arrived, Jennie stubbed out her cigarette. Elder's pasta was fresh and plentiful, the gorgonzola sauce strong but not too sharp; Jennie ate maybe half of her chicken salad and switched to mineral water from wine. "I've got to make a call I'm dreading this afternoon. One of our sales reps, it's just not working out, we're going to have to let her go."

"You'll tell her that over the phone?"

"No. I'll ask her to come in and see me, but she'll know what

it's about. This past quarter she's been on probation. Her figures, they've improved a little, but not enough."

"The price of being the boss," Elder said.

When they were outside on the pavement, Jennie rested her
hand on his arm. "Whatever you find out about Claire, you will
tell me?"

"Yes, of course," Elder said, uncertain if he would tell her
everything.

"I'd better run," Jennie said. A quick squeeze of his arm and,
with a chatter of heels, she was briskly on her way.

Turning, Elder went back inside, time for an espresso before
meeting Maureen to go over what they knew so far.

Chapter 14

1965

HE WAS DRAWING TODAY, DRAWING AND COLOURING, NO stopping him. Covering each new sheet of paper with feverish strokes, thick strong lines across the page, sometimes pressing on pencil or crayon so hard the end would splinter and break. Splashes of colour that he would shade in, then darken. Purple over red over brown over blue.

Alice pushing him all the while. "Tell me about this. I like this. This part here. These dark lines. It's hard to put into words, I know, but try. It doesn't matter what you say, you know that. Tell me."

And the boy not answering.

Sitting skewed at the table, not able to turn his back on her, not exactly, but with his left arm and shoulder round, shielding as much as he could.

"Show me. Let me see. I want to see. And you want me to. You want me to and at the same time you don't."

The boy fumbled for another colour and swore as the crayon spun out of his hand; seized a pencil instead and scored thick lines across the centre of the paper until the lead snapped.

"Perhaps you should take a break now? Have a rest? Maybe that's enough for today, don't you think?"

He grabbed at the piece of paper with both hands, screwed it tight into a ball and threw it across the room.

And started again.

Alice eased back, brought her breathing under control.

Slow and even.

Be patient.

Wait. Just not too long.

The boy's breathing was ragged, loud; his mouth open. Half out of the chair, he was leaning across the table, rocking it with each mark he made.

After what seemed an age, he sat back, letting the crayon he'd been using fall from his hand.

"Let me see."

For a moment, he looked at her, then pulled the paper toward him, against his chest.

"You don't want me to see it. You do and yet you don't."

With a sudden movement, he flourished it before her.

Almost obliterated by a mesh of violent strokes, crude but unmistakable, the figure of a woman sat hunched, holding her vagina wide open. It was as lewd and startling, Alice thought, as a statue on the corbel table of a medieval church, or an image scratched deep into a lavatory wall.

"What is it?" Alice said.

He swung his head away.

"Name it. Give it its name."

No movement.

"It's a vagina."

"No." The voice was quiet, his head still bowed and turned aside.

"It's a vagina."

Suddenly he was looking at her. "You," he said. "It's you."

"It's my vagina, is that what you mean?"

"I said, it's you," he almost screamed. "It's fuckin' you!"

His face thrust toward hers, eyes narrowed, lips parted.

Alice blinked.

"My vagina. Is that what you mean? Is that what you've drawn?"

"Don't. Don't say that."

"Say what?"

"That word."

"Vagina."

"Don't keep saying that."

"It's only a word."

"She says it's wrong."

"Who?"

"It don't matter."

"Your teacher?"

"No."

"Your mother? Your mother says it's wrong to say vagina."

"Stop it."

The boy seized hold of one of the crayons, and biting down into the soft flesh inside his lip, he began to draw thick lines back and forth over the colours that had been there before.

His hand moved faster and faster until the crayon gouged through the page and he hurled it against the wall. Seizing the sheet of torn paper, he ripped it in half and in half again, continuing to shred and tear until there were only scraps that slipped and fumbled through his hands.

Then, crying, he kicked back his chair and stumbled round, stooping to pick up the chair again and raising it above his head before smashing it against the wall with force enough to break one of the legs. Then, with a howl, falling to his knees, he slammed his face down on the desk and covered it with his arms.

At last, Alice thought: at last we might be getting somewhere.

Chapter 15

THE CROWD IN THE GALLERY WAS SMALL, SOME TWENTY to thirty people occupying several rows of stacking chairs: a mixture of students and the generation Elder had been led to believe were gradually taking over the world, those who had passed retirement age with cash in the bank and their brain cells still intact.

"Stieglitz and Early American Photography": an illustrated lecture by Vincent Blaine.

Elder waited, then slipped into an empty seat as the image on the screen changed: a photograph of tall buildings pushing slenderly up from dark, almost black shadow, was replaced by a silvery, largely featureless sky, in which the sun, or possibly the moon, was sleeved behind a smudge of whitening cloud.

Blaine was compact and neat, mid-fifties, not tall, with a trim gray beard and moustache and short graying hair. Not unlike Stephen Singer, Elder noted with interest; at first glance, not unlike him at all. Blaine wore glasses with rectangular frames that he removed sporadically as he spoke.

"Remember," Blaine was saying, "the name Stieglitz gave to the photographic gallery he ran in New York. He called it An American Place. The America of the cities and the America of the natural world."

Pausing, he looked out at his audience, as if making sure they realized this was a significant point.

"It was a name," he continued, "that the poet William Carlos Williams claimed had been inspired by his book of essays, *In the American Grain,* which was itself strongly influenced by none other than D. H. Lawrence. Lawrence, who, as we all know, was born not far from where we are now, in the small mining town of Eastwood. And Stieglitz, who had himself corresponded with Lawrence, came to believe, as did Lawrence, of course, in the primacy of the physical in life as in all creative art. What you touch; what you feel; what you see. The body first and not the mind."

Elder watched as several students hurried to scribble down the final sentence. A sentiment that would reappear, he felt, on the walls of sundry student rooms; encouragement, if such were needed, for various kinds of mindless behaviour.

Along the row, a man with fair hair wisping round his ears, jerked suddenly upright and looked guiltily around, in case any-one had spotted him dozing off.

"Finally," Blaine said, his voice both intimate yet marked by that sardonic distance so beloved of academics, "and lest you should think Stieglitz's passion was fired only by whatever he could observe from his Madison Avenue window, let me leave you with this, a portrait of the artist Georgia O'Keeffe, made in 1918, when O'Keeffe was just thirty-one and Stieglitz was fifty-four."

In the photograph, O'Keeffe was seemingly naked beneath an embroidered robe, her arms across her chest, fingers holding the robe not quite in place; a glimpse of navel, one thumb resting on the suggestion of a breast. The hair, long and unkempt, was that of someone who has just risen from bed.

"O'Keeffe had met Stieglitz in New York when she was a student, barely twenty years of age, a relationship that led to their marriage in 1924, six years after this portrait was made. Between the time of their first meeting and his death in 1946, aged eighty-two, Stieglitz would take more than three hundred pictures of the woman he loved. Photographs of her hands, her face, her neck; photographs of her fully clothed and nude. And this portrait, with its strange, almost haunted quality, is, in my estimation, one of the finest."

Elder continued to stare at the screen as Blaine sat down to more than polite applause, and a slender man with a slight stammer began a short speech of thanks.

It was the look in the eyes that intrigued him most, dark eyes staring out at something above and slightly to one side of the camera's lens, something remembered or not yet seen. Not a portrait, Elder felt, of someone at ease, relaxed, at rest; rather someone anticipating pain, regret.

Around him, people were rising to their feet, pushing back chairs, exchanging words. Several of the students had gathered round Blaine, attempting to engage him in conversation, and for several minutes he stood, collecting together his papers, listening with half an ear, before finally dismissing them with a remark which made them laugh aloud.

Elder waited near the back of the room.

A few last words with the organizer and Blaine buckled the straps of his leather case and crossed toward him.

"I know you," Blaine said affably enough, "but you'll have to excuse me, I can't recall from where."

"Frank Elder."

"No, I'm sorry."

"Eight years ago. I was..."

"No, wait. I have it now. That unfortunate woman who was found dead in her hotel room."

"Irene Fowler."

"Yes, of course. You were the officer leading the investigation into her death."

Elder nodded.

"Detective inspector, I believe."

"That's right."

"And now..." the beginnings of a smile, "now you're interested in photography."

Behind his glasses, Elder noted, Blaine's eyes were blue.

"Not really," Elder said.

"Lawrence, then? That's where your interest lies? His reputation's sadly not what it was, but a fascinating man I've always thought. Misunderstood. Here especially. His own part of the world."

"No," Elder said. "Not Lawrence."

He had tried *Lady Chatterley* once; the rude bits, at least. All they'd succeeded in doing was making him laugh.

"I can't believe," Blaine said, "you wandered into the gallery by chance."

Elder shook his head. "Irene Fowler—I'm taking another look at her murder."

"After all this time?"

"Whoever was responsible, they were never caught."

Blaine looked at him carefully before speaking. "And for that, you feel responsible."

"Not exactly," Elder said. Though to a large extent, of course, he did.

The organizer was hovering near the door, trying not to look concerned. Doubtless there was a caretaker somewhere, ready to complain about the event overrunning, even as he clocked up another hour's overtime.

"Maybe we could talk over a drink?" Elder said.

"You mean now?"

"If that's not inconvenient."

"I'm afraid it is. I've a friend waiting. We're going out to supper."

They crossed the gallery floor, walked through a second room and then down the stairs toward the exit, lights being switched off behind them as they went.

"Some time tomorrow then?" Elder said. "It needn't take too long."

Blaine stopped on the bottom step and gave Elder his card. "I'm afraid I can't recall my schedule exactly. Why don't you telephone tomorrow morning? Any time after eight. I'm sure something mutually convenient can be arranged."

The woman waiting for Blaine had been in the audience, sitting, Elder remembered, at one end of the front row. She was what might once have been called handsome: a strong face, dark reddish hair, a good inch taller than Blaine himself. As they moved away, down toward the Old Market Square, she slipped her arm through his.

THEY HAD TRIED MANY OF THE NEW RESTAURANTS THAT had opened in the city in the past three years, opened and, some of them, closed and replaced; but time after time they found themselves coming back here, to Sonny's, on the corner of George Street and Goose Gate, at the Lace Market edge.

Lively on weekends, but never rowdy, earlier in the week it was a quiet haven of linen napkins and white candles, well-prepared food and hushed conversations.

Flush from the evening so far, Blaine ordered the Felton Road pinot noir.

"So what did you think?" he said. "At the gallery. Your verdict? No beating around the bush."

Almost despite herself, Anna Ingram smiled. For all his demeanour might suggest otherwise, there were times when Vin-

cent needed reassurance as much as a child perched uncertainly on the verge of adolescence.

"You were fine," she said. "It was fine."

"You don't think I went on for too long?"

"No, didn't I just say..."

"Talking about the early Japanese influence, I couldn't help
noticing more than a few eyes glaze over."

"Vincent..."

"I suppose I could have omitted that section altogether. All
that fake *japoniste* Impressionism, who needs it after all?"

"Vincent..." she reached forward and tugged at the lapel of
his jacket, "it was a perfectly good lecture, well judged for its audience; anyone wanting something more specialized can follow
it up on the Internet. Or sign up for one of your courses at the
university. Everyone else will have gone home feeling they've
been entertained and well informed. Now may we please order?
I'm starving."

The waiter was standing a discreet distance back from the
table holding their bottle of wine; having shown Blaine the label
and gotten his approval, he poured a small amount for him to
try. Observing the ritual, Blaine swirled it slowly around inside
the glass, raised it to his nose and sniffed, then sampled, holding the wine against his palate for several moments before al-
lowing it to slip down.

"Very good," he pronounced, with an approving nod.

"Are you ready to order, sir?" the waiter asked.

"Another few minutes, if you don't mind."

Anna Ingram sighed.

Having filled both their glasses, the waiter retired. Blaine pe-
rused the menu again, torn between the salmon fillet and the
liver. Lamb's liver, cooked just enough but not a second more,
was something he loved, and yet could never bring himself to
prepare at home, squeamish as he was about both the texture
of the meat against his fingers and the slow ooze of blood.

Anna had already decided on the marinated squid followed by the rack of lamb.

"Who was that you were talking to?" she asked, once Blaine had finally made up his mind.

"The student, you mean? The tall one with the ring through his nose like a bull?"

"No, the man at the end."

"Oh, nobody in particular."

"It was quite a little conversation—for nobody in particular. And you gave him your card."

"Someone I'd met before, that's all. A policeman."

"A policeman?"

"Yes, is that so extraordinary? Even policemen can have some kind of a cultural life, I suppose."

"And that's why you gave him your card? So you could further broaden his cultural horizons?"

Blaine cast a fierce sideways glance toward a table of four he construed as making too much noise. "Has anyone ever told you, Anna, that you ask far too many questions?"

"Indeed they have. Many, many times. Usually it's you."

"Clearly then I've been wasting my breath."

"Vincent," she said, raising her glass, "you and I, we are what we are. Set in our ways. We'll never change and we both of us, I think, know and respect that all too well. It's why we rub along."

"Ah, I've often wondered why that was."

"And now you know." With a smile, she rested her hand on his and it was several moments before he pulled his own hand away.

Chapter 16

VINCENT BLAINE'S HOUSE WAS IN THE VALE OF BELVOIR, some thirty minutes' drive east from the city. Leaving the A52, Elder took a narrow road that ran, straight as a die, through fields green with spring pasture or yellowing from the first signs of oilseed rape. A succession of small farms clustered close to the old Grantham Canal and beyond the land rose steeply toward Barkestone Wood, the irregular outline of Belvoir Castle clear against an uncertain sky.

As instructed, he turned off along what was little more than a track, and which threatened to peter out among a straggle of hedge ends and little more. Then there it was, sheltered by a covert of slender trees, a two-storey farmhouse in recently repainted red brick, low outbuildings to one side.

"Eleven-thirty," Blaine had said. "That might be best. I've a meeting earlier, here at the house, but it should be over by then."

As Elder turned on to the gravel drive, Blaine was bidding goodbye to a young Japanese man wearing a black and silver jumpsuit, a black leather portfolio at his side. Blaine himself was country casual in the older style, olive corduroy trousers and a checkered Viyella shirt, only missing the cravat.

After much shaking of hands and a small bow, the visitor climbed into a polished but mud-streaked SUV and headed off at some speed back along the track.

"You found it without difficulty then," Blaine said, offering Elder his hand.

"None at all."

"That young man," Blaine said, "has a great talent. A marvellous eye. I'm publishing a book of his photographs toward the end of next year. All taken on the Tokyo subway. There'll be an exhibition here in the city to coincide—the Djanogly out at Lakeside—possibly the Photographers' Gallery in London as well. After that we might arrange for it to tour."

"And that's what you do?" Elder said. "Publish photography?"

Blaine gave him a condescending smile. "That and a little lecturing. What the universities like to call continuing education. The occasional article when I can find the time." He turned toward the house. "Shall we go inside?"

A flagstone porch led directly into a large L-shaped room with a long picture window looking out on to the garden at the rear; at least one internal wall had been removed to help make the interior, despite a low ceiling, seem spacious and airy. At angles to a stone fireplace, and facing a low table neat with magazines, were several pieces of furniture in wood and leather, wood and chrome, more stylish than comfortable to Elder's eyes. Framed photographs, unsurprisingly, dominated the walls.

"You'll have coffee, I trust?" Blaine said. "It should be ready any minute now."

"Thank you, yes."

"One advantage of living here—one of many—you can hear anyone coming from half a mile away. Little chance of being taken by surprise." For a moment, he smiled. "Privacy, Mr.

Elder, in these times more than most, it's something to be cher-
ished, wouldn't you agree?"

Elder would.

"Milk? Sugar?"

"A little milk, no sugar."

Blaine turned smartly on his heels, leaving Elder alone with
the photographs. Prints, Elder supposed, copies of the original,
he wasn't sure how it worked—that he thought must be by the
same person whose work Blaine had been discussing in the
gallery. Stieglitz, was it?

A photograph of the moon passing behind clouds was similar
if not identical to the one Blaine had shown at the gallery, and
then there was a close-up of someone who could have been Georgia O'Keeffe, but framed in such a way it was difficult to know.
The head was angled sharply to the right and cut off above the
mouth. The neck muscle, prominent and central, stretched tight
from below the ear down toward the chest. And at the bottom of
the image were the fingers of two hands, resting on bare skin and
reaching up toward the neck. Whether they were the model's
own or belonged to another person was unclear.

"Beautiful, isn't it?" Blaine said, appearing at Elder's shoulder.

"Is it? I'm not so sure."

"As a study in form, proportion, design, it's fascinating. Close
to perfect."

"And as a portrait?"

"The part for the whole. Sometimes it's enough."

"You don't find it disturbing, then?"

A smile formed along Blaine's mouth. "Up to a point, we all
see what we want to see."

Briefly, Elder's gaze shifted back to the photograph: the way
one set of fingers curved inward, the other pointing straight toward the bulging vein.

"If you want to look at something less troubling," Blaine said,
"come over here."

On the side wall was a photographic portrait, almost full-length, of a woman standing on a wooden porch, looking out. No longer young and not yet old, her face was lined, quite full and round, her waved hair suggesting a visit to the beauty parlour the week before or possibly a home perm. There was even a hint of makeup around her eyes.

The loose cotton dress she was wearing had half sleeves and a brooch fastened across the neck, a white apron tied across at the waist. Her arms hung easily at her sides and her hands, quite large, capable hands, were slightly curled. It was easy for Elder to imagine that what she might be looking at, close by where the photographer must have set his tripod, were chickens pecking in the dirt.

If she had lived a hard life, and almost certainly she had, if she had known sorrow, as certainly she must, she had come through it all composed, relaxed, almost serene.

"When I look at that," Blaine said, "I get a tremendous feeling of peace. And she is beautiful, of course, there's no gainsaying that. Very beautiful."

The coffee was in white china cups, resting on the table on a lacquered tray.

"Try one of the chairs, why don't you?" Blaine said, sensing Elder's hesitation. "Charles Eames. They're more comfortable than they look."

Blaine settled easily onto one.

"Before I answer your questions, Detective Inspector, perhaps you would be good enough to answer one of mine?"

"Of course. But it's not detective inspector, not any longer. I retired from the police force several years ago now."

"Then this is somehow private? Your own crusade?"

"Not at all. I'm working with the Crime Force Directorate— as a civilian consultant."

"An expert."

"If you like."

"I'm pleased to hear it. As we go through life we garner so much knowledge and expertise, whatever our field. The tendency, until recently, has been to allow all that intelligence to go to waste."

Elder let that pass. "What was your question?" he said.

"Nothing untoward, I assure you. Simply this: after so long an interval, why have you focused back on Irene Fowler's death?"

Elder tasted his coffee: it was as strong as it looked. "There was another murder recently, you may have read something about it. Claire Meecham? The circumstances of her death were such as to bring the earlier case to mind."

"She was strangled?"

"Yes."

"And found where? In a hotel?"

"No. At home."

"So not exactly the same."

"There were similarities, as I said."

"Enough to make you think the murders might be linked."

"Yes."

"Carried out by the same person even?"

"It's far too early to say."

"Of course, of course." Blaine set down his cup and saucer on the tray. "To a layman, it's all fascinating. Murder. Detection. Violent crime. Whereas to you, I suppose, it's mundane, everyday."

Elder made no reply.

"These other connections you've noted," Blaine continued, "between the two deaths—you wouldn't be at liberty to tell me what they were?"

A little, Elder thought; a little but not too much. "The victims were of similar backgrounds," he said. "Similar age."

Blaine shifted his position on the settee. "Irene Fowler was, let me see, somewhere in her fifties?"

"Fifty-seven."

"Ah. And this poor woman..."

"Claire Meecham."

"Claire Meecham, she was the same?"

"As I said, they were of a similar age."

"Yes, yes. And I can tell from your voice I've asked a question too many. After all, it was you who came here to question me." Leaning forward, he reached toward Elder's cup. "Let me freshen this up before we continue."

"I'd rather get on, if you don't mind."

"Very well." Blaine released the cup and settled back.

"I wonder how well," Elder said, "you can recall the statement you made at the time?"

"Eight years ago—I can remember the basic facts, of course, but what I said in detail, I'm afraid very little."

"You haven't thought about the evening a great deal then? Since it happened. Run it over in your mind?"

"Yes. I suppose I have. From time to time."

Elder took a small notebook from his pocket; more for show than anything. "Perhaps you could go over for me what you remember. Yourself and Irene Fowler, that evening. The sequence of events."

"If you think it might help, of course, though as I say…"

"Please."

"Very well." Blaine had removed his glasses and now he tapped them against his leg. "I'd come into the city for a concert, that lunchtime. An organ recital at St. Mary's. Bach. In the afternoon I wandered a little around the city, went to the bookshop almost certainly. Waterstone's. Then, in the early evening I saw a film at Broadway. Tavernier, I remember. *Un Dimanche à la Campagne*. That was in the days when they showed such films as a matter of course. Nowadays, more often than not, it's the same American rubbish you'll find everywhere else." He looked at Elder apologetically. "I'm sorry, forgive me, a pet gripe of mine."

"Go on."

"After the film I bumped into a friend. Brian Warren. An accountant. At least he was till he retired. He used to look after my affairs. We chatted for a while and then he suggested going somewhere quiet for a drink. Quite coincidentally, he chose the hotel where Irene Fowler was staying.

"The bar was quite busy and we were forced to share a table with several others. Three or four at first, and then just two. Two women. Irene Fowler and a friend. A colleague. They were attending the conference together." Blaine shifted position slightly on his chair. "It was pleasant enough, if not what we'd intended. After a while Brian decided he had to go."

"You weren't tempted to leave with him?"

"By that time I was feeling quite hungry. I thought I'd stay and have something to eat. I asked the women sitting with us if they'd care to join me. Out of politeness as much as anything else. One demurred, the other agreed."

"And that was Irene Fowler?"

"Exactly."

The occasional flurry of birdsong from the garden aside, it was quiet in the room. A hiccup of water shifting in the pipes, the far-off churning of a tractor.

"How did she strike you?" Elder asked. "What kind of person was she?"

Blaine weighed his words before replying. "We were able to talk easily enough—her job, family, the conference she was attending, things of that nature. She was quite intelligent, I'd have to say; perhaps surprisingly so."

"You didn't talk about yourself?"

"I think I may have mentioned something about photography, but it wasn't really a topic she could pursue."

"All in all, though, you'd say it was a pleasant experience."

"Not unpleasant, certainly."

"Pleasant enough for you to arrange to see her again?"

Something flickered fast across Blaine's eyes. "Why do you say that?"

"I don't know," Elder said, offhandedly. "A man and a woman spend time together, get along, maybe they're both unattached—I should have thought it was the natural thing to do."

"Natural? I don't know. For some people, perhaps it is."

"But not for you?"

"Relationships are more than casual where I am concerned. Not something to be entered into lightly."

"You did find her attractive, nonetheless."

Blaine started to speak, but the words caught on his tongue. "She was perfectly pleasant, yes."

"No more than that?"

"No more."

"After dinner," Elder said, "you had a drink in the bar?"

"A nightcap, yes. Her idea."

"You'd been drinking with dinner?"

"We shared a bottle of wine."

"And before that?"

"I'd had a gin and tonic, that was all."

"Irene Fowler? How about her?"

"I don't really know. A couple of drinks perhaps. But she wasn't drunk, if that's where you're leading. A little merry. In good spirits, nothing more."

"And the invitation to join her for a nightcap, you didn't take this as a prelude to something more?"

"Not at all."

"Some men might have chosen to see it as exactly that."

Blaine bridled slightly. "Do I strike you, Mr. Elder, as the predatory kind?"

"One thing this job has taught me," Elder said, "where sex is concerned, most people are rarely what they seem."

"Sex? Is that what this is all about?"

"I think so, don't you?" Elder drank the last of his coffee. "One way or another, it usually is."

"You and Lawrence would have had a great deal in common," Blaine said, amused. "A phallocentric view of the world."

"You don't think sex is important then?"

"I think in our culture, its importance is exaggerated. And the shame is that sometimes it should lead to this. What happened in that room."

Both men paused as a light aircraft passed low overhead, trailing silence in its wake.

"According to your statement," Elder said, "you left Irene Fowler in the hotel bar."

"That's correct. She seemed in no hurry to go up and by then I was eager to get home."

"The time would have been...?"

"Eleven-thirty, possibly a little later."

"Were there many people, can you remember, still in the bar?"

"Not so many. Possibly a dozen in all. Several more in the lobby, as I recall."

"And when you left her, she was alone?"

"Quite alone."

"And you drove yourself home."

"As you know."

"You weren't worried about the amount you'd had to drink?"

Blaine brought the tips of his fingers together. "It was not, shall we say, the most sensible thing to have done. I believe I acknowledged that at the time and I do so again now. What I should have done was to leave my car parked where it was and take a taxi home; come back and collect the car the next day. As it happened, I was fortunate, nothing amiss occurred." He gave Elder a small, tight-lipped smile. "A lesson learned."

Elder flicked his notebook closed and Blaine rose to his feet.

"I hope what I've told you has been of some assistance," Blaine said. "I'm only sorry I had nothing new to add. No startling revelations."

"Due process," Elder said, rising. "Procedure. That's what most police work is. For me now, it's much the same." He smiled. "Startling revelations, they only usually happen in books."

They were walking toward the door.

"My friend Anna," Blaine said, "Anna Ingram. She was at my talk the other evening. She reads quite a lot of detective fiction. Amongst more serious things, of course. Paradoxically, she claims it helps her to relax. She even persuaded me to read one once. Ian Rankin—she seems to like him especially. His policeman—Rebus, is that his name?—a cantankerous sort. At odds with the world. Not like you at all."

Elder didn't know Rebus, but about himself he wasn't sure.

On the threshold they shook hands. Overhead, the sun was still faltering between the clouds. A pair of blue tits balanced restlessly on the telephone wire that stretched toward the house and then were gone. There were at least two tractors now, out of sight, turning the earth.

"Good luck with your inquiries," Blaine said, as Elder stepped toward his car. "As far as Irene Fowler is concerned, especially. What happened to her, it was terrible. I hope you catch whoever was responsible."

Elder raised a hand, slid behind the wheel and buckled his seat belt, reversed back down the drive, changed gear, and drove away. Vincent Blaine stood motionless in the doorway, watching him out of sight and then continuing to stand, long after the sound of Elder's car had faded clear away.

Chapter 17

WHILE THEY WERE WAITING FOR THE NECESSARY LEGAL
process to be worked through and for the computer geeks to
then uncover Claire Meecham's audit trail, Maureen Prior's
team prioritized three areas: a check of holiday companies,
both local and national, for any booking in Claire's name during
the weekend in question; a canvass of her neighbours for information about any strange or unusual vehicles that had been
seen close to the bungalow in the early hours of the Sunday the
body was found; and a search through records for the names of
any serious offenders with a record of violent or sexual crimes
who had been imprisoned during most or all of the past eight
years.

Maureen Prior, sometimes with another officer in tow, sometimes alone, interviewed Claire Meecham's sister, Jennie, and
her daughter, Jane. She had several long conversations with
Claire's son, James, in Australia.

A five-day, all-inclusive package to Lanzarote, booked in the name of C. R. Meecham, raised hopes briefly, before it was discovered *C* stood for Clarice and not Claire.

Tales of a white van driving around the area eventually yielded two likely lads who were buying fish in quantities in their local Asda, sticking it in the back of a refrigerated 5 cwt. van, and passing it off as fresh fish from Grimsby.

Little else caused antennae to quiver or quickened the blood.

With the names of other possible contacts still locked in the ether, Prior's team made a start on what they had. Norman Prentiss, from Northampton, turned out to be wheelchair bound and severely overweight; Roy James, from Leicester, was a bespectacled thirteen-year-old with permanently sticky palms; Gary Grange, the widower from Kettering, had found true happiness with a special-needs teacher from nearby Corby, and on the weekend that Claire Meecham's body was discovered, they were together on an activity holiday in Aviemore, gorge-walking and canoeing.

Maureen Prior went down to London to talk to Stephen Singer, though without too much enthusiasm. She had spoken to several senior members of the university where he had lectured, but any hopes she might have had that Singer had been guilty of inappropriate behaviour with either fellow staff or students were soon set aside. All the other checks they ran on him had ended up clean.

Singer was polite and courteous, correctly distressed by Claire Meecham's death, eager to be as helpful as he could. A citizen beyond reproach.

Why then, when he pressed a CD of Biber's *Rosary Sonatas* into her hands as she left, a result of a chance remark she had made about the music he'd been playing, did Prior feel a jolt of insincerity in his voice, his manner, his eagerness to please?

She was unable, quite, to shake that feeling from her mind.

———

ELDER, MEANWHILE, AND NOT WITHOUT DIFFICULTY, HAD contacted Christine Dulverton, the woman who had been sitting with Irene Fowler in the hotel bar on the evening that she was killed. Dulverton had moved three times since Elder had last interviewed her eight years before. Taunton, then Dawlish, and currently, St. Albans. She agreed to meet Elder in a branch of the ubiquitous Starbucks, close to the town centre.

Instead of aging since Elder had last seen her, Christine Dulverton seemed, perversely, to have become younger. Diet and callisthenics had slimmed down her figure; Botox or something similar had banished the lines from her face. The rest, maybe, was an attitude of mind. Certainly, she recognized Elder long before he recognized her.

She was wearing blue jeans, low on her hips, a long green and purple open cardigan over a tight white T-shirt that left a good couple of inches of flat stomach exposed. Her hair, which Elder remembered as being of a standard length and cut, was now short and dark and highlighted red and silver. A pair of earrings, shaped like sickle moons, danced a little each time she moved her head. Fifty going on twenty-four.

"You weren't easy to find," Elder said.

"That was the idea," Christine Dulverton replied.

Elder looked at her questioningly and she smiled.

"One divorced husband, one serious ex-boyfriend, both desperate to make do and mend. Neither of them quite to the point where I felt like getting a restraining order, but it came close. Never any children, touch wood, nothing to stop me doing a bunk. I was pretty fed up with my job, anyway. Cold meats and prepacked ham, they can only keep your enthusiasm up for just so long. So I went down to Devon, did nothing for a while, lazed around, eventually bumped into this woman who was making jewellery. Bracelets, necklaces, earrings, that kind of thing. Not expensive. A bit knick-knacky, I suppose. Hippyish, even. I worked with her for a while and then struck out on my own."

"And that's what you're doing now?"

"Even so."

"Those earrings you're wearing…"

"All my own work." She gave her head a lively shake. "They say it pays to advertise."

Elder sipped his coffee; when Christine Dulverton offered him a piece of her skinny blueberry muffin he refused, and the hollow grumbling of his stomach that followed made him wish that he'd accepted instead.

She laughed and, breaking off a piece of the muffin, offered it to him with her fingers. "This is about the murder," she said. "At least, I assume that's what it is."

Mouth full, Elder could only nod.

"You never caught anybody, did you?"

"That's right."

"And now you're looking at it all again?"

"Yes."

"Like one of those—what do they call them?—cold cases. There's that programme on the television, isn't there? A bit far-fetched sometimes, but fun. You know the one I mean?"

"Not really, no."

"I suppose not. Why would you? The last thing you'd want to watch, I imagine." She took another sip at her coffee. "I used to have this friend, worked as a nurse, all these programmes about hospitals and nursing used to drive her up the wall. Couldn't stand them. She'd be there, you know, really long hours, bloody hard work, saving lives, and all these glammed-up nurses on the TV were interested in was shagging some doctor on a trolley. I expect you feel the same." She laughed. "About the programmes I mean, not the trolley."

She offered him the last of her muffin and he shook his head.

Someone was singing, "I don't wanna know 'bout evil," in a quite wavery, high-pitched voice over heavy bass and drums. The same words over and over, the same rhythm: the effect, even on Elder, was quite hypnotic.

"One of the things I wanted to ask you," Elder said. "Irene Fowler's mood that evening, in the hotel—I know it's asking for you to go back a long time—but could you characterize it in any way?"

"Happy, sad, that kind of thing?"

"That kind of thing."

"Happy, I think. Well, maybe not that exactly. But certainly not miserable. Relaxed, I'd say." She laughed. "It's wonderful what a couple of G and Ts will do after a day listening to people droning on about export licenses and VAT."

"And when the two men, Vincent Blaine and his friend, joined you, she was okay about that?"

"Yes, of course. Why not? The place was busy, we were both winding down at the end of the day."

"She welcomed it then, the idea of some male company?"

Christine Dulverton laughed, "Was she on the pull, is that what you're asking?"

"I suppose I am."

"Horrible phrase. Always makes me think of cows being milked. But that regardless, no, I don't think so. I'm not sure whether you can talk of women who are comfortably in their fifties being on the pull, anyway. Having said that, I did get the impression that she might have taken a bit of a shine to one of them."

"Vincent Blaine, you mean?"

"Good God, no," Christine said. "Not him, the other one. Brian, was that his name?"

"Brian Warren. Yes."

"Well, I couldn't quite see it myself, but Irene and him, they really seemed to hit it off."

"Yet she ended up going to dinner with Vincent Blaine," Elder said.

"I know. Brian had gone by then, something about having to get off early the next day I think it was, and this Vincent, he suggested getting something in the restaurant."

"You didn't fancy that?"

"No way. Too full of himself for my taste. One of those men with opinions on everything, you know what I mean? Stuck up, too. I said I was tired, wanted to turn in, and I thought Irene would take that as an excuse, come with me, but instead she stayed."

"You were surprised?"

"Yes, I was." She shook her head. "If only she'd left then, it might never have happened. Or if I'd stayed. I think about that, you know. If I hadn't gone prancing off, how she might still have been alive."

"You don't know that. Neither do we. We still don't know exactly what happened."

For a moment, her hand rested on his sleeve. "Doesn't stop me thinking, does it?"

"I suppose not."

"Blaine," she said, "he was never arrested or anything? For the murder, I mean."

"No."

"You did suspect him, though, you had to."

Elder nodded. "Maybe for a while."

Despite Vincent Blaine's alibi, every inch of the hotel room had been scrupulously searched, hoping for a print, a hair, a thread, anything that would prove he had been inside. Irene Fowler's body and the clothes in which she had been dressed had been examined and reexamined to no avail.

"I don't suppose," Christine Dulverton said, "you fancy another coffee?"

"I'll get them." Elder was already on his feet.

The place was quite full by now and he had to wait in line. The same voice was singing a song about a stolen car. They moved with their coffees to a pair of seats near the window and watched the passersby. Talked about nothing in particular, this and that. Time passed easily, pleasantly. In the end, Christine

Dulverton was the one to say she had to go. On the pavement, they stood facing each other without knowing quite what to do.

"If you're ever in St. Albans…"

"Yes, of course."

"Or in the market for some jewellery…"

"I'll give you a call."

Elder phoned Maureen Prior from the car. "The file on Brian Warren—have someone dig it out for me, will you?"

UNLIKE CHRISTINE DULVERTON, BRIAN WARREN HAD NOT moved at all. When Elder arrived that afternoon, having walked up from the Ice House, Warren was standing in the driveway of the house on Cavendish Crescent South, where he'd lived for the past thirty-five years. Wearing green wellington boots and a pair of sagging cavalry twill trousers, a khaki sweater with holes in the sleeves, Warren was rinsing down his aging Rover with the garden hose. Dark, soapy water gurgled toward the drain. Warren signalled to Elder he'd be just a few moments more, directed the spray toward the last patches of lather clinging to the wings, and then, satisfied, switched off the hose.

He wiped his hands down the sides of his trousers before taking Elder's in a strong grip that belied his sixty-nine years.

"You'll have to excuse me earlier," he said, "on the telephone. Not being able to recall who you were."

Elder gestured to show it didn't matter. "It was quite a long time ago, after all."

"In which case, I should have remembered you well. It's who I met yesterday I have problems with. Not that I met anyone, I dare say. Anyone new, anyway. Come on inside."

There were stained-glass panels in the front door, ornamental tiles on the lobby floor; high ceilings rich with architectural detail, and spools of dust.

"Cleaning woman can't reach up there, bless her soul. Getting on a bit now, like me. I could clamber up with a stepladder,

but I don't bother. Wait till it gets heavy enough to fall down of
its own accord, then brush it away."

Elder followed him past two partly opened doors, along a
wide corridor lined with small framed paintings.

Beside a picture of a white house lodged between misted
hills, Warren paused. "Watercolours. My wife, Sybil. A weekend
painter, I suppose you'd say. Scotland, the Lakes. Every chance
she got. I'd fish a little, play a round or two of golf, stroll. Sybil
would be there all day if she could, working away at her easel,
this great hat like a beekeeper's keeping off the sun. Most of
these I had framed after she passed on."

"They're lovely."

"Thank you."

"How long ago did she die?"

"Ninety-five. October the seventeenth, 1995. Cancer. Merci-
fully quick for her. Too bloody fast for me. All the plans we'd
made for what we were going to do when I retired. And then
that lump was there inside her, eating away at her insides till
there was nothing left. Skin and bones. I'm sorry, it still makes
me angry after all this time."

"That's all right, I understand."

"Do you?"

"Yes, I think so."

Warren studied him carefully. "Yes, perhaps you do."

They sat in the conservatory, surrounded by geraniums that
were showing the first signs of new life and soon would be
strong enough to stand outside. Warren had persuaded Elder to
join him in a sherry, though it was a drink he would usually go
to great lengths to ignore.

"Sherry, a piece of fruitcake, and a wedge of good cheese.
Helps take the edge off the day. Good single malt later on. Bit of
telly. Fast off most nights by half past ten."

Elder sipped his sherry as slowly as he could. "You do remember her?" he said. "Irene Fowler?"

"God, yes. After what happened? Not likely to forget."

"The evening itself, how well do you remember that?"

"Well enough. Like I say, long-term memory, no problem at all." Leaning toward the table between them, Warren cut off a corner of cheese and speared it with the prongs of the knife. "Two of them, weren't there? Irene Fowler and a friend—Christine...Christine..."

"Christine Dulverton."

"That's it, Dulverton. She was younger. Irene, she would have been around my wife's age. Had Sybil lived."

"Is that why you got on, perhaps? Irene Fowler and yourself."

"Did we? I suppose we did."

"You didn't stay and eat with them, though."

"No. Vincent was hungry, as I recall; I was ready to call it a night. Left them to it."

"How did you get home?"

"How? Walked, I suppose. Yes, walked. One of the advantages of living here, nowhere's more than twenty minutes or so away."

"So you would have been home here by ten?"

"I suppose so. Why do you ask?"

"Oh, no special reason. Just filling in the dots."

"It sounds more than that to me."

"How does it sound?"

"As if you're checking up on me. As if, pretty soon, I'm going to need to come up with some kind of alibi. Where were you between the hours of ten and midnight? Like what's-his-name. Inspector bloody Morse."

"And your answer would be?"

"Here. A nightcap most likely, and then bed."

"You weren't tempted to go back to the hotel, have a nightcap there?"

"Good God, no. What on earth put that sort of an idea into your head?"

Elder succumbed to another piece of cheese. "When I was

talking to Christine Dulverton, she suggested Irene Fowler had taken something of a shine to you."

Warren chuckled. "Taken a shine, had she? Poor woman. She'd have been the first and last in quite a while."

"I wondered if it might have gone both ways."

"Afraid not." He reached for the fruitcake, which crumbled against his fingers. "One thing about reaching a certain age, a blessing to my mind, you leave all that sort of thing behind. Oh, not everyone, I grant you. One or two of my contemporaries, there's this club they belong to, for the recently widowed and divorced. Quite a bit of matchmaking goes on there. Another fellow, older than me, wife died less than two years ago, he's getting remarried just next month. But that's for the companionship, you know, nothing else. Can't stand living alone. Probably can't sew a button or boil an egg, poor blighter. Sybil and I, we were never like that, share and share alike, chores along with the rest."

"So you've never felt the need for companionship?"

"We were lucky, Sybil and myself, we lived a full life. I regret that it's over, of course, but I've a great deal to look back on. Grandchildren, too, spread around, but I get to see them once in a while; high days and holidays, I expect you know how it is."

Gesturing with his hands, he inadvertently clipped the top of his sherry glass and, stooping quickly, caught it before it hit the floor.

"Second slip," he said, "that's where I used to field. Good to see some of the old reflexes are still there."

He set the glass back down.

"You're not a cricket man, I suppose?"

Elder shook his head.

"Not many are nowadays. Test matches and these awful twenty-over farragos aside. Coloured shirts and stupid names. Aping the bloody Americans again. But go along to any county game, midweek, and it's like a convocation of the halt and the lame. More time spent between overs talking about hernias and hip replacements than how much the ball's turning from off to leg."

Sprightly out of his chair, he walked Elder out into the garden and round by the side path toward the front of the house.

"There was something on the radio, wasn't there? Local news. A woman over Sherwood way? Found dead in her bed. That's why you're looking back at this other business, I dare say."

Elder nodded.

"Well," holding out his hand, "good luck with it." Again the grip was strong and firm.

Walking back through the circles and crescents of the private estate, Elder had plenty of time to think about the strength still in Brian Warren's hand, the speed with which he had reacted to the falling glass: physical attributes quite at odds with the fading, rather old-fashioned impression Warren sought to give of himself as a man running out of energy and time.

Chapter 18

MANY, IF NOT MOST, OF THE STAFF WHO HAD BEEN WORK-ing in the hotel on the night Irene Fowler was killed had since moved on; some of them had slipped off the radar altogether; others—a few—had proved surprisingly easy to find. The duty manager that evening was now running a small boutique hotel in the centre of the Lace Market; the concierge, a little balder, a shade more portly, was still the concierge; and the barman who had served Irene Fowler and Vincent Blaine their night-caps, and who, at the time, had been a third-year medical student, was now halfway through his surgical rotation at the City Hospital. That morning he was assisting in an operation on a perforated bowel; if all went well, he would be free to talk to Elder between eleven and eleven-thirty.

The traffic on the ring road was more snarled up than usual, and Elder half-wished for a flashing blue light to clear his way through. In any event, the procedure at the hospital had run

into complications, and it was another half hour before Jeremy
Davis appeared, effusive in his apologies and desperate for a
cigarette.

They stood outside under a limpid sky, the building bulked
behind them. Davis was in his late twenties by now, early thirties, a full head of dark, wavy hair, a rugby player's build, stocky
and strong, and tired eyes. There were flecks of dried blood on
his collar, possibly from where he'd shaved, possibly not.

"Hard morning?" Elder said.

"Not too bad." There was a slight Welsh lilt to his voice.

"I'm sorry to be taking up your time."

"That's okay." Davis drew smoke down into his lungs as
though, perversely, his life depended on it.

"Irene Fowler," Elder said. "In the statement you made at the
time, you said you thought she might have spoken to someone
at the bar before leaving, but you couldn't be sure."

"That's right."

"With hindsight, you can't remember any more than that?
Any more detail?"

Davis took another pull at his cigarette. An ambulance swung
past them and slewed to a halt outside Accident and Emergency.
"I've been trying to think, ever since you called. The danger, of
course, because you want something definite, I could convince
myself I saw something I didn't. But like I said before, all I had
was this impression—it was nothing more—of a woman sitting
near the bar, over to the left, a table on her own, and then someone leaning down toward her, as if starting a conversation. And
that's it. That's all. I can't even swear that was all true."

"This man, though—let's assume for a moment there was a
man—was he short or tall? When you see him, in your mind's
eye, just for that moment, what do you see?"

Davis squinted up at the sky. Cars drove up and down past
them, searching slowly for somewhere to park.

"Tall," Davis said after several moments. "The way he was standing; not standing, more leaning over. I'd say, yes, he was tall."

"Fair? Dark? Balding?"

"Dark haired, I think. But no, I can't be sure. I could be making that up."

"What else about him? Was there anything else?"

"Such as?"

"I don't know. Age? How old was he, for instance? Young, old?"

"I don't know."

"Yes, you do."

"Well, not young, I'd be pretty certain of that. If he had been, I think I'd have noticed. That particular bar, that time of night, it's residents in the main. Not kids, clubbers, nothing like that. It's not on the circuit, you know? Least, it wasn't, back then."

"So he's middle aged, probably, reasonably well dressed, you don't pay too much attention because you're busy with other things..."

"That's right. I've got my eye on the clock, making sure all the stray glasses are collected in, getting ready to cash up."

"You're busy so you don't notice him, except that you do. Just for this moment, you do. Something draws your attention, breaks your concentration, whatever..."

"She laughs. The woman, she laughs. When he leans across the table toward her, he says something or other and she laughs."

"You're sure?"

"I'm sure."

"What kind of a laugh?" Elder asked.

"Just ordinary, you know? Not responding to a joke, not like that. More pleasant, friendly. Good humoured, that's what I'd say."

"And after that, after the laugh, what happens next? Does he sit down, join her? Have a drink? Or does she get up and go with him? What?"

"I don't know."

"Try."

"I said, I don't know." Davis dropped his cigarette butt to the ground and checked the watch on his wrist. "I ought to be getting back."

"Of course. And listen, I'm grateful."

"I hope I've helped."

"If you think of anything else..."

"There's a number I can call you? No promises, mind."

Elder had been into Kall Kwik earlier and ordered some cards printed with his name and cell number; for now he wrote the number on a page of his notebook, tore it out, and pushed it down into the pocket of Davis's white coat.

ELDER HAD JUST RETURNED FROM THE HOSPITAL AND was settling down behind a borrowed computer when Maureen Prior spun him round in his chair, her eyes bright and excitement easily discernible in her voice. The cat who had got a scent, at least, of the cream.

"Frank, you remember that loser we were looking at for the Irene Fowler murder? Dowland, you remember him?"

"Richard Dowland. Yes, of course."

The picture that came to Elder's mind was of a sad, round-faced man with bad breath and nervous hands. Dowland had a record of minor sexual offenses—flashing, peeping Tom, stealing women's underwear from garden washing lines. At the time of the murder he had been working as a kitchen porter at the hotel.

"We had him in, I don't know, four times, was it? Got himself so worked up, at one point he pissed himself, right there in the interview room, you remember that? In the end there was nothing to hold him on, nothing to link him to what happened."

Elder remembered Dowland's confused state of mind, the way his words and thoughts stumbled over themselves, helplessly: the pleading in his eyes. If confessing had been an option, something to put a stop, once and for all, to the questioning, it was an option he must have come close to having taken.

"Someone with their eye on the ball," Prior said, "just picked his name off the computer. It seems as if our Richard has moved on from sniffing knickers and getting his kicks at bathroom windows. He was released from Lincoln a little over two months ago. Four years of a six-year sentence."

"What was the offense?"

"Aggravated assault."

"You know the details?"

"Enough to make it interesting. The victim was a fifty-three-year-old woman, working as a prostitute around St. Ann's. Dowland hit her over the head, then did his best to strangle her. She struggled, someone chanced along, lucky for her, and Dowland ran off. That's all I know so far. I've got a meeting with the sex offenders officer later."

"He's out what? On parole?"

"I assume so."

"In which case they'll be keeping pretty close tabs."

"Let's hope. Anything that puts him in contact with Claire Meecham, that's all we need."

Elder shook his head. "He's suspected for the Irene Fowler murder, and now he comes out of prison just a few weeks before another woman's killed in a similar way. It's too good to be true."

"Gift horses, Frank, you know what you shouldn't do."

TOM WHITEMORE HAD BEEN A SEX OFFENDERS OFFICER for three years and hated and relished it with equal measure. He hated it for what it brought him up against, rubbed his nose in, anything to do with kids, especially. That was what got to him the most, the things that could happen to children, some of them so young that even to think of it for a moment fetched bile to the back of your throat. What he relished was seeing the men—they were mostly men, but not all—seeing the men who did those things taken off the streets, locked up inside, and when they got back out again, controlled, looked after, kept, as far as possible, out of harm's way. It was a job that needed doing, and for as long as he could stand it, it was what he would do.

"How much longer, Tom?" his wife would ask, and he'd reply, "I don't know, another year perhaps, six months, then I'll chuck it in. Transfer to fraud. Or traffic, maybe." And laugh.

And each night, no matter what time he got home, he would go into the twins' bedroom and stand beside their beds, watching them sleeping, five-year-old twin boys.

He shared his office with three others, their desks heavy with papers and files, unwashed mugs pushed up against keyboards and computer screens, filing cabinets full to overflowing, action plans and Home Office directives pinned to the wall.

Shirtsleeved, tousle-haired, he levered himself half out of his seat and stretched forward to shake Maureen Prior's hand.

"Throw that stuff off the chair and sit yourself down. Get you anything? There's a machine out in the hall."

"Thanks," Prior said, with a shake of the head. "I don't want to take any more of your time than's necessary."

"Okay. I had this—where is it now?" He rummaged on his desk. "I had this printed out." Finding the pages lodged underneath something else, he pulled them free. "The broad outline's there, you'll see. Because of the nature of his offense, Dowland's file was forwarded to the Public Protection Team prior to his release. The assessment was that though, on balance, he was thought fit for release, there was still some danger he might offend again. So there were conditions laid down, restrictions on his movements. He has to report to his probation officer twice a week, also to me. Regular sessions with a community psychiatric nurse. You know the kind of thing."

"And he's in a hostel?"

Whitemore shook his head. "Should have been. Ordinarily, yes, that would have been the case. But there were no places available at the time. He's in a flat in the Meadows instead."

"How's he making out?"

Whitemore shrugged. "Keeping his nose clean, as far as we can tell. Getting him to talk, it's like getting blood out of the proverbial. But from what you said, you'll know that yourself already. And he's not got any more chatty with age."

One of Whitemore's colleagues, who'd been having what sounded like an increasingly tense conversation on the phone, broke the connection with a curse and immediately dialled another number. A female officer came into the room, dumped her bag on her desk, and went straight out again.

"The offense Dowland went down for," Prior said, "the assault. Can you tell me about that?"

"Let me see if Dave Stockdale's in the building," Whitemore said. "He was the arresting officer. He can tell you better than me."

Stockdale was older than Tom Whitemore by a good ten years, possibly more, one of those officers who finds his level early and sticks with it until he draws his pension. In Whitemore's office, he nodded at Prior, choosing to ignore her rank, and leaned back against one of the desks.

"Dowland had been spotted hanging out in the red-light district on a number of occasions," he said. "Creeping up on cars parked on the Goose Fair site on the Forest. Catching an eyeful, then jerking off. Wonder he didn't get his face fixed by some punter or other. We'd warned him off till we were blue in the bloody face, but that didn't stop him coming back.

"Night in question, he obviously thought he'd do a bit more than look, talked this tart in St. Ann's into giving him short time for a tenner, up by the reservoir, Corporation Oaks. When they got there, no sooner'd she got her drawers down, he weighs into her with this bit of old two-by-four he found laying around. Smacked her round the head real bad and then, once she'd stretched out on the ground, starts strangling her. Would have finished the job if her shouts hadn't roused someone passing nearby. Student, on the way back to his digs. Dowland ran off, but not before this bloke got a good look at him. No question it were him."

"The prostitute, what was her name?"

"Eve Ward." Stockdale laughed. "Been working that patch so long, they'll be raising a statue to her soon. Services to the fucking community. If you get my drift."

Neither Prior nor Tom Whitemore cracked a smile.

"Are there any other instances of him using violence?" Prior asked. "Dowland?"

"Not as far as we knew then," Stockdale said. "A lot never gets reported, mind, you know that well as me."

"And did he ever give any reason for attacking the woman the way he did?"

"Laughed at him, that's what he said. Least, that's what he came out with at the trial. His brief's idea, I'd not wonder. Before that, we had the devil's own job to get him to admit to bloody anything. Tie his shoe, right there in front of you, an' next minute he'd say he didn't. But if that's what it was, spur-of-the-moment-like, how come he had a bit of two-by-four handy? Too bloody convenient by half, if you ask me."

"You think he went out prepared?" Prior asked.

"I bloody do."

"Okay, Dave," Tom Whitemore said. "I think that's all for now."

Grinning, Stockdale shambled to his feet. "Good luck with it," he said to Prior. "Dowland and his like, Tom here'll not thank me for saying so, but to my way of thinking, if you can't castrate the buggers, at least when you lock them up, lose the bloody key." He winked. "Just kidding, of course. My bit of fun."

"Salt of the earth," Whitemore said when Stockdale had left the room. To Maureen Prior it didn't sound like a compliment.

RICHARD DOWLAND'S PROBATION OFFICER WAS BRIDGET Arthur, an experienced fifty-year-old with grown-up children and a husband who was a senior fire officer, both their working lives spent in the same community in which they were born and raised. Bridget was well built and quite tall, tall enough to carry her weight, a haircut that didn't take prisoners, an expression that, normally serious, became almost girlish when she smiled.

As she made herself and Maureen Prior tea, she apologized for the state of the mugs, stained beyond saving. The sugar she stirred with a ballpoint pen.

"Just temporary all this?" said Prior, looking round. The office was in a Portakabin that swayed a little in high winds.

"Yes," Bridget Arthur said. "Right. Four years this coming June."

Prior laughed and accepted a biscuit, a custard cream, to go with her tea.

"Richard Dowland," Arthur said. "What's your interest?"

Maureen leaned back. "Eight years ago he was a suspect in a murder inquiry I was working on; in the end there was nothing to connect him. He was arrested and questioned but never charged. The murderer was never found. Now there's another case, similar…"

"This is the woman out in Sherwood?"

"Yes."

"She was strangled."

"That's right."

"And you think Richard…?"

"It's a possibility."

"Because of what happened in St. Ann's?"

"Exactly."

"There's something linking him to the victim?"

"Not so far as we know."

"So why do you think he might be involved? I don't understand."

Prior drew breath. "Okay. Eight years ago, when Irene Fowler was found strangled, Dowland was working in the hotel where she was killed. As far as we knew then he had no record of violence and we ended up letting him go. But since then the picture's changed, he's attacked this woman, come close to killing her, by strangulation. And now, just a month or so after he's released, there's another attack, another woman strangled. You don't think we should be looking at Dowland?"

"That's not what I'm saying."

"Isn't it?"

"Look, Maureen, I'm not going to presume to tell you how to do your job."

Good, Prior thought. She dunked what was left of her biscuit into her tea and it crumbled apart.

"It's just...Look, Richard, he's not a saint, I'm not saying that. Far from it. Not overbright, not the sharpest penny in your purse. Pathetic, that's what he is. What happened out by the Forest, whatever the reason, it was terrible, of course it was. The poor woman was terrified out of her wits, badly injured, nearly killed. But he's paid for that; he's served his time. He should be given a chance. That's what we're doing, giving him a chance."

"And if he's done it again?"

"If he's offended again, if he as much as steps out of line, his probation will be revoked and he'll end up back inside. All I'm saying—what I'm asking—don't dump on him without reason."

The first drops of rain hit the roof of the cabin and a moment later the windows were rattling.

"Let me ask you something," Bridget Arthur said.

"Go ahead."

"This latest victim, what sort of a woman was she?"

"What sort? Perfectly ordinary, mid-fifties."

"Respectable? Middle class?"

"I'd say so."

"Good job?"

"Yes."

"And the other woman, the earlier murder?"

"Irene Fowler. Pretty much the same. A bit more high-powered if anything."

Bridget Arthur nodded. "Look at the reports, then. Read Dowland's file. All the women he's ever shown an interest in, the trouble he's been in, it's always prostitutes, working girls. There's a restriction on his probation order now, keeping him away from red-light areas, and that's why. All right, these other women, the age might be the same, but that's all. The kind you describe, professional, intelligent. Richard would be terrified. Run a mile."

"I'd like to talk to him just the same."

"Your privilege. But Richard's a vulnerable adult. If you're going to question him officially, someone he knows well should be present."

"Tom Whitemore, will that do?"

"Tom's fine. But if for any reason he can't make it, I'll give you my cell number, you can call me. Or Ben Leonard, that's the community psychiatric nurse Richard's been seeing."

Prior smiled. "Kid gloves, I promise."

For some minutes more they sat there, remains of their tea getting cold, listening to the rain. If it were true, Prior was thinking, the reason Dowland struck out at Eve Ward was that she belittled him; how much more inferior might Irene Fowler and Claire Meecham have made him feel?

Chapter 19

RICHARD DOWLAND WAS LIVING IN THE UPPER HALF OF a small, flat-fronted, terraced house in the Meadows, not far from Wilford Crescent and the playing fields leading down to the Victoria Embankment and the River Trent.

At first glance the place looked clean and tidy, the few bits of furniture uncluttered and Dowland's possessions all neatly in their place. A stained picture of Mary holding the Christ Child above the gas fire in the living room; a cup and cereal bowl still waiting to be cleared away. Only gradually did you realize most of the surfaces were filmed with dust and that there were patches of grease on the backs of chairs, the bed, the kitchen walls.

Dowland stammered a greeting to Tom Whitemore, flushed under Maureen Prior's gaze and turned away.

"I just wanted you to meet Maureen here," Whitemore said, "maybe have a little chat. Although I think you met her before, quite a long time ago."

Dowland said nothing. Whether he recognized Maureen Prior or not, he gave no indication. His face, Prior thought, had the pallor of sour milk. One eye was watery and the skin above the other was swollen and inflamed as if from a sty. Whiteheads ran like rosary beads down one side of his face. He was wearing trackie bottoms and a shiny tracksuit top that didn't match, dilapidated trainers, his hair in need of a comb.

"So, Richard," Whitemore said, once they had all sat down. "How's it all been going?"

Dowland mumbled something under his breath.

"Been keeping out of trouble?"

"Ye-yes." Not looking: looking at the floor.

"Good, good." Whitemore leaned back and crossed his legs. "Last night, for instance, what did you do last night?"

Dowland said nothing; a glance toward Whitemore and nothing more. He was still refusing to acknowledge Maureen Prior's presence.

"Stayed in, did you?" Whitemore persisted. "Stayed here?"

"Yeah. Yes, that's right." Dowland's voice was audible but only just.

"And today?"

Dowland blinked back at him.

"You've got plans for today?"

"No. I dunno."

"You'll be going out, surely? Some time? A walk, at least?"

"Maybe, yeah."

"Bit of fresh air, do you good."

"Yeah, s'pose so."

"Down by the river, perhaps? You go down there at all? It's close, after all."

Dowland's hands fidgeted in his lap. "Yeah, 's'all right."

"How about this evening?" Whitemore asked. "Meet someone later, will you? Go out for a pint?"

Eyes fixed on the carpet between his feet, Dowland shook his head.

"No friends, then, Richard?" Prior asked, speaking for the first time. "You must have friends, surely? Mates?"

The answer, like most of his answers, was slow in coming. "Not here I ain't."

"Where then?"

"Inside. In prison. Lincoln. I had friends there."

"How about a job?" Prior said. "Working at the moment, are you?"

Continuing to stare at the same worn square of carpet, Dowland made no answer.

"Bridget's seeing about a job for you, isn't she, Richard?" Whitemore said. "Talking to someone. On your behalf. Someone she thinks might be able to help you out."

With stubby fingers, nails bitten down to the quick, Dowland was scratching at one of the pimples on his chin.

"This job," Prior said, "hotel, is it? Richard? In a hotel?"

"I don't...I don't know."

"Portering, maybe?"

"I don't know."

"That's what you've done before, haven't you? Portering?"

"Yes." Barely a nod.

"That was when we talked before, you and me, Richard, wasn't it? You remember now?"

For a split second, he looked into her face. "No, not really, no."

"Come on, Richard, I'm sure you do. Something had happened at the hotel, that's why I was there. A woman, a guest, something happened to her. You can't have forgotten that."

Dowland had stopped attacking his spots and instead his fingers were gouging into the soft skin on the inside of his arms.

"You were very helpful then, Richard," Prior said. "I'm wondering if you can help us again."

She waited for the worst of the scratching to cease; long lines, livid on the pale loose skin.

"You see, something similar's happened again. Not at a hotel. At least, not as far as we know. But another woman, she's been found. In the same way..."

Both hands clamped over his ears, shutting out the words, Dowland slid forward from his chair, down on to his knees.

Moving slowly, careful not to distress him further, Tom Whitemore leaned forward and, with his hands beneath Dowland's elbows, raised him back up and eased him back into his chair, then pried his hands away from his ears.

"Tell you what," Whitemore said, "why don't we stop talking for now? You've got milk in the kitchen, have you? You remembered to get some milk? I could fancy a nice cup of tea." This with a glance toward Maureen Prior that said, okay, that's it for now, back off.

THE RIVER CURVED QUITE STEEPLY AROUND THE MEMOrial gardens, the bandstand, and the paddling pool, the green roof of County Hall ahead, and beyond that the floodlit stanchions of both the forest and the county grounds. At their backs, the beginnings of the city clustered low and unpromising, the rounded dome of the Council House just visible in the indifferent light. Overhead, the sky was sealed a uniform bluey gray.

"Wouldn't think it was May," Tom Whitemore said. "Almost halfway through the bloody year. Pair of gloves'd not go amiss."

Maureen Prior had her hands balled up inside the pockets of her windbreaker, collar up.

A six-man boat moved fast past them, parting the water, oars rising and falling in unison.

"Poor bastard's close to falling apart."

"He's on medication?" Prior asked.

"When he remembers."

A couple ran toward them on the lower path, no longer young but moving easily, the man's head slick with sweat nonetheless, the pink of the woman's lipstick matching, almost, the sweatband holding back her auburn hair.

"Ever make you feel guilty?" Tom Whitemore asked.

"How's that?"

"All these people, exercising, keeping fit."

Prior shook her head; any time she felt a little overweight, all she had to do was sit awhile in the Old Market Square and watch the fatties waddling by on their way from Pizza Hut or KFC.

"You don't go down the gym or anything?" Whitemore said.

"Not any more. I did for a while."

She had gone for a couple of nights a week at first, lifted a few weights, a spell on the rowing machine, occasionally a class, aerobics of some kind; in the end it had been too much of a cross between a meat market and a fashion show and she'd quit.

"How about you?" she asked.

"Marianne and I were members at David Lloyd, out at Compton Acres..."

"Marianne, that's your wife?"

"Yes. We kept it going for a couple of years, used it a lot at first, but then...I don't know, things kept getting in the way. Marianne would drive out there, use the pool, that was about all. In the end it didn't seem worth the expense. Now she tells me I'm putting on weight."

"It doesn't notice."

"Thanks." He grinned an almost boyish grin and for a moment Maureen was worried he might think she was flirting.

"Dowland," she said, "how close a watch are you keeping?"

"Between Bridget Arthur, myself, and the rest of the team, he's seeing someone four or five times a week. But there's no kind of surveillance, if that's what you mean. Some cases, we might try and pull in a few extra bodies, cobble something together, keep a closer watch, but only if we thought there was a real risk to others."

"And that's not the case here?"

"I don't think so. Well, you saw him."

"I saw someone who's jumpy, neurotic. A mess."

"But dangerous?"

"Who's to say?"

"Ben—that's the psychiatric nurse—according to him the risk of Dowland resorting to violence again is low. Minimal. Save maybe against himself."

Prior stopped. "I wonder if he'd have said that five years ago? Before Dowland beat Eve Ward about the head and nearly throttled her to death."

They cut back through the gardens behind the statue of Queen Victoria, up past the tennis courts and toward the church in front of which the car was parked. On the far side of the city centre, rain was funnelling dark toward the horizon.

ELDER HAD BEEN OUT AT TOP VALLEY WHEN THE RAIN had started, talking to Irene Fowler's daughter Patricia, who had recently moved up from Market Harborough to take a teaching post at the comprehensive. They sat in the empty classroom, perched on tables, staring out, as the wind blew the rain in swathes across the playground and flung it against the glass.

"I nearly didn't come, you know," Patricia Fowler said. "This job. Here, in the city." Though she was married, she'd kept her family name. "They ask you, when you come for the interview, if we offer you the post will you accept? And for a moment I couldn't answer. Stupid, really. But Mum being killed here and whoever did it..." She shook her head. "Of course, in the end I said yes. You have to put these things behind you, don't you? Move on. And now here you are telling me the case has been reopened..."

"Not that exactly."

"You're looking into it again. Asking questions."

"Yes."

"Trying to find some connection with this other murder."

"Yes."

She turned toward him. "You think it might be the same person?"

"We don't know."

"Oh God! You're all so tight-lipped, aren't you?" Colour flushed her cheeks. "Never giving anything away."

"It's not that."

"That's the way it seems."

"If there was anything definite to tell you, I would."

"Then why tell me anything at all?"

"Courtesy?"

"Just that? No more questions?"

Elder smiled. "Maybe one or two."

There was a constant hum of sound, punctuated by occasional laughter, coming from the rooms to either side. Patricia Fowler got down and walked to the teacher's desk for her bag. She was tall, taller than her mother had been, slimmer, too, but with a distinct resemblance about the face, a strong nose, dark eyes set closely together. She took out a roll of mints from her bag, slipped one into her mouth, and offered one to Elder, who refused.

"What do you want to know?" she said. "What can I possibly tell you now?"

"I've been wondering—I didn't think this at the time, not as seriously as perhaps I should—but I've been wondering if whoever your mother met at the hotel, if it was somebody she already knew."

"From business, you mean? Someone at the conference?"

"No, not that."

"Because I thought you checked everyone who'd enrolled?"

"We did. But, no, I was thinking about someone with whom

she might already have had some kind of a relationship; someone she'd arranged to meet. Or maybe your mother had told
someone where she was going to be and he decided to turn up
out of the blue, surprise her."

"And then he killed her," Patricia Fowler said. She walked to
the window and stared out. The rain was steadier now, less
heavy, beginning to slacken off; some lightening in the sky above
the golf course to the west. "As far as I know," she said, "she
wasn't seeing anybody. Not then. Not that I was aware of."

Elder nodded. The two men Irene Fowler was known to have
had relationships with since her divorce had been questioned
and found to have unshakeable alibis.

"If there had been somebody," Elder said, "somebody new,
would she have told you, do you think? Sometimes, where that
sort of thing's concerned, parents and their children, it can be
a little awkward."

A smile wrinkled the lines around Patricia Fowler's eyes.
"Well, we didn't exactly swap chapter and verse. But after—you
know, after Dad—I think anything else for her was pretty much
a revelation. So, yes, it was something we talked about."

"And she hadn't mentioned that she'd started to see someone
else?"

"No."

The voices were louder now, at the other side of the classroom door.

"The two people she had been involved with," Elder said,
"she'd met them both through work, is that right?"

"Where else was she going to meet someone? I mean, she's
not exactly going to go out clubbing, is she?"

"How about personal columns, the small ads? The Internet,
something like that?"

"No, no way."

"People surprise us sometimes."

"Yes, but Mum...No, never in a million years."

"Okay." Elder slipped to his feet. The sounds of impatience from the corridor were growing louder still.

"This recent murder," Patricia Fowler asked. "Is that how she met him? Whoever it was. Through the Internet?"

"I'm afraid I can't really say."

"Not that you're being tight-lipped."

"Not at all."

The door burst open and the first of thirty or so fourteen-year-olds came stumbling in, others pushing noisily behind.

"Well," Patricia Fowler said, "if you're that anxious, I suppose you'd better all come in and sit down."

A doe-eyed girl with the waistband of her skirt rolled over too many times looked from Elder to Patricia and struck a pose. "Really, miss, you could do better than that."

THE PUB WAS SET BACK OFF THE INNER RING ROAD, MID-way between the Force Crime Directorate HQ and the city centre. Red brick and beams, the once-fashionable Tudor roadhouse look. So far the landlord had held off any kind of refurbishment: the flock wallpaper in the lounge bar brought to mind an Indian restaurant circa 1964, and the floors throughout, instead of being stripped back and sanded clean, were still covered in the same well-worn patterned carpet that gave with a telling softness, almost a squelch, beneath the feet.

Most of Maureen Prior's team were in what the locals still called the snug, debating the whys and wherefores of Forest's relegation from the championship, who to bless and who to blame. Prior herself was standing with Elder, close against the main bar, while behind them a man with a walleye called bingo numbers from a small electronic board. Whenever anyone ventured out of the function room in search of the Ladies or, more usually, the Gents, a snatch of sprightly, slightly old-fashioned jazz followed them through the door.

"Another Jameson, Frank?" Prior asked.

Elder nodded. There was a time, evenings like this, he would have chased it down with a pint of best, but nowadays beer left him feeling bloated and he stuck to shorts, a glass of water on the side to help it on its way, ameliorate the effect.

"Dowland," Elder said, once they'd found a quiet corner, "how did it go?"

"Jumping at false hopes there, I think."

Elder nodded; he'd sensed that her excitement from earlier in the day had abated.

"It's difficult to see Dowland and a woman like Claire Meecham in the same universe," Prior said, "never mind the same room. The same bed beggars belief."

"He could have attacked her, nonetheless."

"She wasn't raped, Frank. Consensual sex, remember?"

"Stranger things have happened."

"In his head, maybe. But, Frank, you should see him. He was a mess before, but now..." She let the thought trail away.

Around the corner of the bar someone shouted out as they scored their pen through the final missing number.

"Scrub him off the board, then?" Elder said. "Or wait a while and see?"

"I want to talk to the woman he attacked. See if I can't find out a little more about what went on."

"She's still around?"

"Apparently. And I've arranged to see Dowland's psychiatric nurse, though that's probably a waste of time. Pretty much forecast what he's going to say now. Dysfunctional this, dysfunctional that: bullied at school, likely buggered at home. Usual set of reasons. Excuses."

"Doesn't mean they're not true."

She fixed him with a look. "Getting soft in your old age, Frank?"

"No more than you're going the other way."

"Is that what you think?"

"No, not really. You've always been a hard woman, Maureen. A hard copper."

"Thanks."

Elder laughed. "About the only person I know who thought the Taliban's hearts were in the right place."

The function room door swung open again, the band squeezing every ounce out of "Take the A Train," and there was Charlie Resnick, detective chief inspector, walking toward them, glass in hand.

"Not interrupting anything, am I?" he said, smiling.

"Case conference, Charlie," Maureen Prior said. "That's all."

"Meecham murder?"

"That's the one."

Resnick nodded. "Up from the West Country for a spell, Frank? Helping out?"

"Something like that."

"Don't know what we'd do without you."

"Frank here," Prior said, goading softly, "has gone west in more ways than one. Fully-paid-up member of the liberal Left."

"Good to hear it," Resnick said, and winked. "Not many of us still around."

"Get you a top-up, Charlie?" Prior said.

"Some other time. I've got to be off home."

"Lynn keeping you on a tight rein these days?"

"Something like that."

A few more pleasantries and he was away, a heavy, broad-shouldered man who still moved, nonetheless, with a certain grace.

"They're still together, then?" Elder said when Resnick was out of earshot. "Him and his young DS? More than just a fling?"

"Staying power, Frank. Stickability. Some people have it, some don't."

It was time to change the subject, Elder knew.

———

BACK IN HIS RENTED FLAT, SURROUNDINGS STILL
strange, Elder flicked through the usual gamut of channels on
the TV before switching it off. The lights of the city burned
bright outside. On the radio, someone was talking about the
war in Iraq, a war that had been won months before and yet still
more people were dying every day. Reflected in the darkened
window, an almost featureless face looked back at him, more
like his father's than his own. *Staying power, Frank. Some
people have it, some don't.* He picked up the phone and was
midway through dialling Joanne's number before he stopped.
I've been seeing him again. Martyn. I'm sorry... Should he
have forgiven her, then? Five years before. *I'm sorry...* Forgiven them? Turned, as it were, the other cheek? For better, for
worse. Instead he had torn the covers from the bed where they
had slept and then, not satisfied, smashed the very bed itself.
Decamped into a hotel with a bottle of Irish whiskey and drunk
himself insensible. Years ago now, yet not so many. Five. Five
years. Not so long out of a life, a marriage. He poured himself a
drink and dialled the number again; stood there, staring at his
reflection, listening to it ring and ring.

Chapter 20

THE DAY HAD STARTED OFF BRIGHT BUT COLD, JET
trails arcing across the sky. There'd been a time, Elder remembered, when, as a young man, he had looked up and wished
himself on board and bound for America, Italy, or Spain. Almost
anywhere: anywhere he'd never been. A time when he had
imagined himself at the airport, staring up at the departures
board, passport in hand, watching the names click round: San
Francisco, Barcelona, Rome. Not knowing how to choose. Now
Paris was a few hours away by rail and lads went to Tallin or
Barcelona for a weekend on the piss, much as he might have
gone to Newcastle or Leeds. And scores of kids with backpacks
were beginning their gap year in Prague or Helsinki, Sydney or
the Great Barrier Reef.

The first time he and Joanne had gone abroad together, 1981,
the year before they married, it had been to a jerry-built hotel
on the Costa del Sol, a package holiday, all they could afford.
Joanne in her bikini on the beach. English food served here.

Fish and chips. Full English breakfast. Warm beer. Skegness with mosquitos and added sun, less wind. On the fourth day, she'd come down with some kind of bug and spent the remainder of the week in bed.

Elder turned left off Bridlesmith Gate and came to a standstill outside the salon. Cut and Dried. Frosted glass across half the window. Lights on inside. If Joanne were there or not, he couldn't see.

When he pushed open the door, faces turned toward him.

Soft, rhythmic music played.

"Em, I was looking for Joanne. I don't know…"

"Frank!" Like some siren in an old-time movie, she stepped through from the rear of the shop, out of the shadows and into the light. Pink, perfect, smiling. "Come in for a restyling? It's never too late."

"No, I thought…" He looked, somewhat helplessly, toward the door.

Amused, she took his arm and ushered him back outside. "Everything's all right?"

"Yes. I just thought, you know, I've hardly seen you and…"

"Coffee?" She was looking at her watch, slim and stylish on her slender wrist. "I could meet you at eleven, a little after."

"No. I was thinking maybe dinner."

"Dinner?"

"Yes, you know, a meal somewhere…"

"You mean, like a date?"

"No. Just, well, dinner. A chance to talk."

"All right."

"Tonight, then? If you're free."

"Tonight? Oh, Frank, I don't know if I can."

"Okay. Never mind. It was just a thought." Head down for a moment, hands in pockets, he stepped away. "Maybe some other time?"

"Yes, of course. Some other time. I'd like that, I really would."
Another moment and she had gone back inside.

Smarting, embarrassed, Elder turned toward the street and began to walk the way he'd come.

Drawing level with Waterstone's, he saw a face he recognized. Vincent Blaine in a green corduroy suit, lifting a book down from the display, then turning toward Elder as he approached. "Mr. Elder, a surprise."

"We do read books, you know."

"We?"

"You know what I mean."

The particular book Blaine was holding was large and, Elder guessed, expensive. "Matisse," Blaine said, "the new biography." Elder shook his head.

"Amazing, that he was still alive into the 1950s. Ten years, almost, after the end of the war. It's difficult sometimes not to think of him as belonging to another century." He smiled, catching his mistake. "But then, of course, he did. So did we all, that century and this." He set the book back on its shelf. "Time, Mr. Elder, it leaves us all behind."

"I was going to contact you," Elder said. "Something else I wanted to ask."

"Ask away. I'm meeting Anna in a short while, but until then…"

"That night at the hotel, when you left Irene Fowler in the bar…"

"Yes?"

"You don't remember, as you were leaving, anyone approaching her, her table?"

"No."

"Or hearing her laugh? You don't recall hearing someone laugh?"

Blaine shook his head. "Not particularly, no."

"And nothing she said, before you left, suggested she was expecting someone?"

"No."

Elder nodded. "Your friend Brian Warren, that evening, how would you say he and Irene Fowler got along?"

Blaine gave it a little thought. "Well enough, I suppose."

"No more than that?"

"No, I don't think so."

"Christine Dulverton, the other woman who was there, she seemed to think they'd hit it off pretty well."

Blaine's face took on a supercilious smile. "One thing I've discovered about women, Mr. Elder, they have an ability to find romance, even intrigue, breeding in the most unlikely soil." He took a half step away. "You've met Brian Warren, I take it?"

Elder nodded.

"Not the most fertile ground for romantic fantasy, I should have thought. And as for anything else..."

"Anything else?"

"Mr. Elder, Brian Warren is not a violent man. A few dead birds on the glorious twelfth, salmon hauled out of some highland stream, those are all very well. Within his natural orbit, shall we say. I also believe that when it comes to bridge, he takes no prisoners. But if you were for one moment considering the possibility that he returned that evening for an assignation that became something darker, I would urge you to think again."

Elder extended his hand. "Thank you, Mr. Blaine. Thank you for your time."

Compared to Warren's handshake, Blaine's was deft and light, as if contact with another person in that way was not something he enjoyed at all.

MAUREEN PRIOR MET EVE WARD IN A CAFÉ ON THE AL-freton Road, last year's calendar still on the wall. Two rows of four Formica-topped tables with only a narrow space between. An elderly Rastafarian stood behind the counter, polishing, with infinite slowness, a battered metal teapot. The only customers, Eve Ward aside, were two young men in hoodies, who got up as Prior entered and pushed past her on their way to the door.

"Some people," the Rastafarian said, "don't feel comfortable with anyone they think might be police." He smiled at her through broken teeth.

Prior assumed that rather than sniffing out her profession from the way she held herself or her self-effacing way of dressing, they had recognized her from a previous occasion. But you could never tell.

Eve Ward was sitting close against one wall, flesh loose on the bones of her face, lipstick bravely rather than wisely applied, her hair hennaed and roughly combed. She was wearing a dark wool coat that had seen better days and, beneath it, a mauve cardigan fastened with a safety pin. Chipped red polish on her nails.

Prior introduced herself and, after asking the other woman what she wanted, ordered two teas. "It was good of you to agree to see me," she said, sitting down. "I won't take up any more than's necessary of your time."

Eve Ward coughed and lit a cigarette. "What you want to waste your breath over that twisted bastard for beggars bloody belief."

Without ceremony, their teas arrived.

"I wondered if you could tell me about what happened? The night you were attacked."

"He went bloody crazy, didn't he? Smacked me round the head and then tried to bloody strangle me. The bastard! Shame he's not still rottin' away inside." She touched her finger ends gently against one side of her head. "Headaches I get all the time. Gettin' worse instead of better, an' all. Doctor says there's nothing she can do, aside from give me pills. Hurts so much sometimes, I want to take a fuckin' knife and gouge it out."

"I'm sorry."

"Sorry! What fuckin' good's that? Sorry?" Angrily, she stirred sugar into her tea.

"Before he hit you," Prior said, "was there anything special that set him off?"

"Ask his bloody psychiatrist, don't ask me."

"You didn't say anything, do anything…?"

"I told you, didn't I? He just went crazy. Lost it altogether. It were nothing to do with me, owt I said or anything." Hand shaking, she lifted her cup. "I don't know what it was got into him that night, but whatever it was he was clear off his head. Drugs, maybe, I don't know."

Prior knew the alcohol level in Dowland's blood that evening had been quite high, not high enough in all probability to make him drunk; aspirin aside, there were no traces of any drug.

"You knew him, then?" Prior said. "You'd been with him before?"

"Once or twice, yes."

"You knew what he liked."

"Yeah."

"Will you tell me?"

A smile twisted one side of Eve Ward's mouth. "Get off on it, will you?"

"I doubt it."

"What he liked was for you to hold him while he rubbed his face against your tits—cuddling, that's what he called it. Suck on your nipples then he would, bite 'em, too, if he got the chance. Then if he hadn't come already, he'd wank over you and then he'd cry. Daft, stupid sod, I couldn't stand him. Used to give me the willies."

"And this particular night, this didn't happen? This was different?"

Eve Ward stirred some more sugar into her tea; she didn't answer right away. "He started off the same, grabbing and moaning, and, I don't know why, it just got to me, like I'd had enough of it, you know? And I asked him what's the matter with him, he didn't want to stick it up like any normal bloke? Was he queer or something? Another fuckin' nance?"

"And that was when he hit you?"

"Yes. This bit of wood lying on the ground."

"When you asked him if he was queer?"

"Queer, gay, yeah. I might've said gay, I dunno."

"A nance? A nancy boy?"

"I think so, yeah."

"Eve, listen—you only think so? You're not sure?"

"What d'you expect? It was five years ago, right? I'm trying to fuckin' forget, not remember. Anyway, what difference's it make what I called him? He tried to fuckin' kill me, that's what fuckin' matters."

Prior pushed her tea aside. A man in painter's overalls came in and ordered a sandwich to take away. Glanced over toward the two women and said something that made the Rastafarian laugh.

"That's got to be worth a bit, in't it?" Eve said. "What I just told you. A tenner at least."

Prior took a five-pound note from her bag and slid it beneath Eve Ward's saucer. "Thanks," she said. "Thanks for your time."

"You know what?" Eve Ward said, when Prior was on her feet. "You ought to lock the bastard back up. Before he does it again. Next time whoever it is might not be so fuckin' lucky."

BEN LEONARD WAS A LIGHT-SKINNED BLACK MAN WITH A small gold ring in his left ear and bleached blond hair cut close to his head. He wore a blue and gold floral print shirt open over a purple T-shirt, black chinos, and red Camper shoes. He had been a community psychiatric nurse for seven years. If anyone ever queried the way he looked, the way he dressed, he grinned and said at least it made his clients seem a shade more sane.

"You know what," he said, once Maureen Prior had sat on the polyurethane chair opposite his desk, "as dysfunctional families go, Dowland doesn't touch top twenty. Not even near. One of those reality TV shows, *Super Nanny,* crap like that, he wouldn't get close.

"Oh, his parents split up, sure, but not till he was nineteen, twenty. Three older brothers, a younger sister, all of them, as far as I can tell, out there holding down regular jobs, leading regular lives. I mean, they're not Einsteins or anything, the closest any of them got to higher education's a couple of NVQs, but they've all got wives, partners, kids of their own. The mother died a few years ago; his father still lives in the house in Kirkby where Richard and the others grew up."

"He sees him?" Prior asked. "The father? There's contact between them?"

"Not any more. Not since Richard went to prison."

"And the mother died when?"

"Six years back."

"A little before Richard attacked Eve Ward?"

Leonard's laugh was rich and warm. "Who's supposed to be the trick cyclist here, me or you?"

"You don't think there's a connection?"

"Of course there's a connection. His mum dies in January, April he's doing his damnedest to help poor Eve Ward shuffle off her mortal coil. At the funeral, apparently, he lost it big time, created this scene, wailing and screaming, like to have thrown himself into the grave if that's what it had been. Right out of *Hamlet.* Took a couple of his brothers to calm him down.

"So, yes, he took his mother's death badly, he was under a lot of strain, regret, remorse, who knows? And when he goes looking for his five minutes of solace and satisfaction, instead of being the compliant body he's paid for, she turns on him, loses her temper, starts calling him names. Consequence: he loses control."

"You think it could happen again?"

Leonard smiled. There was something about the way he smiled that edged her off-centre; something that went beyond what they were doing there, something personal. "I'll tell you," he said, "the more I do this job—the people I see, talk to, day in day out—the more amazed I am there are not more murders out there than there are."

Leaning back, the smile still in his eyes, he ran a smooth hand down one side of his face and something inside Maureen Prior lurched just a little.

"So, yes," Leonard said, "it could happen again, of course it could. If you ask me will it, what the chances are, as a professional man I'll stonewall. Talk percentages at best. But as an individual, a man who likes a wager, a bet, I'd say no, chances are low. There were no similar incidents reported before this and, as far as we know, there've been none since. Whatever anger and frustration Richard's carrying around inside, that's where it stays. In fact you could say, pretty much, he's got it under control." Leonard smiled again, jokey this time, more of a grin. "Just don't quote me, okay, when he goes gaga with an axe and whacks off somebody's head."

"All right," Prior said. "Thanks." Reaching down to the floor, she picked up her bag.

"How about you?" Leonard asked.

"What about me?"

"Are you seeing anyone?"

"Seeing? You mean as in therapy? A psychoanalyst, something like that?"

"Oh, you seem wound a little tight, all right, maybe a few issues you need to resolve, but no, that's not what I meant at all."

Colour flared high on Maureen Prior's cheeks, which were otherwise quite white.

"My business," she said, "is exactly that. My business." And with a swing of her bag, she moved toward the door.

"I'll call you," Leonard said.

But if Prior heard him, she gave no sign: just closed the door behind her, kept on walking, didn't look back.

Chapter 21

1966

USUALLY, BUT NOT ALWAYS, THE SOFT TOYS THAT TENDED
to be used most during Alice's sessions with the younger children were piled back into two large plastic boxes that stood on
the floor to the side of the cabinet of drawers. On these occasions, the boy had scarcely shown more than a cursory interest, dismissing them loudly, almost angrily, as babyish, as if
resenting that they were there.

But on this particular afternoon the earlier session had
slightly overrun and the toys—a motley collection of teddy
bears in various shapes and sizes, soft-fringed lions, cats with
sparkly collars, multicoloured elephants, and long-limbed mon-
keys—were in a haphazard jungle along the top of the cabinet
when the boy entered.

Almost without acknowledging Alice, he turned his back
on her and began to play with them, picking each one up and

petting it, cuddling it against his chest and, sometimes, against his face and neck, before swapping it for the next.

Whatever remarks Alice made were ignored.

After each soft toy had been examined and fondled, the boy began to rearrange them into groups, first dividing them by kind—cat, elephant, lion and so on—and then by size, from the largest to the smallest.

"You do this with your toys at home?" Alice said.

Nothing.

"Give them a cuddle."

"Shut up!" Hissed rather than spoken. The boy on his feet, looking at her, angry, pale skin stretched tight across his face.

"That's what you do," Alice said. "At home. Give them all a cuddle and then arrange them neatly, one by one."

"I said fuckin' shut up!"

"The lion, that's your favourite. I can see."

He was holding the lion against his chest, front paws splayed out on either side of his neck, red strip of tongue flopping from its mouth, the soft tangle of its mane pressed up against his mouth so that he seemed to be talking through it, his own tongue poking at the pale felt as he spoke.

"She made me give them away."

"Your mother made you give them away."

"Yes."

"She didn't like you playing with them."

"'Cause I was too old. That's what she said."

"When was this?"

"When I finished at the juniors. That's when she made me give them all away. Said I didn't need them any more. Said I had to grow up now. You're not a little boy any more, that's what she said." He pulled the lion tighter than ever against his body. "It's time for you to grow up. Be a man."

Alice could see his little erection, pressing against the gray cotton of his trousers.

Chapter 22

THE TEAM HAD BEEN WORKING ON CLAIRE MEECHAM'S audit trail for twenty-four hours and there were still some thirty contacts to be monitored and checked.

Affectionate widowed male, 55, gray/fair hair, medium build, seeks female similar age or younger to share life with.

Not unattractive professional male, late 50s, enjoys cycling, walking and travelling, seeks lady, 35–55, for friendship, maybe more.

Male, early 60s but still young-at-heart, varied interests, seeks female companion for days out, evenings in, weekends away.

Remember Sean Connery and Audrey Hepburn? Robin Hood, straight arrow, long in the tooth but ever hopeful, seeks the perfect Maid Marian with whom to end his days.

Claire Meecham's replies were brief and discreet: she was careful not to give away too much about herself, revealing no more than she felt necessary about her circumstances, keeping her address and the details of where she worked strictly private. Any requests for photographs were either ignored or shunted aside; anything resembling innuendo was given short shrift indeed. Arrangements to meet were always careful and exact, the rendezvous chosen in public spaces always—railway stations, galleries, theatre foyers—locations where there would always be plenty of other people around and that would afford her the opportunity to get a look at whoever she was meeting before they saw her. If necessary, she could fade further into the background and walk away unseen.

It seemed as if there had been occasions when this was what she had done.

Waited outside the Globe for more than an hour and a half. Where were you?

I feel I know the brickwork of the Lyric Theatre rather better than strictly necessary...

Next time you take it into your head to simply not turn up, at least have the decency to phone.

No excuses: no apologies.

Relationships that ended before they had begun.

Once started, however, it was not always so easy.

Maureen Prior read through the printout that had been handed to her for a second time and contacted Elder on his cell. He was in her office fifteen minutes later.

"Stephen Singer," she said. "According to what he told you, the last time he saw Claire Meecham was February?"

"That's right. He wanted to meet her again but she refused. Wrote to her, he said..."

"He had her address?"

"Apparently. He wrote and tried to get her to change her mind. No dice."

"He did more than write," Prior said, "look at these." She swivelled the sheet of paper round on the desk.

There were no fewer than eleven messages sent during a period of seven days in early March; the gist of each was the same: Claire was being unreasonable, unfair, going back on what she'd said, reneging on her word. There was no sign that Claire had reacted with anything other than silence.

And then, a little over a week later, this: *Claire, I'm so sorry for not respecting your wishes and arriving in the way I did, out of the blue. But it seemed the only way I could try and get you to see sense. I'm only grateful that after your initial, and very understandable anger, you have agreed to see things a little more my way. I am looking forward to hearing from you soon.*

"He came here," Elder said, surprised.

"Looks like it."

"To the house, the bungalow."

"Either that or where she worked."

"It would be the bungalow. He talked her into letting him have her address, after all."

"He's been lying, then, hasn't he? Lied to you and lied to me."

"How many days after Singer's last e-mail was it that she disappeared?"

Prior looked back at the printout. "Monday. Five days."

Elder read the message. "One of the things she'd changed her mind about, you think it could have been meeting him that weekend?"

"Only one way to find out." Prior looked at her watch. "There's a train at ten-thirty. We can be in London not long after twelve."

THEY TOOK A TAXI FROM ST. PANCRAS TO SOUTH END Green. The sky, a nondescript gray at the beginning of their journey, was now a speckled blue. The temperature was warmer by five degrees. As they turned off the main road, Elder spotted Singer locking the door to his house, then stooping to retie a shoe.

Surprise showed for a moment on his face, but nothing more.

"You're here about poor Claire," he said when they drew level.

Elder nodded.

"I read about it in the paper. What happened. Not that it said a great deal. A paragraph, little more. I was going to get in touch, ask, but then, well, I wasn't sure..." He looked from one to the other. "Did it seem...I don't know how best...did it seem as if she'd suffered a great deal?"

"I don't think so," Elder said. "Not as far as we can tell."

"Thank heavens for that. For that at least."

Singer cleared his throat. Prior stepped back into the road to let a young woman with a backpack jog past.

"Have you...have you caught whoever was responsible?" Singer asked.

"Not yet."

"If there's anything...well, I suppose, yes, that's why you're here. If there's anything more I can do...I was going for a walk, a stroll on the Heath, but I expect you'd prefer to come inside?"

"We've been sitting for the best part of two hours," Prior said. "Let's walk."

THE PATH LED DOWN TOWARD TWO PONDS AND THEN passed between them, widening as it rose gradually between a ragged avenue of spindly hawthorn trees, tall grass, and nettles thick around their roots, cow parsley standing waist high: the scent of May blossom sweet in the air.

Where the path opened out, the land pushed up more steeply toward a small crowd of people gathered at the summit, staring out across the city, bright-coloured kites flying high above their heads.

Prior pointed to an empty bench on the side of the hill, she and Elder positioning themselves so that Singer sat between them.

"It's beautiful, isn't it?" Singer said. "All this open space. Beautiful. I never tire of it, you know. There's something about it that's different, every day."

He was looking at Elder, but it was Prior who spoke. "You lied to us," she said.

Singer turned his head, mouth open, ready to protest.

Prior didn't allow him the time. "I wrote to her, you said, asking her to change her mind. No more e-mails, just letters."

"And that's true," Singer said. "I did write, several times."

"No more e-mails."

"That's what I said."

"And it was a lie."

Singer looked at the ground.

"Wasn't it? A lie."

"Yes."

"But why? Why lie about that?"

"I...I wasn't thinking. I forgot."

"I find that," Prior said, "a little difficult to believe."

Singer shifted uncomfortably on the bench.

"And there's another explanation," Prior said. "You must have thought there was a chance we'd find the letters, so you had to admit to that. But the e-mails you might have assumed she would have wiped."

"Yes, yes," Singer stammered, "I suppose that's true. But I didn't want you to think...Claire's disappearance, that I'd had anything to do with whatever might have happened."

"What did you think had happened?" Prior asked.

"I didn't know. I didn't know. Of course, I thought—you do— things you read, almost every day now, in the news. I'd thought it might be something terrible...but I didn't know."

"And you didn't see her that weekend?"

"No."

"You're sure?"

"Of course."

"You didn't see her at all?"

"No."

"You didn't go away together? Some small hotel?"

"No."

"I'm grateful you've agreed to see things my way, that's what you said."

"What?" Singer flinched.

"I'm grateful you've agreed to see things my way—in your e-mail to Claire."

Singer's head dropped; sweat slid into the corners of his eyes; his back pressed hard against the bench.

"Agreed to what?" Prior said.

"Nothing."

"Sorry?"

"Nothing. It was just…"

"Was it to see you that weekend? Is that what she agreed to? To see you that weekend?"

"Yes." Head bent low again, scalp beginning to show through his gray hair; Singer's voice was swallowed up by all that space.

"I'm sorry, you'll have to speak up. I didn't hear what you said."

"I said, yes. Yes, that was what I wanted. What she agreed. A hotel, in the Cotswolds. I'd been there before, on my own. I knew Claire would like it. I was certain. That was why I wanted her to come so much."

A woman jogged past in running shorts, pushing a fancy buggy, the child strapped inside cackling and waving. Lower down on the grass, another woman, older, was walking no fewer than half a dozen dogs, some on leads, the others trotting behind, stopping occasionally to sniff.

"Tell us what happened," Elder said quietly.

"She didn't come." The words broke out of Singer from deep in his chest. "We'd arranged to meet at the station. Paddington. Friday afternoon. She'd said she could get time off work. Get away early, beat the rush. I waited...I waited near the information board, where we'd said. At first I thought there'd been a delay, on her train down to London. Or maybe the Tube. I didn't know. I just sat there, waiting. Even after I knew she wasn't coming. After I realized she'd changed her mind." He glanced quickly at Elder. "Perhaps she'd never intended to come, I don't know."

There were tears in his eyes and, taking a handkerchief from his pocket, he wiped them away.

"It's stupid, isn't it? Pathetic. You must think I'm pathetic. A man of my age, carrying on like this. But I thought...my friendship with Claire...we'd only seen each other a few times, I know, but I thought it was special. And it didn't mean anything to her, not really, not at all."

"So what did you do?" Prior asked, trying, not quite successfully, to disguise the impatience in her voice.

"I telephoned the hotel, made some sort of excuse, and cancelled the reservation. They said, in the circumstances, if they got another booking they would return my deposit, but they never did." He looked at her unswerving stare. "That was it. What else could I do?"

"Got angry," Prior suggested. "Lost your temper."

"What for? What would have been the use? Besides, with whom?"

"With her. With Claire."

"She wasn't there. That was the whole point, she wasn't there."

"You knew where she lived."

A firm shake of the head. "I wouldn't do that."

"Do what?"

"Go chasing after her. Just to give her a piece of my mind."

"Why not? You were angry. She'd ruined your weekend."

"No. I couldn't."

"But you knew where she lived."

"Even so. I wouldn't just turn up, unannounced."

"Why not?" Elder said. "You'd done it before."

"When?"

"When you persuaded her to change her mind."

"That's not true."

"I'm so sorry for not respecting your wishes and arriving in the way I did—that sounds like turning up unannounced to me."

Singer sighed and slumped forward, head in his hands, elbows on his knees. A crocodile of small children filed past them wearing brown blazers with gold braid, matching brown and gold caps on their heads, a visitation from an earlier time.

"The more you lie," Prior said, "the worse it gets."

FIFTEEN MINUTES LATER THEY WERE BACK AT SINGER'S flat at South End Green, Elder not remembering the low ceilings quite in time and catching his head a good crack on entering. What had Jennie said it made her feel like? *Alice in Wonderland?* Trapped and unable to escape.

Singer told them he had arrived at Claire Meecham's bungalow late in the afternoon and waited until she returned from work; angry and surprised to find him there, at first she had refused to let him in. Then, when it had become clear he was not going to go away, and not wanting to have a long and possibly intense conversation in front of her neighbours, she had relented. She had insisted he sit in the living room and, without as much as taking off her coat, given him five minutes to say what he had to say and then leave. Singer had pleaded his case well; well enough for Claire to relent a little and remove her coat, sit down with a pot of tea, and talk. She had told him something about her family for the first time, how much she missed her son in particular, off there in Australia. She had spoken of her late husband's illness, his lingering decline. He had wanted to hold her, offer consolation, but she had shrugged him away.

In the end, possibly because she was at a low ebb, or perhaps so as to convince him to leave, she had agreed to change her plans and go to the Cotswolds with him that weekend.

What plans, Elder asked, were those?

Singer didn't know. When he'd asked, she had refused to say.

"You realize," Prior said, "if you've been lying about seeing Claire Meecham that weekend, we'll find out."

Singer nodded, head down.

"If you've lied about going back to the bungalow, or anything else, sooner or later, we'll know."

"Yes."

"So is there anything else you want to tell us before we go?"

For an answer, Singer got up and left the room; a minute later he returned with a postcard in his hand. On the front there was a black-and-white picture of the moon partly shielded by clouds, high above a distant, tree-lined hill. On the reverse was written the word "Sorry," and, below that, the name "Claire."

The postmark on the front of the card read Nottingham, and it was dated Saturday the ninth of April.

The card itself had come originally from the National Gallery of Art in Washington, D.C. A reproduction of a photograph by Alfred Stieglitz, and Elder had seen it, or one very much like it, on the wall of Vincent Blaine's house in the Vale of Belvoir.

"We'll need to take this with us," Prior said, and when Singer began to protest, "we'll take good care of it and let you have it back as soon as we can."

That it had been stamped on the ninth didn't necessarily mean it had been posted that day; it could have been slipped into a box on the evening of the day before.

ON THE JOURNEY BACK THEY DISCUSSED THE RAMIFICA- tions of what they had learned. Claire Meecham had made plans for that weekend, plans she had told Singer she would cancel, then, presumably, had changed her mind. It was more than possible she never intended to do anything of the kind, had simply said so to placate Singer and see him on his way.

And wherever she had been, whoever she had been with, the identity of her companion was quite possibly among those other names from her computer that were still being sifted through.

"You think he's still lying?" Elder asked.

"About seeing her that weekend? It's possible."

"The card, though—if it's genuine..."

Prior nodded and turned her head toward the window.

Elder leaned back in his seat. Instead of the passing scenery, he kept seeing the Stieglitz photograph on Vincent Blaine's wall, knowing that in all probability it was a coincidence and nothing more, that there was nothing to link Blaine and Claire Meecham, nothing at all—yet wondering, all the same, where exactly Blaine had been that weekend.

Chapter 23

THIS TIME THERE WAS NO ONE ON THE THRESHOLD TO greet him. Elder locked the car automatically and as he walked toward the house, raised voices, a man's and a woman's, filtered out through the partly open door.

Elder knocked and waited.

The voices stopped.

The air was still and close, and clouds were beginning to mass toward the horizon.

Blaine was wearing similar clothes as before, a checkered shirt and corduroy trousers, but with a new brightness in his eyes.

"Mr. Elder—a surprise."

"I'm sorry to disturb you..."

"You could have telephoned."

"There's something I wanted you to look at. It won't take more than a moment of your time."

"Very well," Blaine said grudgingly. "Come in if you must."

Entering the room was like stepping into the aftermath of a storm, the tension tangible in the air. The woman Elder recognized as Blaine's companion from the gallery was standing by one of the wood and chrome chairs. Her red hair blazed around her head; her cheeks were full and flushed.

"Allow me to present my friend, Anna Ingram," Blaine said. "Anna, this is Mr. Elder. Mr. Elder is presently working with the police."

Her hand was warm and her eyes, Elder noticed, were big and green. Late forties, he guessed, early fifties. Built, as his father would have said, to last.

"You'll have coffee, Mr. Elder?" Blaine asked.

"As I said, it's just one question…"

"But coffee, nonetheless."

"All right, thank you."

Blaine walked off in the direction of the kitchen, leaving Elder and Anna Ingram alone.

"I can't help but think I've walked in on something," Elder said.

Anna Ingram smiled. "You heard us arguing."

"I'm afraid so."

"Nothing more exciting than the state of contemporary art. A show we saw yesterday. From Africa. These huge and colourful hangings, like tapestries, but made out of discarded bottle tops and cans. It was really vibrant. Exciting. For me, at least. Vincent's appreciation, I'm afraid, doesn't extend much beyond works on canvas or paper. Sculpture's permissible, but nothing more modern than Barbara Hepworth or Henry Moore. Certainly not when it's made from old tin cans."

"Is that what you are then?" Elder asked. "An artist?"

She smiled. "No, I'm afraid not. I'm a curator."

"I'm not sure I know exactly what that is. You look after things? Collect them? Works of art?"

"Not exactly. I organize shows, exhibitions. Supervise their installation. Write those impenetrable little notes that appear alongside."

She sat down and indicated that Elder should do the same.

"I would have offered to make the coffee myself and allow the two of you to talk, but coffee-making's one of those things Vincent believes can only be done in a certain way, and therein, I'm afraid, I am forever doomed to fail." She smiled another self-deprecating smile. "In that, as in so many things."

There were sounds of movement from the kitchen, china against china.

"Whatever it is you want to talk to Vincent about, it's a police matter, I suppose, rather than something artistic?"

"Actually, it's both."

The photograph of the moon and clouds was where he'd remembered it on the wall, next to the close-up of Georgia O'Keeffe with the hands reaching up across her neck.

"I'm sorry," Blaine said, carrying the coffee in on a tray, "sometimes it seems to take longer than usual to filter through. But I'm sure it gave Anna the chance to enlighten you as to some of my foibles." He passed the cups around. "If she were my mother, she'd doubtless delight in causing great embarrassment by showing pictures of me naked in the bath, age nine months."

Anna stuck out her tongue.

"So, Mr. Elder," Blaine said, settling back into his Charles Eames chair, "how may I be of help?"

Elder slipped the postcard, now protected by a plastic envelope, from his inside pocket. "I'm assuming you recognize this?"

Blaine took it carefully between finger and thumb. "Of course. It's one of a set of ten Stieglitz took in the twenties. All very similar. There's a copy of another over there on the wall. As I'm sure you know. It was something he liked to do, shoot pictures from the same setting but in different conditions. A strategy, I suppose you'd call it. There are several well-known sequences he took from the window of his first gallery in New York, for instance."

"One thing you can be sure of with Vincent," Anna Ingram observed, "ask a simple question and you'll be sure to get a lecture in return."

"Actually," Elder said, "I'm not sure my question is so simple. Or if there's a question at all. More like something nagging away at the back of my brain." He paused, looking at Anna before continuing. "At present I'm helping with an investigation into the deaths of two women, Claire Meecham and Irene Fowler, both murdered. Mr. Blaine was one of the last people to see the earlier victim, Irene Fowler, alive. That card was posted by Claire Meecham around the time she disappeared."

"And the connection is what?" Anna Ingram asked, a little incredulously.

"Clearly," Blaine said, tapping the front of the postcard, "the connection is this. Stieglitz. One of my particular interests, as you know."

"But those cards are ten a penny. You can buy them anywhere, any self-respecting art gallery or shop. That this woman chose an image that Vincent happens to have on his wall is neither here nor there, surely? I mean, it isn't even as if she sent the card to him. There's no link to him at all."

"I'm delighted," Blaine said, "that reading all that detective fiction hasn't been a complete waste of your time."

"Just one thought," Elder said, addressing Blaine. "It's not possible Claire Meecham might have been a student of yours at some time? An adult education class, something of that sort?"

"It's possible. But as Anna rightly suggests, cards like those are available everywhere. You don't exactly need to have taken a course in twentieth-century photography to pick one out of the rack, pay over your fifty pence or whatever it costs, and affix a stamp to the back. Nowadays gallery cards are common currency. Seaside postcards for the educated middle class."

"A coincidence, then," Elder said. "Nothing more."

Blaine briefly smiled. "So it would appear."

"I'm sorry," Elder said, getting to his feet, "for taking up so much of your time."

"Not at all. The pleasure was mine. And Anna's too, I'm sure. I'm only sorry I wasn't able to help more."

"Vincent," Anna Ingram said, "why don't you let me show Mr. Elder to the door? I can probably do that without too great a mishap."

With one final glance, Blaine handed Elder back the card.

Outside, the clouds seemed to have dispersed; the horizon was clear. There was a freshness in the air that reminded Elder of Cornwall and, not for the first time since returning, he wished he were there.

"How long have you known one another?" he asked.

"Vincent and I? Seven, nearly eight years."

"You're very protective of him."

"Am I?" She laughed. "If Vincent thought that were true, he'd never forgive me."

"You don't think he notices, then?"

Anna smiled. "For an intelligent man, and that's surely what he is, the things Vincent fails to notice are legion."

"What kind of things?"

"Oh, anything he thinks is beneath him. Anything to do with the heart."

Elder looked at her, but said nothing.

"What? What are you thinking?"

"That perhaps that's a strange thing to say about somebody you've been in a relationship with for almost eight years."

She looked at him with widening eyes. "Are you married, Mr. Elder?"

"Frank, please. And, no, not anymore."

"But you were."

"Yes."

"For how long?"

"Eighteen years."

"Then you'll know all about compromise. The kind of accommodations we make so that things might last." For a moment, her hand rested on his arm. "Vincent and I, we argue about the theatre, about music, about film..."

"About art."

"Exactly. I let him lecture me on wine and, once in a while, he allows me to put on my chef's apron and pretend to be Nigella Lawson. Although, Vincent being Vincent, he'd far rather I were Elizabeth David."

It was a reference Elder failed to grasp, but he let it pass.

"Well," Blaine said, appearing behind them, "still here? Enjoying the view?"

"No," Anna Ingram said. "Talking about you."

"Only good things, I trust."

Anna laughed. "Every scurrilous bit of gossip I could dredge up."

"I doubt then you'd have been here for so long."

"I must go," Elder said, starting to move away. "I've already taken enough of your time."

"There's a show of mine at the castle," Anna Ingram said. "The Staithes Group. Paintings. Even Vincent approves."

Elder raised a hand and carried on toward his car. Disturbed, a magpie rose up with a dry, crackling cry and flew back to where its mate was waiting in the branches of a stunted elm. When he glanced back over his shoulder toward the door, both Vincent Blaine and Anna Ingram had gone back inside.

THERE WAS NO ANSWER AT MARJORIE PARKER'S DOOR. "She went off on her bike about an hour ago," Gladys Knowles said brightly. "Off shopping I shouldn't wonder. I can put the kettle on if you want to wait in mine. No trouble at all."

Elder was saved by the sight of Marjorie Parker's sturdy

stand-up-and-beg bicycle coming slowly into view, burlap bags swaying from each end of the handlebars.

"Organic this and organic that," Gladys Knowles said dismissively. "What's wrong with Asda, that's what I want to know?"

She scurried back across the street in her unlaced sneakers, past the sign that announced Claire Meecham's bungalow was for sale.

"Here," Elder said, as Marjorie Parker brought her bike to a halt at the curb. "Let me take one of those."

In any event, he took both, following her round to the back of the house and waiting while she locked the bicycle in the shed.

"I've some date and walnut loaf in there," Marjorie Parker said. "If you'd like to join me."

"I'm sorry, I'm afraid I can't. There was just one thing I wanted to ask."

"Certainly."

"When you were talking about Claire Meecham before, you said something about her signing up for a course—after a gallery visit, I think it was."

"That's correct."

"You can't remember what the course was, I suppose?"

"Yes, I can. It was an introduction to photography. Appreciation, that is. Not the practical side. I can't recall the exact wording, but that's what it was about. It was linked in some way to the show we'd been to see."

"And this was here in the city?"

"Yes. That small gallery out by the old university. The Weston, I think it might be called. But why? Why is it important?"

Elder smiled. "It might not be. Just filling in a few gaps, that's all."

"Whoever did it," Marjorie Parker said, with a glance over her shoulder, "you haven't yet found him?"

"Not yet."

"That poor woman."

"Yes, indeed." He set her bags down beside the rear door. "One further thing—this course, you can't remember who was teaching it, I suppose?"

A firm shake of the head. "No, I'm afraid not."

"Not to worry. I can easily find out."

Two phone calls later, he did. "An Introduction to the Art of Photography." Eight afternoon sessions. Tutor: Vincent Blaine.

"EVER HEARD THE EXPRESSION," MAUREEN PRIOR SAID, "'grasping at straws'?"

They were in her currently favourite café, late lunch, Prior making short work of a bacon and tomato sandwich, Elder labouring through a slice of apple pie and thinking he should have opted for Marjorie Parker's date and walnut loaf instead.

"I know it's pretty far-fetched," Elder said, "but at the moment, what else have we got?"

"Not a great deal. Singer, possibly. Dowland, remotely."

"Then where's the harm in keeping half an eye on Blaine? Poking around?"

"The harm is if it distracts you from other things."

Elder pushed his unfinished piece of pie aside. "Look, this class Blaine taught, May, June of last year."

"A year ago."

"A year ago. According to the records, there were fifteen people who signed up; two dropped out after the first couple of weeks, the average turnout was a dozen. A dozen students, two hours a week for eight weeks. A man like Blaine who, whatever else he is, is certainly observant. How likely is it, do you think, he wouldn't remember Claire Meecham's name? That, at least."

Prior leaned back. "Okay, let's assume for the moment that you're right. He did remember her name. There's a very good reason, surely, for him not letting on. He's already been questioned over any potential involvement with the Irene Fowler murder. Now here you come along, doing your best to tie him into a second. Why volunteer something that might put you under suspicion if there's no need?"

"Because withholding information's more suspicious still."

"Only if you do your homework and find out. And then if you broach it with him again, all he need say, is oh, sorry, I forgot, I never was very good with names."

"I still don't like it. It doesn't smell right."

"You don't like him."

"I don't know if that's true." He grinned and shook his head. "No, well, it probably is. He intimidates me, that's why. And he knows it, relishes it."

Prior had finished her bacon and tomato and was eyeing Elder's leftover apple pie.

"Where did this appetite come from all of a sudden?" Elder asked, amused.

Prior grinned. "Compensation, I suppose."

"For what?"

She laughed. "Everything."

Elder went back to the counter for two teas.

"So what are you going to do?" Prior asked. "Go out there and confront him?"

"I don't think so. Not right away. I might try another tack instead."

"The girlfriend?"

"There's some kind of exhibition at the castle. The Staithes Group," Elder said, affecting an accent. "They're painters, you know."

"Great," Prior said. "See if you can't get one of them to come round and finish my kitchen."

She was ferreting in her bag for her wallet, when her cell started ringing.

"Okay," she said, after listening. "Right, right. Ten minutes. I'm on my way." And, to Elder, "Best leave off your artistic leanings for a while, Frank. Looks like something serious has cropped up at last."

Chapter 24

WAYNE JOHNS HAD BEEN IN TROUBLE WITH THE POLICE throughtout his teens: petty theft, breaking and entering, stealing and driving away. When he was seventeen he broke into a parked car and was ripping out the CD player and radio when the owner returned. In the ensuing altercation, Johns knocked the man to the floor and kicked him enough to break several ribs and endanger an eye. The magistrates had had enough. Warning after warning had gone unheeded, supervision in the community hadn't worked, and ASBOs had yet to be invented. Eighteen months at Her Majesty's pleasure. The well-known short, sharp shock.

Against all odds, it worked.

Johns came out of prison and, with the help of his probation officer, got a job in a timber yard. A year later, he enrolled in a day-release course at college, further education, a chance to make up for what he'd missed through truanting and playing the fool. Gradually, he began accumulating qualifications, skills. His boss at the timber yard encouraged him to spend half a day each week in the office, observing how things were done—orders, specifications, accounts. By the time he was twenty-five, Johns had struck out on his own, supplying materials for bespoke kitchens, high-end stuff with large profit margins; Johns working with a freelance designer, doing most of the fitting himself at first, then gradually taking on staff who would do that for him.

Come thirty, he was bored: sold out, diversified; a venture or two that failed to spark. Three years followed, running a bar in Portugal, the Algarve. An affair with a married woman that ran aground. Rumours of a scandal that was hushed up, but not before money had changed hands. On the move again, in Barcelona, Johns met a man who was refurbishing an old hotel close to the Ramblas, and after working for him for a month for nothing, showing him what he could do, they went into partnership, the hotel owner having ideas for a new conference centre which he thought Johns would be able to deliver.

He did.

But then boredom started setting in again. Johns thought it might be time to think about moving back home to the UK. Some ten years ago, he arrived back in England, aged thirty-nine. Moderately wealthy. Tanned. Handsome in an obvious sort of way. His hair was starting to fade back at the temples, but otherwise there was little physical change from the man who had left for mainland Europe a decade before. His accent was a mixture of his native East Midlands and a half-jokey Chas 'n' Dave cockney, with the occasional phrase in Portuguese or Spanish thrown in for good measure.

The company he ran now was called BestCon.

www.bestcon.co.uk

Conference facilities provided for venues of any size, from five-star hotels to village halls: furniture and equipment, everything from simple flip charts to interactive white boards and the most sophisticated data projectors.

Their offices were located on the Meadow Trading Estate, not so far from the Notts County soccer ground and the abattoir.

Wearing a white fluffy top that swaddled her breasts and stopped well short of her navel, the receptionist was standing away from her desk, talking to a young man in overalls, when Elder and Maureen Prior arrived.

She broke off her conversation long enough to tell them Mr. Johns was busy.

Maureen Prior showed her warrant card and tried again.

"I said, he's busy." When she turned away the first few inches of her purple thong and her tattoo were visible above the top of her jeans.

Prior moved close enough to get her attention.

"Listen, Kylie, or whatever your name is, if Mr. Johns is in the building, we need to see him now. So stop your chat, pick up the phone and call him, interrupt whatever he's doing, okay?"

"I can't," the girl said almost apologetically, feeling less sure of her ground. "He'll go crazy."

Elder stepped around the desk and knocked hard on the door bearing Wayne Johns's name in gold paint.

"What the fuck...?" Throwing open the door, Johns stopped short, tie adrift, looking first at Elder, then at Maureen Prior, warrant card still in her hand.

"I'm sorry, Mr. Johns," the receptionist faltered. "I tried telling them you were busy."

"'S'all right, no problem. See if you can't conjure up some coffee for our visitors, there's a love." He turned to Elder. "Give me five minutes to finish up here. And you..." jabbing a finger toward the young man who'd been sidling toward the door, "get your skinny arse back where it belongs and stop sniffing round in here or I'll have you out on your ear."

Five minutes, of course, were ten. The coffee was insipid and little more than lukewarm. Wayne Johns's office had a view out toward the waste-disposal unit and the cattle market, a walnut desk with leather inlays and photographs of Johns glad-handing at various functions on the walls.

"Corporate entertainment," he said proudly. "One of the services we provide."

In one of the photographs, he was standing with his arms draped round the shoulders of someone who could have been Phil Collins on a rough night; in another he was kissing a woman with reddish blond hair who Maureen recognized as Carol Decker, formerly lead singer with T'Pau.

"'Heart and Soul,'" Johns said, following her gaze. "'China in Your Hand,' 'Valentine.' Great songs. And she still does a great show, even now."

"Tell us about Claire Meecham," Prior said.

"Meecham? Meecham?" Johns allowed a worried look to pass slowly across his face. "Sorry, no bells. She with some group? A singer, what?"

"She's dead," Prior said.

"Oh, dear. Yeah, well, I'm sorry, I suppose. Whoever she was."

"Fifteenth of October, last year," Prior said. "You sent her an e-mail. Arranging to meet her at the Lace Market Hotel."

"I did?"

"November seventh, another e-mail, dinner at World Service, my place after."

"World Service, eh? Pretty fancy."

"Mr. Johns," Elder said, "stop pissing us around."

Johns looked at them, one to the other and back again. "She never showed."

"What?"

"The restaurant. She never showed."

"You do admit to knowing her, then?"

"Yeah, course."

"A minute ago..."

"I read about it, right? What happened to her. In the *Post.* On the news, wasn't it? On Sky."

"Then you knew we were asking for people to come forward with information."

"People who knew something about what happened, yes."

"And that's not you?"

"No."

"You knew her, that's what you said."

"I met her once. Twice."

"Which?"

"Twice. I met her twice. The time we met at the Lace Market Hotel and another time before that. Some Thai place in Hockley, I don't remember the name."

"And you met her through…"

"That Internet dating thing. I browse it sometimes…" He shrugged a little self-consciously, as if it were something he didn't easily admit.

"The evening you say she didn't turn up to meet you…" Elder began.

"Like I said, she bottled out, didn't show. Left me sitting there with me thumb up me arse."

"And did she get in touch later with a reason, an excuse?"

"She didn't have to."

"Why was that?"

Johns took his time. "That last time we met, right? Some of the stuff that went on…" He glanced uneasily toward Prior. "Nothing that she wasn't up for, no force, coercion, nothing like that, not for one minute. Not once we got going…" He smiled at Elder, almost conspiratorially. "The quiet ones, yeah? Sometimes they're the ones take you most by surprise."

From Elder there was no response, though he could feel the anger coming off Maureen Prior like steam on a cold day.

"She surprised herself," Johns continued, oblivious. "That was the thing. The way she got into it, you know? And it frightened her, that's what I think. The extent to which she let go. I tried to talk to her about it after, but she wasn't having any. Didn't want to know. Supposed to be blokes what never want to talk, but no, next morning she was out of there like the dog after the rabbit, first thing. Wouldn't stick around for breakfast or anything." Johns released a slow breath. "I let it settle, gave her time. Got back in touch. Dinner, I thought, somewhere nice. Quiet." He gestured with open hands. "End of story."

"Not quite," Prior said.

"Eh?"

"This stuff you referred to. Whatever went on between you. You might have to be a bit more explicit."

"If that's what you want." Johns treated her to a broad smile. "It was nothing that much out of the ordinary, I'd say. Depends what you're used to. But, you know, blindfolds, restraints. A moderate amount of pain."

"What kind of pain?" Prior's voice was quick and sharp.

"A good slapping. Across the buttocks. When she was blind-folded. Tied down. It helped her to come."

It was quiet: the sound of three people breathing. Noises fil-tering in from outside: muted voices, the occasional telephone, traffic slowing for the roundabout that leads toward the race-course or into the city.

"It said in the paper she'd been strangled," Johns said.

"That's right."

"And you think what? It might have been someone she met through the Net?"

"It's possible," Elder said.

Johns shook his head. "I wish I could help more. She was all right. A bit uptight. You know, at first. But all right."

"We might want to talk to you again," Prior said, getting to her feet.

"Of course," Johns said, holding out his hand. "Any time. Any time at all."

"One other thing," Elder said at the door.

Johns cocked his head.

"All this physical stuff—restraints and the rest—what was it you said? A moderate amount of pain. I wonder, is there any danger it just might get out of hand? Excitement of the moment? That kind of thing?"

"It's possible, I suppose."

"So what do you do then?"

"Back off, what else?"

"And if you can't?"

Johns held his gaze. "Ever happens, I'll be sure to let you know."

"SO WHAT DO YOU THINK?" ELDER SAID.

They were sitting in Maureen Prior's car in the middle of the almost empty Lady Bay Retail Park, stranded between JJB Sports and Burger King. At least half of the businesses seemed to have closed down for good.

"About what? About Johns?"

"Anything."

"I think it's a shame if that woman died because she wasn't prepare to shrivel up like some old prune."

"Doing what she did, she was taking a risk; she must have known."

"Everything in life's a risk, Frank. Either that or there's no fucking life at all."

Elder looked at her, surprised. In all the time he had known her, he doubted he had heard her swear on more than a few occasions, if at all.

"Stop doing that," Prior said.

"Doing what?"

"Staring at me like that."

Prior pushed out of the car and slammed the door.

Elder watched as she walked off toward the boarded-up furniture superstore, stood there for some moments, then turned and came slowly back to where he was now standing, one hand resting on the open car door.

"Want me to get some coffee or something?" Elder said, nodding toward Burger King.

Prior shook her head. "I'm sorry," she said. "Losing my temper."

"No need."

A maroon Toyota went slowly past and came to a stop by a Staples.

"Seriously," Elder said. "Wayne Johns. What did you think?"

"A chancer. Too full of himself by half. And admitting he knew her, what went on, he gave it up too fast."

"You think he should have held out for longer? Denied it?"

"It's what I would have expected."

"But if he's innocent, nothing to hide..."

"Then why lie in the first place?"

Elder shook his head. "The day someone tells us the truth straight out, something that might implicate themselves, I'll start believing the impossible."

"Claire Meecham," Elder said a few moments later, "she had marks on her wrists and ankles where she'd been tied up."

"Bruises, yes, slight abrasions. Whatever was used was either something soft like a scarf, or else it had been wrapped in material of some kind."

"No traces?"

"Not enough for any kind of identification. At least, that's my understanding. Whoever did this, he washed down the body before putting her clothes back on."

"And we didn't get anything from the soap or whatever it was he used?"

"A slight trace of lavender oil, geranium; other than that, no colouring, no perfume. It narrows it down but not beyond anything you can't buy in any Superdrug or Boots."

"She was tied up, nonetheless."

"So it appears. But there's no knowing exactly when. It could have been the same time as she was murdered, or it could have been before."

"If the bruising was only slight, might that suggest whatever was happening wasn't against her will?"

"It might."

"As if, maybe, she went along with something until it got out of hand." Elder did a little pacing up and down. "What did Johns say? It frightened her, the way she got into it—well, suppose she got over that fear. Went off for a weekend of consensual S and M. And presumably—I don't know—but presumably with those things you push the boundaries a little further all the time."

"Until it's too far."

"Right. Too far for her. And she says stop."

"And he doesn't agree." Prior stepped sharply away from the car. "What did he call it? A moderate amount of pain."

Elder nodded.

"I don't need a coffee, Frank, I need a drink."

THEY FOUND A PUB JUST SOUTH OF THE ROUNDABOUT, on Colwick Road. Even a recent lick of paint had failed to remove the nicotine stains fully from the walls. Maureen Prior had a large gin and tonic and Elder a Jameson with water on the side. There was a signed photograph of the Notts Country team on the wall, the side that had won promotion to the top flight in the early nineties. Tommy Johnson. Craig Short. Mark Draper.

Prior had been glancing through the promotional literature Wayne Johns had given them on their way out.

"Read this and you think, yes, great guy. Successful entrepreneur. All this guff about humble beginnings, picking himself up by his bootstraps—nothing about his police record, umpteen offenses before he was out of short trousers almost; banged up for stomping some bloke half to death."

Elder grinned. "Probably didn't think it would bring in a lot of customers."

"Probably not."

"I'd like to know, though, if he's really been squeaky clean ever since."

"There's nothing on his record."

"Not here. But take a look at this. All this time he spent abroad. Portugal, Spain. We should do a little background checking, just in case."

"When did he come back to England?" Elder asked.

Prior looked at the marketing pack again. "According to this, BestCon was established a little over eight years ago. Some time before that, I'd guess. A year or so?"

"So his company was founded at around the same time Irene Fowler was killed."

"Around then."

Elder swallowed the last of his whiskey and washed it down with water. "The other men on the list," he said, "the ones Claire Meecham arranged to meet, we should see how many shared her sexual preferences."

"You're right, though if Johns is to be trusted, it might be what happened with him was a first. A first in a long time, at least. It could be it was something she'd been holding back, refusing to acknowledge. In which case, the way she responded could have taken her by surprise as much as he said. Frightened her even."

"Johns is what age?" Elder said. They were walking back toward the car.

"Late forties?"

"Claire Meecham was fifty-five."

"So?"

"So isn't it unusual, a man like Johns, a bit full of himself, likely considers himself something of a ladies' man, he's opting to go out with someone significantly older?"

Prior shook her head. "You've seen that photograph of her, Frank, dressed up. Looking like that, he wouldn't have to know how old she was. And besides, maybe there's something about older women that he likes. Feels more comfortable with."

"That they're more grateful, is that what you mean?"

Prior aimed a kick at his shins that only just missed.

ELDER HAD ARRANGED TO SEE JENNIE PRESTON THAT evening, a quick drink in the same bar in which they'd first met. Jennie wearing a black suit with a tapered jacket and flared trousers, a material that shone a little when she moved. Tiredness not quite banished from her face.

She was there before him, a large glass of merlot and a cigarette.

"So," she said, "Frank, how's it going?"

"Slowly. When there's no obvious suspect it takes time. A lot of routine questioning. Checking. Checking again. But I think now we've got one or two leads that are starting to look promising."

"One or two?"

Elder smiled.

"And that's all? That's all you can say?"

He gestured with open hands. "It's still early days."

"Derek said if you don't catch them in the first—what is it?—forty-eight hours, you don't catch them at all."

"Derek's wrong."

"Is he?" Stubbing out her cigarette, she reached for another.

"Look," Elder said, "most murders, the ones that aren't gang related, they're carried out by someone close, husband, wife, lover, someone in the family. What's making it more difficult here is not knowing, any of us, just who exactly Claire was closest to. But there is movement, believe me. The investigation, it's not stalled. Far from it."

"But you can't tell me...?"

"Not at the moment, no. I'm sorry."

Jennie leaned back and closed her eyes. Work finished, a few more people were beginning to drift into the bar. Men, for the most part in suits and ties. Leather cases. Laptops. Laughter that was too false and too loud.

"The police," Jennie said. "I keep trying to find out when they'll release Claire's body. For the funeral. Soon, someone says, a couple of days. Next time I ring, it's 'oh no, we're sorry, it may be a while yet.' I can't get a straight answer out of anyone."

"I'll see what I can do."

"Would you? I just feel this need, you know, to get things organized. As far as I can, move on."

"Yes, I understand."

Jennie finished her wine. "I ought to be going. Early start tomorrow."

Outside, it was still light. The temperature had dropped but not by very much.

"Joanne, Frank," Jennie said. "Have you seen her?"

"Not for a while."

"You should, you know."

"Maybe."

"Frank." She touched her fingers to the back of his hand. "She's lonely."

"I don't think so."

"If that's what you want to believe." She took a step off the curb. "When you've talked to the police about Claire, you'll phone me?"

"Yes, of course."

A scuttle of heels and she was gone.

Elder moved away from the entrance. Something Anna Ingram had said earlier was replaying inside his head. Something about the compromises that relationships, serious relationships, demand. *The kind of accommodations we make in order that things might last.*

In 1989, when Katherine was just three, they had moved from Lincolnshire down to London, primarily so that Joanne could broaden her experience and further her career. Eight years later, with Katherine on the verge of starting secondary school and Elder well settled into the Met, she had urged them to move again, to Nottingham this time, so that she could manage one of Martyn Miles's salons. Katherine had moaned, complained, shut herself in her room; Elder had bit his tongue and complied, agreed.

Now he was back here again.

And why?

Because helping out Joanne's friend had been a way of being close to Katherine, just when he feared they might be losing touch for good?

Or was it something to do with Joanne herself?

Lonely?

Well, there were ways of coming to terms with that, he knew.

Chapter 25

1966

ALICE KNEW SHE WAS TIRED; SHE'D BEEN TIRED FOR THE
better part of a week. Longer. But this was different. Sitting
there, watching the boy first play with the soft toys, as he now
liked to do, then colouring and drawing, Alice encouraging him
to talk, to understand and explain what he was doing, it had
been all she could do to keep her attention focused, her eyes
open.

In the staff room, she fumbled a tea bag out of the tin where
they were kept and into her mug. Damned kettle taking an age
to boil. There was a case conference about the boy and through
the open door she could see Felix Gerber, the consultant child
psychiatrist, already in there waiting.

Jock Mirren, the boy's social worker, nudged her arm as he
came and stood alongside. "Enough water in the kettle for me,
too, I hope?"

"What's wrong?" Gerber said once she'd entered, the words out his mouth before she'd even sat down.

"Just tired, that's all."

But he wouldn't be so easily put off. "It's the boy, isn't it?" he said. "Something's getting to you. Something's up."

Alice shook her head. "It's nothing. Nothing I can put my finger on. It's just something making me uneasy. I can't put it into words."

"Try."

"Yes," Mirren joked. "Articulate. We are the professionals, after all."

"Very funny," Alice said.

"All right," Gerber said, "let's think through what's going on. See if we can't see what exactly the problems are."

"Okay. The problem is," Alice said, "instead of finding it easier to reach him, it becomes more difficult. Every time I seem to be getting somewhere I keep butting up against the mother, and it's like coming up against a brick wall."

"Jock," Gerber said, "you've been seeing the mother."

"Should've been seeing the mother, more like. Three of the last four sessions she's cancelled at the last minute. The one time she did deign to show her face, she turned up twenty bloody minutes late and then found an excuse for leaving early."

"And when she is there?"

"Resentful as buggery she has to be in the building at all. Way she sees it, her little darling's being made a scapegoat by the school because they can't control him—all the usual palaver. Anything other than admit there's something wrong. Something amiss that might need to be addressed."

Gerber tapped ash from the end of his cigarette. "Trust your instincts, Alice. The situation here—what's going on?"

Alice screwed up her eyes. "I think the mother's seducing the child."

"The boy?"

"Yes."

"Oh, come on!" Mirren exclaimed.

"What?"

"Not that again."

"What do you mean?"

"You and bloody Oedipus. It's your answer to everything."

Alice shot him a slashing look, pushed back her chair, and headed for the door.

"Alice..." Gerber said, appealing.

The door slammed shut at her back.

"Oh, fuck!" Mirren said.

"You might," Gerber said, "have expressed that with a bit more tact."

TWO WEEKS LATER A COPY OF A LETTER FROM THE BOY'S mother arrived, forwarded by the school: because of personal circumstances, they were moving to another part of the country and she would, therefore, be withdrawing her son from the school. Unfortunately, this would mean that the therapy would cease.

Chapter 26

ELDER HAD BEEN AWAKE SINCE SOMETHING AFTER FOUR, thoughts chasing themselves haphazardly through what, at that hour, passed for a brain. Coherence all but impossible. Easing back the blinds, he had stood at the Ice House window, staring out. Two murders, years apart. Two women, two deaths, similar but not the same. Maureen had never been as convinced they were the work of the same man.

He made coffee and drank it black. He should write things down again, similarities, differences, a list. The coffee was strong with no more than a hint of bitterness. The book he'd been trying to read lay on the floor beside the bed. *The Fox in the Attic.* Two men, the sea marsh, the mist; a dead girl folded, almost, in two. For him the book had faltered when he was still a good third from the end, casting him adrift amid a tide of German politics he failed to understand. What he would remember always was the image of the dead girl, her heels bouncing off the man's chest as he walked.

You saw what you saw and shucked the rest.

Two men.

Two men, two deaths?

He finished his coffee, showered, and dressed.

Two men or one?

Outside it was cold still, a lingering chill, and he hastened his steps. It was early enough to nod at anyone you passed—dog walkers, joggers, workers coming on or off shift, insomniacs like himself. Sometimes a brief "Morning," hand raised.

When had he last slept past four? Four-thirty at best? His body tense for the call that would alert him to some small catastrophe, some dreadful crime. No matter that it was all a way of life he had sought to leave behind.

Dreadful, he thought again: a word that had lost much of its meaning, except perhaps for himself and others like him.

The photographs were pinned to the office wall.

Irene Fowler's face leaned to one side on the pillow, eyes open and empty; her arms rested across her body, hands touching, a picture of repose and rest. The dress that she was wearing as she lay there was almost without a crease, as if the last thing her murderer had done before covering her was to smooth it evenly down. Beneath it, she wore clean underwear, without spot or stain.

Elder looked again at the ring on her right hand.

At the hand from which the wedding ring had been removed.

The overwhelming impression, the impression Elder guessed whoever had lain her there had been striving for, was one of tranquillity and peace.

Though Claire Meecham had also appeared to be fully dressed, she had been wearing nothing beneath her skirt and blouse. In his mind's eye, Elder saw the murderer carrying the body into the room and lowering it onto the bed.

What then?

Did he linger in the room, gazing down at his victim? And if so, what thoughts were in his mind? Love? Lust? Regret?

The marks around Irene Fowler's neck, where she had been strangled, suggested as little force as necessary had been used; those on Claire Meecham the same.

For a moment another image came to Elder's mind—the Stieglitz photograph on Vincent Blaine's wall, hands reaching up toward the throat, the neck.

What had Blaine said?

Up to a point, we all see what we want to see.

Elder took a step back.

The way the women had been dressed and left was a conscious, careful, bizarrely loving act. An act, almost, he guessed, of adoration.

Elder heard a door open at his back.

"Frank?"

Maureen Prior came to stand at his shoulder.

"The early bird, Frank? Saturday, too?"

He told her what he had been thinking, as clearly as he could.

ANNA INGRAM WAS WEARING AN ANKLE-LENGTH PURPLE linen skirt and a cream cheesecloth shirt over a camisole top, her red hair pinned into a swirl around her face. "So," she said, walking almost the length of the long, central room, "you did come after all."

"You're surprised?"

"I'm not sure."

Elder had been in the museum a good twenty minutes or so, moving between rooms. Paintings of fishing boats at harbour; lobster pots and nets; whitewashed cottages near the edge of the sea.

"You've had a chance to look around?"

"A little."

"And what do you think?"

Elder smiled. "It's very nice" he said, aware of the inadequacy of his reply.

"Here," she said, taking him for a moment by the arm. "Let me show you my favourites."

She led him toward a pair of oils, quite small, not much more than a metre across. In the first, a woman in a purple hat and white apron stood in the middle ground, a basket on one arm; behind her a tumble of buildings rose above a whitewalled cottage with a thatched roof. In the other, the figure of another woman, buckets in both hands, was shown approaching along a narrow alley, steeped in shadow, the wall at her back the only bright thing in the painting.

"Mark Senior," Anna said. "He started painting in and around Staithes when he was in his twenties and studying at Leeds. He helped found the Staithes Art Club in 1901." She smiled. "Hark at me. I sound like Vincent. Lecturing. Droning on."

"No, it's interesting."

"Now you're just being polite."

Elder looked back at the two paintings. To him they seemed oddly unfocused; one even looked unfinished.

"They're good, aren't they?" Anna Ingram said.

"Yes," Elder said.

"I did a dissertation on Mark Senior once, back when I was a student. Now, for my sins, I'm working on a monograph of Harold Knight—that's one of his over there, the woman with her hands together in prayer. He was born here in Nottingham, you know, Harold. Married a girl from Long Eaton. Laura. Laura Knight as she became."

Elder nodded. He'd seen some of her paintings in one of the other rooms.

"Bit of a star was Laura. Still is. Quite overshadowed her husband." Anna smiled again, more broadly. "Nice to know it can be done. Once in a while."

"So why Staithes?" Elder asked, stepping away.

"You know it at all? That part of the coast?"

"Yes." He knew it too well. The village was not so far north of the isolated spot where Katherine had been kept prisoner. So much kept coming back to that.

"Once the railway went there," Anna said, "visitors started coming for more or less the first time. Artists among them. Sea and scenery aside, I think they liked the fact that the village itself still seemed shut off, closed in on itself. There was a rawness about it that appealed. For a while at least." She looked at him keenly. "You haven't really come to see the paintings, have you?"

"Why not?"

"You're not that interested. Not really."

"Then why am I here?"

Anna's mouth slipped into a smile. "Once upon a time I would have been vain enough to think it was because you were interested in me, but it's not that, either."

"What is it, then?"

"It's Vincent, it has to be. You think somehow he was involved with those murders—those women." A firm shake of her head. "It's absurd, absolutely absurd, but I can't think what else it can be."

A couple came and stood close by them, looking at the paintings, and Anna edged Elder away.

"Claire Meecham..." Elder said.

"The woman who sent the card?"

"Yes. No matter what Vincent says, she was in his class at the university. I checked. Just last year. An introduction to photography. Two hours a week for eight weeks. And yet he claimed not to know her, not even to know her name."

"Is that so surprising?"

"Yes, I think so. Twelve students? We're not talking large numbers, after all."

Anna smiled. "You know Vincent a little. You know what he's like. Bound up in himself. When he's teaching, he's even worse. All he can see is the subject. The photography. The work. He could be lecturing to a row of cardboard cut-out dummies and it wouldn't make any difference—just so long as he was able to stand there and talk."

"What about questions? There must be questions. He must pay some attention to them then."

She smiled again. "I'm afraid Vincent's style doesn't exactly encourage participation. He's as likely to treat questions as annoyance as much as anything else."

"Don't the students complain?"

"Occasionally. Some of them. But, for the most part, they love it. They love him. Sit there hanging on his every word."

"Is that what you did?"

"I'm sorry?"

"I wondered if that's how you first met."

"At one of Vincent's lectures?"

"Yes."

"Actually, it was one of mine. Here at the castle. 'Cézanne and His Influence on Late Nineteenth-century British Painting.'" She laughed. "Vincent came up to me afterward and told me all the things I'd got wrong."

They walked through into one of the smaller rooms, pausing here and there to look at a painting. Early in the day, there were relatively few other visitors, and those there were moved quietly and spoke, when they did, in hushed, almost reverential tones. Somewhere between visiting an old-fashioned library, Elder thought, and being in church.

They stopped by a picture of blue sky, clouds, saplings on a rocky hillside torn by the wind. Elder liked it: the life in it. It seemed real to him.

"The weekend of April the ninth and tenth," he said, "you don't happen to know where Vincent was?"

Anna looked at him. "Is that the weekend Claire Meecham disappeared?"

"Yes."

"And that's what? Four weekends ago today?"

"Yes."

"In which case, I do. He was with me. In Dorset. A cottage, it used to belong to his family. Just outside Lyme. We go down there sometimes. Just for a break. Occasionally Vincent goes down on his own. If he has a lecture to prepare, an introduction to a book."

"And you were both there that weekend? Vincent and yourself?"

"Yes. We drove down early on the Saturday. Came back, oh, after lunch on Sunday."

Elder nodded.

"I'm sorry," she said.

"What for?"

"Now you'll have to come up with another theory. What is it? A different line of inquiry."

"Don't worry," Elder said. "There are always plenty of those."

She walked him through the gallery and down the stairs. Outside, they stood for a moment, looking out toward the city, the sun just beginning to edge its way through the clouds.

"Thanks for your time," Elder said. "And for showing me the paintings."

"It was my pleasure."

Had he looked back as he descended the path, he might have seen the shiver that ran through her body, causing her limbs to shake.

Chapter 27

WALKING DOWN THROUGH LACE MARKET, ELDER chanced to glance at what, at first sight, he thought was a regular bookshop, before noticing the Oxfam sign. Fancy for a charity shop, he thought. Regular shelves with everything neatly arranged: books, CDs, videos, DVDs. At the back, clothing, Fair Trade coffee and the like were also for sale. World music playing. A good number of browsers, many of them young. Younger than Elder, at least.

Fiction was ranged along one wall. Now that he'd discarded *The Fox in the Attic,* he was in need of a new book. An old new book. Why pay more than necessary when there were all these going cheap?

Among the selections placed face out on little metal stands was a copy of *Sons and Lovers:* an orange and white Penguin, the kind Elder thought you didn't see much anymore other than in places like this, a phoenix rising from the ashes on the cover and below that the original price, five shillings. Out of interest he checked the date of publication: 1966. Weighed it in his hand.

What had Blaine said about Lawrence? That he had fallen out of fashion? Maybe it was time to give him another chance after all. After reading the first few sentences, a description of a small mining village on the outskirts of the city, he took the book to the counter.

"That'll be three pounds, then," said the assistant. "It's in good nick. Well looked after. Must be forty years old, at least."

Well before you were born then, Elder thought.

Book snug in his coat pocket, he continued on his way. He was crossing toward the ice centre when his cell started to ring. It was Maureen Prior, her voice oddly tinny and distant, though, in all probability, she was no more than a mile away.

"Frank, what are you doing?"

"Not a lot. Not now. I thought I might try and meet up with Katherine later."

"I've turned up some interesting stuff on Wayne Johns."

"Where are you?"

"At the office."

Elder turned on his heels.

MAUREEN PRIOR WAS DRESSED IN WHAT ELDER NOW AS-sumed was her usual weekend wear, blue jeans fraying at the bottom, gray T-shirt, loose-fitting cotton jacket, trainers that had seen better days.

Elder had picked up coffee and a couple of raisin danishes on the way.

"Johns," Prior said, the moment he set the coffee down, "we only asked him about Claire Meecham. Nothing about the ear-lier murder."

"And we should have?"

"I've been doing some checking. It was his company that sup-plied the hotel with all the equipment for the conference."

Elder saw the brightness in Prior's eyes; felt a small quickening of his pulse.

"Frank, he was there that weekend, he had to be."

"Then maybe we should talk to him again," Elder said.

"He's got one of those penthouse flats by the canal," Prior said.

"Now there's a surprise."

WAYNE JOHNS OPENED THE DOOR WEARING AN UNDERshirt and shorts, the shirt dark with sweat. Behind him, on the broad stained boards, was a rowing machine, and, behind that, a treadmill. A leather settee with squared-off arms sat facing a large TV. Speakers hung from the walls. To the right, the kitchen area was separated by a work surface topped with solid wood. There was a low, wide bed at the far side of the room, and, alongside that, a door leading, presumably, to the bathroom.

"Lucky to catch me," Johns said. "Meeting friends for lunch. A quick shower, then I'm gone."

"We'll try," Prior said, "not to keep you too long."

Johns gave her a "fair enough" shrug and walked over to the red, double-sided fridge.

"Water?" he asked, pulling open one of the doors. "Juice?"

When they both declined, he snapped the top from a bottle of some doubtlessly healthy drink and swallowed half of it down. "Thirsty work," he said, "keeping in shape."

Picking up a towel, he rubbed vigorously at his hair.

There was scarcely, Prior noticed, more than an ounce or two of surplus fat on him.

"So," Johns said, flicking the towel into a corner. "What can I do for you?"

Prior gave him one of her second-best smiles. "Stop lying to us, for a start."

"Lying?"

"Withholding information."

"Is that the same thing?"

"Close enough."

Johns's turn to smile. "Sins of omission," he said. "These people I was farmed out to when I was a kid. Used to drag me off to church every chance they got. Figured it was my only chance of salvation, I think. When they weren't beating the shit out of me, that is."

"It worked?" Prior asked.

Johns laughed. "Look around..." Gesturing broadly with both hands. "Clean in thought, word, and deed. And worth a quid or two in the bargain."

"So what was it? The church or the beatings? Which worked best?"

"And made me what I am today? Who knows? Both, I shouldn't wonder. You know, the carrot and the stick. Cruel to be kind."

He wiped some small residue of sweat from his forehead with the inside of an arm.

"No, I'll tell you what it was. Being dragged through a succession of care homes, foster homes, right till I was old enough to get out on my own. No brothers, no sisters, no real family to speak of, I was never in one place long enough for that. What was it that poet bloke said? 'They fuck you up, your mum and dad.' Well mine, they never got the chance, whoever they were, and bless them for it. Stand on your own two feet, look after number one. Only one person in this world going to do a damned thing for you and that's yourself. Lesson learned."

Finishing his drink, he pitched the empty bottle into the bin.

"I must remember to recycle," he said.

"September 1997," Prior said, "a conference here in the city, organized by the DTI. You remember that?"

"One other thing you learn in foster care," Johns said with a quick grin. "Never admit to anything."

"Until you're caught."

"Until you're caught."

He went over and perched, half-leaning, half-sitting, on one corner of the settee.

"It was one of our first big contracts. The one that made me think I was going to be able to make it happen here. In Spain, somehow, it had been different, I'm not sure why. I suppose because there I had somebody else to set out the lay of the land and grease the wheels. Here I was starting off again after what? The best part of ten years? It was always going to be tricky. But then, that conference, everyone was pleased with how it went..."

"The small business of a dead body aside," Elder said, getting a little tired of Johns's self-justifying tone.

"Well, that was bad, of course, but, you know, in the end no skin off my nose. A one-off. Out of all control. Nothing for which we could be blamed."

"Irene Fowler," Prior said. "The woman who died. You knew her?"

"Me? No."

"You didn't meet her that weekend?"

"Not as far as I know."

"But you were there? At the hotel?"

"Of course."

"The whole time?"

"More or less."

"Supervising, making sure things were running smoothly."

"Yes. And like I said..."

"Checking with the participants, I dare say. Getting their take on things. Any problems you could help them with, anything to improve the way things were running."

"Not really, no. That's not the way it works, not for me, anyhow. The management at the hotel, yes, liaise with them. And whoever's responsible for running the actual course. But otherwise, no way. Keep your head down, out of sight, if nobody knows you're there at all, that's the best way. Means it's all going smoothly, like you said." He smiled at Prior. "Like silk."

Prior looked away.

"In the evening, though," Elder said. "You'd relax in the bar, a drink and a chat, not business, social. Winding down."

"Listen," Johns said, "end of the day, my job, check everything's ready for the first sessions next morning. By the time that's done, I'm through. Any winding down I do in my own company, not there."

Neither Elder nor Maureen Prior moved; Johns shifted his position on the settee.

"Look, to the best of my knowledge, I never spoke to the woman—Irene Fowler, that's what you said?—never spoke to her the whole weekend. Till I saw her picture in the paper, I never knew who she was. But then, you're just going to have to take my word for that."

With an agile movement, he was up on his feet.

"And now, if you don't mind, I do have to take a shower. If there's anything else I can help you with, perhaps next time you could call my office. If that's all the same to you."

"COCKY BASTARD," MAUREEN PRIOR SAID. "GOD'S GIFT isn't in it."

Elder laughed.

"What?"

"Watching you get more and more uptight each time he flexed his pecs."

"Arrogant sod."

Elder laughed again. They were sitting on a bench beside the canal, watching a moorhen marshalling its sole surviving chick in slow circles as she fed it from her beak.

"Unfortunately," he said, "it's not a crime."

"What's that?"

"Having muscle tone and a million or so in the bank."

"Well, it should be."

"Amen to that."

"I've had a couple of people phoning round," Prior said. "Men Claire Meecham had been seeing. Unless everyone's being unusually shy, it seems as if, where there was any kind of sexual activity, it was pretty straightforward. No suggestion of S and M or anything like that."

"So if Johns is telling the truth about what happened between them, it could have really taken her by surprise."

"In which case, the question is, did it frighten her off or send her back for more?"

A young woman of no more than sixteen went past, wheeling a small child in a rickety pram. The child, little more than a baby, was crying, snot running from its nose down onto the pacifier in its mouth; the mother, lean-faced, dragging hard on a cigarette, stared straight ahead as she walked, blocking out the sound as best she could.

"I've made contact with the man Johns was in partnership with in Spain," Prior said. "He was cagey at first, worried I might be involved in some kind of investigation of his finances, I think. But he's promised to talk to me again. All the time Johns spent out of the country—it would be nice to know more about that."

They started to retrace their steps, back along the old towpath to the point where it led up from the canal onto the road by the station.

"You still planning on calling Katherine?" Prior said.

"Probably."

She gave him a look that said without doubt he should.

"You know who you remind me of," Elder said, "whenever you give me one of those looks?"

"I'm sure you'll tell me."

"My mother."

"Thanks very much."

"She had this knack of making me feel guilty, whether I was or not."

"Maybe that's what mothers are for."

"To make us feel bad about ourselves?"

"Keep us on the straight and narrow."

"Is that what yours did?"

Prior chose not to answer. "I'm going back to the office for a while."

"Okay. You'll stay in touch?"

"Of course."

At the crossroads, they went their separate ways.

ELDER WAITED UNTIL HE WAS FREE FROM THE TRAFFIC, A small patch of open land off Maiden Lane, benches, shrubs, a few trees. Katherine answered on the second ring.

"You're up then," Elder said.

"What d'you mean up? I've been up for hours."

"Just joking, okay?"

"What is it you want, Dad? Only I'm busy, okay?"

"Doing what?"

"Working, of course."

Music was playing quite loud in the background.

"I thought we might get together," Elder said.

"Dad, get real, yeah? I've got a project to finish. Exams to revise for."

"Okay. I'm sorry."

"You do want me to go to university?"

"I said, I'm sorry."

He took a breath, sensing her impatience at the end of the phone. "How about tomorrow sometime? We could—I don't know—get a bit of lunch? Go for a stroll?"

"Dad, I'll ring you, okay? Only I'm not promising. I'll ring you if I can."

"All right. You do that."

Before he could give her his love, she'd gone.

Elder went into the first café he came to and ordered a ham sandwich and a tea, opened his book, and began to read. Living down in Cornwall, the arse end of the country according to some, stuck out in the middle of some fields between the moors and sea with little company other than your own, people thought that must be hard. But they were wrong. That was the easy part.

Chapter 28

UNUSUAL FOR ELDER, AFTER HE ROLLED OVER HE MAN-
aged to get back to sleep, not waking till close to half past eight.
Showered and dressed, he set about making breakfast: scrambled
eggs on toast, coffee, more toast with marmalade. Late yesterday he'd made a trip to Sainsbury's.

Sitting with a view out toward St. Mary's church, he listened
to the news. Another car bomb in Iraq, children dying by the
thousands in Darfur; closer to home, a pregnant woman shot
and killed as she walked back from seeing friends, a former
boyfriend wanted for questioning by the police. If Louis Arm-
strong came on singing "What a Wonderful World," he thought
he might just throw the radio through the open window.

When the phone rang, he thought Sunday or no Sunday it
was most probably Maureen Prior, but he was wrong.

"Listen, Dad, I'm sorry about yesterday. I was in a lousy
mood."

"Really?"

"All right, don't rub it in. I just called to apologize, okay?"

"That's fine. No need."

"So d'you want to meet for coffee or what?"

"You don't fancy a walk, I suppose?"

A hesitation, then, "Not really."

"Okay, where d'you want to meet?"

"You know that place we went once before?"

"Last week, you mean? Atlas, is that what it's called?"

"I don't even know if they're open on a Sunday. No, upstairs at Waterstone's, remember?"

She had been sitting there reading a magazine when he had arrived, latté and pain au chocolat close at hand. She'd been in a bad mood immediately before that occasion, too.

"Yes," he said, "I think so."

"Half eleven, okay?"

This time it was Elder who got there first. Quite a few of the seats were already taken, parents with small children, a few middle-aged, middle-class types leafing through the *Observer* or the *Sunday Times*. How much of an alternative was this, he wondered, to meeting partners on the Internet?

He ordered his coffee—the third of the day already—and, clearing away the detritus someone else had left behind, installed himself at a small table by the window. When he looked at his watch it was still five minutes shy of eleven. He took out his book and began to read.

Fifteen, twenty pages later, Katherine had still to arrive.

There wasn't another bookshop, was there? Another bookshop with a café? For God's sake, he told himself, calm down. All that caffeine going to his head, his heart, making him jumpy. Then, another page and there she was. The same denim jacket and blue jeans, red basketball sneakers on her feet; bag slung over one arm. Her face breaking into a smile.

"Hi, Dad! Sorry I'm late."

"'S'all right."

"Here. Let me get you another coffee."

"No, thanks. I'm fine."

"Come on. Have something."

"Orange juice, then. But you sit down, let me get it."

"No..." Backing away. "My treat."

The queue was short but slow, and Elder watched her over the top of his book, standing there as if she didn't know. Beautiful, that's what she was. To his eyes, at least. A similar build to Joanne's, if not quite as tall. Her face fuller, a stronger chin. The same eyes. Beautiful.

"What are you reading?" she asked, sitting down.

He showed her.

"*Sons and Lovers?* What on earth you reading that for?"

"Why not?"

She stirred sugar into her coffee. "We had to read it at school."

"You didn't like it?"

"It was okay, I suppose. Bits of it anyway. The beginning, where he's always coming home drunk, the father, from the pit, that wasn't so bad, but later—that bloke—Paul, is that what he's called?—a real pain in the bum, that's what he is."

"He's really that bad?"

"Always whining on about something or other. And the way he goes on about his mother, how he can't live without her. Something wrong with him, if you ask me. And as for the way he treats the girl—what's her name?"

"Miriam?"

"Miriam, yeah. Won't let her touch him, oh, no, naughty, naughty, keep your hands to yourself—yakking on and on about how it's all so spiritual, and then when he does sleep with her, soon as he's had her, he doesn't want to know. Goes off chasing someone else. Her best bloody friend." Katherine snorted. "He got that right, anyway. Lawrence. Blokes, to a *T.*"

Elder smiled. "No one treating you like that, I hope."

"Let 'em try," Katherine said with a grin.

"Anyway," Elder said, "I thought all that had changed nowadays. More equality."

"You mean now we can treat men like shit as well?"

"Something like that."

"Like Mum treated you."

"That wasn't what I meant."

"Maybe not. But she did."

Elder sighed. "It was a long time ago."

"Long enough to have forgiven her?"

"I don't think about it."

"Liar."

He shifted uneasily in his seat. "Look, Katherine..."

"Mind my own business, I know."

"It is your business."

"Well, then."

"It's just...what happened with your mum...and Martyn...I try not to think about it, that's all."

Katherine picked up the book. "In here, right, this woman he has an affair with, Paul, she's married, yeah? In the end she goes back to her husband. Turns out she's loved him all along."

"Thanks," Elder said.

"What for?"

"Spoiling the end."

Katherine looked disgusted. "It's not the book that matters."

Elder changed the subject. Tried, not quite successfully, to find something about sports psychology on which he and Katherine could converse.

"Where you off to now?" he asked, once they were outside on the street.

"Home, I suppose."

"The park or your digs?"

"Digs."

"I'll walk part of the way with you, if you don't mind. Stretch my legs."

"Suit yourself."

At the top of Derby Road, Elder kissed Katherine on the cheek. "Take care," he said.

"You, too. And don't stand there like you usually do."

"How's that?"

"Watching me walk away."

Elder turned first and crossed the road at an angle, cutting through.

THE SECOND SUNDAY OF EVERY MONTH, VINCENT BLAINE had people out to his house for brunch. As he was at pains to point out, it was something of an American tradition, and the Americans had to have had one good idea for civilization since the Boston Tea Party, didn't they? Not that the food was particularly American: There were pancakes, true, as well as grilled bacon, and even, sometimes, maple syrup; it's just that they were never served on the same plate at the same time. And what across the Atlantic were called mimosas were here known as Buck's Fizz.

Blaine being Blaine, the people were not just people. Academics from the city's two universities would mix and mingle with painters and photographers, a scattering of playwrights and novelists, classical musicians, actors who happened to have touched down on a national tour, and members of whichever funding bodies were needed to keep Blaine's publishing endeavours viable.

There were also a few, a very few, old friends.

Food was prepared by outside caterers and served, when the weather allowed, from beneath a canopy set up at the back of the house. Guests wandered in and out, somehow balancing glasses and plates while practicing a certain kind of provincial one-upmanship.

And all the while, Vincent Blaine moved to and fro, adding a footnote to a conversation here, an elegant put-down to another there. If he thought it important, important for himself, that the regional director of Arts Council England spoke to the new visual arts officer for the county, he would engineer it without apparent effort. He ate less than almost anyone else and, the odd glass of chablis aside, drank very little. Everyone's name and function was noted down on the card index he kept inside his head; if they were of no specific use to him now, well, they might be in the future. It was one of the ways he survived financially.

Anna, who knew many of the same people, usually found these occasions pleasant, even though, to her, Blaine's networking was less subtle than he liked to think.

Today, an indifferent spring day, Blaine had opted for black—black trousers, black shirt, black shoes—so that, to Anna, he resembled nothing as much as a spider, weaving purposefully between his guests.

She wanted to talk to him, but knew it would have to wait until later, when, everyone else gone, she would first have to sit and listen as Blaine picked over the occasion with almost total recall.

Moving outside now, into the garden, she was surprised to see Blaine's old accountant, Brian Warren—the first time he'd been at a brunch for the better part of a year.

Warren, shabbily imposing in a Donegal tweed suit, was watching Blaine also, and the moment his quarry came near, he wrapped a firm but friendly arm around his shoulders and steered him toward the far end of the garden where the roses were beginning, reluctantly, to bud.

"Brian," Blaine said, "it's good to see you, naturally, but..."

"We need to talk."

"Yes, of course, but later."

"No, now."

Blaine looked into his face. "Very well."

Only then did Warren withdraw his arm.

"What's so important?" Blaine asked.

"That policeman. Elder. The one who was in charge of that business at the hotel."

"What about him?"

"He came to see me. A week ago."

"He saw me, too. It's nothing. He's just raking over old coals. Not even a proper policeman anymore. It's not important, believe me." Blaine made a move as if to walk away.

"It wouldn't pay," Warren said, stopping him, "to underestimate him as much as you do everyone else."

"That's nonsense," Blaine said. "And besides, what is there to be afraid of? There's nothing."

Warren moved closer, so that he seemed to loom over him. "How long have we known each other, Vincent? Fifteen years? More? All that time and you don't think I know when you're telling the truth and when not?"

Blood rushed to Blaine's cheeks. "Telling the truth about what?"

Warren lowered his voice. "That night at the hotel. There was another woman there, remember? Aside from the poor woman who got killed. Christine Dulverton. Elder went to see her, too. She told him Irene had taken a bit of a shine to me…"

"Well, that's nonsense."

"Is it? I don't think so. You may not have much of a sense for these things, in fact I doubt very much if you do, but I've still got some blood beating in my veins. Least I did, back then. And there was something there, all right. Between us. At least I liked to think there was."

"You're exaggerating. Romanticizing."

"Am I? When you went off for a piss, I asked Irene what she'd think if I came up later to her room. She laughed and touched my hand and said, 'Why don't you try it and see?'"

"It was a joke, that's all. She was just having a bit of fun."

"That's not the way it seemed at the time."

Two of the other guests came cheerily down toward them

and, reading the seriousness of their conversation, turned and went back toward the house.

"After I left you at the hotel," Warren said, "I went home, showered, changed, argued with myself back and forth, should I, shouldn't I? I was excited as hell, just the idea of it, I don't mind telling you. But I knew there was no point in getting back there too early. Had to judge it right. And I thought I had. She was having dinner with you first, after all. When I got back to the bar there she was, sitting all on her own. Delighted to see me, an' all. Laughed out loud. 'Give me half an hour or so,' she said. 'Finish this and then go upstairs, make myself presentable.' I told her she looked fine as she was, but no, she insisted. Gave me the number of her room.

"I went off for a stroll around the block. Took my time. No one saw me come back in, I'm pretty certain of that. When I got up to the room, I knocked, but nobody answered. Thought maybe she was in the shower or something and tried again. Still nothing. So I tried the handle on the door and it came open. An inch or two, no more. They'd put on the chain but forgotten to lock the door. The main light in the room was off, but one of the others—the bathroom most probably—had been left on. And I could see her, with somebody else, on the bed. On top of him. Just the outline. I couldn't see who it was. The man. I stood there for a minute, gobsmacked, then turned round and buggered off smartly, tail between my legs. So randy, I don't mind telling you, I got a cab up to the Forest, got myself a tart."

"A prostitute?"

"Don't sound so bloody disapproving. Clean your pipes as well as anybody else. Better, if you're lucky."

"And this man, the one you say was in the room, you're sure you don't know who it was?"

Warren laughed. "Don't worry, Vincent. Even if I had, I'd never say."

"What do you mean?"

"After I left the hotel I wandered round a bit before I found a cab. Passed your car, right where you'd left it. Still there."

The colour had drained from Blaine's face. "You think...I don't know what you're suggesting...you think that was me? In the room?"

"Could've been the archbishop of bloody Canterbury, for all I know. All I could see. But that yarn of yours about driving yourself home, back by midnight—from where I'm standing, Vincent, that was a lie. And I'd have to say, I wonder why?"

Blaine's throat was dry. "You told Elder all of this?"

"Not a word."

"Why not?"

"And implicate myself in a murder? What would be the point of that? Better to play dumb. There's no way, as far as I can see, they can find out what happened, neither Elder nor anyone else. No one saw me going in or coming out, I'd swear it. And besides, it's best not say anything that might get old friends into trouble, eh, Vincent? Not good form." He winked. "If you got to the trough before me, good on you. More of a man than I took you for. Just wanted you to be on your guard, that's all."

Reaching past Blaine's shoulder, he lifted a branch of the nearest rose bush and inspected the leaves.

"Aphids, Vincent, you want to get whoever looks after this lot to get 'em sorted or you'll see no blooms at all."

SUNDAY AFTERNOON, PRIOR HAD THE PLACE VIRTUALLY to herself. Across the street, somewhat incongruously, someone was playing Radio 3 full blast, Beethoven sailing in through the partly opened windows. The Fifth, the one everybody knew, even if they didn't know exactly what it was. She had called Elder half an hour before and when he arrived it was with two cups of lukewarm coffee and an egg mayonnaise sandwich to share.

"Generosity, Frank? Your middle name?"

Elder grinned.

Prior unwrapped the sandwich and took a bite. "Thanks, Frank. Now pull over a chair and look at this."

The front page of the Spanish newspaper, *El Pais,* was up on her computer screen. Beneath a headline Elder couldn't readily understand were the separate photographs of two men, one with an aquiline nose and dark hair slicked back, a raised scar across his right cheek; the other, younger than when they had last seen him, but immediately recognizable, was a white-shirted Wayne Johns.

"As far as I can make out…"

"Using your fluent Spanish."

"Exactly. They were involved in some sort of fracas in a hotel restaurant. This one here…"

"The one who looks like a bullfighter?"

"He accused Johns of having an affair with his wife. But he isn't a bullfighter, he's some kind of government official. At least he was when this happened. Look at the date there."

"November 1993."

"A year or so before Johns came back to the UK."

"Interesting."

"Earlier today, I spoke again to the man Johns worked with in Spain. Ruiz—that's his name. Speaks perfect English, thank heavens. Seems this wasn't the first time Johns had been in similar sorts of trouble. One of the women he was involved with—and this is interesting—claimed that Johns had had sex with her against her will."

"He'd raped her?"

"That's what she claimed. I asked Ruiz if it had been reported to the police and he said he thought so, but didn't think any charges had been filed. I'm checking that with the Barcelona police. But meantime, I think there's more to learn about Johns than we can get over the phone."

"You're going to go out there? Talk to this Ruiz?"

Prior grinned. "No, Frank, you are. Assuming your passport's still current, that is."

"You want me to go to Barcelona?"

A smile brightened Maureen Prior's face. "How does thirteen forty-five tomorrow sound? From Stansted? Change trains at Luton, I believe. Unless you want to drive."

BRUNCH OVER, BLAINE HAD DISAPPEARED UPSTAIRS. AS much for something to do as anything else, Anna helped the caterers collect the glasses and generally set things in order. By midafternoon they had packed and gone, and Blaine had still not reappeared.

Anna made herself a cup of tea and leafed through a magazine. Eventually, she went up and knocked on the bedroom door. No reply.

Softly, she called Vincent's name.

Still no reply.

Uncertain, she turned away, but at the head of the stairs turned back. The handle of the door turned easily and she stepped inside.

The curtains were drawn across.

A step into the room and she could see his shape beneath the covers, curled toward the edge.

"Vincent."

Moving closer to the bed, she could see his eyes were closed, one hand resting on the pillow, fingers splayed.

Leaning down, she whispered his name again.

She touched his hand and his hand was cold.

"Vincent!"

She shook him by the shoulder and this time he stirred.

"Vincent, wake up."

For an instant he opened his eyes. "Who is it? Is it you?"

"It's me, Anna."

"Anna?"

"I was worried."

He was looking at her now and even in that poor light she could see his face was pale.

"What's the matter? Are you ill?"

She made as if to feel his forehead and he moved his head away.

"I've got a headache. A migraine. It'll go."

"Let me get you something. Some paracetamol."

"No."

"A glass of water then…"

He lurched toward her, seizing her wrist. "What don't you understand? I want to be left alone."

Back outside, in the light, she could see clearly the imprint of his fingers on her skin.

BY THE TIME PRIOR HAD HAD ENOUGH IT WAS ALMOST evening. According to the Barcelona police, a complaint had been lodged against Wayne Johns, but was later withdrawn. She was just leaving the building when she heard her cell phone.

"Hello?"

"Maureen?"

"Who is this?"

"It's Ben. Ben Leonard."

It took her several seconds to realize who he was. "Dowland," she said. "Something's happened?"

"No. That's not why I'm calling."

She pictured him leaning back easily in his chair, phone in hand; the gold ring, the bleached blond hair.

"Then why?"

"I thought you might fancy meeting? A drink, maybe?"

She broke the connection, dropped the phone down into her bag, and hurried on toward her car.

Chapter 29

ELDER SAW THEM AT THE AIRPORT, RAMSHACKLE GROUPS of young men and women, red-eyed from lack of sleep, shambling back into the working week after two days and nights of heavy drinking and relative abandon. "Mel's Hen Party, May 7th–8th, 2005." "Big Coz's Stag Weekend—Away the Lads!" An amiable ginger-haired man of six foot two or three, unshaven, a tattered bridal veil on his head, launched into a chorus of "Jerusalem" as he came through customs, fell to his knees, and kissed the ground.

Elder was glad he was travelling in the other direction.

The plane was no more than two-thirds full, its passengers a mix of business types with laptops and lightweight suits, and holidaymakers in the early years of retirement, some of these, from conversations Elder overheard, with apartments they kept up year-round.

Alternately, he dozed and read his book. Only when he saw, looking down past the wing onto the Pyrenees, the mountains pushing up jaggedly through clouds in a burst of light, did he feel the stirrings of going somewhere new and strange.

The airport at Barcelona was airy and surprisingly uncluttered, more Stansted than Heathrow. He used his card to get euros from an ATM machine, treated himself to a large glass of freshly squeezed mango and orange juice, and followed the signs to the metro. The train was quite crowded but air-conditioned, and he stood, resting back against one of the seats, rehearsing his questions to Juan Carlos Ruiz and running over what he knew already about Wayne Johns.

THE MAIN STREET, THE RAMBLAS, WAS WIDE AND LONG and lined with cafés and bars, shops and hotels. A broad pedestrianized area along the centre was studded with kiosks selling everything from newspapers and magazines to cockatiels and parakeets. At intervals, between clusters of café tables and chairs, a motley collection of jugglers, men on stilts, and human statues panhandled as best they could. Signs in several languages warned visitors about falling for variations of the old three-card trick.

Look for the market, the instructions had said, on the same side as the opera house; just beyond the market entrance take a right. The Hotel Miro, ask for me at the desk.

As it happened, there was no need. An ample man with a full beard, wearing a burnt orange shirt and a green and yellow tie, stepped forward as Elder entered.

"Mr. Elder. It is Mr. Elder? Welcome to Barcelona. Welcome to my hotel."

He squeezed one of Elder's hands in both of his.

"Here, let me take your bag. There is a very nice room on the fourth floor. Why don't you take a little time to freshen up? I will meet you down here in, shall we say, one hour? Then we may talk."

Maureen Prior had been right; his English, naturally accented, was close to perfect.

THERE WAS A FRAMED REPRODUCTION OF A PAINTING ON the wall opposite the bed: a bright blue background on which, it seemed, a small child armed with a white pencil had drawn his impressions of the moon and stars. Elder took a shower and changed his clothes. Just time to stretch out on the bed. Not meaning to, he slept.

Waking dazed from the indistinct clamour of a dream, he feared he had slept too long, but it had been no more than fifteen minutes, maybe less. Ruiz was waiting downstairs, chatting pleasantly to the white-shirted young woman at the desk.

"Come. Let us go."

They crossed the Ramblas, passing into a network of narrow streets that eventually opened out onto an attractive misshapen square. Sunlight spilled down the front of the facing building, red and orange flowers hung behind wrought-iron balcony railings, and, just visible in shadow, small birds perched colourful and silent in their cages. Below were a dozen or so café tables beneath a canopy and, on the near side of the square, several painters were displaying their work beneath large white umbrellas, views of the city and its architecture vying with pastiche Picasso.

"Here," Ruiz said. "This way."

He steered Elder toward the entrance of a narrow bar, on past several young men drinking espresso in the doorway, and into the dark and cool interior. Black-and-white tiles on the floor.

Behind the counter, a short man in a blue polo shirt broke off his conversation to greet Ruiz enthusiastically and shake his hand. Ruiz laughed and said something in Spanish Elder failed to understand. Spanish, or was it Catalan?

Different kinds of olives sat plump under glass on white china trays, on either side of them more trays filled with sausage and tomatoes, squares of cheese, fried chicken wings, anchovies— or were they simply small sardines?—chopped onion, fingers of green chilli. At the centre of the counter there was a tall pump with ornate gold taps for drawing beer and, farther along, bananas and oranges were piled higgledy-piggledy beneath a shelf of pastries and croissants.

When had he last eaten?

Ruiz led the way up a short flight of stairs and offered Elder a seat at the first table, looking out.

A young couple, oblivious of all else, sat by the back wall, morosely holding hands. To the right, an elderly man with a leathered face read the newspaper and smoked a cigarette.

There were heavy, green-leaved plants in corners, small paintings and photographs covering almost every inch of wall; despite the brightness outside, the globed lights descending from the ceiling were switched on, shining a dull yellow; an old-fashioned fan turned slowly overhead.

One of the waiters brought them a plate of mixed *tapas* and a basket of bread, slender glasses of cold beer.

"So," Ruiz said, lighting a small cigar, "Señor Johns."

Elder broke off a piece of bread.

"You know," Ruiz said, "when I first met him it was in here, this bar. I have been coming here for, oh, more than twenty years. I know everyone, apart from the tourists, and there are few of those who venture this far inside; they prefer to sit out in the sun. So this day I was sitting here, my usual place, and I notice this man standing downstairs, drinking brandy, Spanish brandy, and talking to anyone who would listen in a mixture of English and Portuguese with a few words of Catalan for good measure.

"Finally, just as I am about to leave, he comes up to me here and says they have been talking about me downstairs and from what he has heard he thinks there is business we can do together. 'What kind of business is this?' I ask. 'Well,' he says, 'I believe you are in the hotel business and in need of a partner.'

"'What I'm in need of,' I tell him, 'is someone who's prepared to work twenty-three hours a day for a roof over his head and enough food so that he won't starve.'

"'Exactly!' he says, and holds out his hand. 'Wayne Johns. Good to meet you. Unless I'm mistaken, this is a great day for both of us.'"

Ruiz laughed. "I took him to the hotel, the one where you are staying. Then—this is what? Sixteen, seventeen years ago— then it was a burned-out shell, little more. When he saw it, Johns rubbed his hands. 'Twenty-three hours a day is right,' he said, 'if we're going to be open for next summer.'"

Ruiz ate an olive, drank some beer.

"Two years later, he was my partner. Why not? He worked hard, he knew wood, he knew marble, he knew stone, what he didn't know he was prepared to learn. And most of the time he was good company; he told good stories, at least some of which—a few—were true."

"He was a friend," Elder said.

Ruiz spat an olive pit into his hand. "We would share a drink at the end of the day, sometimes a meal, but always, almost always at work, at the hotel, sometimes here, but that was all. He did not come often to my home."

"Why was that?"

"My wife, she did not feel comfortable with him there."

Elder waited.

"She said the way he looked at her, at all women, it was the way men look at beasts when they are at market, for sale, weighing them with his eyes. Before the abattoir."

"You think she was right?"

Ruiz shrugged heavy shoulders and leaned back in his chair. Not speaking, the young couple walked past them and down the stairs. "To some extent, all men, we look at women in this way. I think it is true. Perhaps it is from our history, I don't know. And Johns, he liked women. Not girls, young girls, twenty,

twenty-two, twenty-three, but women, real women. He loved them. Sought out their company. And then he would be charming. Charming, in his way. And his way was always, how shall I say, a little rough. A little—I don't know—not as if to say he came from the gutter, not that, but as if, although he had money and good, expensive clothes, underneath he was just an ordinary working man. A peasant, even, but not quite that, either. It is difficult to explain."

Ruiz leaned closer and lowered his voice. "My wife and I, we have been married for more than twenty years. In that time I have had a few, shall we say, adventures. Not many. Not as many as most men I know. A few. And I think I have learned enough to know there are times with a woman you must show a little tenderness and times when you must show a little strength, even a little force. But never the one without the other. At least that is what I think."

Leaning back again, he drank more beer.

"For Johns, I think, the balance was not there."

"He liked to inflict pain."

"Yes. And some women—I don't know—I don't know why—they find this attractive. It was as if, once they knew, knew what he could be like, they sought him out. There had been a woman, I think, in Portugal, one in particular. I never learned the whole story, but perhaps she pushed him further, to do more and more things. In the end, I think she was one of the reasons he left. I think, even, he was becoming a little bit afraid."

"Of what he might do?"

Ruiz nodded slowly. "Of what he might do."

"And here?" Elder said. "Here in Spain?"

Ruiz turned in his chair and called down for more beer. The man sitting opposite them folded his newspaper closed and lit another cigarette. The conversation from the bar below was quite animated and loud.

"A year," Ruiz said, "after the hotel opened—and it was a

success, a big, big success—I began to talk with some people about something new, a new venture, a conference centre, close to the Placa Espanya. One of these people, he was a minister, you know, in government. There are always certain permissions, paths that have to be smoothed—it is good to have someone in authority, you know, as a friend, someone who can say yes when others might say no."

The beer arrived and Ruiz paused.

Elder ate more sausage and cheese.

"The minister," Ruiz said, "he had a wife. She and Johns, they began an affair. In secret, of course, at first, but after a while it was as if she no longer cared. She would take Johns and flaunt him in front of her husband. Once, at the hotel, he was there with me having dinner. There had been discussions, concerning the conference centre, important discussions, four or five people, and she came up to the table—she had been drinking, perhaps taking something, I don't know, drugs maybe, maybe not—anyway she comes right up to him, her husband, we are all sitting there, and she pulls down the straps of her dress and she shows him the marks—bruises on her neck and arms and breasts—and says, 'This is what he did to me, my lover, you see? That's what a man can do.' And he slapped her and she spat back at him and laughed in his face.

"After that, I don't know, he did everything he could to get his wife to stop seeing Johns. Begged her to think of his position, of their children; she told him she was leaving him, she wanted a divorce. He refused. There was a public scene in which he challenged Johns to a duel. The police heard of this and intervened. Meanwhile, because people knew of his associations with me, they were having second thoughts about my scheme. Finally, what I believe happened, the minister offered Johns money, a lot of money, if he would leave his wife alone, break off the affair."

"And that's what he did? He agreed?"

"So I believe."

"And the wife, she accepted this?"

Ruiz ran his finger down through the condensation on his glass. "She took her own life. An overdose. And, to be sure, she cut her wrists. The minister, he found her in the bath."

"And the scheme? For the conference centre?"

"It went ahead." Ruiz shrugged. "It was business, after all."

Chapter 30

FROM MAUREEN PRIOR'S POINT OF VIEW, THE ONE CLEAR benefit of Wayne Johns's early life being as it was—a litany of minor offenses, council homes, and foster care—was that, though messy, it was traceable. Sad—if she allowed herself for a moment to dwell on it, almost unbelievably sad—but somewhere on file.

One of her team was tracking back to see if there was anything usable, anything that might throw a little more light on where they were now. More urgently, now that she knew of Johns's involvement, she had officers contacting anyone and everyone who had been present at the DTI conference eight years before, those whom Elder had not already spoken to. What she needed was some way of putting Johns and Irene Fowler together during that time, something more than the mere fact they had been under the same roof.

Sitting in her office, late into the afternoon, she thought of Johns and the time they had gone to question him in his penthouse apartment, the cockiness of him in his undershirt and shorts. The smugness she'd have liked to wipe from his face.

Well, between whatever Elder was discovering abroad and what she hoped her team might uncover here, in a few days they might have enough to do exactly that.

She pushed back her chair, stretched her arms out wide and arched her back; she'd been sitting in the same position for too long. As she got to her feet, one of the officers called to her from across the room. "This bloke, been waiting downstairs for you best part of an hour now."

"Which bloke?"

"I don't know. Some bloke. I thought you knew."

BEN LEONARD WAS SITTING LESS THAN COMFORTABLY on a hard plastic chair with metal legs, one of his arms angled sharply upward so that his hand clasped the back of his neck; in his other hand he held a skimpy paperback. He was wearing a maroon overshirt, black T-shirt, loose gray combat trousers, and a pair of New Balance running shoes. When he saw Prior, he smiled.

"Nobody told me you were here," she said.

Leonard dipped his head. "Figured you were busy," he said. "Catching up with my reading. No sweat." For a moment, he held up the book. "You know this?"

Squinting a little, Prior read the title—*Love and Fame*—and shook her head.

"Poetry," Leonard said. "John Berryman?"

Prior shook her head again. Poetry was one of the other things she didn't do.

"He was a drunk. Berryman. A crazy drunk. American. A professor. Manic-depressive all his life."

"Sounds a lot of fun."

Leonard unwound his arm from behind his head. "It gets better. Or worse. His father was always threatening to kill him;

take him into the sea and drown him. Drown the pair of them together."

"Nice man."

"Finally he killed himself, the father. Shot himself."

"And what's-his-name? Berryman? The son?"

"John."

"What happened to him?"

"Jumped to his death off a bridge over the Mississippi River. Misjudged it by all accounts, missed the water and landed on the bank."

"And that's what you're reading about?" An image of someone falling flickered behind Prior's eyes.

"Sort of. I mean, that's not what it's all about. Not directly. And it's funny, a lot of it. Very funny. It needs to be. But, yes, he wrote a lot about dying. Not surprisingly. Death by water. Suicide."

"It's research, then? For you, I mean."

Leonard smiled wryly. "Isn't everything?"

He slid the book into one of the pockets of his combats as he got to his feet. "Where are we going?"

"Who says we're going anywhere?"

Leonard glanced around. "This place has just about outlived its welcome, don't you think? You must have been here— what?—six hours already. Maybe seven."

"Make it eight."

"All the more reason."

"For what, exactly?"

"Coming for a drink."

IT WAS WHAT? NOT A CLUB, NOT JUST A BAR. THE FURNI- ture, comfortable enough, was generally old and scarred. Ciga- rette burns in the vinyl of the settee on which she perched uncomfortably. The place busy for early evening, Prior thought, the beginning of the week. Black, Asian, white. Quite a few men who looked as if they might be gay. Is that what Ben Leonard was? Gay? The earring. The bleached blond hair. She didn't think so. A lot of men wore earrings nowadays. And besides, the way she'd seen him looking at her once or twice. Not hiding it. Her breasts. Her neck. Prior wishing she were somewhere else, anywhere, but if not, if she had to be there, that she were wearing something other than that old faded top and the shapeless cords she'd been threatening to replace for six months now at least.

Leonard had left her there to go to the bar and got stalled on his way back with the drinks, laughing and talking with a couple he knew, the woman beautiful, Prior could see that, dark hair pulled back off her face, light honeyed skin, her hand touching the back of Leonard's wrist as she spoke.

Prior looked elsewhere. Wondered if she might get up and leave. "Come on," Leonard had said. "A quick drink before you go home. Just one. What have you got to lose?"

The music was low in the background, lacing everything together, the same persistent rhythm, the beat. No words. Something electronic. A synthesizer? She didn't know. How could she? The last time she had consciously listened to music, it had been to whom? Fine Young Cannibals? Simply Red?

"Here," Leonard said, handing her a cold bottle of beer before flopping down beside her. "Wasn't sure if you wanted a glass or not."

Prior shook her head. "This is okay."

"Then cheers." Clinking his bottle against hers, he drank.

His leg touched hers.

"So, what do you think of the place?" he asked.

"It's all right." She was holding herself stiffly, fingers clenched.

"Not been here before?"

She shook her head.

"Look," Leonard said, leaning in a little, "the other day. What I said, you know, about therapy. It was...I don't know...it's a bad habit of mine...one of many...saying the first thing that comes into my head."

Prior looked back at him, unsmiling. She wasn't going to make it any easier.

"Anyway, I'm sorry," Leonard said. "I'll try to button my tongue." Taking another swig at his beer, he laughed. "Although, I'd have to say, speaking professionally now, you do seem to be wound a little tight."

Prior was already on her feet. "Thanks for the drink," she said, setting down the bottle, contents largely untouched.

Leonard shook his head and sighed. "Maureen, come on, sit back down."

"No."

"Wait then and I'll come with you."

"What for? Stay here, talk to your friends. Read another poem."

Out in the street, she leaned back for a moment against the wall, hands pressing against the reassuring roughness of the brick.

Chapter 31

DOWLAND BROKE, SWEATING, FROM HIS HALF-SLEEPING, half-waking dream. The grimy sheet wrapped shroudlike around his hip and leg. The hairs on his belly slick and brittle with spunk. Spunk and sweat, the sweet stink of it rancid in the room. The curtains pulled across, closing out what little light there still was. He had lain down wanting to think of someone else—the policewoman perhaps, the one who had come there the week before, asking him all those questions about someone he didn't know, about that time before at the hotel. Yes, hand sliding over his cock, think about her, that's it, a pair of tits on her, no mistake. Something to get hold of, get your mouth round, bite into. That was it. Was it. Yes. But no, when he came, it wasn't her at all. Her face lost in a blur of jism and need. Eve. That fat cow, Eve. Why the fuck was he thinking of her? All the fucking time of her. The way she'd turned on him. All the times she'd been with him before. Loving it. Letting him. Luring him on. Come on, come on, come on.

Christ!

Fuck!

No!

He flicked the spunk from his hand to where it lay now, cold, along the inside of his leg. Always, as he came, the memory of her scabby sprawling flesh against his hands, the choked and stuttering gasps as she gulped for air. Fear and pleading in her eyes.

Please...

Please...

Please...

Oh, yes. Not again. Again.

The skin on his cock beaten red and raw.

With a groan, Dowland pushed himself sideways off the bed. His throat was dry, the backs of his legs were numb. In the bathroom he drank water from the tap, wiped himself down with a scrap of flannel. Closed his eyes, and as he did so, he almost fell. One hand against the rim of the bath, the other against the wall. His head spun and slowly he lowered himself to the floor, forehead pressing against the smoothness of the porcelain. Smooth and cold.

Dowland's eyes closed and, kneeling there, in supplication, he slept.

Five minutes.

Ten.

When he woke he was shivering and hurriedly he dressed. Shirt and trousers. Socks. A coat hanging behind the door. Old trainers: soft soles.

The picture of the Virgin Mary a little lopsided on the wall.

Dowland switched out the light, fingered his keys, locked the door. Outside it was dark enough.

Chapter 32

ANNA INGRAM LOOKED AT HERSELF IN THE MIRROR, THE way the velvet dress she was wearing clung to her hips, to say nothing of the amount of cleavage it revealed, and immediately had second thoughts. Dressing for Vincent was never easy: whether he was more likely to gush forth paeans of praise or condemn her for resembling the loosest woman this side of Nell Gwynn was as dependent on his whim as what she actually wore. But, given the sort of mood he'd been in after the previous day's brunch, caution seemed the wise approach.

She redressed herself in a floor-length linen skirt and cream brocade blouse that buttoned up to the neck. Her hair she coiled into a neat chignon. A touch of lipstick, the merest hint of perfume, soft leather flat-heeled shoes, and she was ready.

The early evening traffic leaving the city had thinned out to reasonable proportions, and she drove with the windows partly open, car stereo turned up high. Puccini. The quartet at the end of the third act of *La Bohème*. As she turned off along the narrow road leading to Vincent's house, the voices rose and fell across the fields and intertwined.

Usually, when Vincent heard her approaching, he would come to the door and welcome her; sometimes, if he had enjoyed an especially good day, with a glass of wine in hand. But this evening, there was no sign.

His car was there, parked just off the drive; the front door was ajar.

"Vincent?"

She stepped across the porch and into the large, low living room. Everything, as usual, was immaculately in place. A book had been allowed to rest on the arm of one of the chairs. In the kitchen, water dripped slowly from the tap. A plate and bowl stood draining beside the sink. A recipe book lay open on the kitchen table. *Finocchio alla Parmigiana.* Fennel and Parmesan gratin. The glass front of the oven was warm to the touch. The smell of cheese and garlic faint in the air.

Anna took down a glass and ran the tap until the water was truly cold; after she had turned it off as hard as she could, it continued to drip. A worn washer, she thought. Something Vincent will never fix himself. The water was cool, and for a moment she rested the glass against her forehead.

When she turned it was almost into Vincent's arms, and she gasped and dropped the glass and it shattered into pieces on the quarry-tiled floor.

"Vincent! For God's sake!"

"What?"

"What on earth are you doing, creeping up on me like that?"

"Creeping? I don't think I was creeping."

"I don't know what else you'd call it."

"Walking into my own house? My own kitchen? It's permissible, I suppose?"

"Where have you been, anyway?"

"Just for a walk. A stroll across the fields. It's quite a lovely evening, but perhaps you didn't notice. Other things on your pretty little mind."

"Vincent, don't bloody patronize."

"Is that what it was? More of a compliment, I'd have thought."

"Stop talking such nonsense," Anna said, "and don't smirk. Let me get the dustpan and brush and sweep up all this broken glass."

TEN MINUTES LATER THEY WERE SITTING IN THE LIVING room, each with a glass of wine. Blaine had set some piano music playing on the stereo: Joanna MacGregor sedately working her way through Byrd and Messiaen, Keith Jarrett's cool interpretations of Handel. A light breeze stirred the curtains and a narrow light slanted across the floor.

"So," Vincent said, "to what do I owe the honour? Monday nights, barring some special reason, we most usually attend to our separate lives."

"If that's what you want, I'll leave."

"No, no, that's not what I mean."

"Are you sure? Because if it is, there are a score of things I could be doing..." She was halfway out of her chair.

"Anna, Anna. Stay. Sit down, please."

Anna did as she was bid. Blaine began to talk about a meeting he was arranging with a Dutch printer he was considering using for a new book—a photographer from the Czech Republic whose work he'd seen a year ago, quite by chance. At this stage, the costs sounded reasonable, and if the quality could be maintained...well, he would have to see.

Anna countered with some gossip about comings and goings in the local arts world, most of which Blaine already knew. When he asked her about the progress of her next project—the contentiously titled "Artists' Wives"—she made a face. "All anyone can talk about is the viability of attracting the right amount of sponsorship. Never mind the quality of the work, or that much of it hasn't been adequately shown for years."

"Verily," Blaine said, "the Mammonites have taken over the world."

"Amen to that!"

"Here," Blaine said, rising to his feet. "Let me refresh your glass."

"Why not?"

When he was leaning close to her, bottle in hand, he said, "Why did you come here tonight? Really?"

"I don't know, I suppose I just took it into my head."

"Anna, you're like me. You don't *just* do anything. Not without thought."

A slight movement of the shoulders. "I was worried, I suppose."

"About what? This new show of yours?"

"No."

"Not about me?"

"When I left you yesterday, you seemed really down. Depressed. Angry, too."

"And you were concerned?"

"Yes. Is that wrong?"

"On the contrary. It's most considerate." Smiling, he moved away. "But you needn't have worried. All those people—it was more of a strain than usual, I suppose. And I was getting something of a migraine. I just needed to be alone. I'm sorry if I was rude."

Anna glanced down at her wrist, remembering the force with which Vincent's fingers had pressed against the skin. "The ex-policeman, Elder, he came to the Staithes show at the Castle..."

Blaine smiled. "A convert."

"He asked me about the weekend that woman disappeared. The one who was found strangled."

"What about it?"

"He asked me if I knew where you were."

Blaine's fingers tightened, almost imperceptibly, around the stem of his glass. "What did you say?"

"I told him you were in Dorset."

"So I was."

"With me."

"What?"

"I told him we were there together."

"What on earth for?"

"I don't know. I just did. I did it without thinking, I suppose."

"But you knew perfectly well I was there on my own."

"Yes, I know."

"Jesus!" Blaine put down his glass with a smack and began to pace the room.

"I could contact him, tell him I'd made a mistake."

"No. That would only make things worse. It's bad enough having him poking his nose into my affairs without giving him a reason to be more suspicious than he already is."

"I could explain I was a little flustered, answering his questions. Tell him it is more usual for the two of us to go together and I spoke without thinking. An honest mistake."

But Blaine was already shaking his head. "If he's any kind of detective, he'll know there's no such thing."

"What do you mean?"

"Honest mistakes, slips of the tongue. In a sense, they're like dreams. It's when we say what we really mean. No, Anna, you told a lie about being with me in Dorset that weekend because, deep down, you're as suspicious of me as Mr. Elder himself. And you thought I needed an alibi."

"Vincent, that's ridiculous."

"Is it?" He came toward her, a sardonic smile in his eyes. "I don't think so." Reaching out, he rested his hand above her heart. "I think somewhere here you believe I might be responsible. Guilty. And I'm touched that, under the circumstances, you think I should be saved."

Bending his head toward hers, he pressed his cold lips to her mouth in a kiss.

ANNA HAD BOUGHT HER HOUSE IN MAPPERLEY PARK JUST before property prices went sky high and had clung to it ever since. In the early days, to help with the mortgage, she had taken in lodgers—usually friends of friends or people she had met through work—but now, most of the time, she lived in her late-Victorian pile, as she referred to it, by herself. Some of the rooms on the upper floor were rarely used, unless some distant cousin fetched up in the city unannounced or a down-at-heel artist, whose work she liked, was in dire need of temporary studio space and a bed.

Ten or twelve years ago it had been a largely prosperous middle-class area, a bastion between the seedier St. Ann's on one side and Sherwood and Forest Fields on the other. But recently things had begun to change, and curb crawlers had become a more frequent sight, tracking the prostitutes who, at night, were taking over some of the streets as their own. In response to neighbourhood complaints, the police had begun clamping down for brief periods of time, stopping motorists and issuing warnings, making a show of noting down their registration. A week later the patrols were gone and the punters were back.

One of Anna's friends, who had moved into the area at around the same time, had just announced that she and her family were selling and moving out. Anna had done her best to dissuade them, but with no joy.

"If you had a thirteen-year-old daughter who was constantly being leered at by men from cars, asked if she was looking for business and how much she charged, you'd be going, too."

Anna thought she was probably right. She'd been trailed more than a few times herself, propositioned, too. It all lent to an atmosphere she grudgingly had to admit she liked less and less.

She arrived home from her visit to Vincent feeling distinctly off-key. He hadn't been angry, not in the same way as the previous day after his conversation with Brian Warren at the brunch, but, more importantly, he hadn't denied that her suspicions had any grounds.

Was she suspicious?

In her heart of hearts?

Her eyes closed for an instant as she remembered Blaine touching her, his hand fast across her breast...*somewhere here you believe I might be responsible. Guilty. And I'm touched that, under the circumstances, you think I should be saved.*

His kiss on her lips.

Suddenly she felt stifled; wanted air. Pulling on a coat, she went outside, slamming the heavy door at her back. In the short time she'd been inside, it had become dark. Patches of pavement showed up dull orange under the streetlights, with areas of deep shadow in between. Thick hedges and stone walls. Blackened trees.

Anna set off eastward, a route that took her quickly across two roads and then along a steep incline that rose toward the Woodborough Road. The houses here dwarfed her own: massive six- or eight-bedroom dwellings that had long since been converted into flats, each with long gardens that pushed them well back off the road.

A third of the way up she passed a woman walking slowly toward her close to the pavement edge, touting for business. As they were passing, the woman looked impassively into her face and then hastily away, and Anna realized she was little more than a girl. Seventeen? Eighteen at most. A pretty face, but pale with buried eyes.

Behind her, Anna heard a car slow almost to a halt before ac-
celerating slowly away, and, instinctively, she quickened her
pace.

She didn't know whether she wanted to blank all thoughts of
Blaine from her mind, or try to think rationally through what
little she knew. What she felt. Despite what she'd said to Elder,
she didn't believe, if Claire Meecham had been in one of his
classes, he would not, at the very least, have remembered her
name. No matter how self-absorbed he might be, he would have
known that, surely? So why then deny it outright? Unless there
was something there, something he wished to hide.

As she walked on, an image of the two of them, Blaine and
this woman whom she had never seen, other than in a patchy
newspaper photograph, formed clearly in her mind. The cottage in Dorset, high on a cliff overlooking the sea. A white
bedroom flooded with light, white walls, white tasselled cover
across the bed, the sound, rhythmic and repetitive, of the waves,
his hand on her skin...

Anna jumped, startled by a sound at her back, and turned.

A shadow moving close against the wall.

A sheet of discarded newspaper lifting in the wind.

Far down the street, the muted headlights of a car.

She hesitated, uncertain whether to turn around or go on.

If she reached Woodborough Road there would be more traffic, more people; she set off again up the hill and only a short
distance on heard behind her the fall of footsteps other than her
own.

The skin at the backs of her legs froze cold.

Looking over her shoulder she saw something—someone—
sliding from sight into the gateway to one of the gardens, an
arched gap in the high stone wall.

Anna held her breath and waited.

Nothing happened. No sound.

"Hello? Is there anybody there?"

Her voice sounded flat and small.

She took a pace back down the hill. Another. Still nothing. The sound, faint, of someone's breath, but was that her own?

One more step brought her level with the gateway, and as it did, a face materialized out of the dark.

Anna gasped and stumbled back, swung clumsily round and started to run. Not daring to stop, not daring to look round. Her arms flailed as she neared the point where the road levelled out and air choked raw from her lungs.

As she reached the corner a large shape loomed suddenly in front of her, and, even as she screamed, her arms were caught and held fast. She wriggled and kicked and screamed again.

"Anna? Anna, is that you?"

Recognizing Brian Warren's face, she threw herself against him and sobbed.

THEY SAT IN THE HIGH-CEILINGED SECOND-FLOOR LIVing room of Anna Ingram's house, every available light in the room switched on and the heavy velvet curtains drawn closed. Anna sat with a brandy glass in one hand, the other tight around her upper arm. Brian Warren sat across from her, his long legs angled somewhat awkwardly away from the restored chaise lounge, a glass of good whisky within reach.

Anna had washed her face in cold water, changed her top, brushed out her hair, waited until her pulse had steadied, then poured them both drinks and sat down.

She had said nothing to Warren other than the fact that something had spooked her and now she told him, as clearly as she could, what she had heard and seen.

"He meant you harm, then," Warren said when she'd finished. "That's what you think."

"It's not rational, I know. I mean, why should he? He could have thought I was a prostitute and wanted...I don't know, it could have been no more than that."

"You know prostitutes sometimes get attacked."

"Yes, I know."

"And, clearly, you thought he might attack you."

"Yes, but as I say, not for any reason. Not really. I just allowed myself to become scared, that's all."

Warren picked up his glass. "It's a shame, I realize, but perhaps you have to think again about walking around here after dark."

"Brian, it's where I live."

"I know."

"I can't allow myself to be marooned."

Warren nodded, understanding. "You'll report it to the police?"

"I don't know. I don't think so. I mean, what is there to really say?"

"I suppose you're right."

"Anyway, what were you doing round this way?" Anna smiled. "Aside from waiting to rescue damsels in distress."

Warren smiled an easy smile in return. "It's my bridge night. The club up on the Mansfield Road, near where the old lido used to be. One of the other members is a bit wonky on his pins. I usually walk him home, make sure he gets back safely. He's just around the corner from you here."

"Well, I'm glad you were there."

Warren raised his glass. "Me, too."

When he had finished his drink, Anna asked him if he would like another and he shook his head. "Very kind, but perhaps I'd better not. I can stay a bit longer, though, if you'd like. If it would make you feel any easier."

"No, it's all right."

"You're sure?"

"Brian, it's nice of you. But I'm fine now, really."

"Just as you say."

He hauled himself to his feet.

"There is just one favour," Anna said.

"Anything."

"Don't mention this to Vincent. You know what he's like. He'll only fuss."

"Of course not." He placed a finger across his lips. "Not a word."

At the door, he turned and kissed her gently on the top of the head.

"Goodnight, Brian. And thanks again."

"Goodnight."

When he had passed through the gate and out of sight, she locked and bolted the door and stood there for several moments before climbing the stairs.

Chapter 33

THE FLIGHT BACK FROM BARCELONA WAS TWICE DE-
layed, giving Elder ample opportunity to resist buying cheap
booze or overpriced cologne and to treat himself to another
chunk of *Sons and Lovers*. As he read on, he found himself beginning to sympathize more and more with his daughter's view
of Paul Morel, who was in danger of becoming a right little
know-it-all. Katherine was correct, too, he thought, about the
way Paul was messing about this girl he was seeing, this
Miriam—never knowing what he wanted and, it seemed to
Elder, too scared of the consequences. And his mother not
helping, not able to hide her resentment, one of her sons dead
by then and Paul, her favourite, being, she felt, taken from her.
Jealousy, that's what it was, plain and simple. The mother and
Miriam pulling in opposite directions and Paul dithering in the
middle. Not pulling any punches, either, the mother. What was
it she said to Paul when they were arguing? I've never had a
husband, not really. Then kissing him. Fervently, is that what
Lawrence had said?

Elder wondered how many times his own mother had kissed him after he was past the age of twenty or so? Oh, a peck on the cheek at Christmas, birthdays, the increasingly few times they met. As if, having done her job and brought him up as best she could, she—she and his father both—had been happy enough to step aside. Step back. Let him get on with his life just as they got on with theirs.

He had buried them both a little over ten years ago, his mother first, cancer; and then, little more than nine months later, his father, a heavy fall and with it the onset of pneumonia that stubbornly resisted antibiotics for too long; a catalogue of ensuing ills, too much pressure on his heart.

Elder folded down a corner of the page and slipped the book into his pocket; his flight had at last been called.

IT WAS EVENING BY THE TIME HE WAS BACK IN HIS FLAT in the city. There were three messages on his cell: Joanne, Jennie Preston, and Maureen Prior. When he phoned Joanne back all he got was her answerphone; Jennie Preston the same. Maureen Prior picked up at the second ring.

"Frank, we need to meet. Tomorrow, first thing." No niceties, no "Did you have a good trip?" "The super's got a meeting with the assistant chief constable at eleven; I've got to brief him before then."

"Usual place?"

"Half eight. Bacon cobs are on me."

Elder poured himself a small whisky and sat facing the blank, dark glass of the window, trying to marshal his thoughts. Only when his arm slipped off the edge of the chair and he jerked awake did he realize he'd dropped off to sleep.

Ten minutes later he was in bed, fast off.

MAUREEN PRIOR WAS THERE BEFORE HIM, PLACING HER order at the counter. "Bacon and tomato?" she asked Elder as he entered. "Bacon and sausage, or just plain bacon?"

"Plain bacon."

They sat in the farthest corner, the café quiet at that time; Prior smart today in a black trouser suit, black cotton top, black boots, her hair pulled back.

"It's the usual bullshit, Frank. Pressure trickling down. The force has not had a good press these last twelve months, you know that. Several high-profile cases dragging. What they need is a result. A good result. The super's going to be on me like a ton of bricks."

Elder nodded, sighed. HP Sauce with his bacon cob, yes or no? Having decided yes, no matter how hard he shook the bottle, no sauce would come out.

"Frank!"

"Yes?"

"Pay attention, will you?"

"I'm sorry, it's just this..."

"Here. For pity's sake give it to me." Taking the sauce bottle from him she hit her hand smack against the bottom.

"Thanks."

Maureen shook her head. "Johns—what do you think?"

Elder leaned back. "I just don't know. The whole business, I don't know if we're any closer or further away. And what I learned about Johns—all right, there's a clear pattern of sadistic relationships, sadistic on his part at least, women held almost in thrall. But all that does is confirm what we more or less know."

"That's not what I want to hear."

"I'm sorry."

"Singer, Dowland, your pal Mr. Blaine..." She shook her head. "Johns was our best bet."

"Maybe he still is."

Prior released a long, slow breath. "Is that what I tell the super? Is that the best we've got?"

"For now."

"Jesus, Frank."

"All right, we keep digging at Johns. And meantime, retrench, regroup. Start going through everything again. From the beginning, if necessary. See what we've missed."

Prior pushed away her plate. "I haven't got the taste for this any more."

JENNIE PRESTON REACHED HIM MIDMORNING AND HE DID his best, without any great success, to reassure her about the progress they were making.

"Claire's daughter," Jennie said, "Jane. She's coming up to stay with me. For the funeral."

"They've agreed to release the body, then?"

"Yes. I never said thank you, did I? For your help."

"That's okay. I don't think it was down to me at all."

"James is coming over from Australia. They'd like to meet you. Talk about the investigation."

"I don't know..."

"I thought, if you were coming to the funeral."

"I'm not sure. They might be better off talking to someone else."

"They want to talk to you."

Elder was silent.

"You will come, though?" Jennie said. "To the funeral?"

"I'll try."

"Wilford Crematorium, twelve o'clock, Friday."

"All right, if I possibly can."

"Joanne's promised to come. She said she might try and bring Katherine."

"Like I say, if I can."

Elder phoned the salon and asked for Joanne.

"She hasn't come in today," the receptionist said, "she wasn't feeling too well."

Elder walked through the centre of town, along Warser Gate and Bottle Lane, down past St. Peter's church, and then across

Maid Marian Way and into The Park. At first he thought there was nobody home. It was only after he had rung and knocked several times that Joanne came to the door.

She was wearing a cream-coloured robe, tied at the waist, bare feet just showing underneath. Her hair was held back by a broad green band.

"Frank," she said, surprised, and he smelt the alcohol on her breath.

"They said at the salon you weren't well."

"And you came round to see how I was, how sweet."

"What's the problem?"

"Oh, you know." She wafted a hand vaguely through the air. "One of those days. Didn't feel up to it, I'm afraid."

Elder stood his ground, feeling slightly foolish, not knowing whether to stay or leave.

"Well," Joanne said, stepping back. "I suppose you'd better come inside."

Going into the living room she slipped and Elder steadied her, his hand on her arm.

There were magazines open on the settee and scattered here and there on the floor. A few old newspapers. A copy of *The Da Vinci Code.*

"Having a bit of a clear-out?"

She looked at him as if through a haze. "A drink, Frank. Since you're here, let me get you a drink."

There was a wineglass, a third full, next to a bottle of unoaked chardonnay. There were other glasses, last night's blurred with lipstick, on different surfaces around the room. Ashtrays in need of emptying.

"I'll just get you a fresh glass," Joanne said.

"It doesn't matter."

"Don't tell me you're drinking it out of the bottle now?" Said with an attempt at a smile.

"For Christ's sake, Joanne, it's scarcely eleven in the morning. I don't need a drink."

"God, Frank, you're such a prude." Her hand shook slightly as she filled her glass. "In fact, you've got worse. You know that? Since you went down to that fucking place. Fucking Cornwall. You used to know how to have a good time, have fun."

"Is that what this is?" he said, looking round the room. "Having fun? Hanging around the house half-dressed because you're too pissed and pilled up to go to work? Suddenly that's your idea of fun?"

Sitting down on the settee, she misjudged the height and landed awkwardly, spilling wine over her hand and down the front of her robe.

"Suddenly, Frank? I don't think it's so sudden, do you?"

Slipping the catch, he slid back the glass door to the garden, letting in fresh air. "Why don't I make some coffee?" he said.

"Because I don't want any fucking coffee."

"Suit yourself."

In the kitchen, he found a jar of Carte Noire and set the kettle to boil. There was milk in the fridge but little enough else. Butter, several small yoghurts, mineral water, a tub of what might be hummus, half an avocado turning brown.

He made two coffees regardless and took them back in. Joanne was sitting at one end of the settee, her legs angled tightly up in front of her, smoking a cigarette.

Elder put her coffee on the table within reach and carried his own across to one of two S-shaped chairs.

For a while neither of them spoke.

Joanne stubbed out her cigarette and picked up her coffee. One sip and she made a face. "Sugar, Frank. There's no sugar."

He fetched sugar.

When he came close she caught hold of his hand. "I'm not always like this, you know. I'm really not. Well, you know. I think you know. I mean, I couldn't be. The job and everything. The salon. It's just that sometimes…"

Her voice drifted away. When he freed his hand, her nails had made small indentations in his skin.

"Sometimes it gets to me, you know." A wan smile for a moment lightened her face. "All this."

"It was what you wanted."

"Was it, Frank?"

"The salon, the house. Martyn."

Joanne's laugh broke harsh from her throat. "Two out of three, then, Frank. I suppose that's not so bad."

Tears appeared at the corners of her eyes and began running slowly down her face; instead of going to comfort her, Elder stayed where he was. He'd made the coffee too strong; it was acrid but strangely without taste.

Joanne found a screwed-up tissue in the pocket of her robe; sniffed, dabbed, blew her nose. "No use crying over spilled years, eh Frank? What do you think?"

Elder was remembering a game he used to play as a kid: ten places you'd rather be than here.

Joanne put the coffee aside and reached for the wine. Another cigarette. "Jennie, Frank. She manage to get hold of you?"

"Yes."

"She wants you to go to the funeral, I think."

"She said."

"You'll go?"

"Maybe."

"You should. She's nice, Jennie. I like her."

"Yes."

"Attractive, don't you think?"

"I suppose so."

"She likes you, Frank. Sympathetic, that's what she said. Handsome, too." Joanne smiled. "Play your cards right and you never know."

He knew he shouldn't say it, but he did. "She's with someone, isn't she? More your style, that, than mine."

"Touché, Frank. But as it happens, Jennie and Derek…these last couple of years, pretty much like brother and sister, the way I understand it."

"That's their business."

"Suit yourself." With a swish of robe, Joanne got to her feet. "I meant what I said, you know, about you coming round. It was a sweet thing to do." She was standing close to him, close enough for either of them to have reached out a hand. "What you said before, about going out for dinner…you don't fancy this evening, I suppose?"

"I can't, I'm afraid."

"Never mind, it was just a thought."

"I ought to go."

"Yes, all right."

At the door, he stopped and turned. "You'll be okay?"

"No, I'm going to sit in the bath and slit my wrists. Of course, I'll be okay."

Perversely, the sun was shining as he stepped out onto the street. The trees in blossom or in bud. A young woman walked past pushing a small child asleep in a buggy, head to one side. An elderly man with a dog said hello as Elder passed. Ordinary people leading ordinary lives.

ELDER ATE AN EARLY SUPPER AT THE ITALIAN CAFÉ IN Sneinton Market, helping the pasta down with a bottle of wine. It was just beginning to darken by the time he had wandered home. Strange to call it that: a strange sort of home, with little in it, aside from clothing, that was his.

He tried to read but found himself unable to concentrate, the earlier encounter with Joanne forever sidling into his mind. The usual rubbish on TV. He picked up the book again, but soon set it aside.

Outside, the temperature had dropped again, and he walked briskly to keep warm, down past the ice arena to the round-about and the canal, along the towpath to the Trent. He stood for a while, leaning on the bridge, looking along the river past the forest grounds toward the east. How many miles before it flowed into the sea?

A shiver ran through him and he turned and headed back, collar up against the wind.

Indoors, a shot of Jameson to help him sleep.

He was just drowsing off when the phone startled him back to life. The body of a woman had been found in some allotment gardens just north of St. Ann's, not that far from Mapperley Park.

Chapter 34

IT WAS A CIRCUS. UNIFORMED POLICE, PARAMEDICS, scene of crime officers, detectives from both regular CID and Force Crime Directorate. Close between a patch of new crop potatoes and some burgeoning shallots, a tent had been erected enclosing the body. Lights running off a small generator. Enough white protective clothing to suggest a revival meeting of the Ku Klux Klan.

Lewis Reardon, recently promoted to detective inspector, was in charge; his first murder as senior investigating officer and perhaps making himself heard too much as a result. Probably not keen on Maureen Prior being there either, though so far she'd been careful to stand aside, only offering advice when asked.

It had been Prior who had called Elder. No certainty there was any link with their own investigation, but she wanted him on hand in case.

Spotting him at the edge of the cordon she waved him through.

The dead woman was of mixed race, most probably in her forties; she was lying on her back in a shallow trench, with one leg twisted beneath her, her head at a sharp angle to the rest of her body. From the waist down she was naked; her blouse had been torn open to expose her breasts, her bra pulled down. Her eyes were open.

"Poor woman," Prior said softly, her breath just visible on the night air.

"Do we know who she is?" Elder asked.

Prior shook her head.

A short way off, Reardon was talking to the pathologist, the crime scene manager standing beside them. Every now and then there was a small flash from inside the tent as photographs were taken. Crime scene officers were beginning to take swabs and samples.

His initial briefing over, Reardon came to where Elder and Maureen Prior were standing. He was an inch or so below six foot, broad shoulders but slim hips, a body that seemed to taper away till it reached his black leather shoes, polished earlier, but now blotched with mud.

"Dead less than three hours," Reardon said. "Rigor's barely started."

Elder looked down at his watch: it was fifteen minutes past midnight, Thursday morning.

"You know Frank?" Prior said.

"By reputation," Reardon said.

He and Elder shook hands.

"What are you thinking?" Prior asked. "She was on the game?"

"Looks that way. One of the PCs is pretty sure he's seen her round and about. Cranmer Street, Mapperley Road."

"And she brought her punters here?"

"It's possible. Either that or the body was dumped. Once

we've had a proper look at all the marks and tracks, we might know better."

"What did the pathologist say about cause of death?" Elder asked.

"Strangulation."

"Ligature or manual?"

"Manual, looks like," Reardon said.

He caught a glance pass between Prior and Elder.

"Something I should know?"

Prior told him about Richard Dowland.

AN HOUR LATER, NO MORE, THE TELEPHONE DRAGGED Tom Whitemore from his bed.

"Don't answer it," Marianne, his wife, said, reaching out an arm toward him as, sluggishly, he pushed aside the blankets and rolled his legs around till his feet touched the floor. Blankets and sheets—somehow a duvet was never quite comforting enough.

Standing, Whitemore listened, grunted a few monosyllabic responses, then put down the phone.

"What is it?" Marianne was sitting up now, tugging free the undershirt she slept in from where sweat had stuck it lightly to her body. She liked to sleep with the window open, Tom with it closed. The last thing he did each night was go round all the downstairs windows and make sure they were locked; bolt and lock both doors: He knew too well what was out there and she did not.

"One of mine," Whitemore said, zipping up his trousers, tucking in his shirt.

"In trouble?"

"So it appears." He sat down on the bed to pull on his socks.

"Serious?"

Leaning across, Whitemore kissed her on the forehead and gave her arm a squeeze. "Get back to sleep."

Switching on the upstairs light, he pushed the door to the twins' room quietly open. Andy lay almost sideways on the upper bunk, thumb stuck in his mouth; underneath, Felix had wriggled himself fully upside down and wrong way around, one of his feet pushed under the pillow, the other on top. Carefully, Whitemore eased his son's thumb from his mouth and kissed them both.

Downstairs, he lifted a well-worn leather jacket from the crowded set of pegs near the front door and pulled it on. Outside, the air struck cold and the car spluttered twice before the ignition caught and held. There were precious few stars in the sky.

The rendezvous was in the Portland Leisure Centre car park, off Meadow Way. Lewis Reardon and two other detectives, Maureen Prior and a man Whitemore failed to recognize. A civilian?

Reardon he knew by sight—a coming man. Prior introduced Frank Elder and the two men shook hands. There was a set of Polaroids in Reardon's pocket and, for Whitemore's benefit, he spread them across the roof of one of the cars.

Whitemore looked and nodded.

"We know who she is?" he asked. The same question Elder had asked before.

By then they did.

A shoulder bag had been found several allotments away, chewed up a little by one of a pair of goats that was kept tethered there. Condoms, KY Jelly, cigarettes and a disposable lighter, a couple of ready-rolled joints, a credit card in the name of Ms. L. Carne.

Lorraine Carne. Known to her pimp and boyfriend as Lo. He had the grace to shed a few tears as he asked the officer who'd rousted him from his bed where the cash had gone from her bag. Hundred, hundred and fifty she'd've had in there, no question.

"You really reckon Dowland for this?" Whitemore asked.

"After what happened before," Prior said, "Eve Ward—it's got to be at least a possibility."

Whitemore looked at Reardon.

"Worth a pull," Reardon said. "That at least. 'Less you got reason to say otherwise."

Whitemore shook his head.

They got into their cars.

A FOX LOOKED TOWARD THEM FROM THE END OF THE street, temporarily blinded by the lights. Red brush aglow. It stood a full half minute before trotting nonchalantly on, into the narrow alley and out of sight. Hunters, but not for him.

Fists hammered on the door.

A woman's voice sang out from the house opposite: if they didn't shut it she'd call the fucking police.

Reardon knocked again and a downstairs light came on. A few moments later a scrawny ginger-haired man in T-shirt and boxer shorts dragged open the door, yawning, and scratching between his legs.

"Not you," Tom Whitemore said, and the man stood to one side.

Pushing past him, they went quickly along the narrow corridor and up the uncarpeted stairs. Whitemore knocked on the door and called Richard Dowland's name. There was a sound, not easy to decipher, from inside, but no clear reply.

The door moved open at Whitemore's touch.

Dowland was huddled, crouching, in the farthest corner, hands across his mouth, babbling, his face wet with tears and snot.

"Richard," Whitemore said, cautiously approaching, his voice low and even. "Richard, it's okay."

With as much care as he had earlier taken his son's thumb from his mouth, he moved Dowland's hands away from his face.

"I've been a bad..." Dowland said, blinking. "I've been a bad boy."

THE NEAREST INTERVIEW ROOM WAS AT THE CENTRAL Division police station. Dowland was cuffed and put into the back of a car, white faced and frightened. He shivered waiting for the car to drive off, and when it did he began crying; when he got out of the car at the station, the crying had stopped, but he was still shivering. Tom Whitemore took off his jacket and put it round Dowland's shoulders but it didn't appear to make any difference.

Whitemore took Reardon to one side. "Before you start questioning him, I want to make sure there's somebody there he knows."

"He'll have a solicitor, what more's he need?"

"I said, someone he knows. Someone he can trust. He'll likely go to pieces else and then what good'll he be? Or anything he says."

Reardon grudgingly agreed. "Just make it sharpish, that's all."

Whitemore called Ben Leonard on his phone.

THE DUTY SOLICITOR WAS WAITING AT THE POLICE STA-tion entrance, eating a kebab from the late-night kiosk near the square. A queue of mid-week clubbers, mostly students, stood waiting for taxis at the far side of Mansfield Road, by one of the entrances to the Victoria Centre.

"This my client?" the solicitor asked, licking chilli sauce from his fingers.

Raising his eyebrows, he screwed up the paper from his kebab and, not seeing anywhere to dump it, pushed it down into his briefcase with his papers and his phone.

Dowland was hurried inside.

"Get you anything?" Reardon said, once they were in the interview room.

Eyes down toward the floor, Dowland shook his head.

"Tea," Whitemore said. "Richard likes a cup of tea. Two sugars, that right, Richard?"

At a nod from Reardon, the uniformed officer who'd been standing just inside the door went off in search of a brew.

Elder and Maureen Prior were sitting in an adjacent room. "Hang about if you want," Reardon had said. "No skin off my nose."

They had elected to stay.

Ben Leonard arrived, minutes later, had a quick conversation with Tom Whitemore, spoke quietly to Dowland and took a seat close to his side.

Using his thumbnail, Reardon broke the cellophane wrapping on two audio tapes and stripped it away, slotted the tapes into place in the dual recorder fixed to the wall.

"This interview," he began, "started at one forty-seven, Thursday the twelfth of May."

After the usual admonitions, Reardon cleared his throat. "So, Richard, where were you earlier this evening?"

No answer.

"Richard? You going to tell me?"

No answer.

"Earlier this evening, where were you?"

No answer.

Reardon repeated the question, with slight variations, another half a dozen times, eliciting the same response.

"You might tell your client, Mr. Logan, it would be in his best interests to answer my questions."

"My client," said the solicitor, leaning forward, "is within his rights not to say anything." There was a piece of meat wedged between his back teeth and, try as he might, he couldn't pry it free.

"Why don't you drink your tea, Richard?" Ben Leonard said, leaning toward him. "No sense letting it get cold."

Reardon scowled.

Dowland looked at the mug of tea as if seeing it for the first time; his hand was shaking so much when he picked it up that it spilled down his fingers and back along his wrist.

"Jesus!" Reardon muttered beneath his breath.

Two gulps and Dowland set the mug back down.

"This evening," Reardon said, impatiently. "Where were you?"

"N...n...nowhere."

"Nowhere? You had to be somewhere?"

Dowland turned toward Leonard, mouth open, eyes wide.

"What did you do this evening, Richard?" Tom Whitemore asked. "Stay in? Watch TV?"

Dowland nodded.

"Went out for a bit later, though? Stretch your legs? Get a bit of air? Not a bad night for a stroll."

"I'm sorry," Dowland said, so quiet it scarcely registered on the tape.

"Say again?" Reardon said sharply.

"I'm sorry," Dowland said, louder this time.

"I bet you are," Reardon said. "I just bet you are."

Dowland glanced at him briefly, then let his head drop back down.

"Tell me what happened," Reardon said. "When you went out."

Dowland's hands were interlocked but moving, bitten-down fingernails scraping back and forth across the insides of his wrists, scoring the skin.

"Take your time, Richard," Ben Leonard said. "Take as much time as you want."

Reardon shot him a look that said keep the fuck out of this.

"Take your time," Leonard said again, resting a hand for a moment on Dowland's shoulder.

"I...I went for a walk," Dowland said.

"A walk?" Reardon echoed.

"Ye-yes."

"Where did you go?"

Dowland looked round at Leonard then at Whitemore, but this time neither of them intervened.

"Tell us where you went, Richard," Reardon said, trying for the same modulation Whitemore had used earlier. "Where you're not supposed to go, was it? Where you know you're not supposed to go."

"Yes."

"Where's that exactly, Richard?"

"You know. He knows."

"Tell me. Won't you tell me?" Reardon knowing they needed it on the tape.

"Up round, you know, St. Ann's, the Forest." The answer slow in coming, accompanied by more scratching, Dowland's head moving agitatedly from side to side.

"And that's where you went? St. Ann's?"

Dowland nodded.

"Richard, that's where you went this evening?"

Nothing.

"Richard..."

"Yes. Yes."

"It's okay, Richard," Leonard said. "Take it easy." Reaching slowly across the table, he laid one of his hands on Dowland's. "Don't do that. You're hurting yourself."

The inside of Dowland's left wrist was raw, pinpoints of blood showing through the skin.

"Tell us what happened," Tom Whitemore said. "In your own time. Okay?"

They thought he would never start and then he did.

"I never meant to go up there, you got to believe me. Don't know how I even got there, the graveyard, you know? Cemetery, up by Mansfield Road. I'd had a drink, a drink or two, down in town and just sort of wandered..."

He looked at Tom Whitemore as if for guidance and White-more nodded gently back at him and waited.

"Course I saw the girls, all down Forest Road, you know, where they go. Standing round, waiting for cars and that, and I thought no, that's not right, you're not allowed, you mustn't go there and so I suppose I crossed the other way and..."

"The other way across the Mansfield Road?" Reardon asked.

"Yeah, that's right, must've been. I was just walking, right? Like I said. Didn't mean nothin'. Walkin' an' I saw this woman. I'd seen her before. Followed her. I know I shouldn't. But I followed her. She never saw me, not then. An' I watched her. Watched her and..."

Dowland's hands came up to his face as the tears returned in gulping sobs that shook his body. His head moving side to side behind his hands. "I'm sorry, I'm sorry..." The words muffled, mumbled, blurred.

Ben Leonard looked across meaningfully at the solicitor, and the solicitor said, "We should take a break."

"Yes, yes." Reardon was already on his feet. "This interview suspended at two-thirteen."

THIRTY MINUTES LATER THEY WERE BACK. DOWLAND had made some attempt to wash, to wake himself up in the interim; the front of his shirt was wet and so was his hair.

"You okay now?" Tom Whitemore asked. "Okay to carry on?"

Dowland nodded.

"Good," Reardon said. "Now, Richard, you were telling us about this woman, the one you followed—where was that? Where did you see her, can you remember?"

Dowland shook his head.

"Somewhere to the right of Mansfield Road, you said. Is that correct? Just because of the tape, if you could answer properly..."

"Yeah. Yeah, that's right."

"Mapperley, then?"

"Yeah."

"You remember the name of the road? The road where you saw her first?"

"No. I'm sorry. I dunno."

"And you followed her, that's what you said?"

"Yes."

"She was looking for business?"

"Yeah. Course. What else she be doin'?"

"So did you speak to her or what? What happened?"

"No, I just...I just followed her and then, then I hid like, in this garden, watching."

"You were just watching her or watching her with somebody? Was she with somebody? You were watching her with someone?"

Dowland shook his head emphatically. "No, no. Not like that. I never done that."

"And this garden? It was, what, like an allotment? An allotment garden?"

"No, I dunno. I don't think so. You mean like all veg an' that? No, no, I don't know. It might've been, I dunno."

"And the woman, did she see you watching her? Is that what happened?"

"Yeah, she might. I never meant her to, but yeah, she might've, yeah."

"So what happened then? Did she get angry? Start shouting?"

"No, not shouting, no."

"Calling you names? Did she start calling you names, maybe? Lose her temper?"

But Dowland was shaking his head again, pushing his fingers up through his hair, scratching the spots on his face. Starting to rock, forward and back, on his chair.

"Is that when you hit her? Is that why? Because she was angry, calling you names?"

"No. No." Dowland slammed his forearms down hard against the tabletop. "Why're you saying that? Don't say that. It's not right. It's not fair. It's not fair."

"Richard, it's okay. It's all right now. You can tell me. Tell me."

Dowland lowered his face into his arms. "I'm sorry," he said, just audibly. "I'm sorry," through a slew of tears.

Ben Leonard stayed with Dowland, attempting to comfort him, a uniformed officer looking on. The solicitor was back outside, smoking a cigarette. Along with Tom Whitemore, Reardon joined Elder and Maureen Prior in the small adjoining room, their faces, all the faces save for Lewis Reardon's, pale in the artificial light.

"So," Reardon said, "we get a warrant, right? Search his flat."

SEVERAL HOURS LATER, MORNING TRAFFIC BUILDING UP outside the building, buses logjammed front to rear in every direction, two of Reardon's team arrived back with broad smiles on their faces and, each one secure inside plastic, a pair of broken-down size nine no-name trainers with dark mud caught between the grooves of the sole.

Chapter 35

IT WAS THE SAME YOUNG OFFICER AS BEFORE, ENJOYING the chance to wind up a superior. "Your boyfriend's downstairs again," he said, and ducked back before Maureen Prior could throw anything.

Ben Leonard was the most conservatively dressed she'd ever seen: dark blue chinos and a pale green shirt, a plain gray baseball cap covering most of his blond hair.

"Dowland," he said. "You're not going to charge him. You can't."

Prior shook her head. "It's not my case."

"It's your concern. It bloody should be."

Two officers walked casually past, feigning disinterest.

"Here," Prior said. "If we're going to talk, let's not do it here."

There was a small windowless room along the corridor that was used by temporary support staff in emergencies. Now it was a quarter full of reams of copy paper and old files. No chairs.

"You saw what he was like," Leonard said. "Something like this, you can't believe he was responsible."

"He's done it before."

"That was a one-off."

"That's what you believe?"

"Yes. Yes, I do."

"I don't see how you can be so sure."

"Look, someone like Dowland, it's all up here." Leonard tapped the side of his head. "Fantasy. Okay, he'll watch, if he can. Get close. But where it plays out, it's in his head. Whatever happened with Eve Ward, whatever triggered him off, in part that was down to the fact that he knew her, he'd been with her before. In his mind, they had some kind of relationship. Lover, mother, whatever. Ask me, that's why he reacted as extremely as he did when she turned on him, why he snapped."

"I still don't see why that couldn't happen again."

"This woman," Leonard said, "Richard didn't know her, did he?"

"We don't know that."

"You ought to. Somebody ought to."

Prior shook her head again and sighed. "You're talking to the wrong person. Lewis Reardon, he's the SIO. Talk to him. Or Tom Whitemore, you know him after all."

Leonard looked at her; drew a breath. "Okay. I'll talk to Tom."

The conversation was over but neither of them moved.

"The other night…" Leonard began.

"Don't…"

"The other night…I really should learn to bite my tongue. I'm sorry."

"It doesn't matter."

"It does. To me." He grinned, the tension broken. "I was having a pretty nice time…"

"Well, thanks."

"I enjoyed your company."

"I can't think why."

Leonard smiled. "You want me to count the ways? All right. You're your own person, that's one. That's important. You're dedicated to your job, I like that, too. I like talking to you. It's hard work sometimes, but that's okay. I don't mind that. I'm used to it, you could say. And you're attractive." He laughed. "I think you do your best to hide it sometimes, but it's true."

Prior was shaking her head. "You know what?"

"What?"

"You're full of shit."

Leonard clung to his smile. "So are we all."

"Yes, well, I've got enough shit of my own, thanks very much. I don't need somebody else's."

"Sometimes it helps."

Prior's mouth set in a line before she spoke. "I don't want analyzing, Ben. That's not who I am. A prospective client, is that what you call them these days? A customer? Someone to be analyzed and saved and, okay, if you can screw them on the side, that's a bonus."

"Maureen, listen. That's not..."

"Because I've been analyzed. Five years of it. More. And, as for me, it was all a waste of space and time and I'm not about to go down that road again. I'm not going to get even close. Is that clear?"

"Yes, I suppose..."

"Is that clear?"

"Yes."

"Good. Now what I suggest you do, you're really worried about Dowland, get in touch with Tom Whitemore ASAP."

"Okay," Leonard said quietly. "I'll do that. Thanks."

Once he'd left, Prior went to the Ladies and locked herself in one of the cubicles so that no one could see her tears.

AFTER SEVERAL HOURS OF INDECISION, ANNA INGRAM phoned Elder and left a message on his cell. Fifteen minutes later, he called her back. "Last night's murder, you said you might have some information."

"It may not be anything," Anna said, "but when I heard about what had happened on the radio..."

"Where are you now?"

"At work. At the castle."

"Okay, I'll come to you."

"You're sure? Because I can always..."

"No. Give me half an hour. I'll be there."

Elder broke the connection and dialled Maureen Prior's number. "I've just had a call from Anna Ingram..."

"Blaine's friend?"

"That's right. She says she's got some information about last night."

"You passed her on to Reardon?"

"I thought I'd go and talk to her myself. Only thing, I don't want Reardon to think I'm going behind his back, poking my nose in."

"I shouldn't worry. He's busy sweating Dowland. But I'll make sure he knows what you're doing. Anything pertinent, you'll pass it on?"

"First thing."

ANNA INGRAM'S OFFICE, WHICH SHE SHARED WITH TWO others, was at the top of several flights of winding stairs and along a high, narrow corridor. When finally you arrived, the panelled door opened on to a good-sized room with ornate plasterwork in need of some significant repair. In one corner, a bucket stood ready to catch the drips which came quite liberally through the roof whenever the wind drove the rain in the wrong direction. A large vase of dried flowers stood at the centre of a tiled fireplace. Exhibition posters hid any suggestion of damp on the walls.

Anna was wearing the same purple skirt as when Elder had

last seen her, this time with a loose-sleeved lavender top; her red hair had been allowed to fall, long, to her shoulders.

One of her colleagues was down in London, a meeting at the Hayward; the other, at Anna's request, was enjoying a longer-than-usual coffee break in the cafeteria.

"I hope this isn't going to be a waste of your time," she said, shaking Elder's hand.

"I doubt that," Elder said, and smiled.

From where he sat, partly facing the window, he could see strips of pale cloud straggling across the sky.

Anna fidgeted with some pencils on her desk before beginning, her voice unusually hesitant. "What it was," she said, "something happened the other evening. Monday. I wasn't going to say anything about it, report it or anything, but then after what happened..."

Breaking off, she looked at Elder uncertainly.

"Go on," he said.

"Well, I was out walking, where I live, Mapperley Park. It was quite late, I suppose. Half past eleven, perhaps. I'd just come back from seeing Vincent, and there'd been a bit of a row. I felt I needed to clear my head."

"Uh-huh."

"It was when I was walking up toward the Woodborough Road; I had this feeling—I don't know—not that I was being followed exactly, but that someone was watching me. Silly, really. I mean, I looked around and there didn't seem to be anyone there. All the same, I got sort of spooked, and then I thought I heard this sound, behind me, and out of the corner of my eye, I saw something moving—farther back along the street, but close, quite close, behind this doorway, and when I looked—maybe I shouldn't have, I don't know, perhaps it was foolhardy—but there was somebody there, staring out. Staring back at me. And I ran. I didn't think, I just ran."

"And what happened? He followed you?"

"No. No. I don't think so. I didn't see him again. I just ran and ran on down the hill until I bumped into Brian."

"Brian?"

"Brian Warren. He's Vincent's accountant. At least he used to be. Until he retired. They've been friends for years."

"And you bumped into him?"

"Yes. On the corner of Cyprus Road."

"What was he doing there?"

"He'd been playing bridge. The club where he plays, it's not far away."

"So he was what? On his way home?"

"Yes. He'd just walked a friend home first."

"And then he met you."

"Yes. You can't imagine how relieved I was, seeing him. Well, not at first, of course. When he grabbed me…"

"He grabbed you?"

"To stop me crashing into him. I was running full pelt."

Elder shifted his weight on the chair. "The other man, the one whose face you saw, do you think you'd be able to recognize it again?"

"Oh, yes, I think so."

"Can you describe him now?"

"I can try."

"Was he white? Black? Asian?"

"White, definitely white. His face was thin; sallow, I suppose you'd say. Pale. His skin was pale and sort of yellowish, though that could have been the effect of the street light, of course. And he had what looked like a swelling around his eye. His left eye."

"How about his hair? What colour was his hair?"

"I don't remember."

"And how old was he, would you say?"

Anna looked toward the fireplace. "That's difficult. It was one of those ageless faces. You know, not young, not old."

"Thirties, forties?"

"Thirty rather than forty, I suppose. I can't be more definite than that, I'm sorry."

"You would recognize him, though? You're certain of that?"

"I think so, yes. It is important, then?"

"It might be."

"You think he might be the same person who attacked that poor woman?"

"It's possible."

Anna shuddered. "Do you know who he is?" she asked. "Do you have any idea who he is?"

"We might."

She sighed. "I just hate the idea of being frightened; frightened to go outside my own home."

"I know."

"And I hate it when all these people go on about how everywhere's becoming more violent, more dangerous. You know, how you daren't go into the city centre on a Friday or a Saturday night. If you do go out, be careful not to look anyone directly in the eye, don't speak to anybody you don't know. It's ridiculous. You can't live like that; I don't want to live like that. And I'm always telling people it's not really that bad, you're exaggerating. But then something happens—that man, for instance, it was in the paper just a few days ago—somewhere innocuous, Nuneaton, I think—he remonstrated with this group of youths who were damaging his sister's car and they turned on him and killed him. Just like that. Beat him until he was dead. It's unbelievable. You'd like to think it was unbelievable, but it happened. It's happening."

She was shaking a little and there was a suggestion of tears in her eyes. Elder made to go and comfort her, but she waved him away. "It's all right, I'm all right."

"Do you want to go and get a cup of coffee or something? Some fresh air?"

Anna smiled. "Now that I have an escort, you mean?"

Elder smiled back. "I'm sure you'll be safe here."

Anna pushed back her chair. "If a woman can't feel safe in her own castle, where can she?"

They walked down past the swathe of lawn and the ornamental flower beds, along the path toward the bandstand, trees on either side.

"So," Elder said, remembering, "how's the work on Harold Knight coming along?"

"Oh, slowly. More slowly than it should, I'm afraid. My publisher's already let me slip past one deadline and now it seems I might have to try and renegotiate another."

"Your publisher? That's not Vincent?"

The thought made Anna smile.

"Not his kind of book?" Elder said.

"Not really. Photography, that's Vincent's niche. And he does well at it. As well as a small publisher can. But the idea of having yet another way to earn Vincent's disapproval..." She laughed. "It doesn't bear thinking about."

A little way past the bandstand, they stopped and sat on one of the wooden benches. Despite a wavering sun, there was still a clear nip in the air. Anna had slipped a cardigan over her shoulders when she left the office and now she put her arms through the sleeves and buttoned it at the front.

"When we were talking before," Elder said, "you mentioned something about yourself and Vincent having a row."

"Oh, yes..." Anna wafted a hand. "It was nothing."

"But enough to upset you."

"Did it upset me? I suppose it did, a little."

"Enough to give you a headache. Send you out of the house to clear your head."

Anna waited until a slow crocodile of small, blazered children had filed past.

"I can't even remember what it was about now, what set him off. Nothing probably." She made a slight sighing sound. "It doesn't seem to take much nowadays. Mondays especially."

"Why Mondays?"

"It's when he goes to see his mother. Margaret. Every Monday without fail. Sometimes other days as well. But Mondays always."

"And this is in Dorset?"

"Oh, no, Derbyshire."

"I thought you said something about a family place in Dorset? Maybe I misunderstood?"

"No. That's right. It's been in Vincent's family since, oh, the twenties. Earlier, perhaps. But they moved up to Derbyshire when Vincent was ten or eleven, I think, and that's where he lived until he went off to university—not that you'd know it to hear him speak. The house in Dorset they kept on for holidays."

"And Derbyshire's where his mother still lives?"

"Yes. Quite a way north, between Buxton and Bakewell."

"His father...?"

"His father died when Vincent was quite young. I suppose that's one of the reasons why he and Margaret have always been close. Despite everything."

"What d'you mean?"

"Oh, nothing too unusual, I suppose. She was in a nursing home for a while; she'd been finding it difficult to cope on her own. But she was never really happy there, and somehow Vincent found the money to have her looked after at home. I don't think it's been easy for him."

"Financially, you mean?"

"Not just that. I've only met Margaret a few times and she's not what you'd call an easy woman. That's my impression, at least." Anna gave a rueful smile. "Like mother, like son. And what makes it worse, sometimes now I think she hardly recognizes him. Mistakes him for his father, things like that. Babbles on, you know, about the past. When Vincent's father was still alive. And then at other times she can be completely rational. So Vincent finds it hard; he doesn't say much, but you can tell. I can tell. So much depends on whether his mother's had a good day or a bad."

Elder nodded, thinking that he understood.

"How about you?" Anna said. "Your parents, are they still alive?"

Elder shook his head.

"I'm sorry."

"You?"

"Oh, yes. My father still plays golf and swims year round. My mother's on the local church committee and flirts happily and quite openly with the vicar, despite his being married with seven children and that he's had his right leg amputated below the knee. My not-quite-whole holy toyboy, she calls him. I think she's paying Daddy back for all the silly little flibbertigibbets he used to fool around with when he was younger."

They could hear the bell on the roof of the Council House sounding the hour.

"I should go," Elder said. "I've taken enough of your time as it is."

They walked together toward the Castle gate, and at the point where the path went off in different directions, Anna stopped. "It was nice to see you again," she said. "Even in circumstances like these."

Elder looked in her face. "There's nothing else you want to say to me, is there?"

"What about?"

"I don't know. Vincent, perhaps?"

She tried to hold his gaze, but failed. "No," she said. "No, I don't think so."

WHEREVER MAUREEN PRIOR WAS, SHE WASN'T AT HER desk, she wasn't answering her phone, her cell was switched off. At the third attempt, Elder managed to get Lewis Reardon on the line.

"I've just been talking to a woman who was frightened by someone up in Mapperley," Elder said. "Monday night. He was following her; stalking her, I suppose you could say. Maureen Prior was meant to have told you."

"I got a message, yes." Reardon sounded impatient, tired.

"From the description she gave me, I'm pretty sure it was Dowland."

"She'd ID him?"

"I think so."

"Okay, thanks. Maybe useful, maybe not."

"How come?"

"Could be too late for that," Reardon said. "Got the okay from above, hold Dowland another twelve hours. Way things are going he's gonna cough. Nice little confession. Murder of Lorraine Carne on a plate. Thanks very much." Reardon chuckled. "I'll make sure you get invited to the piss-up, Frank. Help us celebrate."

Chapter 36

THE CEMETERY WAS ON THE SOUTHERN PERIMETER OF
the city, bordered by trees; gravel paths wound between grave-
stones, carefully tended flower beds, and close-cropped grass.
When the trees were in leaf, the crematorium, close by the Garden of Remembrance, was out of sight from the road.

Jennie Preston, wearing a smart black suit and a black hat
with a broad brim, was standing with Claire Meecham's children, greeting guests as they arrived, accepting condolences.
Guests? Was that the word?

Claire's daughter, Jane, was tall and slim, dark haired, stooping a little when she spoke; Claire's son, James, still feeling the
aftereffects of his long flight, was stockier, rounder of face, less
than comfortable in a suit borrowed or bought for the occasion.

Elder had spoken to them earlier, done his best to reassure
them about the progress of the investigation, without laying out
too many false hopes and promises. Jane had looked at him
throughout with flinty eyes, disbelieving. James had nodded,

smiled, crushed his hand in his, and thanked him for everything he was doing. "Just get the bastard, eh?"

When Elder dipped his head to kiss Jennie's cheek, he had
been startled by the depth of shadow around her eyes. Organ
music drifted, faint, from inside the chapel, underscoring the
hushed and stilted conversations, the sporadic chatter, and song
of birds. Jennie's partner, Derek, was standing out on the perimeter, silent, smoking a cigarette.

Glancing at his watch several times, Elder thought that
Joanne had changed her mind, but then, as people were starting to file inside, she arrived, almost elegant in a long black coat
and red shoes, dark glasses with large frames that covered
much of her face. There was no sun and scarcely a patch of blue
in the sky.

"Katherine not coming?" Elder said, crossing to meet her.

"She had lectures," Joanne said, then shook her head. "She
didn't want to."

Death, Elder thought, still a bit too close to her for comfort.

He and Joanne sat together, listening as the clergyman spoke
in a soft Irish voice of Claire's life as a wife and mother, her
quiet devotion, the unstinting, uncomplaining way she had
nursed a loved and loving husband. Then Jennie herself spoke
with affection about the childhood she and Claire had shared
and the way in which Claire, as the older sister, had looked after
her when the need was there. More like a mother than a sister.

"Perhaps the saddest thing for me," Jennie said, finally, "is
that after half a lifetime spent looking after others, Claire was
just beginning to forge a life for herself when that life was taken
away."

Throughout the hymn that followed, Jane Meecham's tears
were brittle and loud.

Elder's thoughts drifted to his own parents' funerals, his
mother cremated as she had wished, but his father buried in
hard, cold ground. A granite headstone marked the grave. A

plot Elder visited seldom and never without feelings of grief
and regret: things he had said, things he had thought but left
unspoken.

His father's coffin had been closed, the dead separated already from the living, screwed down safely beneath expensively
bought and burnished wood.

Better that way?

When he was still only a child—eleven? twelve?—his
mother had taken his hand and led him into the heavily curtained front room—the parlour—of his grandmother's house,
where the older woman lay, eyes closed, in an open coffin. He
remembered staring down at her empty face, noticing the way
her lips puckered in as if drawn together by an unseen thread.

When he didn't think his mother was looking, he had touched
a finger against his grandmother's cheek and immediately pulled
it back, the tip white from the powder dusting her face.

"Say goodbye to your gran, now," his mother had said. And
then, "You can kiss her if you want."

Elder hadn't wanted.

Unable to get back to sleep this morning, in the early hours
he had read the scene toward the end of *Sons and Lovers,* in
which Paul Morel gazes down, by the light of a single candle, at
his dead mother as she lies on her bed, waiting for the under-
taker to come. The sweep of the sheet—what does Lawrence
say?—like a clean curve of snow. And the mother, to Paul's
eyes, young again and beautiful, as if a kiss might wake her: a
fairy tale that, when he did kiss her, was shattered by the un-
forgiving coldness of her mouth.

Kiss her if you want.

Elder's mind ran back to Claire Meecham as she had been
when first he'd seen her, her body laid out at the centre of the
bed, her own bed, her clothes arranged just so, her hair neatly
brushed and combed.

Laid out.

Joanne nudged him and he bowed his head for the final prayer.

HE LEFT A MESSAGE ON ANNA INGRAM'S ANSWERPHONE, but she failed to call him back. At six-thirty he assumed she might be home from work and looked up her number in the directory. It seemed to ring for a long time and he thought she wasn't going to answer, but then she did.

Apologizing for disturbing her, Elder asked if they could talk.

This evening?

This evening.

He found the house without difficulty, set back, as most of those houses were, a little way from the road behind blackening stone walls overhung with greenery. The house itself seemed a little tatty round the edges, in need of some exterior repair. A number of small squares of tile were missing from the path leading up to the door. The large circular bell push, fatter than his thumb, looked to have been there since the house was built, well over a hundred years ago; Elder wondered if it still worked, yet it did. From the suddenness with which Anna Ingram appeared, he thought, in all probability she'd seen him approach and had been waiting in the hall.

The second-floor living room was spacious and tall, framed posters and what Elder took for original paintings on the walls. A large bookcase that sagged a little under the weight of its load. Velvet curtains that, here and there, had faded. A deep red carpet on the floor.

"I was just having a glass of wine," Anna said. "Nothing special, but if you'd care to join me." She laughed nervously. "I suppose it depends on just how official this is."

"A glass of wine would be nice," Elder said.

Eschewing the old-fashioned settee with no support at one end, he chose an armchair that proved less comfortable than it looked.

The wine was pale and slightly sharp and he sipped it and set it aside. Anna Ingram fidgeted with one of the small pearl buttons on the sleeve of her blouse.

"Vincent Blaine and his mother," Elder said. "I was just wondering if there's anything else you can tell me."

Anna looked surprised. "I don't know," she said after a moment's hesitation. "I really don't know that there is. I don't know what kind of thing you mean."

"You implied there was some kind of tension between them."

"Well, yes, there is a little now, this last year or so, ever since he agreed to take her back out of the nursing home..."

"And that's because of what? The expense?"

"That's part of it, certainly. That and the worry. Finding anyone qualified who'll stay for any length of time isn't easy. His mother's moods can vary a great deal and sometimes she can be very rude indeed. People won't stand for it, being spoken to that way; they leave. And at nighttime often all Vincent can get are slips of girls without any real training who try to smuggle their boyfriends in whenever they can."

"And the responsibility for this, it's all Vincent's? There are no brothers or sisters?"

Anna shook her head.

"It seems a shame," Elder said, "he can't persuade her to go back into some kind of care."

"Vincent and his mother..." Anna smiled. "She's the one person he can't bully or cajole or shame into doing what he wants. A real old-fashioned matriarch, that's Margaret. Too used to having her own way. But if I ever dare to say as much as a single word against her..."

Anna sipped some wine.

"When they moved," Elder said, "from Dorset up to Derbyshire, was that after his father died?"

"Not straight after. I don't think so. No, in fact, I'm sure of it. Vincent's father died when he was only three—a car accident. He scarcely seems to have any memory of him at all."

"And they moved, I think you said, when Vincent was ten or so?"

"Yes, ten or eleven. But why? Why do you want to know all this?"

"You know what it was," Elder went on, sidestepping her question, "that caused them to move?"

Anna shifted in her chair. "Not really, no."

"Something to do with his mother's work, perhaps? I assume she worked. Or maybe at the time she thought she'd sell the place in Dorset for some reason? Move right away."

Anna shifted again, unsettled by Elder's gaze. "I think...I think...Vincent said something once...I think perhaps it had something to do with the school. Vincent's school."

"What? It wasn't good enough? Poor results, that the kind of thing?"

"No, I think Vincent...he'd been in some kind of trouble..."

"Trouble?"

"Yes."

"He doesn't seem like the kind." Elder smiled. "Unless it was for knowing more than the teachers, that is. Taking over the class."

Anna smiled back. "He was always bright, of course. I think that may have been part of the trouble. You know, he got bored, misbehaved, children do. Maybe he was trying to get noticed, get attention, I don't know, I'm only guessing."

"Do you know what kinds of things he did?"

"Not really." Anna reached for her glass of wine. "You've got to understand, it's not something we've talked about a great deal. Hardly at all." She laughed. "Being excluded from school—not exactly one of the high points of Vincent's illustrious academic career."

"He was actually excluded? Suspended?"

"For a while. I don't know how long, but not long. I think it was a gesture as much as anything else. To convince his mother the problems were serious."

"And that's why they moved? A new school somewhere else?"

"Not immediately. Vincent was referred for some kind of treatment, therapy. He really won't talk about it. But it went on for quite a while, I think. The best part of a year?"

"It didn't work then, the therapy?"

"Who's to say? As far as I know, he didn't get into trouble later on, after they'd moved, so perhaps it did. Or maybe it was just the change of school, who knows?"

Elder leaned back in his chair. "My daughter," he said, "Katherine, when we moved up to Nottingham at first, she was just about to change schools anyway, junior to secondary, but at least in London she'd have been moving up with a lot of her friends, whereas here..." He leaned forward again and lifted his glass from the floor. "We practically had to carry her to school the first week or so; it took her ages to settle in. Ages."

"But she did in the end?"

"Yes. In the end it was fine."

"It's difficult, things like that. When you're young. Changes. For some people it can be really traumatic."

Elder nodded. "I think that's right."

"Can I offer you a refill?" Anna said, nodding toward his glass.

"No. No thanks. It was very nice, but I'd better not."

"Just as you wish."

Five minutes of inconsequential chat and she was escorting him back downstairs.

Chapter 37

AT AROUND THE SAME TIME THAT ELDER WAS GETTING himself ready to attend Claire Meecham's funeral, Lewis Reardon was strutting around in a sharp suit, loud shirt, and spotted tie, exchanging high fives up and down the Force Crime Detectorate building: the rat, as someone observed, that'd gotten the cream. Not exactly flavour of the month with everyone, Reardon, since he'd piggybacked his way over several others on his way to promotion, though, as even his detractors grudgingly admitted, one way or another the bastard got results.

"Maureen, thanks for the help, yeah?"

Maureen Prior, who'd helped, in her estimation, little if at all, shook the proffered hand. Pumped up as he was, even Reardon realized she wasn't about to join him in a high five.

"All the forensics in, then?" Prior said. "Signed and sealed?"

"Got him on tape, haven't we? That's what matters. Pleading to it, the whole fucking works. Begging for forgiveness at the same time. Pathetic bastard!"

"You've charged him then?"

"Bet your fucking life."

There was spittle, damp, round Reardon's mouth, reddening the small cut where he'd nicked himself shaving.

"You'll be down at the pub," Reardon said, more of a statement than a question. "Later."

"I'll see what I can do."

"Come on, get yourself legless for once. Never know..." Reardon winked, "you might pull if you're lucky."

THERE WERE THREE CALLS FROM BEN LEONARD ON HER cell, and when Prior arrived back at her own office she half-expected him to be waiting to ambush her in the lobby.

Instead, it was Wayne Johns.

Johns, just outside the building and looking as if he'd come straight from the gym. "This where I make a complaint?" he asked with a cocky grin. "Spying, defamation of character, that sort of thing?"

"No," Prior said, "that would be County Police headquarters. Make an appointment first, if I were you."

She made as if to walk past him, but Johns shifted position and blocked her path.

"Get out of my way," Prior said.

Still grinning, Johns stayed where he was.

"Get out of my fucking way."

"Naughty, naughty."

The grin had become a leer. Prior's hand had formed into a fist.

"Sending that mate of yours off down to Barcelona," Johns said, "sniffing round. Seeing what bits of dirt he could dredge up. You didn't think I'd get to know about that?"

Prior said nothing.

"Little birdie tipped me the warning," Johns said. "Abrogation of my human rights, that's what I've been told. Slap-on-the-wrist-time from your chief constable at the very least, once my lawyer gets on it. Lucky to hang onto your job."

"Look," Prior said, "you're not funny, and you're wasting my time."

"Funny? No, I'm not being funny. This is serious, yeah? Barcelona, that's not the half of it. Going round my customers, seeing what you can dig up. Old girlfriends. Neighbours. Stirring up trouble, talking to people who might have a grudge. All behind my back. You want to know anything about me, you come straight to me, right?"

"For the last time," Prior said, "get out of my way."

"You know what?" Johns said, moving closer. "You get a real glow on you when you're riled. Attractive that. Makes me think we could get a little thing going, me and you—'less, of course..." he laughed, "you're tied up already."

Prior brought her right leg up fast and hard and Johns gasped and staggered back, hands clutching between his legs.

"What's the matter?" Prior said. "I thought you got off on a little pain? Or is it just when you're handing it out?"

"You bitch," Johns said through gritted teeth.

"You got that right," Prior said.

FOR THE REST OF THE DAY, SHE FELT A WHOLE LOT BETTER. Better enough that, come four o'clock, she returned Ben Leonard's call.

"Thanks for getting back to me," Leonard said. "Can we meet and talk?"

"We can talk now."

"This is important."

"Then say what you have to say."

There was a sigh of exasperation at the other end of the line. Then, "Richard Dowland, it doesn't make any sense."

"Go on."

"I've been talking to him, once, twice a week. All that stuff he's got going round in his head, that's where it is, where it stays. Like I said before, it's all fantasy. Pure fantasy."

"Not so pure."

"You know what I mean."

"And you know what I'm going to say, the same as I did when we had this conversation last—what he did to Eve Ward wasn't fantasy. If you don't want to believe that, maybe you should talk to her instead of him."

"You're convinced then, is that what you're saying? The murder the other night—he was responsible for that?"

"I'm not saying anything."

"Because I don't think you believe it, any more than I do."

"Don't tell me what I believe."

Prior held the phone away from her ear for a moment and looked across the room. Officers with heads bent over sheets of paper, the now eternal filling in of forms, or peering at the small print on their computer screens, scrolling up or down. The number of cases the unit was dealing with increasing daily, hourly it sometimes seemed, the number that got solved, sorted, resolved, diminishing to the same degree. Bernard Young had been banging on in his office the other morning: "What I need's a result, a nice fat headline-snagging result, something that will get the ACC feeling good about himself, take the vultures off the chief constable's back, and give the press department something to scream about. And if you can't give it to me, God'll bless whoever will."

"You've talked to Tom Whitemore," she said to Leonard, "like I suggested?"

"He told me it's out of his hands; there's nothing he can do."

"There's your answer then."

Leonard cursed softly at the other end of the phone. "Jesus, Maureen, come on. I don't believe you're just going to sit there and let this farce go ahead."

"It's not my case. Not my call."

"It's the rest of a man's fucking life."

"Ben, Ben, if it's wrong, if it's not safe, that'll become clear."

"When?" Leonard scoffed. "Like that poor sod got released a few weeks back? After ten or more years inside?"

"There's a call on the other line," Prior said. "I've got to go."

Breaking the connection, she leaned back into the relative silence.

AWARE HER ABSENCE WOULD BE NOTED, PRIOR SHOWED her face at Lewis Reardon's party, having first persuaded Elder to join her. Just a quick one, Frank, two at most. Now it was her turn to get them in, and, flushed with the afterglow of a successful result and a succession of single malts, Bernard Young kept her talking at the bar. Behind them, in the far room, karaoke was in full swing, Reardon up on the small stage and giving his best Elvis, chest puffed out, shirt front undone, "Suspicious Minds."

"Dowland," Elder said, once Prior had finally sat back down. "What do you think?"

"Don't you start."

"I'm sorry."

"It's none of our business, right? Somebody else's concern, not ours."

Elder shrugged and lifted his glass.

Reardon, hips gyrating, sweat falling off him, had switched to "Jailhouse Rock."

Earlier, Elder had taken a quick look at the postmortem report: the pressure exerted on Lorraine Carne's neck when it was twisted to one side had been sufficient to snap several vertebrae. Did Dowland, even worked up as he would have been, have that kind of strength?

"I'd like you to run a couple of checks for me, Maureen, if you would," Elder said. "A couple of favours you might call in."

Reardon, on his way back from the Gents and less than

steady on his pins, intercepted Elder later. "Frank, Frank..." throwing his arm round Elder's shoulders, "didn't expect to see you here, don't know why."

"Just looked in," Elder said. "Congratulations."

"Great result, Frank. For all of us. Me especially, no getting round it. First murder since I made inspector." He was slightly slurring his words. "Trouble is, now they'll be expecting me to do it every fuckin' time. Still, any luck, I'll end up with a reputation like yours." He punched Elder lightly on the shoulder. "Cover meself in fuckin' glory."

"First murder case I ever had," Elder said. "This squad, eight years back now, never solved. No one was ever as much as charged. Still open to this day."

"Shame that, Frank. Fuckin' shame." Reardon laughed. "Maybe it's you should be takin' a leaf out of my book, eh? See how it's done."

Against her better judgement, Prior had said yes to another drink and now sat hemmed in by a bunch of her colleagues with no early chance of escape.

"You won't forget," Elder called out as he was leaving.

She wouldn't forget.

Chapter 38

IT WAS FOUR, FOUR-THIRTY IN THE AFTERNOON, THE SUN still quite strong and the light not yet beginning to fade; what little breeze there was came off the water, bringing with it a smell of the ozone, faint but unmistakable.

Alice Silverman had moved along the coast when she retired, but not far, a thirties house overlooking the sea just outside Weymouth. By rights it was too large for a now elderly woman living on her own, although there were nieces and nephews who occasionally came to stay when they wanted a cheap holiday, and once in a while her old colleague Jock Mirren would turn up on her doorstep, virtually unannounced, and occupy the spare bedroom for weeks at a time, keeping her awake with his snoring and leaving the room stinking of cigars and whisky and worse.

When she turned sixty-five, Alice had started to have trouble with her hip, especially when climbing stairs; bursitis, the physiotherapist said, though he didn't seem entirely sure, and the exercises he prescribed alleviated the pain for a while but no more; her GP had offered an injection of steroids in the chance that might work, but it was a chance Alice had, so far, not opted to take. Stairs she was prepared to take slowly, especially if there was a banister, and normally, as long as she could take her own time, she could manage the slow climb home; it was only those occasions on which the pain afflicted her suddenly, when she was out in the street—on her way back from the library, for instance—and turned her into a crippled old woman, wincing with pain, that she hated it and wanted it gone.

An old woman. She supposed, to many eyes, that's what she was: a skinny old woman with white hair.

Frank Elder had phoned ahead and asked, as persuasively as he could, if she might be prepared to spare him a little of her time; it had been the devil's own job tracking her down and now that he had found her he hadn't wanted her to slip through his fingers.

Perhaps he need not have worried: since time was what Alice Silverman had the most of, she had agreed with little hesitation. If it were convenient for him, why didn't he come for tea? The bulk of her shopping she had delivered, and there was a rich fruitcake that Jock was wont to say, as he cut himself another slice, went down a treat. It was a long while, longer than she might have liked to admit, since she'd had a conversation, a proper conversation, with anyone, and she did like to talk.

The house was on a hill, and by the time he arrived, Elder, who, uncertain of his bearings, had parked his car down in the town, was jacketless, his shirt sticking to his back.

"Mr. Elder?"

"Yes."

"Please come in."

They sat in the living room: a small table by the picture window, wicker chairs. Tea in white china cups, quite delicate. The cake sat on a Susie Cooper plate Alice had picked up in a charity shop for far less than it was worth; chipped on the underside of one edge, but a bargain for all that. She cared about such things now that she had the time.

"Mr. Elder, you're with the police you said?"

"In a way, yes."

"You have some kind of identification, of course?"

There was a letter, signed by the chief constable, inside his wallet.

She read it carefully then passed it back. "So, how may I help?"

Elder settled his cup back into its saucer. "Vincent Blaine," he said. "Does that name mean anything to you?"

Alice Silverman was cutting the cake as Elder spoke and the knife slipped just a little in her hand.

"Vincent," she said, recovering. "Yes, of course. I can't claim to have remembered every one of my patients—as the years go by they tend to merge—but Vincent, yes, I do remember him."

"I wonder why that is? That you remember him so clearly?"

"I really can't say. Some faces, some people, for whatever reason, they stick with you and, as I suggested, some it's almost impossible to recall."

"And this was, what, forty years ago?"

"Almost. Nineteen sixty-five it would have been, when Vincent was first referred to me." She sipped her tea. "It was April, I think, near the end of the school term. He was quite small for his age, slightly built; for the first session, the first two sessions, he wouldn't say a word. Didn't do anything, wouldn't play with anything, wouldn't draw, wouldn't colour in; he just sat there, head turned away. And then, every so often, he'd look right at you. Suddenly. When you were least expecting it. He wore those glasses, the old National Health kind, round with wire frames, and you could never quite see where his eyes were focusing, except when he was staring straight at you. And then you knew."

"He frightened you."

"Did he? Yes, I suppose he did. Something...there was something about him I found unnerving."

"Can you say what that was?"

Alice Silverman smiled. "If I'd been able to do that, I might have been more successful. With Vincent, I mean. Even in the relatively little time we had. But I think...let me try...I think in part it was a sense that he knew more than you, better than you—that it was all a game and he knew how to cheat the rules."

"So you thought he was manipulating you?"

"Yes, I suppose that's true."

"Is that so unusual?"

"No. Not at all. I'd say in most cases it happens to some degree."

"But with Vincent it was different?"

"Yes."

Alice Silverman took her time, drank some more tea; when she offered Elder a slice of cake he held out his plate.

"The thing with Vincent," she said, "his guard was up most of the time; there were relatively few occasions when it came fully down. And when it did, you saw what in a way you expected: he was letting you know he understood all the paraphernalia of the sessions, what it was all for, what I was trying to do, and, for now, he was agreeing to play along. But there was more to it than that. On those occasions he showed more. More of himself. Without meaning to, I think, but I was never certain, not even of that."

"And it was, what? Sexual?"

"Sexual, certainly. At this age especially, the beginnings of adolescence, it's what you'd expect. But no, there was something about him at those moments that was dangerous. That's what I remember thinking. Feeling. Dangerous and in some way threatening."

"He did frighten you, then?"

"A little, yes, as I've said. Not all the time. But, yes."

"You thought he might attack you?"

The answer didn't come easily. "Yes, I suppose I did."

"There in the room?"

"Perhaps, but that's a risk you always take and there are pre-cautions...No, I thought...this might sound a little ridiculous, I know...but I thought he might attack me later, outside, when I was alone."

"Attack you how?"

"Well, physically..."

"Sexually?"

"Partly, yes. Possibly."

"You thought he might try to rape you?"

"Yes." Alice Silverman closed her eyes.

Elder waited. "But none of this ever happened?" he said.

"No. I never saw him outside that room."

"And these fears of yours, did they lessen in time? As you got to know him?"

"Not entirely, no. It changed, my feelings changed, but I think I was always uneasy—it's difficult to explain."

Nodding, Elder broke off a piece of cake. "All in all, for how long did you see him?"

"Just over a year. Until the family moved away."

"Long enough to know the cause of his problems?"

Alice Silverman smiled. "Now I think you're asking for more than I can give."

"Miss Silverman, as I said when I called, I wouldn't be asking any of this if I didn't think it was important."

"Lives at risk, I believe that's what you said."

"Yes. I don't think that's an overstatement. More lives could be at risk."

At the word "more," Alice Silverman narrowed her eyes.

"What could you tell me," Elder said, "about Vincent's rela-tionship with his mother?"

Despite her best intentions, Alice Silverman found she was smiling. "Perhaps you've missed your calling, Mr. Elder?"

"Anything you think you could tell me," Elder said, "it might be useful."

Alice Silverman turned her head away toward the window; there was a large container ship just visible on the horizon. Much of the earlier blue had been bleached out of the sky. Were lives really at risk, or was that an exaggeration?

"The way he behaved toward me," she said slowly, still not looking Elder in the face, "some of the things that emerged in the course of the therapy, they led me to the conclusion that he'd been seduced by his mother. Or, at the very least, that he thought he had."

"Isn't there a big difference?"

"No, not for someone like Vincent. Reality or fantasy, they're just as real. As long as he believes what happened to be true." Neatly, she brushed the cake crumbs from her own plate onto the larger one. "I think I've said far more than I should. I only hope it can be of help."

"If I could just ask one more thing?"

"Mr. Elder, really..."

"It is important."

Alice Silverman hesitated a second too long.

"Someone in the situation you describe, someone who grew into adulthood thinking he'd had sex with his mother, would he be able to control that, forget about it, keep it suppressed?"

"Hypothetically speaking?"

"Hypothetically speaking."

"He might, he might well. Much of the time. You can never tell. I suspect it would be difficult. But there are ways, strategies someone in that position might adopt."

"Such as?"

"He might, if it were possible, live his life in a very ordered way, keeping everything very tightly under his own control.

And that would include relationships, of course, relationships with others."

"Other women?"

"Yes."

"He would be able to maintain a satisfactory physical relationship?"

"Yes. Up to a point. The danger would always be that the Oedipal tension he's been able to control would become unmanageable."

"And what might cause that to happen?"

"It could be one of any number of things. Something about the particular situation, the woman concerned. Her appearance, for instance, the way she'd done her hair, the clothes she was wearing; a scent, even, a smell, something that would remind him quite vividly of his mother. It might be, also, that his own defenses had been weakened, by alcohol, say, or drugs. What might happen, given that combination, would be that the woman, instead of simply being like his mother, would, to his eyes, become his mother. The 'as if-ness' disappears. And that would bring back all the intense feelings of guilt he'd been keeping at bay."

"With what result?"

"It would depend. But one way or another, he would need to lose that guilt and restore equilibrium."

"One way or another?"

Though she was sitting and not walking, no hill to climb, the pain in Alice Silverman's hip was quite intense. "As well as his own guilt, he might feel extreme anger toward the woman— toward his mother, because at that moment, then, that's who she is."

"Enough that he might want her dead?"

"Oh, yes."

The voices of children were raised on the street outside, laggardly on their way home from school.

"If we can assume for a moment that the man's anger has been such that the woman has been killed, once that anger has dissipated, which I assume in time it would, how might he then feel?"

"About himself?"

"Yes."

"More guilt, I suppose. But relief, too. Perhaps, above all, relief."

"And the woman, the victim, how would he feel toward her?"

"Solicitous, I think, caring. Tender, even. She is his mother, after all."

Chapter 39

THE CASE AGAINST RICHARD DOWLAND WAS UNRAVEL-
ling. While soil of the same kind as was present on the allotment had been discovered in the cleats of his trainers, it was
matted together with that from a number of gardens in the area.
He had been close to the murder scene, almost certainly, but
when was a matter of conjecture rather than proof. More cru-
cially, although traces of three different kinds of semen had
been found on—and in—the dead woman's body, in no instance did the DNA match Dowland's.

"So what the fuck?" Lewis Reardon blustered. "He used a
fucking condom, didn't he? Either that or he didn't shag her at
all. Couldn't get it fucking up. Why he topped her, more'n likely."

And if any of his team raised a questioning voice, Reardon
shouted them down.

"It's all here, right, on tape. I killed her. Strangled her. You
want more proof, get off your arses and find it. I got the confession, you get out there and get the fucking evidence to back
it up."

But even the confession was starting to look shaky. While not attempting to withdraw it, not exactly, Dowland was becoming less certain in his pronouncements, and frequent mentions of following a woman with red hair were worryingly off track.

"Time for a rethink?" Prior said in passing, a not altogether unfriendly question.

"When I want advice from you," Reardon said, "I'll fucking ask for it."

Anything less aggressive, more contrite, she might have felt a smidgeon of sympathy. But now there was none.

She was seeing Elder at eleven.

ANNA INGRAM WAS ON HER WAY TO THE MAIN STAIRCASE when she saw Elder waiting and had to resist the irrational desire to turn around and walk the other way; either that or keep on going, pretend somehow that he wasn't there.

There's nothing else you want to say to me, is there?
What about?
I don't know. Vincent, perhaps?

He straightened and came toward her, a slight smile and a nod, almost apologetic.

"You're not here to take another look at the paintings?" Anna said.

"No, I'm afraid not."

She took a step away. "I've got a meeting scheduled for ten-thirty."

"I won't detain you long."

Anna started to say something, but the words caught on the back of her tongue.

"That weekend," Elder said, "in April. The one when Claire Meecham disappeared. You weren't with Vincent, were you? At the cottage?"

Anna was already shaking her head.

"As far as you were concerned at the time, he went there on his own."

"Yes," she said. "Yes, that's right."

She thought she might cry, but looking back at Elder, no tears came.

"THIS FUCKING GOVERNMENT," BERNARD YOUNG SAID, "has become so obsessed with fucking targets, it's all they ever fucking see. And in consequence, we're cursed with spending all our time filling in form after form with figures and percentages for a bunch of gimcrack quangos to analyze in minute fucking detail, so they can tell us, down to the most infinitesimal decimal fucking point, by exactly how much we're failing. Instead of which, if they sacked their half-arsed focus groups and all the rest of the sycophantic hangers-on, and allowed us to take on more officers instead, we might have a cat in hell's chance of solving the occasional fucking crime."

From her seat on the other side of the superintendent's desk, Maureen Prior nodded silent agreement; she had heard it all before and would hear it again. Alongside her, Elder continued to study the tops of his shoes.

"All right," Young said, "tell me what you have."

When they'd finished, Elder doing most of the talking, the superintendent angled himself back in his chair and ran it back through in his mind.

"What you've got," he said, several moments later, "is Blaine at the site of one murder—Irene Fowler—something we've questioned him about before without much joy—and other than the fact he seems to have been lying to his back teeth, precious little to connect him to the second. Your gut feelings, Frank, aside. No firm evidence, no witnesses to place him within half a mile of Claire Meecham at or around the time of her death, no forensics—what you're basing your case on are the theories of some antique psychotherapist who hasn't set eyes on Blaine for forty years. Is that right? Or am I missing something?"

"No," Elder said. "Not a thing."

Young unfastened the final button of his jacket; too much

lunch too fast and, for once, the bloody Rennies didn't seem to be working. "So," he said, "what do you want to do?"

"What I'd like," Elder said, "is a chance to look round Blaine's place in Dorset. See if we can't find some evidence Claire Meecham was there."

"And I can see the look on the magistrate's face when I ask for a warrant. No, what we do, bring him in, let Maureen question him, see if we can't make him sweat a little. Take it from there. Okay?"

"Okay," Elder said, grudgingly. He had hoped for more.

"Before you go, Maureen," Young said, "this investigation of Reardon's, the tom out amongst the cabbages, what the fuck's going on?"

"Not my case, sir," Prior said.

"Stop being so prissy," Young said. "You've got your ear to the ground. Coming apart at the seams, isn't it? Close to. The whole bloody shooting match."

"I think all he's got now's the confession and even if he can persuade the CPS to go ahead on that, I'd be doubtful if it'd stand up as safe."

Young scowled and shook his head. "One-trick fucking pony, that's Reardon. Can't see past the fucking blinkers."

"I think there might be another angle," Prior said. "Frank here had an idea."

"What's this, then, Frank? Some other bit of Freudian sooth-saying? Another touch of the Melanie Kleins?"

"Not exactly," Elder said, without knowing who on earth Melanie Klein was.

"You want me to have a word with Reardon, sir?" Prior asked. "See if I can't steer him in another direction?"

"Not yet. Let him stew in his own juices a bit longer. Learn the hard way but at least he might learn." Young slapped both hands down hard on his desk. "Let me know how it goes with Blaine. Keep me informed."

PRIOR WENT OVER IT ALL WITH ELDER BEFORE THE IN-terview, making sure she was fully briefed. Elder himself would be watching, listening, unable to directly intervene.

After some deliberation, she had decided to take Anil Khan in with her; Khan was a detective sergeant who'd moved across from Charlie Resnick's squad at Canning Circus, and, to Prior's eyes, would have been a better candidate for promotion than Lewis Reardon, though she was sure his time would come.

Khan ushered Blaine into an interview room and then they left him there for close on twenty minutes, watching him fume.

"Mr. Blaine," Prior said when she finally entered. "Sorry to keep you waiting."

"If you're going to drag me along here for neither rhyme nor reason and then abandon me without cause or explanation, you might at least have the good grace to apologize."

"I just did."

Blaine looked back at her sharply, but for once held his tongue.

"What it is," Prior said, "there are one or two points from previous statements you've made that we'd like you to clarify."

"Before we do that," Blaine said, "just to be clear, it is the case that I am under no obligation to answer any question, should I choose not to?"

"None at all."

"And I can leave at any time?"

"Absolutely." Prior angled her head invitingly toward the door; other than that, nobody moved. The air in the windowless room was stale, the faint smell of disinfectant seeping from the corners.

"I believe," Prior said, "when you were asked if you knew a Claire Meecham, you said that you did not?"

"That's correct."

"Despite her being a student of yours last year?"

"Was she, indeed?"

"A continuing education course in photography."

"Well, if you say so, of course I'm happy to take your word."

"This course, Mr. Blaine, it would have lasted how long?"

"Eight weeks would have been the normal time."

"And how long would each session have been?"

"Two hours."

"A dozen students? More?"

Blaine shook his head. "No more. A dozen at most."

"And yet you still claim not to know Claire Meecham?"

Blaine smiled with his eyes. "The brain, it's a funny thing. Attention. Memory. What, without willing it, we focus on and what we don't."

Prior nodded at Khan, who took out a photograph of Claire Meecham and pushed it across the desk.

Blaine looked at it carefully. "There," he said, "you see, now that I look at it I do have at least a vague sense of having seen this person before, of knowing that face, but I would still never have been able to say for certain where from or when it might have been."

With a last glance at the photo, he pushed it back toward Khan. "I'm sorry I can't be of more help."

Prior shrugged as if to say never mind and watched Khan sliding the photograph back into its envelope. "There's one other little thing you can perhaps help me with," she said, making it seem like an afterthought.

"If I can."

"Your friend, Anna, why d'you suppose she lied?"

Just for a moment, behind his glasses, there was a look in Blaine's eyes that didn't show there often: the look of surprise.

"I'm afraid I don't know," he said, "what you're referring to."

"What I'm referring to is the weekend of April ninth and tenth, when, according to Anna Ingram, the two of you were at your family cottage in Dorset?"

Blaine sighed theatrically. "Dorset, yes. What of it?"

"Miss Ingram has changed her tale. She now says, rather than going with you to Dorset, she stayed here, in the city, and you went on your own."

Blaine held his breath: two seconds, three. "I see."

"So which version is true? Did you go together or, as Miss Ingram now says, did you go alone?"

Blaine removed his glasses and set them deliberately down. "I went alone."

"If that's so, why did you want us to believe otherwise?"

"I didn't."

"You said..."

"No, no. Listen to me. Anna told me that, in a moment of confusion when she was being questioned, she said the pair of us had travelled down to Dorset together, as we more usually did. I knew she would be deeply embarrassed if I turned around and said something else. So I went along with her story. I couldn't see that it was doing any harm." He paused. "If I lied, I lied for her."

"If you lied..."

"As I said, I didn't think it really mattered, one way or another."

"A woman was murdered."

"And whether I was in Dorset with Anna or on my own bears no relevance to that whatsoever." When he repositioned his glasses, they almost slid out of his hand.

"Let me ask you again," Prior said, "why do you think Anna Ingram felt it necessary to lie about that weekend?"

"And I've told you, it was a mistake, natural confusion, a slip of the tongue."

"I think she did it because she wanted to give you an alibi."

"An alibi? What on earth for?"

"That weekend is the weekend Claire Meecham disappeared, the weekend she was murdered. And for some reason, I believe, your friend Miss Ingram thinks you were involved. She lied to protect you."

Blaine laughed theatrically. "This is preposterous."

"I'm sorry you think so."

"A farrago of half-truths and false accusations." He pushed back his chair. "You said I could go at any time?"

"That's your right."

"Very well. I shall exercise it." Pushing the chair back further, Blaine got to his feet and, without looking at either Prior or Khan directly again, walked out of the room, out of the police station and out onto the street.

"What do you think?" Prior asked Elder moments later, when he came into the room.

"I think he was with Claire Meecham that weekend. I'm sure of it."

"In Dorset?"

"I'd say so, wouldn't you?"

"I think we should go back to Bernard Young," Prior said. "See if we can't talk him into changing his mind."

BLAINE WENT STRAIGHT TO THE CASTLE AND SAID HE was there to see Anna; the man at the desk, recognizing him, phoned up to her office.

"She's on her way down," he told Blaine and smiled.

Blaine met her on the first landing, Anna's expression changing when she saw the set of his face.

"Vincent, is something wrong?"

"You stupid, stupid woman. You stupid bitch!"

"Vincent!"

He struck her with the back of his hand and then again with the palm, the force of the blows so strong that, off balance and taken by surprise, she was spun around and, losing her footing, fell hard against the banister and then down half the flight of stairs.

Chapter 40

WITHOUT KNOWING WHY, ELDER HAD BEEN EXPECTING something a little more roses-round-the-door. Beech Cottage was more a house to his eyes than a cottage, though the name was engraved on a stone lintel above the door. Standing on its own on perhaps a quarter acre of land, within sight of the coast path leading out of Lyme, it was square, brick, the upper half of the front and side walls painted white. There were white curtains at the windows. Presumably, someone local was paid to keep the garden under control; shrubs, hardy perennials, a few late-flowering daffodils; the single beech tree at the farthest corner would block some of the sea view when it was in full leaf.

When they'd mentioned Dorset to Anil Khan, he had looked blank, and Prior had vowed to take him along; herself and Elder, two crime-scene officers, and now Khan.

Gaining access was a breeze.

"If Claire Meecham was here that weekend," Prior told them, "there'll be some sign. Even after all this time. Doesn't matter how small."

With infinite patience and painstaking care, whoever had
been responsible for the deaths of both Irene Fowler and Claire
Meecham had managed to remove or erase every trace of himself from their bodies or their clothes: But this was a whole
house, where, they believed, Meecham had sat and walked,
washed and slept.

"The bathroom," Prior said to the scene of crime officers,
"why don't you start there? The bedroom next."

"You got it," one said. The bathroom first, what else did she
expect?

They set to work.

Elder walked slowly through the downstairs rooms. At some
point, he thought, much of the furniture from when it had been
a family home had been removed. What remained was simple
and plain, echoing the pale colours of the walls. Living room,
kitchen, dining room; the dining room, at the back, was shaded
from the light.

Instead of the walls being plentifully hung with photographs,
as in Blaine's Vale of Belvoir home, there were only three,
arranged in a triangular pattern on the living-room wall opposite the door. Three photographs of Blaine's mother, Margaret,
he had little doubt: the resemblance was there. And not only
that between mother and son. The longer he stood in front of
the photos, taking in aspects of the mother's appearance—her
features, the set of her head—the more he noticed—no, it was
not his imagination, not entirely—a resemblance between her
and the first victim, Irene Fowler, a resemblance he had not noticed at first glance.

Elder was certain Blaine had taken the larger, central photograph himself, it was so deliberately posed: The similarity to the
Stieglitz photograph of the woman in a cotton dress he had
made a point of showing to Elder could be no mere coincidence.

And she is beautiful, of course, there's no gainsaying that.
Very beautiful.

Blaine's words echoed inside his head.

He looked more closely at the photograph on the left, unusually in colour: Blaine's mother when she was younger. She was wearing a plain blouse with a full, rounded collar, open to show off her necklace, a simple silver chain with a single pendant, a ruby stone in the shape of a teardrop.

The last time Elder had seen it, it had been around Claire Meecham's neck.

AFTER LITTLE MORE THAN AN HOUR, THE SCENE-OF-crime officers had found three hairs, darker than Vincent Blaine's gray, in the U-bend beneath the bathroom sink. And then, almost an hour later, another, snagged on the hinge of the wardrobe in the main bedroom.

"All we need now," Khan said, "is a match in the DNA…"

Prior scowled. "A DNA match places Meecham here at best; it doesn't prove anything more; it doesn't prove Blaine caused her death. All right, he can say, I admit it, I lied. I was slipping around, a little extracurricular activity on the side. A score of reasons for trying to keep it quiet."

"How about the necklace?" Elder said.

"The necklace?"

"If I'm right."

"If you're right," Prior said, "maybe there are hundreds of them, thousands, all made in Taiwan; the kind you get on the shopping channel, Ideal World or Bid TV, a bargain at nineteen ninety-nine."

Elder had a momentary vision of Maureen Prior at home on the settee, just her and the remote.

"Okay," he said, "and maybe they gave them away free inside packets of Shredded Wheat. But I don't think so, do you?"

Prior grinned.

"Tell me honestly," Elder said, "what we know, what we've seen, what we can surmise—you still don't think Blaine's guilty?"

"What I *think* doesn't matter."

"It's your investigation, I'd say it does."

"I'm not Lewis Reardon," Prior said.

"Thank the Lord for that."

"I'm thinking ahead: What we've got, is it enough to satisfy the CPS? If it is, then what happens next? What's Blaine's barrister going to do to us in court?"

"Maybe that's not our concern."

"Frank..."

"All right, okay, but we're going to bring him in again for questioning, that at least?"

"We?"

Elder's turn to smile. "You know what I mean."

"You're a civilian, Frank, remember? If there's any bringing in to do, Anil and I will do it. Right, Anil? If he's good, we'll let Frank come along and watch."

"I was hoping," Khan said, "while we're here, I'd get a chance to go down to the—what's it called? the Cob?—some bit of harbour Meryl Streep walks along in that old movie, it was on TV..."

"Dream on," Prior said.

ELDER WATCHED WHILE PRIOR AND KHAN KNOCKED AND rang and all three of them waited for Blaine to answer his door. It was late in the afternoon by the time they arrived back at the Vale, early evening almost, the sun, what remained, darkening like a blood blister over the horizon. High above the fields, the faint skeleton of the moon was visible in the sky.

"What do you think, Frank?"

Elder shook his head. "In town having a meal? Lecturing somewhere? Who's to say?"

"That woman..."

"Anna?"

"He could be with her?"

"It's possible."

But when Elder rang Anna Ingram's number there was no reply other than her recorded voice asking him to leave a message.

"So what do we do?" Prior said.

Elder shrugged. "Leave somebody here in case he comes back?"

They were both looking at Anil Khan.

"Oh, great!" Khan said. "Stuck out here without any transport while it gets darker and darker."

"Not afraid of the dark, are you?" Prior said.

"Rumour is," Elder said, "there are still wolves in the Vale of Belvoir."

"Bollocks!"

"No, it's true. Been a while since they attacked anyone, though. A few sheep, but no humans. Not recently, anyway."

"I'll send someone out," Prior said, smiling. "Keep you company."

"Get them to bring a pizza, yeah? Anything with anchovies. And a can of Lilt or Seven-Up."

"Sweet, isn't he?" Prior said.

Elder laughed.

WHEN ANNA INGRAM CAME, CAUTIOUSLY, TO HER FRONT door, it was immediately clear why she hadn't answered the telephone. The lower half of her jaw, dislocated when she had been sent headlong against the iron banister at the Castle, had been reset and was now partly encased in plaster and wire. Her left elbow had been chipped and badly bruised when she was sent reeling down the stairs and her forearm now rested in a sling. There were other bruises to her face, the foremost of which, a vivid purplish yellow, surrounded the lump above her right eye.

"Jesus!" Elder muttered, below his breath.

Anna Ingram's hearing was unimpaired. "It will be a while," she said, "before I can get around to turning the other cheek."

The words sounded as if they were having to squeeze past a large stone in the centre of her mouth, and Elder could only just make out what she had said.

He followed her as she gingerly climbed the stairs. In the living room, she had arranged several cushions on the settee and she lowered herself carefully onto those.

"I'd like to think this was an accident," Elder said.

Though it pained her to do so, Anna shook her head.

"It was Vincent," Elder said.

This time it was a nod.

"I should have warned you. I'm sorry."

Anna blinked.

"You'll press charges?"

"What for?" It came out as "got gor."

Elder nodded, understanding. "I don't suppose he said anything?"

Anna tried to force her face into a rueful smile. "He said, 'You stupid bitch!'"

"We're looking for him," Elder said. "He's not at his house. There's somebody there, waiting to intercept him, but they haven't called." He waited, watching her. "I don't suppose you've any idea where he might be?"

She looked back at him with bruised eyes.

"His mother's address," Elder said, "you know what it is?"

After a moment, Anna Ingram stretched out her good arm and pointed to a pencil and a pad of paper on the table.

Chapter 41

SQUAT AND SOLID, THE HOUSE HAD BEEN BUILT FROM local stone that had blackened and weathered with wind and time. Turned away from the other houses and facing into the valley, it was at the farthest end of the village, the hills of Dark Peak massing at its back.

Once he had made up his mind what to do, what was necessary, Blaine had decided there was little need to rush. At Buxton he stopped for coffee before sauntering along to the opera house, where he spent some twenty minutes checking through the programme for the forthcoming season.

Old habits...

The lights were on in the house when he arrived, visible as he turned off the narrow, winding road into the lane. The girl's bicycle was resting up against the wall close by the front door. When he had interviewed her for the post, she had hardly been able to string two sentences together, scarcely looked him in the eye; a child of her own when she was sixteen, and a few pathetic qualifications not worth the paper they were written on; clever enough, just, to ignore his mother's eccentricities and her more abstruse requests, make her bedtime Horlicks, lift her on and off the commode in her room when necessary.

When Blaine let himself into the house, she was in one of the downstairs rooms, watching TV.

"You can go," he said.

"But I haven't..." She looked at him, confused. "She'll need help to get washed and ready for bed...then there's her bedtime drink..."

"Just go. Now. Go."

Scrambling up her things, the girl backed toward the door. "I will still get paid, the full twelve hours?"

But Blaine had already dismissed her from his mind.

His mother was upstairs in her room, the door ajar. The locks and handles had been removed. The bathroom aside, she rarely strayed to other parts of the house.

When Blaine eased back the door, she was singing.

At first he didn't recognize the tune and then he did.

"Alice Blue Gown."

She had been singing it when first she met his father, some sixty years before.

A story she had told him many, many times.

Standing now as she was, before the dressing-table mirror, she turned slowly toward him, a smile frescoed on her face. The cotton robe she was wearing sagged open; her breasts, like sad, deflated balloons, hung down against her chest.

"Howard," she said. "How nice. What a lovely surprise."

He had written it all out by hand, pen and ink, of course, not Biro, not felt-tip; the same neat italic script as always, slight flourishes in the upper case. His confession, signed and sealed. He wanted to explain it all to her, nonetheless; unburden himself. Ask for forgiveness. Absolution.

"It's not Howard," he said. "Not my father. It's me, Vincent."

"Vincent, of course. You think I didn't know? My own son."

A few unsteady steps toward him and she folded him in her arms. She smelt, as she always did now, of stale urine and face powder, lily-of-the-valley.

"Come and sit here," she said, her voice modulating into a soft, antique croon. "Sit by me on the bed. Rest your head on my lap. There. There."

The bone of her thigh was hard against his cheek; the flesh around it had fallen away to the point at which he could have encircled it, almost, with one hand. The fingers she patted him with were swollen purple at the knuckles, otherwise thin like brittle twigs. When she ran them through his hair, did she notice it was almost as gray in places as her own?

Blaine closed his eyes.

"I've been less than good," he said. "I've done some terrible, wicked things."

"It's all right. You can tell your mother. You can tell me everything."

NOT KNOWING THE PEAK DISTRICT WELL, ELDER LOST his way twice, on one occasion having to reverse along a quarter-mile of narrow lane, a sheer drop to one side, a high stone wall to the other. By the time he arrived at the village, it was shrouded and quiet, a handful of disconsolate youths hanging around outside the only shop, trading sexual threats and cigarettes and drinking cider from a can; the shop itself was closed for the night, a pale light shining in its almost empty window.

When Elder asked for directions, they ignored him at first, and when he persisted, one of them grudgingly pointed the way before, head down, letting a slow dribble of spit falter toward the ground.

Elder parked behind what he recognized as Blaine's car.

Moths jousted in the space between the frame and the open door.

The downstairs rooms were dark.

Elder called Blaine's name, waited, then climbed the stairs.

The sound, faint, of singing directed him along the landing.

Blaine's mother was sitting at the foot of the bed, her son's head cradled in her lap. The blood had splashed up across her face and breasts and collected, dark, between her legs; her hands were steeped in it where they touched his face.

"My Vincent," she said, looking up at Elder, "has been a bad, bad boy."

Not trusting the two vertical cuts he had made in his wrists, Blaine had slashed one side of his throat across, from below one ear to beneath his chin. An old-fashioned open razor lay on the folds of his mother's robe, close by her leg.

"It's Howard's," she said, smiling gently as she followed Elder's gaze. "My husband's. He would never use anything else."

The envelope, addressed to Elder, was resting against the dressing-table mirror, its contents clear and to the point. Elder read it twice then left the room, reaching for his cell as he went. As he stepped outside, a barn owl screeched and flew past, its white face lit up by a sleeve of moon.

FROM WHERE HE STOOD, HE COULD SEE THE EMERGENCY vehicles, like giant fireflies, making their way slowly up the valley. Prior was in the lead car when they arrived, her face taut and pale.

"Take a look," Elder said, inclining his head toward the house. "Tread carefully."

The first ambulance was coming cautiously along the lane.

"My God, Frank," Prior said, when she emerged. And then, "It's what I think?"

He handed her the envelope, the letter.

When she had read it, they stood side by side, not speaking. Swaddled in blankets, Blaine's mother was led slowly toward the nearest ambulance; at the hospital in Chesterfield she would be examined thoroughly, and if there was nothing physically wrong, passed into the care of Social Services.

Vincent Blaine's body would be removed later, after the medical examiner had done his work.

One of the officers, standing a short way off, had lit a cigarette, and Elder, for the first time in years, wished he still smoked. He wished for—no, he craved, a drink. In one of the cupboards in the long, flagged kitchen, he found a bottle of blended scotch. Rinsing a pair of glasses under the tap, he poured two good measures and carried them back outside.

Prior had been reading Blaine's confession again.

"Irene Fowler, Claire Meecham, he admits killing them, washing the bodies, laying them to rest—that's what he calls it—laying them to rest. He says nothing about why."

Vehicles were reversing down the lane to allow the first ambulance to leave. Disturbed, a few birds were making an unseen racket in the trees. Prior set her empty glass down on the stone and went back inside the house, leaving Elder standing there, staring out into the unchanging dark.

Chapter 42

AS IF FURTHER PROOF WERE NEEDED, ANALYSIS OF THE DNA from the hairs found in Vincent Blaine's Dorset cottage showed a match with Claire Meecham.

Blaine had kept a trunk of his mother's old clothes at the cottage, and, while she was there that weekend, he had persuaded Claire to wear one of her dresses—a full-length ball gown in brilliant blue. There were several photographs of her posing in it, among others found in a drawer of a small bureau at the house outside Nottingham; the expression on her face, even as she tried to smile for the camera, was one of uncertainty and concern. She was wearing the same necklace that would later be discovered on her body.

In a number of the older photographs in a family album, Blaine's mother was shown wearing a ring that looked identical to that on Irene Fowler's dead hand. Perhaps in her case, the ring and the facial resemblance had been enough.

Enough to tip Blaine over the edge.

What had Alice Silverman said?

Enough for the "as if-ness" to disappear. No longer a fantasy: a game. At the height of his passion with both women, Vincent Blaine had believed he was making love to his own mother.

When Elder talked later to Jennie Preston, trying, as best he could, to explain, it was as if she understood the words but not what they really meant. And she herself had changed. Although everything about her was superficially in place—the bright and perfect makeup, the hair, the clothes—her sparkle was gone. It was somehow as if, now that she knew what had caused her sister's death, the life had been sucked out of her, leaving a richly decorated shell.

As if.

Given time, Elder thought, Jennie would bounce back; the resilience he had sensed in her would bring the spring back to her step, the brightness to her eyes. For now it was as much as she could do to squeeze his hand and thank him in a faltering voice for all that he'd done.

"YOU THINK HE REALLY DID, FRANK?" PRIOR ASKED. "Have sex with his mother when he was a lad? A youth? You think it really happened?"

"I don't know." Elder shook his head. "I doubt we ever will."

They were in a pub around the corner from the Central Police Station, the occasionally raucous rise and fall of overlapping conversations sealing them in.

"If it did...If she did..." Prior was staring into her glass. "The mother...it wouldn't have been easy...for her, I mean. She would have had to try and deal with it, too."

"Perhaps she was more able to shut it out. Forget. Pretend it never happened. If it did."

She looked at him. "Stuff that's happened between you and Katherine—no, listen. Don't get me wrong—things that have happened between you. Times you've been especially happy, or had a blazing row. Even ordinary things that don't seem to mat-ter at the time. Do you forget?"

"No."

"Not even when you're down in Cornwall, say? Miles away. Katherine out of sight, getting older, growing up."

"No."

"Christ!" Prior said vehemently. "Being a parent, having kids..."

Elder could see the tears in her eyes. When she continued, her voice was so low he had to bend his head forward to hear.

"When I was seventeen, just seventeen, I fell pregnant. This bloke, he was older, twenty-six, twenty-seven. My parents—you can imagine—they were tearing their hair out, doing everything they could think of to stop me seeing him, and, of course, that only made me want to see him all the more. True love, Frank, that's what it was. True fucking love. And him—he didn't give a toss about me, I was just someone to screw when he wasn't screwing somebody else.

"Then, when the penny dropped, when I couldn't pretend any longer, three months along—even if I'd wanted an abor-tion, by then it would probably have been too late. And of course, he didn't want to know. Laughed in my face when I told him. Raised the can of whatever it was he was drinking: 'Here's to the little bastard's health!'"

Prior wiped her face with the back of her hand.

"You had the baby," Elder said.

"I had the baby. A baby boy. Six pounds, five ounces. Christopher, that's what I called him. In my head. I don't know what he's called, really. I only saw him...I only saw him for..." She swallowed hard. "I only saw him for a moment, a few mo-ments. His foot, I can remember touching his foot. With my hand. The palm of my hand." She sniffed and for a moment turned her head away. "He was adopted. Young babies, new-borns. There's never a shortage of people waiting, can't have kids of their own. A blessing, really." She smiled askance through what remained of her tears. "Saves them all the hard work, mum especially. All that push, push, push. The pain."

She picked up her glass, but it was empty.

"I could do with another drink, Frank. I really could."

While he was at the bar, she went to the Ladies and splashed cold water on her face; reapplied some makeup, as much as she ever used. When she came back out, she looked much the same as she had earlier, restored; except to Elder she would never look quite the same again.

They sat, mostly silent, five minutes, ten; he couldn't leave it alone.

"Are you in touch at all or … ?"

A quick shake of the head.

"His adoptive parents … ?"

"I don't know where they are, where he is, anything."

"You could find out."

"I could put my hand in the fire. I don't."

Elder looked away.

"He'd be twenty-three," she said, a moment later. "This year. A man."

She looked bereft. Elder wanted to put his arms around her and give her a hug, but the space between them was too great.

"THIS CHAP LEONARD," HE SAID, ONCE THEY WERE OUT on the pavement. "Ben, is it?"

"God, not you as well."

Elder grinned. "It's a small town, Maureen. You said so yourself."

"There's nothing going on, okay?"

"He seems a nice enough bloke."

"They're all nice, Frank. For a while."

She had collected together the information he'd asked for: details of persistent curb crawlers, car registrations, names, addresses. Thanking her, he folded the envelope and pushed it down into his inside pocket.

"Dowland's been kicked free?"

"Yesterday."

"And Reardon?"

"Tail between his legs. Looking for someone to blame. Aside from himself, that is."

"He'll learn."

"Let's hope." She rested a hand on his arm. "Frank, what I told you…"

"Not a word," he said. "You've got my promise."

"Thanks." She squeezed his arm, then stepped away. "You sure you want to do it this way?"

"Sure."

Prior nodded and, with a half smile, turned away.

BY THE TIME ELDER HAD WALKED UP THROUGH THE Park, it was starting to get dark. Lights showing through blinds and between partly drawn curtains. Glimpses of other lives. A wind moving the trees. There were lights in Brian Warren's house, too, upstairs and down.

When the bell didn't seem to work, Elder used the heavy iron knocker, shaped into a horse and rider, at the centre of the door. While he was waiting, he checked his watch.

There were footsteps inside and then a shadow on stained glass.

Bolts and then the lock.

"Mr. Elder?"

Warren was wearing normal gray trousers with a striped pyjama top, slippers on his feet.

"Not too late to call, I hope?" Elder said. "Didn't disturb you getting ready for bed?"

"You did as a matter of fact. But come in, come on in. Always good to see a friendly face."

Elder followed him into a long kitchen at the back of the house. There was an ancient Aga range facing the door, black paint starting to crack. A dresser, some eight feet wide, took up most of the side wall, and a large oak dining table, its top several inches thick, dominated the centre of the room. There were plates and glasses here and there, mostly clean; a wine rack stood on the tiled floor; another on the solid wooden counter above. Nearby were several bottles of port and sherry, a bottle of single malt.

Warren reached for glasses from a shelf.

"You'll join me? Drinking in company, more pleasant than drinking alone."

He pushed aside a pile of newspapers and magazines: the *Times* and the *Telegraph*, vintage cars and contract bridge. On top, the local paper was folded across Vincent Blaine's picture, his gray hair surprisingly dark, a whiff of arrogance in his stare.

"Mud in your eye," Warren said.

Elder raised his glass.

"That woman," Warren said, "the one that was murdered. Your investigation. And the other one, too. Irene. I couldn't believe what I read in the paper. Vincent—I mean, never in a million years."

The whisky was a little peaty for Elder's taste, but went down easily enough nevertheless.

"If it were only that simple," Elder said.

"How's that?"

"To be able to tell—at a glance."

"Even so, a man like that. Cultivated. Civilized. It's not what you expect. And as for Anna—poor Anna. She must be gobsmacked. Shaken, too, bound to be. There but for the grace of God." Warren added a dash more whisky to his glass. "All that time they spent together. A lucky escape."

"Like the other night."

"Sorry?"

"Monday of last week. Didn't she run into you near where she lives?"

"Of course. Run into is right. Almost sent me flying. What with all this business about Vincent, it'd gone clear out of my mind."

Elder smiled. "Your chance to play knight errant."

"Absolutely. Not that I think she was in any actual danger. More perceived than real. Tarts, that's what he was interested in, that fellow. Dowland, that what he's called?"

"They've released him," Elder said quietly. "The police. You'd maybe not noticed it in the paper. Tucked away among the small print, I dare say."

"Done it before, though, hadn't he, according to what I read? A few years back. Some kind of compulsion, that's how it sounded. Shame, if you ask me, they ever let him out. Of course, I'd have seen the bugger hang, if I'd had my way; castrated him, at least."

"The evening you bumped into Anna Ingram," Elder said. "Was that when you noticed Lorraine Carne first? Or had you been with her before?"

Warren was staring at him, fingers fast around his glass.

"Cars seen in the area," Elder said, "records of curb crawlers, potential punters. I've been checking back through the reports. Six months. A year. More. That old Rover of yours, it turns up a number of times. Always with an excuse. On the way back from this or that. Dropping off a friend. But now the police have been out talking to the girls, showing them a description." Elder leaned away. "You've been a good customer over the years."

Some of the colour left Warren's face. "Men my age, left alone, there's no sin in seeking out that kind of relief, no crime."

"When the forensic team does a proper search, they'll find something. They generally do. Mud from the allotment on your shoes, a splash of it on your clothes."

"This is all nonsense and you know it." Warren's hand was still steady, but the conviction was fading from his voice.

"You know what first made me think of you?" Elder said. "Reading the pathologist's report. Lorraine Carne's neck, snapped with a single wrench of the head. Someone with strong arms, strong hands."

Letting the glass fall, Warren drove his right fist toward Elder's face, and, ready for it, Elder threw out an arm and forced the blow wide. He was unprepared for the next, a fast looping left that caught him on the edge of the jaw and propelled him out of his seat, spinning toward the floor.

Before he could pull himself up, Warren had wrenched open the door into the garden and disappeared from sight.

Elder righted his chair and sat back down, ruefully rubbing his jaw. There was still a finger of whisky left in his glass. Anil Khan, he was sure, would have taken the precaution of stationing officers front and back. "Let him have the chance," Prior had said. "Show what he can do."

Through the open door, Elder could hear raised voices, the sound of a scuffle; then something louder, duller, like something heavy being thrown against the side of a car.

More shouts.

Silence.

Khan's grinning face at the door.

Chapter 43

THE WEEK LEADING INTO THE WHITSUN BANK HOLIDAY was suddenly sunny and warm, topping twenty-three degrees. On the Wednesday evening, Elder had somehow contrived to be in a crowded pub, staring with disbelief at the big screen while Liverpool clawed their way back from being three goals down to win the European Cup. And then, the next night, Joanne had surprised him with tickets to see Elvis Costello at the Royal Concert Hall, a present, she claimed, from one of her customers; the first time Elder had been to see any kind of rock music live since he'd grudgingly agreed to accompany Joanne to see Rod Stewart in 1989, the year they had moved to London.

Costello he could remember from his time in Lincolnshire, when he was just a young officer in CID: "Oliver's Army," "Pump It Up," "Watching the Detectives." The last a bit of a natural favourite. Despite the almost total inappropriateness of its lyrics, he and Joanne had slow-danced to "Alison" at their wedding.

"Come on, Frank," Joanne had said when he demurred. "Enjoy yourself for once. Doesn't pay to get old before your time."

He and Costello, Elder had to remind himself, were more or less of an age. Difficult to believe after watching Costello thrashing away at several guitars for more than two hours without a break, singing himself hoarse in front of a three-piece band.

Elder wasn't sure if he found all that energy intimidating or inspiring. And although much of the music slammed abrasively past him, there were songs he recognized and happily tapped his feet to: a heartfelt "Shipbuilding," originally about young men caught up in the Falklands War but just as sadly appropriate now; and, of course, there was "Alison," Joanne sliding her hand over his and giving it a squeeze.

"You'll still be here Saturday, Frank?" she asked when he'd walked her home.

"Probably."

"Come round for dinner, then. I'll ask Katherine."

He kissed her cheek and it was warm; the keys were in her hand.

"You won't come in?"

"I don't think so."

Joanne smiled. "Saturday, then."

"Yes, sure."

ANNA INGRAM WAS SITTING IN HER GARDEN, SHELTERED from the sun by a large umbrella. The swelling on her face had gone down significantly, though there was still a clear residue of bruising; her jaw was out of plaster and she could talk, albeit slowly. She offered Elder biscuits and homemade lemonade, both of which he gratefully accepted.

"How are you feeling?" he asked.

"I'll live," Anna said, and then shivered, realizing what lay behind the words.

"You'll be able to go back to work?"

"Soon. Too soon, probably." She gestured about her with her hands. "A life of leisure—I could get used to it, given time."

The garden was coming into flower; soon everything would be at its best. Not for the first time in the past days, Elder caught himself thinking of his part of Cornwall, small pink and white flowers in profusion between stone walls, the fuchsia virulently in bloom.

"Once," Anna began, "not long after we started seeing one another, as a couple, Vincent asked me if I would wear a dress that had belonged to his mother. Of course, I refused, it seemed totally bizarre, and he passed it off as some kind of joke. He never mentioned anything similar again."

She paused: speaking was less than comfortable.

"Then there was one occasion when we were…we were making love. It didn't happen often, not even then. And I can't say I minded when it stopped more or less completely. But on this occasion, Vincent, he…this isn't easy for me…he seemed more excited than usual. I mean, normally it was all very ortho- dox, he had to be absolutely in control, sex by the numbers, but this particular evening, for whatever reason, it was as if he lost himself in what was happening, totally, and just as he was about to climax he called out his mother's name: 'Margaret! Mar- garet!' And then, afterward, he curled up in my arms with his head against my breast and cried. And I cuddled him, as if he were a little child."

Anna was crying herself at the memory.

At what she now thought it meant.

"I should have told you sooner," she said. "Shouldn't I?"

"It doesn't matter," Elder said. "We got there in the end."

"He was good company," she said. "Vincent, when he wanted to be. He was intelligent, opinionated—the most opinionated person I ever met—but he never patronized me. I liked that. I liked it when we argued, about art or literature or the theatre. I liked being able to hold my own. And it was never boring." She righted herself in her chair. "Now I feel I've just woken from a dream. You know, that strange half-shocked state you're in when the dream's just broken."

"I think so," Elder said.

"I suppose you'll soon be heading back down to Cornwall?" Anna said.

"Yes. Just a few more things to tie up first."

"You like it down there?"

"It suits."

She insisted on walking him, however slowly, to the gate. "That gallery, Tate St. Ives, have you ever been?"

"Once, with my daughter."

"I keep telling myself I should go down, take a look. The building itself is supposed to be really special."

Elder wondered if there was something he was supposed to say.

"But it is a long way," Anna said with a smile.

"Yes, it is."

They shook hands.

BERNARD YOUNG HAD THANKED HIM PUBLICLY IN FRONT of the squad and then privately in his office over a glass of Lagavulin.

"There's always a job for you here," the superintendent said. "You know that."

"I'll keep it in mind."

"And not just here. You know Bob Framlingham?"

Elder did, indeed. Robert "Farmer" Framlingham, head of the Metropolitan Police's Murder Review Unit. They'd worked together in the past.

"He's got the go-ahead to set up a national team, shadowing the new National Crime Squad, looking at cold cases, ones that go across normal boundaries, advising. Kind of thing you've done once or twice before. He'd like you to be in there with him, at the start. Help set it up. Told me to let you know."

"I'm flattered," Elder said. "Be lying if I said otherwise."

"So I can tell him you're interested?"

"I don't think so."

"For God's sake, Frank..."

"This unit, where would it be based, for one thing?"

"London, I imagine, initially. After that—well, national means national. Could be anywhere."

"But probably not Cornwall."

"Probably not."

Elder finished his scotch. "I'll keep in touch, Bernard. Next time I come up to see Katherine, we'll meet and have a jar."

"Right, let's do that."

Within a year or so, Bernard Young would retire to the York-shire Dales, and Katherine would be away studying at Lough-borough or Sheffield. It was life: it was what happened.

KATHERINE WAS ALREADY AT THE HOUSE WHEN ELDER arrived; she and her mother drinking gin and tonics in the kitchen, while Joanne put the finishing touches to a generous salad. Pots were simmering on the stove.

"I hope you're hungry, Frank."

"I'll do my best."

The salad dressing made, but not applied, Joanne excused herself to go upstairs and change. Elder accepted a glass of white wine and quizzed Katherine gently about any plans she had for when she'd finished her degree.

"I'm going to go to Africa," she said. "Work with one of these projects teaching gymnastics to little kids in Zimbabwe or somewhere."

"You're not serious?"

"No. But I probably should be."

Joanne reappeared in a sheer, pale blue dress with a slashed front and slit to midthigh at one side. Katherine whistled approval and Elder looked vaguely embarrassed.

For starters there was an onion tart Joanne had picked up at a fancy deli close to where she worked; lamb stew with thyme and anchovies was served with couscous, and there was salad to follow. For dessert there were little individual ramekins of crème caramel, courtesy, also, of the delicatessen. There was cheese that nobody really wanted or had room for.

White wine was followed by red, and then Joanne produced a small bottle of dessert wine at the end. The conversation, a little stilted at first, soon ran to tales of small embarrassments and misdemeanours, in the way that family conversations often do.

A family: these past years it had been all too easy to forget that's what they still were.

Although she'd tried to insist it was perfectly safe for her to walk back to her student room, Elder had insisted Katherine take a cab. At the door, he kissed her and held her close.

"Wherever you finally decide to go, to do the degree, you'll let me know?"

She grinned. "I doubt it."

He slipped a fiver into her hand for the fare.

When he got back inside, Joanne had cleared most of the things from the table and he carried the last few glasses into the kitchen.

"You want me to help with those?" he asked.

"I've got a dishwasher, Frank. No need."

He grinned. "It used to be me."

Joanne smiled, remembering.

"That flat in Shepherd's Bush," Elder said. "The kitchen was so small we couldn't both be in it at the same time."

"Without a squeeze," Joanne said. "Not that that was such a bad thing."

Kissing him, she slipped one hand behind his head, her fingers touching his neck, her breasts against his chest. Eyes closed,

Elder kissed her back, and for a moment there was nothing else: the feel of her body against his, her breath, her kiss. No memories, good or bad.

"Jo," he said, when finally she stepped back.

"I know, I know."

"The dinner, it was great."

Looking down, she shook her head.

"I mean it, the whole thing. Kate. You. It was lovely. A lovely evening."

"Frank, if you're going, just go."

His coat was in a walk-in closet off the hall.

Joanne had poured herself a glass of brandy and lit a cigarette. She was standing by the window, outlined against the dark.

"When are you back down to Cornwall?"

Elder shrugged his shoulders. "Tomorrow? The day after?"

"Drive safely."

"I will."

He was at the living room door when she stubbed out her cigarette. "Don't go, Frank. Stay."

Elder took three more steps, stopped and turned around.

Acknowledgments

Writers, as Alan Bennett suggests, are not nice people. All the more reason to be grateful to those who stick their heads above the wire and offer encouragement, advice, and the occasional admonition: my thanks, therefore, to my exemplary editor, Susan Sandon, and to my agent, Sarah Lutyens; to Mary Chamberlain for her painstaking copyediting, and to Justine Taylor and others at Random House too numerous to mention; to both Sarah Boiling and Graham Nicholls (yet again) and, especially, to Bernard Ratigan, without whom this book would scarcely have been possible. The faults, as they say, are all mine.